THE LAMBS

In 1914, Kevin Flynn had hardly given the war a thought; everyone said it would be over by Christmas. Instead, desperate to impress a girl called Mary, Flynn and his friends, like thousands of fellow Irishmen eager not to miss the adventure of a lifetime, and keen to help set their country free, they begin a journey that leads inexorably to suffering beyond imagination. Confronted by the harsh realities of war and rising hostility at home, Flynn finds his courage, loyalty and love tested to the limit making him question whether it was worth becoming a lamb to the slaughter.

THE LAMBS

THE LAMBS

by

Peter James Cottrell

Magna Large Print Books
Long Preston, North Yorkshire,
BD23 4ND, England.

British Library Cataloguing in Publication Data.

Cottrell, Peter James
    The lambs.

    A catalogue record of this book is
    available from the British Library

    ISBN   978-0-7505-4045-2

First published in Great Britain in 2014 by Robert Hale Limited

Copyright © Peter James Cottrell 2014

Cover illustration © Collaboration JS by arrangement with
Arcangel Images

The right of Peter James Cottrell to be identified as the author
of this work has been asserted by him in accordance with the
Copyright, Designs and Patents Act, 1988

Published in Large Print 2015 by arrangement with
Robert Hale Ltd.

Magna Large Print is an imprint of Library Magna Books Ltd.

Printed and bound in Great Britain by
T.J. (International) Ltd., Cornwall, PL28 8RW

In memory of the tens of thousands of Irishmen who served in the 10th and 16th Irish Divisions during the Great War of 1914–1918, as well as their fellow countrymen in the 36th (Ulster) Division.

*Go ndéana Dia trocaíre ar
na n-anamacha dílse.*

HISTORICAL NOTE:

The book's title, *The Lambs*, is taken from one of the regimental nicknames of the Royal Dublin Fusiliers and whilst the book, like its sequel *England's Janissary*, is a work of fiction, its key events are firmly rooted in fact. Whilst Kevin Flynn is fictional, all of the officers and the majority of soldiers mentioned in the book actually served in the 9th Battalion, the Royal Dublin Fusiliers. I took the liberty of basing one of the chapters on the DCM citation of my Irish great-uncle, Sergeant William Driscoll, but the majority of historical events are based on surviving records relating to the 9th Battalion's activities between its formation in September 1914 and the attack on Ginchy two years later.

Over 210,000 Irishmen served in the British armed forces between 1914–18, and although the 49,400 who died are remembered on the Irish National War Memorial in Dublin it is impossible to know how many more never recovered from the mental and physical scars of war. The majority were

Irish Catholics, over 27,000 were former members of the pro-Home Rule National Volunteers and the majority saw the 1916 Easter Rising as a 'stab in the back'. When they returned home they found a country utterly changed; a country that viewed them as an embarrassment to be effectively airbrushed out of Irish history. That is, until the Good Friday Agreement in 1997 made it possible for those in the Irish Republic to remember those who had fought and died in the Great War.

PROLOGUE

Sunday 26 July 1914, Bachelor's Walk, Dublin

If he lived, Private Tam Lennox of the King's Own Scottish Borderers knew that today would be etched as firmly in his memory as the boot-print on his face. Blood and gritty fragments of tooth flooded his mouth as he sprawled on the wet cobbles beneath the rich, spleen-filled canopy of Dublin curses. He tried to rise. A boot slammed into his jaw, sending him reeling into darkness.

'Quick! Grab the Jock bastard's gun!' someone shouted behind a flail of feet.

'Get back!' Lennox opened his eyes. A shadowy figure stood over him, rifle ready, bayonet fixed. It was Captain Hugh Cobden, his company commander. Others joined him: khaki-clad Jocks, bayonets glinting in the wet sunlight. 'Back, I said!' barked Cobden, cowing the mob momentarily as, sullen-eyed, they edged from the licking blades.

Despite the adrenalin, Cobden felt tired, bone-weary even, as he eyed his fellow Dubliners circling like hyenas. It was days like this that reminded him why he'd left, why he'd joined a Scottish regiment – to get away from Ireland and its bloody politics! The country was a mess, teetering on the brink of civil war over Home Rule. Going to Howth had been a fool's errand. If the Home Rulers wanted to land a load of obsolete old rifles to march around with, let them. The police should have turned a blind eye, like they did up in Ulster for the Unionists. Instead, he was stuck in the middle of a riot.

'You all right, Lennox?' he asked, keeping his eyes on the crowd. Something sailed towards him. He ducked. It brushed his cheek. There was blood.

'Aye, sir, I've had worse,' growled Lennox as Lance Corporal Finney pulled him to his feet. Cobden didn't doubt it; his Jocks were hard men. The crowd had been dogging them all day, hurling insults and cobbles in equal measure, and Cobden prayed he could get them away before they did.

'The bastards didn't get my weapon, sir!' Lennox added, grinning despite a swollen eye. His face was numb. The pain would come later.

Major Haig, the second in command, had brought reinforcements: the entire under-strength battalion crowded onto Bachelor's Walk – a mere 200 men. They were outnumbered three to one. Lennox hawked up a gobbet of blood. There were people on Ha'Penny Bridge and Liffey Street. They would be cut

12

off soon.

'Tell them in Sparta,' muttered Cobden, beginning to feel like Leonidas at Thermopylae. He shuddered. Thermopylae hadn't ended well.

'Will you look at the arrogant English shite,' hissed Martin Fallon, his desiccated features, cured beneath the harsh Indian sun, egging the mob on from the safety of its depths. Nine years in the British Army had taught him to make the best use of cover. It had also taught him to hate officers. He scowled at Lennox's swollen face. By rights he shouldn't have got back up. Next time he wouldn't. Next time he'd get the Jock git's rifle too. A .303 would do nicely; better than the German rubbish they'd landed at Howth that morning. He'd be a big man in the Volunteers with a .303. He hurled a cobblestone at Cobden. The captain's cricketer instincts made him swerve. Fallon cursed. The cobble swept harmlessly by, then it struck Major Haig, sending him staggering. The crowd cheered. It was enough. The storm broke. The crowd surged like a tidal wave. Fallon lunged at Lennox's rifle. The Scotsman twisted, jabbing hard, his solid fist crashing into the Irishman's nose. It snapped.

'Shit!' cursed Fallon, his mouth suddenly coppery. He staggered.

'You all right, Marty?' asked a friendly voice, helping him to the rear. Fallon nodded, spitting blood. He stepped into a doorway, wiping snot and gore on his sleeve. The rifle would be good, but not worth dying for – he'd leave that to the amateurs, the ones crying out to be martyrs. The mob eased back; jeering, steeling itself for another rush.

Major Haig summoned Cobden. He was pissed off. His uniform was ruined, stained with God knows what; utterly ruined. This wasn't the Sunday he'd anticipated. He hated Dublin.

'Hugh,' Haig said, 'take twenty men and form two ranks across the street. You're the rearguard. I'll stay with you. We'll hold here until I give the order to fall back on Gilbert's line.' Down the street Second Lieutenant Gilbert Hammond was forming a second firing line near Ormond Quay. 'We've got to be quick, Hugh, or we'll never get out of here.'

Cobden nodded then barked, 'Corporal Ludlow. Twenty men. Two ranks. Here. Facing that way.' Cobden gestured at the angry mob. 'Quick as you can, please!' The corporal shoved twenty men across the street in two ragged ranks. Lennox was with them along with his mucker Jimmy Porter. Porter was scared, new to all this, his face pale. He was shaking. Haig stepped out. Porter's head was swimming. He'd been hit by a rock, blood stinging his eyes. He could see Major Haig waving his sword, shouting.

'If you do not disperse at once I will order my men to open fire.' Open fire! The words swirled through Porter's befuddled mind. He raised his rifle. It thundered, kicking like a mule. He palmed the bolt, firing again; his senses flooded with cordite. Others joined in. Rioters fell. 'Cease firing!' Haig screamed. 'For God's sake, cease firing!' His cry was taken up by Ludlow, leaving an ominous, ear-ringing silence echoing across the blood-soaked cobbles. Fallon crouched in a shop doorway, dusted with glass. The crowd had scattered. There were bodies everywhere; forty at least. A woman lay face down, a ragged, fist-sized hole in the small of her back.

'B-but he said to open fire,' mumbled Porter, red-eyed with fear and shock.

'Yer murdering Brit bastards!' someone screamed as the mob re-formed and Lennox knew that today really would be etched as firmly in his memory as the boot-print was on his face.

CHAPTER 1

September 1914, Dublin, Ireland

Kevin Flynn hated his job. In all his nine-teen years he couldn't remember being so bored, his mind listless behind his intelligent grey eyes. He kept thinking about the Sherlock Holmes story left half-read on his bedside cabinet. It was much more interesting than the papers stacked neatly on his desk. He wasn't a very good shipping clerk. He could have gone to university – he had the brains, and besides, his parents were good for the fees. Instead he'd wasted his schooldays letting his laziness get the better of his intellect. His father had got him the job. It had prospects, he told him. It was the sort of job he could be proud of. The problem was he hated it. It was dull. Shifting uncomfortably in his chair, he listened to the martial music booming by, rattling the windows to strains of 'Rule Britannia' and 'It's A Long Way To Tipperary'.

The clerk opposite, Terry Gallagher, looked equally bored. He seemed oddly out of place in the office, thickset like a navvy with dark-brown eyes and a mop of unruly brown hair, barely contained by liberal applications of pomade. He came from Bridgefoot Street, down by the Liffey, and sat awkwardly scratching entries into a weighty ledger. He seemed a simple soul, always playing the fool, but behind the buffoonery lay a quick wit and a dry sense of humour. Flynn liked him. He liked Gallagher's sister Mary even more! Gallagher put down his pen, glancing at their ageing senior clerk, Mr Byrne, who sat perched behind his desk billowing pipe-smoke like an idling steam engine in a siding. Gallagher rolled his eyes theatrically, cracking a toothy grin in Flynn's direction.

'Mr Byrne,' said Gallagher, 'they say this war'll be done by Christmas.'

Byrne harrumphed from behind his smokescreen. 'Do you not have enough work to be getting on with, Mr Gallagher, to stop you wasting the firm's time with your gossip?' he asked, before deigning to peer over the rims of his half-moon glasses. There was still a hint of Kerry in his voice despite twenty or so years living in Dublin.

'That I have, Mr Byrne,' replied Gallagher, beaming angelically. Byrne eyed him suspiciously, reminding Flynn of a sour old schoolma'am. 'I've a brother in the Irish Guards,' Gallagher added. 'He's in France banjaxing the Hun. He says they'll all be home soon.'

'Does he now?' said Byrne from behind his spectacles.

'It's terrible what the Germans are doing in Belgium, Mr Byrne; says so in the papers. Even Mr Redmond says we must do something. If we don't it'll be Ireland next.' Byrne didn't look convinced. 'Will you be joining up, Mr Byrne?'

Byrne frowned. He was obviously too old for the army. 'Did he now? Mr Redmond may have got Home Rule through parliament for us but the old fool stopped talking sense the moment he started backing the war. People should know better than to encourage young *eejits* like you to go running off playing soldiers. Besides, I wouldn't go believing everything you read in the papers,' grumbled Byrne sourly.

'But the world is passing us by whilst we pore over manifests and drink tea!' persisted Gallagher.

Byrne put down his pen, tugging at his walrus moustache. He sat back, suddenly feeling every minute of his fifty years. He needed a drink but resisted the temptation of the brandy flask in his top drawer. He could almost feel the fiery liquid pooling in his gut. The noise of the band grew louder.

Gallagher raced to the window as it passed below belting out 'A Nation Once Again'. 'That'll be more lads off over the water whilst we're stuck here!' he cried.

Byrne ignored him, his eyes resting on Flynn. 'And would the firm be paying you

18

to daydream, *Mr* Flynn?' he asked. Flynn blushed. Gallagher grinned. Byrne harrumphed again.

'I was thinking...' Gallagher said.

'Lord help us!' snorted Byrne. Gallagher was just about to speak when the door flew open, crashing into the wall, sending papers flying. It was John Riley, their skinny fourteen-year-old office boy.

'In the name of God, Master Riley!' spluttered Byrne.

'I'm sorry, Mr Byrne, but will you not be coming to see the band?' he gabbled, hopping from one foot to the other like a desperate man in a toilet queue. 'There are soldiers and everything!'

'Ach, isn't it all brass bands and soldiers these days!' snapped Byrne. They were looking at him, like puppies. He had little time for soldiers, unlike his brother Martin, but he was long gone, buried beneath South Africa's red dirt; killed at Colenso. 'Black Week' they'd called it. The telegram had come just before Christmas. It had broken his mother's heart and he hated the army for it. 'Away with you then if you must,' he sighed. 'I'll be expecting you back by three or I'll be docking your wages!' he called after them but they'd already vanished. Byrne reached into his desk for his flask, unscrewing the cap slowly. Outside, the autumn sun shone down on the crowded street packed with enthusiastic well-

19

wishers cheering the soldiers on their way. '*Eejits,*' he muttered before taking a long pull on the flask's contents.

Flynn smoothed his wavy dark hair and cocked his straw boater at what he thought a rakish angle before striding off after Gallagher, who had a fearsome pace for a short fella. Thankfully, his own loping gait closed the gap in a few steps.

'Some of us are thinking of joining up,' said Gallagher, meaning the members of the Gaelic football team he played in. Flynn didn't play football – of any sort; he preferred reading. 'Will you be coming with us?' The band struck up another chorus of 'It's A Long Way To Tipperary'. People sang; girls darted from the pavement to plant kisses on unsuspecting soldiers' cheeks who swaggered towards the docks. Only months before, rioters had been gunned down by soldiers on the same streets, the country sliding into civil war, yet now everything seemed forgotten, subsumed beneath the carnival façade of bands and billowing bunting. 'C'mon, Kev, do you want to be the one who misses it?'

'It's all right for you, Terry, your family's full of soldiers. My parents gave my cousin enough stick when he joined the Volunteers. God knows what they'd do if they saw me in a red coat!' replied Flynn, unconvinced.

'Are your folks Fenians then, Kev?' asked Gallagher.

'It's not that, it's just that, well, soldiering isn't respectable, that's all,' said Flynn awkwardly.

'Jaysus, Kev, have you never wanted to shake the world? This is different. It's not like we'd be regulars like our Mickey or me Uncle John, it'd only be for the duration! Let's face it, you're as bored as I am, it's all over your face. Besides, it'll be a laugh. Think of it as one of those adventures you keep reading about. Do you really want to end up like Byrne, eh? Done nothing, seen nothing, been nowhere? Christ, it'll be over by Christmas – if we don't join up now we'll miss everything!'

'You're bloody serious?' spluttered Flynn.

'Look.' Gallagher pulled a leaflet from his pocket. 'It says here that if you join up with your pals the army will keep you together. We'd be together and, besides, the colleens love a fella in uniform! Isn't that why half them fellas joined the Volunteers in the first place? They won't get a look-in now. Who knows, even our Mary might give you a kiss too! Everyone knows you're soft on her.'

Flynn flushed pink, his ears glowing as the band faded into the distance as they headed over the Liffey into town.

'You're late!' snapped Rory Gallagher suddenly from the shade of King William III's imposing equestrian statue on College Green. Gallagher grunted something as his younger brother fell in beside him. They were like chalk and cheese. Rory was Gallagher's exact opposite: tall, fair, lanky and thin-faced. 'Will you be coming with us, Kev?' asked Rory.

'Terry seems to think so,' replied Flynn. In truth, he didn't know what he would do when they reached the recruiting office.

'I'm up for it!' squeaked Riley, the young office boy.

'They'll never take you, you're a kid!' said Flynn but Riley puffed up his sallow chest indignantly.

'I'm tall for my age and I'll tell 'em I'm nineteen, so I will. You'll back me up, won't you, fellas?' Riley implored, looking at Gallagher for support.

'Does the wee fella here not put you to shame, Kev?' laughed Gallagher.

'My old man'll kill me if I join up,' said Flynn.

'Well, you'll be the only fella left if you don't cos they was queuing round the block up at City Hall when I left so we best get a spurt on!' declared Rory, leading the way.

'There's thousands of the beggars,' gasped Flynn as they rounded the corner revealing City Hall in all its neoclassical glory. The queue of recruits was massive. It was as if every man in the British Empire's second city was there: rich and poor. Here and there National Volunteers in green uniforms helped the police marshal the babbling crowd. The city had already raised two battalions for the Royal Dublin Fusiliers, the Dubs, and now it looked like she would easily raise a few more.

'You, lad, will you answer your king and country's call?' barked a nicotine-stained voice with the merest tint of Mayo in it. Flynn could see a white-whiskered Irish Guards sergeant, a recalled reservist, brandishing a cane like a sideshow barker at a group of what looked like Trinity College students. A scarlet sash added a splash of colour to the man's immaculate khaki uniform. 'Will you let them Boches get away with attacking poor little Belgium?'

'No!' chorused hundreds of cheering voices.

'Over there!' shouted Rory, pointing out a tall man who Flynn recognized as Gallagher's next-door neighbour, Joe Carolan. He was tall, sparsely built with sensitive green eyes, with a shock of bright red hair that contrasted starkly with his pale skin, making him look a bit like a lit match.

'I've kept you a place!' shouted Carolan, beckoning them over with one of his shovel hands. He was grinning, like the rest, and as they drew nearer Flynn recognized the other members of Gallagher's Gaelic football team. They really were all joining up together. 'You coming too, Kev?'

'Couldn't keep him away!' joked Terry, slapping Flynn hard enough on the back to nudge him into the milling crowd. Riley slip-streamed in behind him.

'What the hell! It'll all be over by Christmas anyway,' said Flynn. The players cheered as myriad hands slapped him on the back. Gallagher smiled and Flynn nodded, their friendship somehow made stronger by that one simple act. For the first time Flynn felt part of something, something bigger than himself. Gallagher noticed a stocky Royal Dublin Fusiliers lance corporal ushering the recruits in through the door as they reached the top of the steps.

'Uncle John?' he gasped.

'Recalled me, didn't they? Your Auntie Joy is furious. She says I'm too old for these shenanigans,' replied the soldier who bore more than a passing resemblance to Gallagher. 'I'm to be with the new 8th Battalion,' he added, puffing up his chest proudly. 'Do your parents know you are here?' Gallagher shifted awkwardly, avoiding his uncle's gaze. The soldier nodded. A dark-haired sergeant with an abrasive Derry accent and clipped moustache shouted to keep them moving. 'Aye, Sar'nt,' replied Uncle John before glancing back at his nephew. 'Whatever happens don't you go telling your dad you saw me. He'd kill me for not stopping you,' he added, letting Terry and his friends past with a wink. 'Oh, and don't go letting them put you in anything but the 8 Dubs, d'you hear? That way I can keep an eye on you.'

'Is there anyone in your family who isn't in the blasted army?' Flynn asked as they shuffled into the atrium.

'Well, it's a bit of a family thing. My dad's the only one who didn't join up. Uncle John was in South Africa with the Dubs, fought at Colenso with that old woman Byrne's brother. I think that's why Byrne gave me the job in the first place, cos Uncle John was with his brother when he was shot.' Flynn gave Gallagher a puzzled look. 'Did you not know Mr Byrne's younger brother was killed in South Africa?'

'I guess that'd explain why he's not keen on the bands, then,' Flynn replied.

'Hold it right there!' barked the Derry sergeant, barring the way with a glossy cane. He was looking at Riley. 'How old are ye, sonny?'

Riley hesitated.

'I'm nineteen, sir,' he declared, puffing up his sallow chest as best he could.

'Are ye now, son?' replied the sergeant. 'When were ye born?'

'July thirteenth,' replied Riley.

The sergeant stepped back, dropping his cane. He beckoned Riley forward with a curt flick of his head. Riley stepped forward. 'Oh, just one more thing.' Riley paused. 'What year?'

'Er ... nineteen ... er ... no, eighteen ninety ... er ... six!' he gabbled, flustered.

'That's what I was thinking. I'm sorry, sonny. I'd be coming back when ye're older, eh?' he said gently, ignoring Riley's protests.

'Is there a problem there, Sergeant Devlin?' asked a flat Staffordshire accent. Devlin swung round to confront the moustachioed Englishman at the foot of the main stairs. His uniform was immaculate, the man composed, quintessentially professional from his obsidian boots to the slashed peak of his Service Dress cap.

'Who's he?' Terry asked his uncle.

'Him? Sar'nt Major Clee. He's some old donkey walloper.' Terry looked puzzled. 'A cavalryman, 12th Lancers – till last week, that is. Now he's slumming it in the poor bloody infantry.' Sergeant Devlin shot Uncle John a sharp, narrow-eyed look.

'And what age are ye, then?' Flynn heard the Derryman growl. He paused then he realized the sergeant was talking to the man next to him – a willowy, soft-featured lad dressed in a well-made pinstripe suit.

The boy looked at Devlin with large, crystal-blue eyes, like a hare caught in the beam of a poacher's lamp. 'Er ... I'm nineteen ... er ... Sergeant.' Devlin looked sceptical. 'I've my birth certificate and a letter from my

26

parish priest,' said the boy in a reedy voice. He thrust a wad of folded papers at Devlin, who unfolded the sheets, reading to himself, his lips childishly tracing the words.

'So it would seem ... er ... *Mister* Patrick Cronin. Best ye get a move on and stop blocking the door, then.' Cronin stuffed the papers back into his pocket, following Flynn towards a bank of tables manned by over-worked clerks.

'Sign here,' drawled one of them wearily.

'It says here three years or the duration,' Flynn said, his pen hovering above the freshly filled-in enlistment form.

'And your point is? Look, either sign or piss off,' the clerk snapped. Someone muttered impatiently behind him. He signed. It was done. 'Over there. Next!'

'Coats off; roll up your sleeves and answer the doctor's questions when he asks you,' barked a medical orderly. He snatched Flynn's paperwork. Up ahead, Gallagher, Rory and Carolan were chatting as they shuffled towards a thin white line of doctors. Cronin stood quietly behind him. The man in front turned slightly, flashing Flynn a toothy, bright white smile and thrust out his hand. He was about Flynn's height and fashionably dressed, dapper even, with his boater cocked at a jaunty angle and a large carnation ostentatiously thrust through the buttonhole of his lapel.

'Hi, I'm Séamus, Séamus Fitzpatrick,' the man said in a distinctly un-Irish accent. Flynn looked puzzled. 'I'm from Boston, Boston Massachusetts in the US of A! I'm an American!'

'American? I didn't think America was in this war,' Flynn said.

'It sure ain't,' Fitzpatrick replied. 'Hell, if it was this thing'd be over by now! Why, Uncle Sam ain't lost a war yet!'

'Really?' Flynn replied, unsure what the man's Uncle Sam had to do with it, before hesitantly taking Fitzpatrick's hand and introducing himself.

'Well, I'm sure pleased to make your acquaintance, Mr Flynn. Say, you got any folks in the States?' asked Fitzpatrick. Flynn shook his head. 'Heck, I thought everyone here had folks in the States.'

'Not me. I've people in Tasmania, though.' Fitzpatrick didn't look too impressed. 'So what brings you here?' Flynn asked.

'Well, you see, I'm Irish too,' Fitzpatrick began, obviously enjoying retelling his tale. Hooking his thumbs under his lapels, he puffed out his chest. Flynn felt his heart sink; another American fixated with his Irish heritage. 'I was over, seeing the old country. You see, my people are from Kildare; Milltown, as it happens. Evicted by the English during the Famine, they were, went west to America. Fine country; a man can be free there. Anyway, when I heard the National Volunteers were forming I thought I'd join up; see if I could help throw off the Saxon yoke like we did back home in 1776. Then old Redmond told us Volunteers to join the British Army so here I am ... here we are.' He pointed at several others. 'I guess the old fella knows what he's doing but, gee, will my old man be pissed when he hears I've become a redcoat!'

'Does your old man like the drink, then?' Flynn asked.

'Er ... never touches the stuff,' replied Fitzpatrick, leaving Flynn wondering how a teetotaller could get drunk. They lapsed into silence and it was almost a relief when Flynn found himself in front of the doctor. He began unbuttoning his shirt. Cronin looked worried.

'No need for that,' mumbled an aged doctor, clenching a pipe in his teeth. 'Any coughs or colds? No, good ... open wide,' he said, forcing a wooden depressor into Flynn's mouth, counting his teeth. 'Let's have a listen to your heart, then.' He placed a stethoscope over Flynn's heart, the sound muffled by the double layer of shirt and vest. 'Good, good, now touch your toes. Excellent, you'll do. Grade one,' the doctor said, scrawling his signature on Flynn's paperwork.

'Is that it?' Flynn asked but the doctor was already examining young Cronin as an orderly shoved him towards the exit. An ageing reservist slapped a Bible in his hand and before he knew it he'd sworn allegiance to King George, his heirs and successor in front of a rather fusty-looking old officer with red tabs on his tunic collar and a red band around his cap. The officer pressed a silver shilling into his hand before the NCO ushered him out of the side entrance with instructions to report to St Stephen's Green at nine o'clock the next morning. In a strange way it seemed like a bit of a let-down, an anticlimax almost, as he stood unnoticed on the corner of Castle Street watching other freshly sworn-in recruits tumble into the street. Gallagher and the others appeared, looking troubled.

'Rory failed the fecking medical! They said he had a dickie heart of all things, said he was unfit for service,' said Gallagher. 'Now he's taken off in a sulk.'

'Shouldn't we look for him?' Flynn asked.

'No, he'll show up,' replied Gallagher, somewhat deflated by the turn of events. He stuffed his hands deep into his pockets, biting back the disappointment.

'Mr Byrne wanted us back by three,' said Flynn.

Gallagher looked at him and nodded. 'Aye, I suppose we had, but before we do, Kev, I could murder a drink. How about it, lads? There's a pub round the corner and this king's shilling's burning a hole in my pocket. Byrne can wait.'

Predictably, one drink became two and two became three, and by the time they finally managed to stagger back to work it was well past three o'clock. To their surprise, Mary Gallagher was sitting in the office, her eyes raw with tears and her usually neat long blonde hair a dishevelled froth. 'Wha' yous doin' here, Mary?' Gallagher slurred. Flynn fought back the urge to puke, regretting all the whiskey Gallagher had been pouring down his throat all afternoon.

'It ... it's our Mickey, Tel, he's been killed,' she sobbed.

Suddenly Flynn was sober; very, very sober.

CHAPTER 2

September 1914, Dublin, Ireland

'Damned fool!' was all Flynn's father could bring himself to say to him during breakfast. It had been a sullen affair, all painful silences and clattering teacups. His mother blamed Gallagher. They always blamed Gallagher when he did anything wrong; said he was a bad influence, that they always knew he would lead him astray. They didn't approve of their friendship. The Gallaghers were from the wrong part of town. They certainly wouldn't approve of Mary. That was why he never mentioned her. They would find out soon enough, if anything came of it. They didn't say anything when he left but he could feel their eyes on him as he scuffed his way down the street.

Bridgefoot Street was quiet. Mr Kinsella the postman was returning from his round and Flynn tried not to throw up as he said hello. The postman gave him a knowing, sympathetic look. It was a soft day; grey and overcast like Flynn's mood by the time he reached Gallagher's house. He was glad he'd worn his overcoat. His mouth still felt foul with stale whiskey despite toothpaste and a good breakfast and his head ached. He rapped on the door, nestling into his coat. There was silence. He thought of knocking again, then he heard fumbling. The door eased open a crack, revealing a clear blue eye, puffy from lack of sleep. It was Mary. Flynn felt something warm inside. He smiled. Her skin was smooth, pale against the pallor of the morning, and despite being Gallagher's twin sister he couldn't help thinking she was beautiful, even in grief.

'Oh, it's you,' she said, opening the door.

'H-hello there, Mary, I've come for Terry,' he stuttered awkwardly. Utterly inappropriate thoughts barged to the front of his mind as he looked at her. He blushed.

Usually she laughed at Flynn's awkwardness around her but today wasn't a laughing day.

'May well you look shamefaced.' For an awful moment he thought she had read his mind. 'I thought you had more sense. You're a pair of *eejits*,' she rebuked half-heartedly, mercifully oblivious of the real reason for his blushes. So much for a kiss, thought Flynn as he stepped into the musty hallway, following Mary's backside to the kitchen. The smell of tea, fried bacon and tobacco embraced him as he entered the small cluttered room where Mr Gallagher slumped in a chair staring at the slowly congealing fry-up turning to grease in front of him. Gallagher was finishing his breakfast. Mrs Gallagher fussed pointlessly amid her pots and pans. Flynn loitered in the doorway, abandoned by Mary, feeling guilty about his inappropriate thoughts amid the Gallaghers' grief.

'I'm here for Terry, Mr Gallagher,' Flynn said. Mr Gallagher seemed smaller. He didn't look up, instead staring intently at the neat, looping letters on the lilac paper in his hands as if he couldn't quite make out what it was. Flynn guessed it was the letter from Mickey Gallagher's wife.

'There was a big battle on the Marne,' mumbled Mr Gallagher. Flynn had read about it in the papers. 'Maybe they got it wrong. A battle's a confusing thing. Maybe our Mickey'll show up somewhere.'

33

'Here's hoping,' Flynn said rather lamely.

'Will you listen to you? What would you know about a battle?' snapped Mrs Gallagher, slamming down a pan. 'The army couldn't even tell me, his mother! We had to rely on Janet writing!'

'Well, she is his wife, Brigit, darling,' offered Mr Gallagher, taking Mrs Gallagher's hand.

'He'd never have joined if it wasn't for your blasted brother with all his stupid war stories and now they've taken my Terry too!' she moaned. 'Well, at least they'll not be getting my Rory, thank God!'

'Thanks for reminding me, Mammy,' snapped Rory as he stomped into the room. 'I'll be getting white feathers from all the girls in Dublin now!'

'Better that than six foot of Belgian dirt!' sobbed Mrs Gallagher. Rory slammed the door like a clap of thunder.

'He'll get over it,' said Gallagher before glancing at the clock over the kitchen fireplace. 'We'll be late!' Rain rattled off the window heralding an almighty downpour. The Irish 'monsoon' season was in full swing. Gallagher snatched his cap from its peg and kissed his mother goodbye. She looked at the floor. 'Let's go. Joe will be wondering where we are.'

'Away with you now,' said Mrs Gallagher. She was crying.

'Do you think they might have got it wrong about Mickey?' asked Flynn as they left the house.

Gallagher shook his head.

'Janet said they found a load of her letters on the body,' replied Gallagher. He sniffed. 'So how'd your folks take it?'

'Let's just say you're off their Christmas card list,' said Flynn.

'And there was me thinking I was on it!' Gallagher grinned. They knocked on Carolan's door. He looked sheepish, subdued even: another one whose news had not gone down well.

'My girl Lizzie's furious,' Carolan said as he slipped out the door, turning up his collar. 'I thought she'd be happy with me bringing in some extra money but she said I'd get myself killed before we had a chance to wed. She said I was as bad as them Jocks who shot up Bachelor's Walk last summer. Ma and Da weren't impressed either. Me ma went all Fenian on me, ranting about how the redcoats pitch-capped me great-granddad back in '98 before they strung him up with his own belt.' Carolan thrust his hands deep in his pockets. Despite the deluge, the air stank of the nearby Guinness brewery but at least the rain had eased by the time they reached City Hall. Flynn's shoes were sodden as they trudged through College Green and the sun was shining as

35

they ambled past Trinity College.

Grafton Street was busy as usual, Union flags fluttering from its tall buildings. Posters of Lord Kitchener pointed at them as they mingled with the knots of young men making their way towards St Stephen's Green where they'd been ordered to report. Gallagher beamed shamelessly at every shop girl who caught his eye. They didn't seem to mind. Some even smiled back. Flynn really didn't understand how Gallagher did it. He was more than a little envious. As they reached Fusilier Arch, Flynn noticed a sharp-featured lad about his own age leaning against the park railings pretending to read a paper as he watched the assembling throng with angry eyes. A band played in the park.

'Do you think he's a G-Man?' Flynn asked Gallagher, referring to the Dublin Metropolitan Police's detective branch. Carolan shook his head. 'What?' Flynn was confused.

'He's too young and, besides, do you really think a G-Man would be seen dead all scruffy like that and reading anything but the *Irish Times?* No, a tanner says yon corner-boy's a Shinner,' Carolan replied as they strolled past the man, who wrinkled his nose in disgust.

Gallagher spun around. 'What you looking at?' he snapped, pale as death.

'I'm looking at a traitor to his country. That's what I'm looking at,' sneered the

36

man, folding his paper and sticking it in his pocket. He was smiling. 'Fitting, is it not, that they get you all to pass through Traitor's Gate to join up?' he added, referring to the Fusilier Arch by one of its local nicknames. Flynn could feel the violence brewing as Gallagher's short fuse began to smoulder.

'You what, you slasher gobshite?' growled Gallagher, picking up on the man's County Longford accent.

'Jackeen shite! At least Judas took thirty pieces of silver, not a measly shilling, to become a traitor,' retorted the stranger. Heads were beginning to turn. Gallagher's fists balled. The stranger drew himself up, a head taller than Flynn's friend, his eyes burning like coals.

'Is there a problem here, lads?' It was a policeman, thickset, truncheon in hand, his face weather-beaten, hard, his smile utterly devoid of warmth. He seemed deceptively relaxed. The stranger licked his lips, a flicker of recognition in his eyes, and for a fleeting moment Flynn thought that maybe the stranger was a G-Man after all. 'Move along there, McNamara, before I take you down the station,' said the peeler, firmly. It wasn't a suggestion. Another policeman, slab-featured and raw-boned, sidled up beside the first, his thumbs hooked into his belt.

'Is there a problem, Constable Dolan?' the new arrival asked.

Dolan shook his head. 'This young *gentleman*–' emphasizing the word like a bad taste, 'was just leaving, weren't you, *Mr* McNamara, Constable Gough.'

McNamara paused, glaring at the two peelers and then back at Gallagher.

'May you die in Ireland, you West Brit bastards,' spat McNamara before sloping away to melt into the Grafton Street crowd. A flock of gulls shrieked overhead, dispelling the silence along with the tension that slipped into the gutter and washed away.

'Some would say he was right. Ironic even,' mused Flynn as they passed beneath the Fusilier Arch into St Stephen's Green. Carolan gave him a curious look.

'You know, ironic, like we were told in school; when you says something and mean the opposite,' Gallagher explained, seemingly incongruously academic.

'You *eejit*, I know what ironic is! I mean what is he on about?' Carolan retorted, jabbing his thumb at Flynn.

'That some people call this Traitor's Gate when half the city seems to have relatives in the Dubs,' observed Flynn.

'Your problem is you think too much,' Gallagher replied with a wry grin.

'YOU!' brayed a harsh Derry accent, bulldozing its way across the park towards them. It was Devlin, his face puce. 'What the hell do ye think ye're doing?'

'Someone's for it!' chuckled Gallagher. Devlin oscillated with rage.

'Christ, Terry, I think he's shouting at us,' said Flynn. Devlin exploded into life, jabbing his lacquered pace-stick in their direction. Flynn felt sick.

'Us? Away with you,' replied Gallagher as he flashed Devlin one of his innocent schoolboy smiles. Devlin went a darker shade of puce as Gallagher pointed at himself, mouthing the word 'me'. Devlin exploded, storming towards them like an angel of death.

'Aye, you, the three feckin' musketeers! Move it! Jildy!'

'Who's Jill Dee?' asked Carolan.

'I think my Uncle John knows a Jill Dee,' said Gallagher.

'Christ knows, but she doesn't sound like a nice girl!' replied Flynn.

'WHERE DO YOU THINK YOU ARE, BLOODY SCOUT CAMP? AT THE FECKIN' DOUBLE!' Devlin screamed.

'Move where?' Carolan quailed in terror, desperately fighting the urge to run.

'There!' Flynn snapped, pointing at a marquee sporting a signpost that said 'Orderly Room'.

'What's an orderly room?' Gallagher asked. Devlin was close now.

'I don't flaming know but it's better than standing around here!' Flynn replied. Then they ran. They burst into the tent. It stank of mildew and damp humanity. There were a few familiar faces. Fitzpatrick and Cronin were there.

'What now?' asked Gallagher. There were tables at one end piled with papers. Smart, moustachioed NCOs snapped like terriers, keeping the lines of recruits moving. Nearby a clerk stood poring through a clipboard of papers.

'Let's ask this fella,' said Flynn. 'Excuse me, but what do we do now?'

The soldier, red-faced, looked up. 'Name?' he snapped.

'Kevin Flynn.'

'Over there.' He pointed at a desk marked 'D-F'.

'Don't mind Garvey, he's a miserable old bugger,' said the clerk at the 'D-F' desk. He took Flynn's papers. Gallagher was at the next desk: 'G-H'. 'Now let's see,' muttered the clerk. 'Ah, yes, Flynn K. Well, Private Flynn, it looks like you've been allocated to B Company. You'll be somewhere on the north side of the pond. It's signposted.' He handed Flynn a brown envelope. 'Your papers and pay book are inside. Whatever you do don't lose them.'

'And my pals, can you tell me what company they've been put in?' Flynn asked, worried that they could be split up. 'The leaflet said we'd stay together.'

The soldier smirked knowingly. 'Believing

that clap-trap was your first mistake.' Flynn looked worried. 'All right, let's see, then,' relented the clerk. 'What are the names?' Flynn told him. 'Carolan J and ... er ... Gallagher T ... um ... yes, it looks like your chums are in B Company too.' Flynn felt a surge of relief wash over him. 'Well, what are you waiting for? Off you go, then, jildy doh. Next!' Flynn hesitated. 'Yes?'

'What does jildy mean?' he asked the clerk.

'It means quickly, comes from India.' He pronounced it 'in-juh'. 'Now jildy, eh? There's a good lad.'

Flynn stepped out of the marquee, armed with his papers and his first piece of army slang. Gallagher was nowhere to be seen.

'Hey, buddy, I heard you was looking for Company B,' said Fitzpatrick, who was behind Flynn in the queue. 'Me too, buddy. Some fella said it was this way. Just stick with me.' They made their way along the north shore of the lake until they reached an off-white, open-sided timber pavilion. A crowd of maybe 200 men chatted excitedly and Flynn felt a sudden surge of relief when he saw Gallagher and Carolan gathered with the rest of their footballing mates. Company Sergeant Major Clee was there too, at the edge of the pavilion, his 12th Lancers cap badge replaced by a Royal Dublin Fusiliers one. His spurs were gone too: only field officers and the adjutant wore spurs in the infantry al-

41

though Clee still wore his horse soldier breeches. Two sergeants hovered nearby. Flynn recognized the old Irish Guardsman. He was wearing an RDF badge too. The prickly Ulsterman was there, also, looking sullen and dangerous. Young officers in freshly tailored uniforms stood in the shade whilst an ancient colonel and a white-haired captain sat on horseback, the pair an island of calm amid the chaos. Then Clee stepped forward and saluted the colonel with elbow-cracking precision before climbing onto the steps in front of the milling crowd, jamming his cane tightly under his left arm.

'QUI-ET!' His voice ripped through the crowd, stilling the hubbub. 'Right, now that I have your attention,' he sneered. 'My name is Company Sergeant Major Clee. When you speak to me, you *will* call me *sir*. From this moment on you belong to me. You do not do anything, do not take a shit without my say-so. Is that clear?' he barked, making the veins of his purple face bulge. There was a ragged response. He scanned the recruits with theatrical disdain. 'Jeezusbloody-Christ, and I thought you people were supposed to be the fighting fucking Irish? Answer me like fuck-ing soldiers, not a bunch of girlie-bloody-guides. My bloody daughter can do better than that. Now, I said DO YOU UNDER-STAND?' he roared.

'YES, SIR!' they bellowed.

He seemed satisfied. 'Now we've got that out of the way, let's get down to business, shall we? Is there anyone here with previous military experience?' There were a couple of hands. 'Right then, get out here. You lot are now NCOs – report to Sergeant Mahon for your stripes.' He pointed at the old Irish Guardsman who stood with a box of armbands which he dished out, catapulting recruits to the heady heights of corporal or sergeant depending on their experience.

'We're still divvy, sir,' Mahon informed Clee, who nodded, examining the remaining armbands, his lower lip poking out in thought. The officers looked on, aloof. The colonel nudged his horse closer, followed by the captain, their spurs and swords glinting in the sun.

'Ah well, beggars can't be choosers, Sergeant. I suppose we'll have to make some of the National Volunteer fellas up,' announced Clee. He didn't have much time for weekend warriors like the Territorials let alone a load of politicized paramilitaries like the Volunteers. Mahon gave Clee a look that betrayed his own suspicion of amateur soldiers. 'At least they'll be able to march.' The Guardsman wasn't convinced. 'Right, Sargent Mahon, sort it out,' he added, stepping back to let Mahon get on with it, and half an hour later they were formed into platoons and sections.

Then they were set to drilling but at least Flynn was amongst friends. Gallagher, Carolan and Fitzpatrick were all in his section. So was an odd-looking lad with an aquiline nose and brown hair called Wellesley who rather predictably became known as 'the Duke' after that other Irishman of the same name. The Gaelic football team's half-back Mickey Doyle was also in their section along with the willowy Cronin. There was Jim Docherty – Fitzpatrick knew him – a fellow Volunteer who'd grown up in the Monto, Dublin's notorious red-light district, whose harsh slum accent sounded like a foreign language to Flynn. Then there was their section commander, Corporal Martin Fallon.

'Right, you shower of shite, let's start at the very beginning, shall we? I want the tallest on the right ... er ... that'll be you, Private ... er ... Carolan and the shortest on the left. That'll be you ... er ... wee Private Gallagher. The rest of you fill in the middle. MOVE!' snapped Fallon. His grating whiskey- and nicotine-stained voice, made worse by his broken nose, jarred like nails down a blackboard.

'Best we tread carefully with this fella,' Flynn muttered to Gallagher out of the corner of his mouth as Fallon strutted up and down in front like a threadbare old peacock in a worn brown suit that stank of stale sweat, cheap tobacco and yesterday's whiskey.

'Silence in the ranks!' snapped Fallon, his beady eyes fixed on Flynn. He'd already developed a dislike for the tall, wavy-haired youth with his well-made suit and la-di-da middle-class accent. 'I'm watching you, Flynn!' His weathered face hovered inches from Flynn as he poured out a tirade of spittle-laden abuse before turning on the others. 'Jesus, Mary and Joseph, that was pathetic! My flaming daughter could do better!' Flynn began to suspect that soldiers' daughters were unnaturally proficient at military evolutions. Then, Clee's scalpel voice sliced through the park, bringing the company to a sudden, bone-jarring silence. They stood to attention. The white-haired captain, Henry Stirke, spurred his horse forward. He thought his soldiering days were over but they'd dug him out of the reserve to be the battalion's second in command. He felt a tingle of pride as he eyed the silent ranks and Flynn could hear the leather creak as Stirke leant forward in his saddle.

'Looks like Sar'nt Major Clee's whipped 'em into a frenzy, sir,' Stirke quipped dryly as he surveyed the silent ranks of motionless men. The colonel gave a curt nod; at fifty-nine and after a lifetime in the Indian Army, Charles Harman had rather hoped for a quiet retirement. Instead they'd given him a battalion. He stood in the stirrups, addressing his men.

'Men of B Company, let me welcome you to the 9th Battalion, the Royal Dublin Fusiliers.'

'Hang on, I thought we joined the 8th?' Gallagher whispered.

Suddenly Devlin was at his shoulder. 'Shut it, stumpy! If I ever catch you yapping whilst the CO is speaking I will shove this' he jabbed his pace-stick under Gallagher's chin 'where the sun don't flaming shine!' The colonel paused. Clee made a note. Devlin moved in; close enough to kiss Gallagher's cheek if he'd wanted to. 'I've got my eye on you.' Then he stomped off.

'What's his problem?' Gallagher muttered.

'I may be wrong but I think he's our new platoon sergeant,' Flynn whispered back.

'Oh great, just feckin' great,' moaned Gallagher, rolling his eyes in despair. 'That's all I need.'

CHAPTER 3

November 1914, Royal Barracks, Dublin

'Ah, there you are. Corporal Fallon wants you,' Gallagher called to Flynn. The open row of ablutions stank, the acrid stench singeing his nose hairs. 'Jaysus, is that you?'

he spluttered.

Flynn shrugged. His sense of smell was not good at the best of times and, besides, he was past caring. He folded down the top corner of the page of the Sherlock Holmes novel he was reading and glanced up wearily.

'Can't a fella take a crap in peace?' grumbled Flynn as he tore off a sheet of cheap, shiny toilet paper. 'It's no wonder people call this rubbish scratch and polish!' he added ruefully.

'Will you get a move on or yer man will have another of his hissy fits,' spluttered Gallagher, looking away, still not reconciled to the army's utter lack of privacy. Flynn wasn't so finicky, but somehow he still thought of the lavatories as some sort of sanctuary – holy ground, even – to relax and read despite the lack of toilet cubicles. Gallagher heard the toilet flush and then the rush of water as Flynn washed his hands.

'It's a wonder, isn't it?' Flynn mused as he wrestled with the buttons of his Kitchener blue tunic, a stopgap until the war office could supply enough khaki Service Dress uniforms for the battalion. They looked like postmen.

'What is?' Gallagher sighed wearily.

'You know, old Hackett over in stores told me that when the army builds a camp it assumes that the average man produces two pounds of shite a day.'

'What are you on about now?' Gallagher asked.

'Like I was saying, old Hackett over in stores–' Flynn persisted.

'What would that old bugger Hackett know about anything?' replied Gallagher.

'Old Hackett's almost as old as this place,' Flynn said with a sweep of his arm. 'He knows his shit! So, c'mon, Terry, how many fellas do you reckon live in this barracks?'

'How should I know?'

'Go on, how many?' Flynn urged.

'I don't know; there's a load of 7th Battalion's lads, a few odds and sods from the 8th and us lot, so ... um ... maybe 1,500 fellas, give or take a few. Anyway, what's this got to do with Fallon?'

Adjusting his Glengarry cap in the full-length mirror by the door, Flynn noticed how easily the cap adhered to his head since his unruly curls had been inexpertly shorn away by the garrison barber.

'All right, let's say 1,500...' Flynn's tongue protruded slightly from the corner of his mouth as he tallied something with his fingers. 'That means that this barracks churns out almost a ton and a half of shite a day.'

'Isn't that truly a load of shite,' Gallagher replied briskly.

Slapping his friend on the back, Flynn laughed. 'Well, that's the army for you, Terry, me old mucker! Now we're on the subject of shit, what does that lazy bastard Fallon want anyway?'

'Don't ask me, I'm only the bloody messenger!' Gallagher grumbled. Outside the air was stiff and cold, a soft day. Bawling NCOs rifted the latest recruits, lobbing sarcasm like hand grenades reverberating off Royal Barracks's 200-year-old walls. The 7th Battalion, the Royal Dublin Fusiliers, were almost ready for war.

'At least they've got proper uniforms,' observed Flynn.

'We'll get our khaki kit soon enough,' Gallagher said. 'These fellas have only got theirs cos they are off over the water soon.'

'So how come Fallon's got a proper uniform?' Flynn grumbled.

'Cos he's an ex-reg, I guess.'

'That's the flaming ARABs for you,' Flynn replied. Gallagher frowned. 'You know, ARABs – Arrogant Regular Army Bastards – they take care of their own. Anyway, old Hackett thinks we won't be long after them.'

'Does he, now? And did he pick up that gem when he was taking tea with Lord Kitchener himself, then?' Gallagher asked. 'He probably thinks we're still at war with bloody Napoleon, he's been here so long!'

'So you don't think we're off overseas soon, then?' Flynn asked.

'What do you think? If that old soak knew his arse from his elbow he wouldn't still be a private at his age! Why should we? The rest of the battalion are out in the sticks, somewhere near Cork, so it stands to reason we'll be joining them sometime,' replied Gallagher.

'So why d'you reckon our platoon was left here as battalion rear party when the other lads left?' Flynn asked.

Gallagher shrugged. 'Maybe Corporal Fallon didn't fancy emigrating to County Cork,' he suggested with a wry smile. 'After all, it's pretty cushty here.'

'Aye, so where is the miserable beggar anyway?' asked Flynn.

'Oh, over in the stable block. He's got us mucking out the Ruperts' gee-gees,' Gallagher said, just as the gloomy stables came into view. There was a tang of warm horse-flesh and urine in the air as they crossed the empty yard.

'I told you, more shit!' said Flynn, but Gallagher's attention was elsewhere.

'Steady, Kev, here comes trouble,' he muttered just as Fallon, resplendent in khaki, emerged from the shadows. He braced his fists on his hips, staring in sullen silence. Flynn sensed the man's rodent eyes following him from beneath the peak of his cap.

'Where the hell do you think you've been, you idle bastards?' Fallon shrilled. Just as they reached the stable door he blocked their path. 'DOWN!' he barked. Flynn and Gallagher hesitated, glancing at the matted morass of excrement and hay. 'I said down. You owe me twenty for being late!' Gallagher's face darkened, his eyes narrowing.

'Easy,' Flynn muttered quietly to Gallagher; he'd been in the army long enough to know that striking an NCO would be just about the worst thing his friend could do, short of deserting. Gallagher gave an almost imperceptible nod of his head and dropped into the press-up position. Brown sludge oozed between his fingers. Flynn joined him.

'I said down!' shrilled Fallon, shoving his foot hard down on Flynn's back until his face vanished beneath the mire. 'Now give me twenty, you useless feckin' *eejits!*' he ordered. He lit a Woodbine and leant back to watch their exertions, barely concealing his enjoyment of the moment. The stink of cheap tobacco melded unpleasantly with that of the stables. Flynn straightened his arms. Gallagher did likewise, his thick biceps distorting his tight sleeves. The press-ups were easy; after all, press-ups were the small change of a recruit's life, a way of earning remission for sins real or imaginary. No, it wasn't the push-ups that bothered him but the effluent-stained cobbles that soiled his tunic with every dip of his arms. It was bad enough he looked crap; now he smelt of it as well! 'Now you've done down there you can get inside,' Fallon added, flinging down a long-handled shovel.

'Very good, Corporal,' Flynn replied with studied civility, anxious to get Gallagher away from the corporal before he did anything stupid. Fallon's eyes narrowed, disliking Flynn's tone.

'Still here?' growled Fallon, exposing nicotine-browned teeth that reminded Flynn of something unpleasantly feral.

They darted inside. The stable was gloomy and the stench slapped Flynn in the face. Nearby, a huge horse snorted, stomping its hoofs, sparking off a flurry of activity from the other horses occupying the stalls along the wall.

'Easy there,' cooed Carolan, soothing a horse's nose with his large hands. He had a way with animals. They seemed to trust him.

'Jesus, they're big bastards,' Flynn muttered.

'Irish Blacks, the best cavalry horses in the world,' said Carolan.

'I'll take your word for it,' Flynn replied.

'Shut it, Flynn, and get to work,' snarled Fallon as he shoved the door shut, leaving dust-laden shafts of light to lance across the cavernous space.

'Christ, I stink,' Flynn moaned as his boots squelched past a steaming, sweating mountain of horseflesh. 'And there was me thinking I'd joined the infantry, not the flaming cavalry!' They laughed.

'Even the infantry need horses,' Carolan

replied, patting his horse admiringly. 'How can you not say he's beautiful?' The horse's large brown eyes shone in the gloom as it nuzzled Carolan's hand.

'Easy. Can't stand the bloody things,' Flynn snorted.

'Hey, I thought the Irish loved horses?' Fitzpatrick chipped in. There was more laughter. Gallagher leant on his spade and stared at the chirpy American.

'Look, Séamus, you may be a cowboy but I'm a Dub. What would I know about horses 'ceptin' they deliver the milk?' There was more laughter. Fitzgerald gave Gallagher an indulgent, long-suffering look, not bothering to explain that he came from Boston not Arizona.

'Them Frenchies eat them,' the Duke interjected.

'Away with you, that's ... that's...' Carolan gawped in horror.

'That's what they do,' chipped in Cronin just as the stable door flew inwards, flooding the space with light. It was then Flynn noticed Cronin's delicate face was marred by a livid, blue-black welt. The boy flinched.

'Shut it and get about yet work. The officers' horses won't muck themselves out!' Fallon barked angrily before slamming the stable door shut once more.

'Pat, how'd you get that?' Flynn asked Cronin. He wasn't the fighting type. In fact

Flynn wasn't sure exactly what type he was. He kept himself to himself, rising before the others, never complaining. None of them could place his accent; it was neither here nor there, although since September it had finally come to rest in Dublin. Flynn repeated the question but the boy merely looked away, suddenly intent upon his work.

'Just tell us who done it and we'll leather the bastard,' Gallagher growled.

'Reckon ye'll be on a fizzer if you try,' said the Duke. For a moment Gallagher looked puzzled, then his face dropped in epiphany.

'Away with you, don't tell me that Fallon done this?'

Cronin shifted awkwardly, avoiding their gaze.

'That's a serious accusation, Duke,' said Flynn. 'It's against King's Regs!'

'And your point is?' asked Carolan.

'It just isn't right; there's gotta be something we can do about it,' replied Flynn.

'Like what?' Gallagher asked.

'Maybe we could report him to Devlin?' suggested Flynn.

'Oh, aye, and he'll be taking our word over a full-screw? Wake up! Regulars like Devlin and Fallon stick together like flies around a steaming great turd. No, if you go grassing him up to Devlin you'll just be making it worse, especially for young Pat here,' observed Carolan. Of course, he was right.

'And to think we volunteered for this and all we get is treated like shit. Well, I hope the great Irish public are bloody grateful when this blasted war is over!' Flynn muttered angrily.

'Let's face it, the Ruperts couldn't care less what the NCOs do to us as long as we do what we're told,' Gallagher grumbled.

'Isn't your uncle a corporal?' Fitzpatrick asked.

'That's different,' snapped Gallagher.

'So what makes you think Devlin isn't different too?' asked Flynn.

'Because ... er ... because...' Gallagher started then the door banged open once more, making him jump. It was Devlin, framing the doorway, legs braced, hands on hips. They pretended to work in a flurry of activity as the sergeant scanned the stable, looking for something. His face was impassive, masking the thoughts behind his hard eyes.

'Where's Corporal Fallon?' There was a dangerous edge to the sergeant's voice, like a keen blade.

'Is he not outside, Sergeant?' Gallagher replied politely, his heels together in a vague semblance of attention. Devlin came at him in a haze of starch and boot polish until his face hovered inches from Gallagher's, then he sniffed, his face pale as death in the gloom.

'Now, would I be in here with you lot looking for him if he was?' Gallagher stepped back, as if pushed by some invisible hand. Flynn shivered. Time stood still. A horse snorted. Devlin's gaze fell on Cronin, who stared woodenly into the middle distance. The sergeant's eyes narrowed. Then he was gone, the stable door rattling angrily on its hinges like a badly oiled machine gun behind him.

'Well, someone's not happy. Do you suppose he heard us?' Gallagher asked nervously. Flynn shrugged. They went back to work. Half an hour later the door burst open. It was Fallon, his face flushed purple. He'd been running.

'All right, you lot, get back to the block at the double!' he rasped.

'What's happening, Corporal?' Flynn asked.

'OC wants to speak to the platoon – now MOVE!' Fallon barked.

'I bet this is it!' Gallagher said, breaking into a broad, boyish grin.

CHAPTER 4

November 1914, Royal Barracks, Dublin

They were off to Buttevant in the morning to join the battalion. They'd been granted leave, on the proviso they got past the discerning eye of the orderly sergeant. Flynn resigned himself to staying in, bitter that Fallon had ruined both his tunic and his last night in Dublin, but then Gallagher saved the day with one he'd scrounged from old Hackett in stores. It had cost him.

'I owe you,' Flynn had said as he squeezed into the jacket. It was slightly too small. He didn't care. It would do beneath his great-coat.

'Aw, it was nothing. We're a team, we stick together; we don't leave anyone behind, do we, fellas?' replied Gallagher dismissively. The others agreed and it wasn't long before they'd got past the orderly sergeant, an immaculate Connaught Ranger sporting a luxuriant moustache and boots like glass. He eyed them disdainfully, resenting being prised from his warm guardroom.

'You'll do for a bunch of bloody fusiliers,' he'd grumbled. 'Now piss off, and try and not get arrested.' They didn't wait to be told twice, marching briskly towards the main gate past the postbox and the guardroom cells. Behind them the barrack lights flickered in the thickening gloom whilst ahead the lights of Kingsbridge Station blazed from across the Liffey. Flynn turned up his greatcoat collar against the chill rolling up the river from Dublin Bay. When they reached the station they stopped, basking in the warm blast emanating from within. Gallagher leant against the wall, lighting up as if on watch.

'I could murder a drink,' declared the Duke, stamping his feet against the cold. Gallagher beamed, his teeth shining in the lume of the streetlamp.

'I got to see my Lizzie first,' said Carolan.

'Say, what time you got?' asked Fitzpatrick. The station clock said it was just past five. 'Ain't it a bit early for a drink?' They gave him a queer look. 'What?' he asked.

'And you call yourself a Dublin Fusilier?' gasped Gallagher, summoning a volley of laughter from the others.

'I was just thinking we should get some scoff, that's all,' said Fitzpatrick.

'Yer man's got a point. Drinking on an empty stomach's just tempting fate,' opined Doyle. They agreed.

'Tell you what. Me folks live nearby. I'm sure my mammy won't mind rustling up a few sandwiches and some tea,' said Gallagher, doing his best to ignore the icy offshore wind.

'I'd better drop by my parents first. It is our last night,' said Flynn.

'So you'll not be seeing our Mary?' asked Gallagher. Flynn shuffled awkwardly. Gallagher was grinning like a buffoon.

'That's not what I said,' replied Flynn. 'I'll only be a few hours. Where shall I meet you?' he asked. Someone suggested the Brazen Head, sparking a brisk argument about the merits of the city centre's various drinking dens. Gallagher insisted he'd wait at the house; that way he could make sure Flynn found the right bar as well as seeing Mary before they left in the morning.

As Flynn strolled to the tram stop, it started to rain. It was still raining when he reached his parents' house, a smart detached building on the North Circular Road.

'If you must go playing soldiers, couldn't you apply to be an officer? We can always help you with your mess fees,' said his father.

'You'd be amongst decent folk, not all those common soldiers,' interrupted his mother. Flynn rolled his eyes.

'Your mother's got a point, Kevin. At least you wouldn't be a common soldier.'

'I like being a *common* soldier. I'm with my mates,' Flynn snapped, suddenly realizing how true that was.

'I told you no good would come of getting

him that blasted job,' his mother spluttered. 'He should have gone to university, made something of himself.'

'It's a good job,' protested his father.

'That may as well be but if he didn't work there he'd never have let that Gallagher boy stuff his head with all this army nonsense,' she added, bitterly. Flynn bit his tongue, nursing a cup of tea in his hands. 'Will you look how the lad can't hold a cup of tea decently anymore?'

He'd had enough. 'I've got to get back,' he lied, making a show of looking at the clock on the mantelpiece. His mother stared at him, red-eyed, at a loss for words. He felt awful. 'Look, we're only off somewhere down south.' She didn't say anything. 'They say it'll be all over by Christmas.' He knew he sounded foolish.

'Take care,' said his father. 'Keep your head down and don't do anything stupid.' He pressed something into Flynn's hand. It was a crisp white £5 note. Flynn noticed his father looked tired, worn out, and even their clasped hands weren't enough to bridge the invisible chasm that had opened up between them. He closed the front door, his mother's sobs haunting his thoughts as he made his way back to the tram stop. It was raining but by the time he reached the city centre it had stopped. It was late and as he strolled towards Gallagher's house the strains of melancholy rebel songs ghosted from shabby bars. A shaft of light stabbed the gloom as a figure tumbled into the street followed by another. Flynn didn't know why but he suddenly felt the urge to hide. He slipped into the shadow of a shop doorway, the rush of blood pounding in his temples. A match flared; lighting a cigarette. It was Fallon.

'Fecking gobshite, I told you I'd get the information for you,' slurred Fallon.

'Make sure you do,' replied his companion menacingly. He sounded familiar but Flynn couldn't place the voice. Then the door flew open once more disgorging drunks, bathing the men in light.

'Curiouser and curiouser,' Flynn mumbled softly to himself. It was the man from the park, the one the policemen had called McNamara.

'Did you not understand your orders, you old sot?' snapped McNamara, drawing close to Fallon. Flynn thought he would hit him. 'What good are you to the Movement if you can't even gather a bit of information about what your battalion's up to?' Fallon cringed and Flynn strained to hear his reply as McNamara shoved the dishevelled corporal against the wall. Even from across the street, Flynn could see the hatred in the old soldier's eyes as he glowered at McNamara, but he did nothing, remaining unnaturally silent. McNamara spat noisily in the gutter before flipping up the collar of his jacket and stomping off down the street. Fallon vanished into the pub. McNamara paused, thrusting his hands deeper into his pockets. He looked like he was listening. He stepped into the gutter. Flynn pressed deeper into the shadow, his heart pounding. Something touched his leg. McNamara was staring in his direction. A cat meowed, brushing his leg. Ever so gently he shoved it away. It wouldn't go. McNamara took a step closer. Fallon shoved the cat again. It shrieked, scuttling into the light. McNamara hesitated, watching the cat's approach, then he pulled his cap low, shading his face before walking away.

McNamara's footsteps faded into the night, leaving Flynn alone with the sound of his own breath. He paused, trying to make sense of what he'd seen; trying to work out what Fallon was up to. He stepped into the street, sparing a cursory glance up and down it before loping off to meet Gallagher at his house. He moved quickly, not noticing McNamara slip from the shadows, closing the gap as deftly as he could; unnaturally silent. Flynn paused at the end of Bridgefoot Street. It was better lit. Something made him look round. He thought he saw a shape in the darkness. The moon drifted behind a cloud, deepening the guttering shadows. He clenched his fists, half tensed, sensing something was amiss. A boot crunched on the cobble.

'You took your bloody time!' declared Gallagher cheerfully.

'Jesus!' gasped Flynn, spinning around, his fists raised.

'Easy there, big fella!' Gallagher replied, raising his hands.

'What are you doing creeping around like that?' asked Flynn.

'The others got sick of waiting ... left me as the rearguard ... they'll be calling time soon if we don't hurry,' Gallagher burbled. He'd already been drinking. Flynn glanced up the street to Gallagher's house. 'You're too late, me old mucker, Mary got sick of waiting and went to bed.' Flynn's heart sank; he'd wanted to see her. 'I know, I know, so much Guinness and so little time,' effused Gallagher, mis-reading his friend's disappointment.

McNamara followed them to the bar but didn't enter. It was too full of soldiers for his liking, despite the free-flowing stout. Besides, he wasn't much of a drinker anyway; not when there was work to be done. He would speak to Fallon.

The next morning Flynn felt like something had crawled into his mouth and died. Breakfast was a chore; he forced down a greasy fry-up between mouthfuls of strong orange tea. Something made him look up from his plate past Gallagher, who was shovelling down food with gusto. Fallon was watching him, exposing his crooked, stained teeth in a humourless rictus grin.

'I meant to tell you I saw Fallon last night,' said Flynn. Gallagher grunted, barely looked up from his food. The door slammed open. Devlin stood in the doorway, sharp and shiny, his cane tucked under his arm like an idle shotgun.

'All right, you useless lot, outside! Mr Murphy wants you formed up and ready to move in ten!' he bellowed, his words ricocheting off the walls like shrapnel. It was cold outside, still dark, and the chill struck Flynn's face like the back of a hand, stinging life back into him whilst they formed up in full kit waiting to go. Devlin barked. They stamped to attention, a crescendo of heels.

'At ease, lads,' said their platoon commander, Will Murphy, as he returned Devlin's salute with a casual tap of his peak. He tugged his moustache, ruminating over his words. He had a lived-in face, rather too old for a subaltern. It didn't matter: Kitchener's Army didn't play by the Regulars' rules. He'd hoped for the Leinsters – he was a Carlow man – but the Dubs were short-handed so here he was. He didn't mind. They were a good bunch of lads. He began to speak. Flynn wasn't listening. Then it was over; another casual salute and a volley of orders from the Ulsterman. They turned right, like a well-oiled machine, swinging their way across the gravelled yard and down to the main gate.

'Get your bloody heads up and swing your arms!' shouted Devlin. 'You're supposed to be the Royal bloody Dublin Fusiliers! Give it some bloody swagger!' So they did, all the way to Kingsbridge Station. The policeman on the station steps didn't even look; he'd seen it all before. Dublin was full of soldiers these days. Even the shop girls, walking to work, were less enthusiastic than Gallagher had hoped. No one kissed him. Flynn noticed Murphy was already there, leaning on his blackthorn. It puzzled him how he'd got there before them. They were herded onto the crowded platform, their blue uniforms standing out amid the khaki. Murphy chatted to a captain with a cut-glass English accent. It was warm inside, bathed in engine smoke, the air buzzing with excitement. Men chatted, men slept, some just stared into space: killing time.

'That'll be us soon,' Gallagher enviously observed, looking at the khaki-clad soldiers arriving to be shipped over the water to the war. A young woman carrying a small boy draped herself around a self-conscious sergeant's neck. They kissed. Flynn felt a pang of jealousy; missing Mary already.

'You look like you could do with one of

these,' said a beaming young nun, handing Flynn a steaming mug of tea. The tin mug scalded his lips. Nearby the Duke was wedging a chunk of fruit-cake into his mouth.

'Fecking *eejit*,' grumbled Fallon as he barged past Flynn, slopping his tea down Cronin's tunic. 'I've an eye on you, sonny,' he added, a menacing glint in his glassy eyes before shambling off, keeping a wide berth of the two well-dressed civilians at the edge of the platform surveilling the throng. Obviously G-Men. Cronin scooped a mug from the nun's tray. 'It's all right, Kevin,' he said. 'It'll dry. We'll be here a while yet anyway. Haven't you learnt the army's all hurry up and wait?' For a moment Flynn wondered how Cronin seemed to know so much about the army. He was about to ask when his heart skipped a beat: it was Mary.

'And did you think to be slipping away to play soldiers without saying goodbye, Kevin Flynn?' she teased, wrinkling her nose and smiling. His cheeks flushed as he fumbled for words. She looked sad, despite the smile. She took his hands. They were cold but their softness sent his skin tingling. She stepped closer. She smelt of soap. 'So what have you got to say for yourself?' she added, looking up, her head cocked to one side.

'Er ... I came round last night ... um ... Terry said you'd gone to bed,' he stumbled. She smoothed the lapels of his greatcoat,

66

drawing even nearer. He could smell her hair; it was tied back with a green silk ribbon. Her breath was warm on his cheek. 'Look, Mary ... er ... I mean ... um ... I was thinking ... ah ... would you mind if ... you can say no if you want ... er ... I'd understand...' She pulled him close and kissed him, pushing her tongue into his mouth. He melted into her arms, ignoring the barracking cheers and wolfwhistles.

'That's enough of that,' snapped Devlin, like a malevolent *sidhe* through the steam. The others were boarding the train. Gallagher was grinning manically from a carriage window.

'You make sure you write, Kevin Flynn,' said Mary, pulling away from him. The train whistle shrieked. 'Now get away with you. You're no good to me on the run for desertion.' The train began to stir, making Flynn run through the bank of smoke and steam. He felt Gallagher's hand on his shoulder, heaving him through the door. When he looked back she was gone, leaving a warm, lingering memory to sustain him on his journey.

CHAPTER 5

January 1915, Buttevant Camp, County Cork

It was early, but that didn't bother Flynn. Since arriving at the camp, their day'd always begun before the dawn. He'd got used to it. He'd got used to the ablutions too. They were dark and draughty but at least there were cubicles giving a semblance of privacy and a place to sit and read. Cronin was already there, wiping away the last dregs of shaving soap from his pink chin. He was always there before everyone else. He kept himself to himself. Flynn just assumed he was an early riser or one of those people who was uneasy with the intimacy of communal living.

'I don't know why you bother shaving – your chin's like a baby's arse,' Flynn quipped light-heartedly as he lathered his stubbly jaw. In a way he was jealous. He hated shaving, especially in cold, peaty water, knowing he would cut himself as usual. Flustered, Cronin muttered something about King's Regulations, suddenly eager to leave. Flynn started to shave, the razor stinging his wet flesh as Cronin headed for the door.

'Out of my way, you *eejit*,' snarled Fallon as he barged in, deliberately sending the slightly built youth flying. Flynn didn't know what the corporal's problem was with Cronin but he'd been picking on him ever since Dublin. He'd had enough.

'Leave the wee fella alone,' snapped Flynn, turning.

'It's *Corporal* to the likes of you, *Private*,' replied Fallon, his eyes flicking to the razor in Flynn's hand. He stepped closer, close enough for Flynn to smell the stale whiskey on his fetid breath. 'Are you threatening a superior officer?'

'No, but I am,' said Gallagher, his stocky, khaki-clad frame blocking the doorway. It looked like the rest of the section was with him.

'I'll have you all up on a charge!' shrieked Fallon, his face pale with rage.

'It's amazing how easily accidents can happen on these wet washroom floors,' Gallagher replied, calmly. 'Isn't it, lads?' The others nodded and Flynn thought he saw Fallon shrivel under the realization that he was quite alone. Flynn sniffed and packed his things, slowly, deliberately, before walking to join the others.

'What do you think he'll do now?' asked Flynn as they crunched through the snow back to the wooden hut they now called home.

'What can he do? It's his word against the rest of us,' replied Gallagher. Flynn knew he was right. 'Jaysus, I'm bored!' he added, lobbing a pebble at a nearby barrack wall. A face appeared at the window, frowning, before disappearing once more. 'The war will be over at this fecking rate!'

'At least they trust us with guns now,' said the Duke as they watched a platoon march off to the ranges, belting out sentimental old rebel songs. Somewhere Sergeant Mahon's parade-ground voice was putting someone through their paces. Flynn liked drill. In a bizarre way it was relaxing; you didn't have to think, only do. He got the impression the army didn't encourage thinking: not from lowly privates anyway. It was probably for the best.

'Here we are, fellas, home sweet home!' declared Fitzpatrick, pushing open the door to their hut. A large, blacked-iron stove squatted in the middle of the hut, its grate open, empty and unused. Carolan lay curled on his bunk ensconced in a balaclava and greatcoat beneath two grey army blankets. The rest of the bunks were empty beneath angle-iron frames that served as a boot rack-cumwardrobe and three pegs beneath which new Lee Enfield .303 rifles nestled in iron brackets. They trooped in. Fallon's bed was at the far end, screened off by a washing line of purloined blankets.

'I said to Sergeant Devlin there was no point having a stove if we've no turf or coal to burn in it,' complained Doyle. For once his pasty slum complexion looked positively rosy against the wintry backdrop as he stamped his feet for warmth.

'And what did the good sergeant say?' asked Flynn.

'He said organize some,' replied Doyle.

'What the feck does that mean?' said Gallagher. Doyle shrugged.

'Well, I've had enough. I'm off to see if I can nick some coal from behind the guardroom,' said the Duke, snatching up the coal bucket. Carolan had his back to them and Flynn assumed he was looking at something pornographic under his blankets.

WOOF!

'What was that?' asked Flynn.

'Nothing,' Carolan replied rather too quickly.

None of them looked convinced.

WOOF! There was a brief scuffle as they wrenched away Carolan's blankets, revealing two large, chocolate-brown eyes surrounded by a ball of black and tan fluff. It was a dog; a Yorkshire terrier, to be precise. Just about the scrawniest, scruffiest Yorkie any of them had ever seen. Its tongue lolled. In fact it bore an uncanny resemblance to Carolan. 'I found him wandering around the camp. It's cold outside; I couldn't just leave him,' protested Carolan.

'If you've not noticed, it's bloody cold in here too!' said Gallagher, fending off the yipping puppy's excited advances.

'He could be our mascot,' offered Carolan. 'All the other Irish regiments have them.'

'They have wolfhounds, not a useless ball of fluff,' joked Flynn as he tickled the pup's belly, its stick-like legs flailing in the air.

'I called the wee fella Spud,' said Carolan.

'You called it Spud?' spluttered Gallagher.

'Sure I did, he's all dirty with eyes!' Carolan said defensively. 'So what do you say, lads, do we keep him?'

'Fallon won't like it,' Flynn said.

'Bugger Fallon!' snapped Gallagher.

'To be honest I'd rather not,' replied Flynn, reducing the others to renewed fits of juvenile laughter.

'By the way, this arrived for you,' said Fitzpatrick, remembering he'd collected the section's mail that morning.

It was a letter from Mary. Scraping the ice from the window, he angled the paper, making the best use of the thin light to read. He could hear them talking about a corporal called Dempsey who dropped dead in training.

'That's two, three if you count the old CO we've lost, and we haven't even left Ireland yet,' moaned Gallagher.

'They'll be after a new corporal,' Fitzpatrick mused. Spud yipped.

'What's the new CO like?' asked Doyle.

'Colonel Connolly?' Gallagher said. 'Well, they say he's a decent enough fella. He's a dugout like the old fella was, some sort of Marine.' Gallagher noticed Flynn was quiet. 'So what's that sister of mine got to say for herself?' She didn't write to him.

'Not much. Rory's still mad about his medical,' Flynn said, scanning the page. 'She says she's off to London to stay with your Mickey's Janet now that the baby's due. She says she doesn't know when she'll be getting back.' He felt dejected as Gallagher lumped his hand on his shoulder.

'Why the long face, you great *eejit*? We're bound to pass through London on our way to France. Maybe you'll see her then?' Flynn was about to speak when the Duke burst in, clutching a bucket of whitewashed coal. He'd been running.

'Quick, get a bloody match to this stuff,' he gasped. They could see the provost sergeant not fifty yards off. He was squared up to Devlin. Neither looked happy. Fitzpatrick snatched the pail and emptied its contents into the stove then Carolan stuffed it with paper. Gallagher struck the match. They were partners in crime. The coals smouldered, crackling into life. Spud skipped over, stretching like a suckling pig waiting to be roasted. Doyle and Docherty busied themselves doing nothing on the ends of their bunks. The door banged open. It was Devlin, immaculate as usual in heavily starched khaki and gleaming brass. The Duke nudged the grate shut with his knee.

'I see ye managed to organize some coal, Private Doyle,' he said, inspecting the flakes of whitewash in the bucket with his stick. 'Best ye get this cleaned out. Don't want no sloppy soldiering, do we, sonny?' He sniffed, warming his hands on the stove. 'Funny, but the provost sergeant was just bending me ear that some ne'er-do-well had lifted some coal from behind his guardroom. Upset that lads on punishment won't have anything to paint.' They did their best to look innocent. Spud yipped. He looked down. 'By Christ, it's a bloody boot brush!' he said, breaking into a broad grin as he squatted down to pet the dog. It was the first time any of them had seen the sergeant smile. 'Don't bother explaining; just keep the wee fella out of the way.'

'So we can keep him?' asked Fitzpatrick.

'Did I not just say that?' he sighed. Then he looked around the room as if looking for something. 'Where's young Cronin?' His voice was stern once more. Flynn realized the youngster was missing. 'Where's Corporal Fallon?' Devlin added.

'They're outside, Sar'nt,' said Flynn. He could see them on the path outside. Fallon

74

was jabbing the boy in the chest. He gave Fallon something. Flynn couldn't see what. Devlin's face darkened, his eyes hard as he strode to the door. Then they heard shouting, lots of shouting, sending them to the window like children outside a sweetshop. Spud stayed by the stove. Moments later Cronin came in, pale and red-eyed on the cusp of tears: more childlike than ever.

'You all right there, Pat?' Flynn asked as he sat down next to the boy. 'Is that bastard picking on you because you lied about your age?' Cronin began to protest. 'Look, none of us give a damn if you did; you're one of us now and we look after our own,' he added, hesitantly putting his arm around the boy's slight shoulders. The boy wiped his nose on his sleeve and smiled weakly, suddenly childlike behind his large blue eyes. For some reason Flynn felt awkward, unsure what to do. His father had never been tactile. The others tumbled from the window.

'Shit, it's Mr Murphy!' cried the Duke as he dived for his bunk and began studiously shining a brass belt buckle. Carolan stuffed Spud into his backpack whilst Gallagher, Doyle and Fitzpatrick engrossed themselves in small talk about polishing boots. Cronin began cleaning his rifle. They looked guilty as sin. Flynn walked to the window. Murphy was talking to Devlin whilst Fallon stood rigidly to attention, his gaze in the middle distance.

'What's the craic?' asked Gallagher, glancing up from a toecap.

'Fallon doesn't look a happy chappie. Murphy's taking them somewhere,' he replied. Spud poked his head from Carolan's pack.

'What now?' Doyle asked.

'This is the army, me ol' mucker, so we march to the last command,' replied Gallagher as he pulled a chair up by the stove.

'But we've not been told to do anything,' said Carolan.

'Precisely!' declared Gallagher with a cheesy grin, warming his hands. Flynn re-read Mary's letter. The door flew open, drenching them in an icy blast. It was Fallon. They tensed but he said nothing; instead he marched inside, pursued by two provost corporals barking like irate terriers. For a moment Flynn thought they were about to be arrested for what had happened earlier, but then he realized they were barking at Fallon. He was hatless and beltless, his stripes gone: under arrest.

'Private Fallon will be collecting his kit,' said Devlin from the door.

'Serves the gobshite right,' muttered the Duke.

'Wind yer neck in, Wellesley,' snapped Devlin before shouting at Fallon to move

76

faster. Moments later their nemesis was gone, doubling through the snow in full kit with his rifle above his head.

'So who's our new corporal, Sarge?' asked Docherty, fiddling casually with his sandy moustache. Devlin chose to ignore his familiarity; for now. Instead he scanned the room then rummaged in his pocket. His gaze fell on Flynn, who shifted uncomfortably.

'Why are ye out of uniform?' asked Devlin. Flynn checked his uniform, giving Devlin a puzzled look. 'Mr Murphy, in his wisdom, has decided to put ye in charge of this shower of shite so you'd better put these up,' he added, tossing a set of corporal stripes at Flynn. He felt sick as the colour washed from his face. Gallagher laughed. 'I don't know what ye're laughing at, ye Jackeen *eejit,* cos he's made you a lance jack!' Gallagher stared at the two braided chevrons that landed on his bed. 'Now, you've got ten minutes to get them sewn on and outside – full marching order. Mr Murphy wants to take us out for a stroll!' No one moved. 'Well?'

'Marvellous,' groaned Gallagher.

Outside it began to snow.

CHAPTER 6

September 1915, *MV Cambria*, Dublin Bay

The lord lieutenant and the GOC saw them off on the morning tide. Flynn had never been to sea before. Overhead, circling gulls screeched. The weather deck was crowded, throbbing beneath their feet as the *Cambria*, one of the vessels that regularly ferried soldiers across the Irish Sea, slipped its moorings into Dublin Bay. A lone piper, up in the eyes of the ship, skirled a lament.

'Well, the Wild Geese are flying,' said Flynn quietly as he watched the grey smear of land shrink on the horizon.

'Them's gulls not geese, you *eejit*,' replied Gallagher, scanning the sky. Flynn didn't bother to explain. His cap was on the back of his head, letting wisps of oiled hair dance in the wind. 'How long is it?'

'That's a rather personal question,' quipped Flynn.

'No, I mean how long is it since we joined up?'

'A year,' replied Flynn.

'At least we'll get a chance to show the Kaiser what the Irish can do,' added Fitzpatrick. 'Wasn't this all supposed to be over by Christmas?'

'Yes, but no one said which Christmas,' said Flynn. It was a weak joke but it made them laugh every time.

'Seriously, though, things have changed,' said Doyle, leaning on the guard rail. 'When I was home on leave I got plenty of funny looks–'

'It's them bloody Shinners,' interrupted Carolan. Flynn noticed him fiddling self-consciously with his wedding ring; he'd married his girlfriend, Lizzie, on his last leave and for a moment he felt jealous. Not of Lizzie (though she was nice enough), nor the extra money (although that would be useful), but because Carolan had found someone special, someone to share his life with, and for a brief moment he toyed with asking Mary to marry him when he saw her next. Then he glanced back at Carolan, who was gazing mournfully in the direction of home, and dismissed the thought: maybe after the war.

'No, it was the lads in my old Volunteer unit. They said I was an *eejit;* a traitor even, for doing England's dirty work,' added Doyle. The war had split the National Volunteer movement but the battalion, indeed the division, was full of them, none the less. 'Remember that day we were marching down in Cork, came across a load of Volunteers drilling outside Ballyhooley? You know, the ones who turned their backs on us as we marched by? You mark my words, there's trouble brewing.'

'Not that old *England's adversity is Ireland's opportunity* nonsense,' said Gallagher. 'The Fenians haven't done anything since they cocked it up in '67,' he said, referring to the last failed Irish rebellion almost half a century before.

'But England wasn't at war then,' said Docherty.

'True,' said the Duke. 'But surely there's no point in rebellion. All we've got to do is win the war and we'll have Home Rule. It's as good as in the bag. A rebellion would fuck it up for everyone.'

'Lieutenant Reid says Jerry was a holy terror in Belgium; bayoneting women and children. He was in the Volunteers and he says we've got to do something and if we don't, then who will?' asked Gallagher.

'I'm just saying what I heard,' replied Doyle.

'What about the Prods from up north? Those fellas are as Irish as you and me. Maybe they think if they help win the war the government will kybosh Home Rule?' said Flynn.

'They've only got one division,' answered Fitzpatrick, meaning the Unionist 36th Ulster Division, 'whilst we've got two: ours and the 10th. The English will owe us twice as much. Besides, not all Prods are the same. Lieutenant Callear's one and he don't seem to mind taking orders from Captain Murphy. Maybe this war will finally show that we can get on together.' Murphy had recently been promoted, Callear his replacement.

'Orange and Green meeting in peace, like the Shinners' flag?' asked Flynn.

'It's a thought,' said Fitzpatrick.

'It's bollocks,' replied the Duke. 'Mr Callear's not a proper Prod. He's like Wolfe Tone: one of ours. Not like them fellas from up north.'

'Anyway,' said Doyle, 'Protestant, Catholic, whatever, we're all a bunch of Micks to the English.'

Flynn sighed. He'd heard this discussion a thousand times and still it depressed him, hating both the Anglophobia and sectarianism of his country's politics. Cronin, until now quiet, jack-knifed noisily over the rail, retching violently despite the dead calm, just as the battalion's padre, Father Doyle, emerged from the crowd.

'There, there now, my son,' soothed the middle-aged Jesuit, rubbing the boy's back. 'You'll be better for a lie-down,' he added as the boy mustered a weak, vaguely vomit-smelling smile before wiping his mouth with his sleeve. 'We'll be ashore soon.' Cronin tottered away, helped by Carolan. It was three hours to Holyhead. Spud yapped at the

Jesuit's feet and he squatted to pet his fur as he chatted to the lads, offering cigarettes and comfort. The boys seemed to like him. The wind picked up and Flynn gathered himself into the depths of his greatcoat, staring at the grey skies. 'You look troubled, Corporal?' Father Doyle asked.

'Just hungry, Father,' replied Flynn, more interested in the CO up on the bridge-wing deep in conversation with the ship's bearded Welsh captain. He wasn't much of a Catholic. The padre offered him a humbug. Spud yapped, wagging his approval. 'If you'll excuse me, Father, I think I'll see if there's any scoff on this rust bucket.'

'How come he knows when we are talking about scoff?' asked Gallagher as they made their way below.

Nearby, in the lee of a lifeboat, Fallon watched them go. 'You know, they're the shites who cost me my stripes,' he told his round-faced companion, Aiden Collins, who stood puffing on a briar pipe. Fallon flicked his fag end overboard, ferreting through his pockets for his cigarettes.

'There'll be time enough to get even,' said his companion, his Corkonian accent incongruous amid all the Dubliners. 'The Italians have a saying, Marty, that revenge is a pudding best eaten cold. They'll get their just deserts.' Then he laughed.

'What's so funny?' asked Fallon.

82

'Just deserts? Did you see what I did there?' said Collins.

There was a swell building. Below decks the throb of the engines was louder, rattling off the bulkheads to mix with the hubbub of milling soldiery. Flynn and Gallagher found what they were looking for: a galley serving thick sweet tea and doorstop bacon sandwiches dripping in grease. Flynn forced it down, savouring his tea. Even Cronin tried to eat, although he still looked like an anaemic panda, whilst Carolan slipped Spud a few scraps. So did the others. Flynn went back on deck. By the time they reached Holyhead, it was raining.

As soon as they tied up, Clee was on the quayside, with the RSM and the other sergeant majors, preparing to unload the battalion. The CO and officers stood aloof, leaving the work to the NCOs. Flynn got his boys ashore, his legs unsteady on the firm ground beneath the weight of his kit. At least Cronin looked happier to be on dry land. Devlin kept them moving, over the road to the huge railway terminus where Mahon was waiting, sickeningly smart. Gallear sauntered over, his uniform rumpled.

'The trains here aren't like the ones back home,' he said. 'They'll not hang around so keep the boys moving. I'm not looking forward to London. Once we're at Euston we've got to get on the underground to Waterloo in

83

time for the connection to Aldershot.'

'I'll try not to lose any,' said Mahon, who knew London well and had fond memories of the city from his time in the Irish Guards. Devlin was no stranger to the place either. Flynn couldn't help wondering how many Irish soldiers had passed through its doors on the way to God knows where. A battered old locomotive in London and North Western livery sat steaming in the station. Someone handed him a mug of tea which he drank quickly, scalding his mouth but warming his guts. He pulled out his watch, a half-hunter given to him by his father.

'It'll be the middle of the night by the time we reach London,' he complained.

'Then sleep on the train,' growled Devlin.

He didn't reply, preferring to find a seat and snuggle into his greatcoat, staring at his reflection in the window, his thoughts drifting to Mary. Spud was sticking out of Carolan's coat, who was being quizzed by Docherty about what it was like to *do it* with a woman. They were always asking him since he'd got married and he always declined to answer. Gallagher was already asleep. Fitzpatrick broke out his cards. He was trying to teach them Pinochle. They preferred Twenty-Five. The train lurched, starting to move, its motion rocking Flynn to sleep. By the time he woke they'd arrived. It was still dark.

Euston Station was cold and in chaos.

Bleary-eyed soldiers, labouring under all they owned, swarmed around its red brick confines. There were stretchers laid on the icy stone floor, their burdens huddled beneath blankets being ministered to by orderlies and nurses in crisp, starched uniforms. A row of men sat silently on nearby benches, their faces masked by bandages: gas casualties awaiting the next hospital train. Here and there angry-looking military policemen stood surveying the scene, anxious to apprehend anyone with thoughts of running. Flynn needed the toilet. He'd already been several times on the train but the raw night air was proving too much for his bladder. The toilets were closed.

'So are the pubs,' Gallagher grumbled. It was five minutes past three. 'Why does the army do everything in the middle of the blasted night?'

'Because the pubs are closed, *eejit?*' offered Carolan, cheekily.

'That's *corporal eejit* to you, Joe,' said Gallagher with a grin. Flynn slipped away to find somewhere out of the way to relieve himself. Nearby a policeman stood looking bored. Soldiers were no longer a novelty in London either. Outside a police whistle shrilled. Others took up the cry. The policeman glanced out into the gloom, deciding to ignore it. It was someone else's problem.

'Incredible, isn't it?' observed Flynn as

they were herded towards the underground; another precaution against any of them slipping away in the dark. Dublin had nothing like it and whilst Gallagher seemed disinterested – he wanted a drink – there were others who were equally overawed.

'My uncle helped dig this. This is good Irish workmanship, not any of your English rubbish,' the Duke said, raising a laugh as they descended into the bowels of the earth.

'Heck, this is nothing! We got a subway like this back in Boston,' Fitzgerald added rather too smugly.

'You don't say?' said Carolan. They were used to Fitzgerald telling them how things were much better and bigger in the States. 'I bet it was built by the Irish too!' Devlin waited at the foot of the stairs, clipboard in hand. Murphy was there, aloof, puffing on his pipe whilst Clee saw to the details.

'Keep them together,' Devlin told Flynn as they jostled onto a platform between two tracks. He didn't notice Fallon squeezing in behind him. They were close to the edge. A blast of cold air tore through the tunnel, burgeoning ahead of the oncoming train. Fallon eased forward. Flynn glanced down at the track. He felt something sharp in his back, shoving him forward as the noise of the train overwhelmed his senses.

'Steady there, Kev, you almost fell!' cried Gallagher, yanking his friend back from the edge just as the tube train came squealing to a halt.

Flynn was shaking. 'Someone pushed me!' he gasped.

'Don't be daft. It's a good job I was there to catch you, eh?' said Gallagher as he bundled Flynn onto the train.

The lights flickered as the tube train lurched into life, clattering past a tatty old Ovaltine poster. A face leapt from the mob: Fallon. Flynn felt his eyes bore into him, dripping with malice. Then they were gone, leaving Flynn to the musty odour of damp serge, sweat and tobacco.

'Anyone know where the hell we're going?' asked Carolan, petting Spud.

'Blackdown, near Aldershot,' grunted Gallagher.

'I heard Devlin and Mahon call it Aldershite,' said the Duke.

'Marvellous,' replied Flynn.

Back on the platform someone pulled out a mouth organ and started to play 'A Nation Once Again'. Fallon slumped against the station wall, lighting a cigarette.

'Are you all right, Marty?' asked Collins.

Fallon nodded, a sneer playing on his thin lips. Next time he'd try harder. Next time he'd get it right. Next time Flynn would pay. He started to sing.

CHAPTER 7

December 1915, Woolwich, London

'Terry says you're off overseas soon,' she said.

'You know, they don't do chips like they do back home,' said Flynn. He'd looked forward to seeing her but felt awkward now, groping for something to say that didn't involve the war. Even the air stank of the war, the enormous armaments factory that dominated Woolwich. There was a nip in the air; that nip all cities seem to have after sunset as the masonry cools.

'It's just chips and a scrap of fish,' she laughed, looking up at him. She thought he looked different; less lanky but as gawky as when she'd seen him last; more man than boy. Her brother had changed too. She put it down to the army. She traced his corporal stripes with her finger, pulling him closer, making his skin tingle. 'Is that all you do? Go on about missing Dublin?' she asked. Flynn gave her a sidelong glance, half hoping she wouldn't notice whilst secretly hoping she would. He loved her smile, although she seemed more careworn than he remembered her. She was beautiful, none the less.

'They make sure we don't get enough time to get homesick,' he lied. 'We're run ragged from dawn till dusk. We were lucky to get leave as it is.' His voice faded, as he realized that he had no idea when he would see her again after the weekend. Gallagher was right: they were off soon. She sensed his discomfort, looking into his pale-grey eyes.

'Do you miss nothing from home?' she asked, wide-eyed in mock innocence.

He blushed. 'Not at home,' he replied, haltingly. She wrinkled her nose, beaming before unexpectedly pecking him on the cheek. 'I think we better get back before this lot gets cold,' he said, floundering. 'Do you think you should be living round here?' he asked as they turned into the street where Mary shared a few shabby rooms with her brother's widow, Janet. It was a no-man's-land of drab red brick punctuated by chipped windows and grubby net curtains. It reminded Flynn of those bits of Dublin his parents didn't approve of. Not because they were run down but because of their scions.

'I didn't know you cared?' she teased.

'Is it safe from the Zeppelins here? What with the arsenal so close?' he asked. 'Didn't they bomb the place recently?'

'They did, and the docks as well as up town,' she replied dismissively.

'Why don't you and Janet go back to

Dublin?' asked Flynn.

'Janet's English and, besides, what would we do? Sit around and listen to my mammy go on about Terry playing soldiers or Rory moan about not being able to? I'd rather be here. I've a job and some money of my own to do with what I want,' she said. 'Sure it's long hours but I'm doing my bit.' Somewhere a dog was barking, ignored by the two policemen strolling down the other side of the street. 'Anyway, shouldn't it be me worrying about you?'

'I'll be fine. Besides, it'll all be over by Christmas,' he joked.

'Away with you,' she said, slapping his arm. 'Do you want to fight?' It was a strange question. Despite a year in training, he hadn't really thought about it. He didn't know what to say, realizing that part of him really was looking forward to going to France, that part of him was afraid it would be over before he got there.

'We're here,' he said, changing the subject, stating the obvious. Mary narrowed her eyes, pouting in thought. Flynn scanned the street, unconsciously watching her back. He could smell her hair. The door swung inwards unleashing a waft of unwelcoming musty air. She turned on the light. The hall smelt damp; candy-striped wallpaper blistered from the walls. Dog-eared letters lay discarded on an old sideboard. Flynn realized it wasn't just the Zeppelins that made him uncomfortable about Mary's lodgings. A door at the far end of the hall creaked open a crack. A face peeped out, then it swung open, unleashing a blast of old socks. A thin, colourless man in a greasy cardigan stepped into the hall. He looked older than his years, a pathetic scrape of hair doing nothing to mask his baldness. Flynn didn't like the way he looked at Mary, blatantly undressing her with his watery eyes.

'Good evening, Miss Gallagher,' said the man. 'I don't approve of my ladies having ... er ... *gentlemen* callers,' he said. Flynn didn't like his tone.

'Mr Daiken, what are you suggesting? This isn't a *gentleman caller*. This is Corporal Flynn of the Royal Dublin Fusiliers and he's an old family friend. He's here with my brother to see how we are before they go off to fight for king and country,' she replied.

Daiken didn't look impressed. 'Maybe so, Miss Gallagher, but this is a respectable house!' Daiken said, doing little to hide watching Mary's backside in anything but a respectable fashion as they climbed the stairs.

'Who's he?' asked Flynn testily, balling his fists.

'Never mind the old lech; he's only the landlord,' she replied.

'I don't like the way he looks at you,' Flynn said.

91

'Just ignore him, he's a harmless old fart,' she teased as they reached the third landing where the rooms she shared with Janet and her children were located. 'Here we are, home sweet home,' she announced. The door was cracked, flaking in places, and smelt like old cabbage.

'You will write, won't you?' he suddenly blurted.

'Don't I already?' she asked as she reached up, touching his face, grazing the hint of stubble on his chin with her fingertips.

'It's just that I ... I ... er...' he stammered, blushing, suddenly lost for words.

'I know you do, Kevin,' she said softly, cupping his face gently in her hands, reaching up to kiss him. He pulled her nearer, savouring her warmth, crushing their fish suppers between them. There was a thud. Flynn jumped, pulling away from Mary suddenly. Gallagher stood in the doorway in shirt-sleeves, his grey army braces hanging down either side of his khaki trousers. He was nursing a half-drunk bottle of Guinness in his ham fist.

'Jaysus, Kev,' Gallagher blasphemed un-ashamedly, 'will you put my sister down, I'm starving like my throat's been cut.' He held up a bottle of stout. 'You know, this stuff isn't nothing like the stuff back home!'

'Will God save us, if it's not another of you bleating on about how much better things are back home!' said Mary, rolling her eyes and laughing as she barged past.

'What?' Gallagher asked, following the appetizing aroma in his sister's wake. The room was all dancing shadows, threadbare in the guttering gaslight, but neat. Janet kept an orderly house. There was a table, piled with plates, in the centre of the room whilst tea brewed in a garishly cosied pot at its heart.

'You took your time,' said Janet Gallagher, giving Mary a knowing look as she bounced a toddler – a mini version of herself – on her knee. The little girl yawned, exposing a smattering of milk teeth, rubbing her eyes. 'I think someone needs a nap.' She lay Daisy in her cot near the window, wiping her hands on her apron before brushing away a brown curl from her sad, dark eyes. She was only twenty-five but looked older; worn down by widowhood and three children. A picture of Mary's brother stood on the mantelpiece next to a bundle of letters bound with a black velvet ribbon. He looked like a taller version of Gallagher. They were so alike that one of the children, Davey, had mistaken him for his dad. Who could blame him, as the boisterous six-year-old's memories of his father began to fade? Eventually he accepted that Gallagher was his uncle, whatever that was, and spent the rest of the day amusing himself with the brightly painted lead soldiers Gallagher had given him. He especially liked the one on a horse in shining armour and a scarlet tunic. He also liked wearing his uncle's khaki cap. Davey's other sister, four-year-old Lizzie, all auburn hair and beamy smiles, sat swinging her legs at the table, balancing her chin on her little hands, watching the packets of food with keen, intelligent eyes. Money was tight. Mickey Gallagher had married Janet without permission, which meant no extra money, no married quarters and now not even a widow's pension. That was why she'd got a job at the arsenal and why Mary had left Ireland to help.

'Come on, everyone, dig in!' said Flynn, throwing his coat over the sofa. He wasn't really hungry. 'What's this, then?' he added, waving a bottle of lemonade. Lizzie squealed with delight as he sloshed the fizzy liquid into the children's cups, pausing for a moment as he wondered if he would ever do this with his own children.

'Do they feed you well?' Janet asked as she cut up Davey's food.

'Aye, mostly bully beef and chips with everything,' replied Flynn.

'I like chips,' Gallagher said through a mass of food.

Flynn snorted. 'You'll eat anything! There was this time back in Ballyhooley...'

'I really don't think the girls would want to hear it!' choked Gallagher, making Flynn laugh all the harder. Mary and Janet laughed too whilst the children picked through the scraps like vultures.

'So when do you have to report back?' asked Janet, suddenly sombre.

'Tomorrow afternoon, Mrs Gallagher,' answered Flynn.

She smiled. 'I've told you to call me Janet,' she said, clearing the plates.

'Leave those, Janet,' he said. 'We'll clean up, then we'll get back to Waterloo station. There's a place there we can stay the night.'

'You'll do no such thing–' Janet started to say.

'It's only the plates,' replied Flynn.

'Stop talking nonsense! You ain't seen Mary for almost a year. You'll stay here and that's the end of it,' she chided. 'I've plenty of blankets.'

'What about that Daiken fella?' Flynn asked.

'Sod him,' she replied. Secretly, Flynn was relieved. He didn't fancy traipsing across London in the middle of the night in search of a bed or, worse still, a pub if Gallagher had his way.

In the end a pub wasn't needed and by ten o'clock Gallagher was snoring gently, slumped in an old armchair after his fifth bottle of Guinness.

'Just like back home,' joked Mary from the sofa next to Janet. Flynn sat at the table, gazing at the fire smouldering in the grate bathing the room in a flickering glow.

'Well, I'm off to bed,' announced Janet. 'Thank you, for tonight,' she said, resting her hand on Flynn's shoulder and smiling, and he wondered how many countless other women's lives had been ruined, would be ruined, by the war. She closed the door, leaving him alone with Mary and her brother's snores.

'Don't worry, he's dead to the world with a drink in him,' said Mary, patting the space next to her. 'Now come here and talk to me.'

'It must be hard for her,' Flynn said.

'It's hard on all of us,' she replied. 'It must be terrible for him, buried over there away from his kin.' She squeezed Flynn's hand, looking into his eyes. 'Will you visit his grave for me?' There were tears in her eyes. Flynn pulled her close and she nestled her head on his chest and sobbed. He nodded. 'You will take care of this one too?' she finally said, looking at her brother sprawled in his chair beneath a tartan picnic blanket.

'I'll try,' he replied awkwardly, desperate to avoid making promises he couldn't keep.

'And take care of yourself or I'll kill you,' she added, giving him a peck on the cheek. He kissed her, pulling her close, feeling the warmth of her body through his clothes. 'I suppose I'd better be getting to bed myself,' she finally said, doing nothing to end their embrace, letting him smooth her unruly blonde hair. He closed his eyes, blotting out the world as she snuggled up closer, wriggling in his lap, making him stir.

'Mary...' he began but her lips cut him off. When she finally left him, he sat gazing at the fire's dying embers, unable to sleep as he listened to the old building creak. Her scent lingered on his skin, her taste on his lips, and when he finally closed his eyes her image was behind them. Being so close made him warm. Then he remembered the war, waiting for him across the Channel. Gallagher farted, filling the room with a terrible stench. Flynn didn't know whether to laugh or cry.

By morning the smell still lingered so he opened a window to freshen the air.

Gallagher let rip another thunderous fart. 'Gas! Gas! Gas!' he chuckled like a naughty schoolboy before nestling deeper into the folds of his blanket.

'Has something died in your arse?' gasped Flynn. 'You need pulling through.'

It came to something when city air smelt good. He could smell the Thames as well as the arsenal. It was peaceful, quiet even, save for a painfully emaciated horse in the street below struggling to pull a milk float. All the good horses were gone.

BANG! Both soldiers jumped as the children's door exploded inwards disgorging a jumble of squealing kids that crashed into Gallagher's seated form. Janet stood in the doorway, balancing Daisy on her hip. 'Tea?' she asked.

Breakfast was frugal; tea and toast supplemented by a large tin of plum and apple jam 'organized' by Gallagher from the QM's store, which Davey ate straight from the tin with a spoon. He'd 'organized' some tins of bully beef too, but it was the slab of dark army chocolate that truly sent the children into wide-eyed rapture. Conversation was scarce. Time passed too quickly and it was with great reluctance that the two men gathered their kit to leave. Gallagher gave the children thruppence each before self-consciously stuffing a ten-bob note into Janet's hand.

'I'll try and send you something,' he said, making Flynn think of his father's fiver still unspent in his wallet.

'If it were done when 'tis done, then 'twere well it were done quickly,' Flynn announced, quoting Shakespeare. It was a habit in awkward situations.

'Don't worry, he's always talking like this,' explained Gallagher as they strolled through the streets to the station. Despite their company, Flynn felt alone; like a man taking the short walk to the gallows, each step a step closer to the inevitability of an inescapable fate.

'I'll write,' she reassured him, squeezing his hand. He clung to her like a drowning man on flotsam. She was crying; fat, salty tears as if already mourning him. They kissed. The war had changed everything; no one noticing such a public display of intimacy. Then they parted and he trudged reluctantly to the waiting train, their separation seeming so final. Flynn tried to look like he wasn't going to cry and Gallagher pretended not to notice.

CHAPTER 8

December 1915, Golden Harp public house, Kilburn, London

Few saw beyond Mick Collins's boyish charm and cheap brown suit to see the dedicated revolutionary. That suited him fine. Like all members of the secretive Irish Republican Brotherhood, Mick had spent ages cultivating influence amongst the city's Irish diaspora and wasn't keen to be seen in the company of men wearing the king's uniform; even if one was his cousin in the back of a smoky pub. Anonymity suited him.

'Where I come from a man is taught to be ... er ... cautious about who he talks to,' Mick said warily, his thick west-Cork brogue fresh off the ferry untainted by five years of London life, as he handed his cousin Aiden Collins a pint of Guinness. He was smiling, his listless hazel eyes flitting to his cousin's wizened companion. Fallon made a discreet gesture. Mick paused, ignoring his own drink, his cigarette flaring before responding, partially satisfied that the man was also a member of the IRB.

'Maybe it's you who should be asking what I could do for you?' suggested Fallon before taking a draught of stout, draining a third with a loud deep swallow.

'And what would you do for me?' replied Mick.

'*Tiocfaidh ár lá*,' Fallon said in his native Irish, sitting back smugly. Mick raised an eyebrow, surprised that a Dubliner would be *Gaeilgeoirí*, a native speaker.

'Our day will come,' he repeated in English.

'Aye, and when it does, me and Aiden here are perfectly placed to do our duty and help free the old country from the English yoke,' replied Fallon.

'So says the redcoat,' Mick quipped.

Fallon bridled at the barb. 'I've my orders,' he sneered.

Mick simply smiled, betraying nothing that went on behind his hard, dark eyes. 'It'll not be long before there's another rising, what with the war and all, and when it comes there'll be plenty of lads in the Dubs who would be willing to come in with us and help. I've heard talk of an Irish Brigade being raised from the boys taken prisoner by the Germans at Mons and the like.' Mick said nothing. He'd heard the rumours too that Sir Roger Casement, the renegade ex-British Diplomat and co-founder of the Irish Volunteers, had travelled to Germany to try and raise an 'Irish Brigade' from amongst Irish prisoners of war. He'd also heard it was a failure, attracting less than sixty recruits to its ranks: hardly a brigade at all.

'What's that to me?' Mick asked, playing his cards close to his chest. He didn't trust Fallon, just another revolutionary wannabe. Ireland was cursed with them, men who could neither hold their drink nor their tongues, sending too many good men to England's gallows.

'My division, the 16th Irish, leaves for France this month,' said Fallon, sliding a tatty envelope across the beer-stained table towards him.

'And why would I be interested in that?' asked Mick.

'In there's everything. Movement orders; timetables; supply dumps; the lot. It wasn't easy to get but if we moved quick we could get a few rifles and ammunition for the cause. Who knows, maybe Jerry would be interested to know too,' replied Fallon before sitting back and draining his glass. He banged the empty glass down smugly, causing a lull in the hubbub, and drinkers turned their shadowy faces to peer through the fuggy air at the fuss. Mick didn't mind. The Golden Harp may well be down at heel, shabby even for a backstreet pub, but it was safe Fenian ground and that was all that mattered.

A hulking shape loomed from the shadows. 'Is everything all right there, Mick?' asked the man, cradling a dark polished *shillelagh* in his brawny arms.

'We're just grand, Charlie,' Mick said, waving the man away, then he smiled. 'Tell you what, Charlie, would you fetch us a couple more drinks?' Charlie nodded and slipped slowly back into the smoky gloom. The envelope remained untouched on the table. Mick didn't even look at it, feigning disinterest as he weighed up the odds of this being some sort of Special Branch set-up. The Brits were always looking for fellas willing to sell out their countrymen; they were the bane of his life. He was naturally cautious. 'I might know someone who knows someone,' he eventually said, slipping the envelope into his inside pocket.

'Knows someone who knows someone, what kind of *eejit* do you take me for?' Fallon snapped. Mick resisted a reply. He'd been warned about Fallon by his contacts in Dublin. He'd been a good man once, ruined by drink. Now he was a liability. 'Look, sonny,' Fallon sneered. 'Either you're for sticking it to the Brits or you're not, so stop wasting my time,' he slurred, worse for the drink. Mick's cigarette flared and for a second Aiden thought he saw his cousin's jovial façade slip, revealing the cruelty within, and he realized that if looks could kill, the old soldier was already snug in his grave.

'*Slán abhaile.* We'll not meet again,' said Mick. He chose his words carefully – safe home – a phrase used by Irish-speaking Republicans to speed the English on their way. The irony wasn't lost on Fallon as he sat in the king's khaki.

'Your gobshite cousin's telling us to piss off,' snapped Fallon.

'I'm wishing you a safe journey home, that's all,' explained Mick, all smiles once more. Aiden relaxed, reassured by his cousin's words.

'Sure you are,' growled Fallon dangerously, his fists balling as Mick scraped back his chair. Fallon lurched to his feet, swaying after a hard day in his cups. Ruefully Collins shook his head and turned to go, ignoring Fallon's rheumy eyes on his back as he strode through the swirling tobacco fog. For a second Aiden thought Fallon would go after him but he was distracted by the two glasses of stout that Charlie plonked down on the greasy, beer-stained table. Licking his lips, Fallon slumped into his chair, knocking back half a pint of Guinness in one deep, open-throated swallow.

'Leave the punk go,' muttered Fallon but Aiden ignored him, following his cousin. He caught up with him by the door.

'Marty's a good man, Mick,' he said.

'Maybe, but how do you know ye can trust him? He's a drunken *eejit* now, whatever he was, and you're better off shot of him,' said Mick.

'But he got you the division's movement plans,' added Aiden.

Mick sighed, giving his cousin an indulgent look. 'I'll tell you what, keep the drunken *eejit* out of my way until I've had a chance to take a look at these; see if they're any use. If they are, well, I'll be in touch. *Sián go foil*, Ade,' he said, pulling on his coat as a wailing air raid split the night. 'Ach, if it isn't them bloody Zeppelins!' he muttered, flicking up his overcoat collar against the chill. Then he was gone, leaving Aiden alone in the dark.

CHAPTER 9

31 December 1915, Ploegsteert, Belgium

It had been warm in the train, huddled together in the cattle wagons, leeching heat from each other, but now, outside, the night was raw. Even the fillings in Flynn's teeth seemed to ache as he jumped from the carriage, stretching his stiff limbs as the battalion coughed and spluttered into something resembling a long khaki slug next to the railway line. Gallagher wiped his nose on the back of his greatcoat sleeve, red-eyed from lack of sleep.

'Are we downhearted?' someone shouted, trying to rouse the Irishmen's spirits with a song, but the lack of response spoke volumes. Then it started to rain. He could hear the RSM venting his ire on someone. He wasn't sure who he feared most: the RSM or the Germans. The sky rumbled like approaching thunder.

'There's a storm coming,' Doyle grumbled, pointing at distant flashes.

'That's not thunder,' growled Devlin as he strolled by, leaving Doyle to slip into sullen silence beneath the weight of his pack, his eyes drawn to the flashes like a moth to a candle flame. Predictably, it started to rain and by the time they reached their destination, a cavernous barn, they were soaked. Flynn didn't care. He was tired and wanted to sleep so he buried himself in his sodden greatcoat, closing his eyes. The cold seeped up from the ground into his bones. He sensed movement, opening his eyes. Two little round eyes like jet beads stared into his. They were close, disturbingly shiny, even in the gloom, and he felt something soft brush his nose. It was a rat: a large, smug, fat, self-satisfied rat. Nose twitching, head cocked, it studied him from its plump haunches, smoothing down its greasy fur with its paws before gnawing one of Flynn's leather ammunition pouches.

'Jesus Christ,' he muttered as he swept the plump, cat-sized rodent from his kit, sending it skittering like a drunk across the hard dirt floor, pursued by Spud, who disappeared through a hole in the wall in hot pursuit of his plump prey. Flynn sat up, rubbing his extremities. Propping himself against the damp wall, he fumbled for a cigarette with numb, gloved hands. The gloves, woolly, thick and brown, were a Christmas present from an unnamed Maryborough schoolgirl, along with a pair of warm socks encasing his feet. They were cold and heavy, like lead.

It had been a bleak Christmas, their first out of Ireland, and whilst food had been plentiful no amount of tinned stew could make it any less miserable or distract him from thinking about Mary. She'd written, of course; her loopy, childlike handwriting doing nothing to ease his misery. She'd sent him a picture too, which he slipped in his wallet, to keep it safe. Gallagher had got a fruit-cake – his mother was known for her fruit-cakes – and he guarded it like the crown jewels from his comrades' envious stares.

He watched Spud haul the rat's plump,

limp corpse back through the hole, dragging it towards where Carolan lay, peering from his groundsheet. Spud looked pleased with himself, if dogs could look pleased, and his scrawny tail whipped furiously as he dumped his kill next to Carolan's head, tongue lolling as he patiently awaited his master's response. Flynn took a slug of water from his water bottle, sluicing the brackish fluid around his mouth before spitting it onto the dirt floor.

'Go easy with the water, Corporal Flynn,' chided Devlin, who was already up, making tea over a small, evil-smelling kerosene stove. Nearby, Mahon sat bulling his boots to an inappropriately glossy shine whilst Devlin poured a steaming stream of dark-brown liquid into a battered enamel mug just as Flynn joined him.

'You may talk o' gin and beer when you're quartered safe out 'ere, an' you're sent to penny-fights an' Aldershot it; but when it comes to slaughter you will do your work on water, an' you'll lick the bloomin' boots of 'im that's got it,' said Flynn. Devlin looked at him blankly. 'Kipling; *Gunga Din.*' Devlin thrust a steaming mug into his gloved hands. Even through the wool the heat burned his palms but he resisted the temptation to hold it by the handle, masochistically savouring the warmth leeching into his palms. It was hot and sweet, laced with condensed milk. He could have sworn there was rum in it.

Devlin smiled.

'Don't mind him, Sarge, he goes all poetic on us every now and then,' said Gallagher. 'Do you like Kipling, Sergeant?'

'How would I know? I've never kippled,' retorted Devlin with a grin.

'Very funny,' Flynn groaned between mouthfuls of sweet, hot tea, amazed that no one had gone *'Boom! Boom!'* Gallagher held out his empty mug, an expectant smirk plastered across his face.

Devlin shook his head. 'Am I ye brew bitch now?' he grumbled, sloshing a liberal dose of the steaming brew into Gallagher's mug. Flynn noticed that Devlin treated him and Gallagher differently now they were NCOs, realizing that all the time Devlin, Mahon and now even himself were simply playing the parts expected of them by officers and men alike. It was a game.

'It looks like we're just in time for tea,' said Captain Murphy with Lieutenant Callear in tow. Instinctively, Flynn and Gallagher braced up, feeling suddenly uncomfortable in the officers' presence, but Murphy gestured for them to stand at ease. Flynn was wary of officers even if Murphy was all right. Officers were usually bad news, full of bright ideas like *'Let's go stick it to the Hun'*, and Flynn had a sinking feeling that it wasn't going to be a quiet New Year.

'Any news, sir?' asked Devlin, handing the

officers a mug of tea each. 'The boys are getting bored sitting around.' He knew what to say; how to play the game. Murphy slurped his tea, his dark eyes fixed on some distant point, mulling over both tea and response in equal measure.

'The general thinks it'll do us good to have a wee taster of trench life before we get a sector of our own so we're going into the line for a few days. Plugstreet's pretty quiet right now so I doubt we'll come to any harm.' Devlin started draining his tea. 'No, no, Sar'nt, no need for that, we've plenty of time. Make sure the lads have some hot food inside them; it may be their last chance for a couple of days. I want everyone formed up outside in full kit at nine ack-emma sharp! We've got some trench stores to collect and we need to bomb up but with a bit of luck we'll be in the line in time for a spot of luncheon, eh?' Murphy said. Flynn felt his heart sink. Mahon nodded, breathing on the toecap of his boot before renewing his efforts to buff up the shine. Something in the old NCO's eye told Flynn he shared his reluctance despite his studied, calm demeanour. Devlin flicked away the last dregs of tea before stowing his mug in his knapsack, suddenly serious. Somehow, the distant rumble of the guns seemed ominously louder than before.

'Well, this is it at last,' gasped Gallagher, rubbing his hands with glee.

'Yes, this is it,' muttered Flynn, wondering if he and Mahon were the only ones having reservations.

'Well?' growled Devlin, reverting to type. 'Ye heard the captain; we've a war to be getting on with!' The officers smiled politely, finished their tea and left. Breakfast was tasteless – fuel, nothing more: a greasy mess of some sort of pork fritter and scrambled reconstituted eggs. Gallagher drowned his food in brown sauce. Flynn chewed mechanically, forcing the slimy lumps down with gulps of cold tea. Cronin, pale and waiflike as ever, seemed relieved. Flynn had never seen the boy so happy, as if he truly relished the prospect of entering the line. Spud sat proudly atop his rat watching the cacophony, tail wagging furiously as Father Doyle passed by, patting his scruffy little head before moving on to a corner of the barn where he had erected a makeshift altar and was quietly hearing confessions. Ignoring the priest, Flynn delved into his tunic pocket, feeling the hard wood of the rosary his mother had given him. It wasn't that he wasn't religious; he just couldn't be bothered putting in the effort of being devout. He couldn't even remember the last time he'd recited a decade, let alone the whole sequence of prayers he'd been forced to learn as a child.

'Do you have to do that?' Flynn asked, watching Gallagher repack his kit for the fourth time. All around them others were doing the same, going through mindless rituals – psychological comfort blankets to pass the time. Flynn worked the bolt of his rifle, its click-clack perversely satisfying as the oiled steel slid smoothly into place. He worked it again and again and again.

'Do you have to do *that?*' snapped Gallagher, who was midway through his fifth repack.

'So what do you think it'll be like?' asked Flynn.

'Ye'll find out soon enough,' said Devlin softly, his voice an island of calm amid the buzz of excitement. Unlike the rest he wore webbing, not leather equipment, marking him out as a regular soldier not a wartime volunteer. His rifle's furniture glinted in the morning sun, lovingly polished and oiled, an oilskin cover guarding the working parts against the slurry of sleet tumbling down from the leaden sky. Mahon stood nearby, his middle-aged frame bolt upright despite the weight of the kit draped about him like a lethal Christmas tree. His boots gleamed, flashing in the sunlight as he moved. Gallagher farted loudly, grinning childishly as he wrenched his cap off to scratch his head. His hair was cropped close at the back and sides but hung long across the fringe, flopping over his eyes. Flynn thought it looked strange, reminding him of the haircuts sported by medieval Irish warriors, but it was a popular trend amongst Kitchener's men.

'Christ, my head's cold,' whined Gallagher as they stepped out into the crisp morning air. It had snowed, dusting the area with filthy, grey-brown slush, a cruel easterly wind chilling their bones. Whilst most of them had taken the wire stiffeners from their caps, Gallagher had managed to acquire a battered old 'Gor Blimey' trench cap from somewhere. It was tatty, stained and shapeless, reminding Flynn of an old flat cap. It was obvious that he was desperately trying to cultivate the impression that he was some sort of grizzled old veteran rather than a new arrival.

'Serves you right for getting such a bloody stupid haircut,' said Flynn, who had resisted the temptation to follow suit and have his hair cropped like Gallagher's.

'Dukey here told me they were all the rage over here,' answered Gallagher. The Duke shuffled his feet, trying not to catch Gallagher's eye. 'Didn't you say you were going to get one yourself, eh, Dukey?'

'*Said*, you great culchie *eejit*, I said *said*,' chortled the Duke, ostentatiously raking his fingers through his thick mop of unruly hair. Before he knew it, Gallagher was on him, whooping with glee and slapping him around the head with his battered cap.

'That'll be *corporal* culchie *eejit* to you!' Gallagher chuckled.

112

'For the love of God, will ye give it a rest? We've work to do, ye blathering Jackeen *eejits!'* snapped Devlin, slinging his rifle over his shoulder. Beckoning Flynn over, he led him out of earshot of the others. 'I know this is your first time, Kevin, but it's theirs too, and as long as ye've them stripes on yer arm they'll be looking to you if anything happens, so try not to look so bloody worried. Smile, joke and make them think ye've not a care in the world. I don't give a shit if ye're crying inside, nor will they; if ye look happy, they'll be happy too,' Devlin said softly, patting Flynn on the shoulder. Flynn nodded, forcing himself to smile. By the time they'd loaded up with picket posts, barbed wire, bombs, ammunition, food, water and the myriad of other bits of awkward, unwieldy junk so innocuously labelled *'trench stores'* on the QM's inventory, it was almost midday. The guns had stopped, probably for lunch according to Carolan, and the snow had redoubled its efforts, leaving a light frosting on caps, packs and shoulders.

'Gosh, fellas, this stuff weighs a fricking ton,' grumbled Fitzgerald.

'For the love of God, will you stop bitching? You're a flaming Yank – you aren't even sup-posed to be here!' snapped Doyle grumpily. Devlin smiled to himself: as long as they were complaining, he knew their morale was good. It was when they stopped that he'd worry.

'Come on, ye miserable bastards, sing!' Devlin shouted. A voice from the back of the column boomed out *'Whiter than the whitewash on the wall...'* joined by dozens answering *'...on the wall! Oh, wash me in the water that you wash your dirty daughter in and we will be whiter than the whitewash on the wall!'* Devlin belted out the chorus, urging others to join. There were Tommies lining the road: grey, sallow-faced, fatigue etched into their bones, wallowing in the sheer luxury of inactivity. Here and there one smiled or even waved but for the most part they sat staring blankly. Swirls of snow whipped up around their feet as the Irishmen swaggered past, singing gustily, drawing nearer to their destination. Flynn couldn't help notice the subtle change in the bleak winter landscape as nature's desolation gave way to man's.

'Jakers, what's that stink?' gasped Carolan, gagging violently. Flynn smelt it too, a putrid stench clawing at the contents of his convulsing stomach. Then they saw it: a shambles of bloated, rotting flesh that used to be a horse, its front legs torn away, its glassy eyes staring in disbelief. 'Poor bugger,' he muttered as they passed, the singing trailing away into uneasy silence. There was a ramshackle farmhouse nearby, a casualty clearing station. A ragged hole marred the roof; shrapnel scars gouged the walls. They had only come a mile or two at most but it was

114

another world. A doctor stood in the door-way in shirtsleeves despite the cold. His rubber apron was splashed with blood and he watched them with little more than casual professional interest, exchanging meaning-less pleasantries with Murphy as they passed. Men whistled as they dug in the field behind. A plane circled overhead like a mechanical bird of prey.

'What are they digging trenches here for?' asked the Duke.

'They're not trenches,' muttered Gallagher, leaving the rest unsaid as they came to a halt. Flynn noticed a group of mud-caked soldiers watching them from further up the lane. One of them, a young-looking sergeant with a wispy blond moustache, sauntered over, saluting Murphy. He stank like a farmyard, his 'Gor Blimey' cap perched on the back of his head unleashing a shock of blond hair.

He wore a goatskin over his coat.

'My name's Sergeant Kay, sir. I'll be tak-ing you up into the line,' he said in a rolling Lancashire accent. Murphy returned the salute. They said something Flynn couldn't hear and then they were off, following the sergeant's easy, economical, infantryman's stride. The noise of the guns grew louder and the slushy mud grew deeper till it slurped over the tops of their boots.

'Join up, they said... See the world, they said...' someone muttered from the anony-

115

mity of the ranks, drawing a grim look from Clee. Then they were silent.

'Copped it last night, sir,' Kay told Murphy as they passed a tarpaulin covering three bodies, their mud-caked boots sticking out from beneath it. Flynn tried not to look – he'd never seen a corpse before – but he couldn't help it. 'A stray whizz-bang got them,' he added, matter-of-factly, as if being emotional was too much effort. 'It's pretty cushty really, sir,' said Kay, but his words lacked conviction. It wasn't long before they reached the communication trench, passing a battered sign ominously declaring *'Beware of the Snipers'*. It didn't take long for Flynn to lose his bearings as they snaked along the wet clay gutter decked with cracked boards. At least Kay seemed to know where he was going. Something rent the air, sending skittish fusiliers ducking for cover beneath showering dirt. Flynn was on his arse.

'A fecking banshee!' quailed a whey-faced Gallagher.

'And since when did you get all culchie, believing in banshees?' chided Flynn.

'Show's over, let's get moving,' said Devlin, calmly ignoring their baptism.

'It's not the ones you can hear that will kill you,' said Kay with a smile that was at once weary and knowing, indulgently shaking his head. Flynn struggled to his feet, his hobnails skidding. The iron wire pickets he'd been given bit into his shoulder despite the layers of serge and flannel between them and his flesh. There were more loud bangs, more dirt. He was slick with sweat despite the snow and a lump grew in the pit of his stomach like a badly digested meal. Devlin's words, *'They'll be looking to you,'* swirled through his mind, crushing him beneath the weight of responsibility.

CHAPTER 10

31 December 1915, British front line, Ploegsteert, Belgium

In a few hours it would be 1916. Flynn's lips were dry. They'd been ordered not to touch their water and for the first time he really got what Devlin had meant about conserving it. War made you thirsty; very thirsty. They'd been told not to touch their iron rations either. Murphy said there'd be hot food waiting. Flynn didn't believe him. Gallagher still had his fruit-cake, buried in his pack, and some chocolate too. No one asked where he got it from as long as he shared. He always did and Flynn savoured his square as he walked. It took his mind off his blisters and the nipping cold. Then they stopped. They were there.

'Could be worse,' said Devlin, looking sickeningly happy. Flynn wondered if the Ulsterman was as miserable as the rest of them. The trench was a shambles; a potpourri of unwashed humanity, decaying matter and discarded food tins. Kay's Lancastrians had obviously done little to make the place habitable. 'We'll soon have this sorted.' Doyle skidded on a greasy duckboard, almost losing his boot in the viscous slurry.

'Well, at least it's not raining,' chipped in Kay.

The heavens opened and a lazy stream of opaque effluent began to slide, rather than flow past, before oozing into the entrance of a nearby dugout, slithering down its steps. Flynn pulled his groundsheet over his head, watching Kay, Devlin and the officers vanish around a traverse. His feet were like ice and he knew if he didn't change his socks soon his feet would begin to rot. Gallagher flopped down next to him, disappointed that his chocolate was all gone.

'This place makes the Liffey smell good,' he observed.

'And what exactly did you expect?' Flynn asked.

'Dunno, it's...' replied Gallagher, shrugging his shoulders, drinking in the scene. Here and there the trench's sides had collapsed under their own waterlogged weight or shell-fire, despite the best efforts of dilapidated corrugated iron and rotten wood. It was an open sewer in every sense of the word and together they watched what looked unmistakably like a turd drift slowly by before eddying into an oily, semi-frozen pool of slushy filth to nudge against a discarded, rusty bully-beef tin. Gallagher offered Flynn a cigarette.

'Why not? Maybe it'll get rid of the smell,' Flynn replied. It didn't.

'See anything?' asked Cronin as he scrambled up beside a bucktoothed sentry who looked barely out of short trousers. They peered into no-man's-land, looking like children playing soldiers. Keeping his eyes on the wasteland, the sentry shook his head. Cronin looked excited, his eyes shining. He was enjoying himself.

'Jerry's up there,' said the sentry, pointing up at the crest a few hundred yards distant. 'The buggers have all the high ground round here; pump the bloody water out so it runs downhill into our trenches every time it pisses down.' There was a series of dull crumps off to the left and Flynn fought the urge to dive for cover. Gallagher began dishing out the last of the cake. More explosions followed.

'Some poor bugger's for it,' muttered one of the Englishmen. Then it stopped as suddenly as it began and for some inexplic-

119

able reason Flynn felt the urge to climb up onto the fire step and take a look for himself. Tufts of grass thrust up around the picket posts amid the dirty snow. Somehow it was nothing like he'd expected. It was, well, ordinary. Rusty barbed wire sagged beneath its own weight, swaying in the gentle breeze. Harmonica music drifted down the hill towards him. It was almost peaceful.

'What's that?' he asked.

'Jerry. They always seem to be singing or the like; musical little bleeders, them lot,' observed the sentry.

'No, I mean what's that?' repeated Flynn as he craned up to get a better view of the misshapen bundle sagging the wire. There was something vaguely familiar about it. Something long and white – bleached in the sun – protruded from it.

'Oh, that? That's a Jerry too,' the sentry informed him, matter-of-factly. Crack! Thump! Flynn felt something hot zing past his cheek.

'Get down, you bloody idiot!' bellowed Sergeant Kay, doubling towards them, followed by Devlin, but Flynn just looked stupefied, unable to comprehend what had happened. Then Gallagher grabbed his belt and heaved him down. Several more rounds zipped overhead. Crack! Thump! Crack! Thump! Crack! Thump! It was a bit like being in the butts back on Ash Ranges outside Aldershot. A machine gun joined it for good measure,

120

sounding like tearing canvas. 'Now look what you've bloody done!' Kay snapped angrily. Gallagher flashed Flynn one of those looks he used to reserve for when Mr Byrne told them off back in the office. It seemed a lifetime ago. Crack! The rifle shot cut Kay short. Everyone turned to stare at Cronin, who stood on the fire step, grinning like the Cheshire cat.

'Gotcha, you filthy Hun swine!' he muttered, his eyes bright with elation. The machine gun had stopped as suddenly as it had begun. There was a ragged cheer.

'Well, look at you. Here five minutes and you've already potted a Hun,' Gallagher crowed proudly as he slapped Cronin on the back. Beaming, Cronin applied his safety catch and got down.

'It's a terrible thing to kill a man,' muttered Mahon.

'Weren't you in the South Africa war?' asked Flynn.

The old soldier gave Flynn a doleful look, as if some long-forgotten memory had awoken.

'I was, and I saw my fair share of killing. The Boers were the enemy, that's all. It was him or me. I took no pleasure in it. Once you've killed a man, there's no going back. It changes you.' He sniffed before walking off.

'Well, when ye've quite finished trying to win the VC perhaps ye can do something useful like sort this dump out – it's a flaming disgrace!' barked Devlin, snatching up a long-handled spade and tossing it at Gallagher, who just managed to catch it without dropping his cigarette.

'You heard the man, let's get to work,' said Flynn, hopping gingerly into the slime that oozed over his ankles and into his boots. 'Hey, Mickey, you were a chippy.'

Doyle nodded, running an expert eye over the cracked timbers.

'I've not got my tools but I'll see what I can do,' he said, tapping one of the beams with his muddy boot. They began digging out the trench, chucking spadefuls of slurry over the parados. It was a thankless task as the evil-smelling burgoo slid back into the trench. Flynn's spade struck something. He didn't look too closely.

'What's that?' he asked Flynn, pausing to listen to a muffled clack-clack-clack sound coming from the German front line.

'That'll be Jerry pumping out his trenches,' answered one of the Englishmen.

'Marvellous, absolutely bloody marvellous,' sighed the Duke, hovering in mid-scoop. 'So why do we fecking bother?'

'Because, me old china, it'd be a bloody sight worse if we didn't!' chortled the Englishman. 'Now let's see if we can shovel faster than them buggers can pump!' By sunset the trench still looked like a sewer. At least Doyle had managed to do some good with the woodwork and whilst the rain had stopped the darkening sky threatened more to come. Murphy, Gallear and Clee were in their traverse. Clee was cradling an earthenware jar in his arms: rum. Flynn licked his lips. He could do with a tot.

'Stand to!' bellowed Glee.

'Holy cow, are the Krauts coming?' cried Fitzgerald, his face blanching as he flung himself at the fire step.

'Didn't you listen to a word they said in training?' said Carolan. 'It's just trench routine. We stand to at sunset and sunrise, just in case Jerry tries to have a crack.'

'Do y'reckon the Boche is doing the same over their side?' asked Doyle.

'That they are,' replied Carolan.

'Silence!' snapped Devlin from behind them. Flynn felt lightheaded, the blood pounding like thunder in his ears. It may be quiet but as soon as it was dark the front lines would come alive with work parties and patrols. His eyes were drawn to the bundle on the wire fading into the dark as if it were being sucked back down to the underworld where it belonged, and began to fidget, reading the letters and numbers stamped into his rifle's metalwork. He could hear the others breathing. Somewhere out in the thickening dark the wire creaked and the grass rustled. Whoosh! A green flare lanced into the sky,

123

stripping out his night vision before wafting gently earthward beneath its parachute. The flickering canopy of light set shadows dancing amid the wire pickets and Flynn's thumb drifted towards his safety catch as he fought the temptation to slip it off. Half an hour later they were stood down. Food arrived: battered green Dixies full of tepid 'all-in stew'. They wolfed it down none the less. Then there was tea: orangey-brown tea sweetened with condensed milk and a splash of rum.

'All right then, I need two volunteers to man a listening post,' announced Devlin when they'd finished. No one moved. Everyone knew manning the listening post was a vital job but when it came to it no one wanted to do it.

'Never volunteer for anything,' muttered Gallagher out of the corner of his mouth to Flynn. He'd learnt that much about soldiering already.

'Now you bloody tell me,' replied Flynn with a brisk laugh.

'Well done, Corporal Flynn, you'll do!' called the sergeant.

'I'll go, Sarge,' Cronin said, picking up his rifle and groundsheet as a collective sigh of relief rippled down the trench.

'Good man!' Devlin beamed, leading them to a sap. 'I'm told there's a shell hole about thirty yards in front of us. Just follow this here cord and ye can't miss it.' He placed a length of thick string in Flynn's hand, then handed him a Very pistol. 'If ye hear anything suspicious fire this straight up, then keep your heads down or ye'll get 'em blown off. Keep an eye on the boy and don't go doing anything stupid, understand?'

'How long do we stag on?' Flynn asked.

'I'll yank the cord once when it's time to come in, you yank twice to say you're coming. The password's *Cúchulainn*. Jerry'll not get his mouth round that one,' said Devlin, smugly.

'And you think a load of Dubs and English fellas can?' asked Flynn.

'Then 'tis just as well I'm here and ye're out there,' replied Devlin as Flynn and Cronin shed their leather equipment and caps. They waited as someone moved the timber and wire knife-rest barring the end of the sap before slipping off into the darkness. It was a starry night. The cord led to a gap in the wire wide enough for a man to crawl. Flynn felt like Theseus following the thread in the Minotaur's labyrinth as he slithered into no-man's-land followed by Cronin. They ended up in a painfully shallow scrape behind a meagre burr that left Flynn feeling painfully exposed, his guts like water. He tried not to puke. Cronin, on the other hand, looked disturbingly calm; unpleasantly at home where they lay.

'Get a grip,' Flynn silently chided himself, seeing monsters flit amongst the creaking wire and shadows. Another pale green flare whooshed skywards. He froze, fear icing his bones. Never volunteer for anything. The flare fizzled out. Darkness seeped back, over-whelming his brain. He shifted his weight. He could feel the warmth of Cronin's body next to him smelling of soap. Time became meaningless. Crunch! 'What was that?' Flynn hissed, sure he could see something; a move-ment deep in the wire. Cronin eased off his safety catch. It clicked gently. The noise stopped. He eased his rifle into his shoulder; his breathing even, measured, controlled. Sweat streamed down Flynn's face as the Very pistol's butt slipped into his hand and he inched it from beneath him. Crunch! He raised the pistol, heaving back the hammer with both hands. Crunch! Something loomed from the dark. 'Shit!' squealed Flynn, his voice skipping up an octave. Panic pulled the trigger, sending the red flare rip-ping across the ground on a flat trajectory. There was a scream. One of the shadows erupted in a shower of sparks. Cronin fired, sending a white flash jabbing through Flynn's skull, deafening him. He fired again, and again, and again. Flynn's ears were ringing, his nose bleeding. He rose to his knees, rifle loose in his hands; his head was spinning. There was a bright flash, then darkness.

When he opened his eyes it was light. His face hurt and he groaned, closing his eyes, and for a fleeting moment he imagined he was back in Dublin recovering from a terrific hangover. It wouldn't be the first New Year he'd begun in pain. He opened them again. He was in the trench. It wasn't a hangover. He was disappointed. There were boots next to his head. He was on the fire step. 'You're still with us, then?' said Gallagher. Flynn struggled to sit up. 'Easy there, big fella,' Gallagher said, easing him back down. 'I thought you'd copped it.' There was a dressing on his face. 'You'll have a cracking scar, you jammy bugger,' Gallagher added. 'The colleens'll love it.' There was genuine envy in his voice.

'What happened?' Flynn asked.

'Christ knows what happened. One minute everything's cushty and the next Jerry's everywhere. If you hadn't got that flare off when you did they'd've been all over us. There was shite everywhere; a proper fireworks display. Harry Mason copped it and that Kay fella,' Gallagher explained, looking dog-tired.

'So ye've finished yer nap, then?' said Devlin, forcing a weary smile. His face was pale and pinched, betraying the emotional strain of the night's exertions. 'Ye can thank young Cronin for your skin. He brung ye in,' he added, waving vaguely towards Cronin, who was sitting like a grubby elf cleaning his rifle. He looked up, smiled and then carried on working contentedly, humming tunelessly. Devlin handed him a water bottle. 'This'll put the hairs on ye chest,' said Devlin. Flynn took a swig; it seared his throat. 'Whoa there, that's none o' ye southern shite; that's a decent drop of medicinal Bushmills, so go easy!' laughed Devlin, retrieving the canteen.

'Where the heck did you get whiskey from?' Flynn asked.

'Could I not be having a wee tint, Sarge? After all, is it not New Year's Day?' interjected Gallagher, licking his lips, his eyes large and childlike as he watched the sergeant replace the stopper. Devlin sighed, rolling his eyes as he unplugged the bottle once more. Gallagher grinned, snatching the canteen with trembling hands before taking a long pull. 'Well, then, fellas, here's to 1916,' he declared with a wry grin.

CHAPTER 11

St James's Park, London

Mary folded Flynn's letter, a talisman in her slim, discoloured fingers, its whiteness dazzling against the sulphur-stained yellowness of her flesh as if it somehow brought her closer to him. The newspapers called the girls in the munitions factories *'munitionettes'*; it made them seem more glamorous somehow than canaries, which was what most called them because of their waxy-yellowed complexion, the byproduct of handling so many dangerous chemicals. At least none of her teeth had fallen out. Not yet, anyway. She sat back, letting the sun's warmth play on her skin, half-hoping it would give her back her natural colour. It was Sunday, her day off, and somewhere a brass band thumped out yet another patriotic tune. People were singing and for a fleeting moment she squinted at the sun, wondering if somewhere over in France Flynn was doing the same: sharing a moment, bridging the gap on a quiet afternoon. Unfolding his letter, she read it for the umpteenth time, consuming Flynn's spidery, thoughtless scrawl. It was the words this time, not the chemicals, that made her sick and no matter how often she read it, no matter how much she mumbled prayers to the Virgin Mary, the words remained the same. He'd been wounded. A scratch, he said, but she couldn't help worrying. She sat back, leaning heavily on the park bench, toying with the letter, when she heard voices nearby: Irish voices.

Her eyes were drawn to a group of soldiers in hospital uniforms; invalids out of Milbank military hospital enjoying the park's clean air. Some were in wheelchairs, limbless detritus of some distant battlefield, others hobbled along, the click-clack of their crutches echoing from the tarmac pathways, herded benevolently by stern-faced nurses in crisp, starched uniforms. Mary couldn't help thinking there was something painfully familiar about one brown-haired soldier. He limped along, head down, leaning heavily on a walking stick that he held in one gloved hand, curled like a claw. She felt her stomach tighten. It couldn't be? One of the nurses paused, looking puzzled as she broke into a run, shouting 'Mick!'

'Aren't we all Micks here, darling?' called a ruddy-faced Irish Guardsman, sweeping his cap from his ginger hair in a sweeping cavalier bow, referring to the regiment's nickname. 'What brings a Dublin girl to this mucky old town?' he added, exposing his tombstone teeth. The others had stopped too, ribbing the jilted redhead as she ignored him, swerving past after the one who kept limping on.

'Mickey!' she gasped, placing her hand on the soldier's arm. He stopped and turned, exposing scarified flesh snagging his mangled mouth into a sneer. The left side of his face was gone, the eye covered by a patch. The right side was flawless, unmistakable. His right eye was a well of sorrow and infinite sadness. He turned to go but she

130

didn't release his sleeve. 'Is it you, Mickey?'

'Mary?' he whispered. His voice was like the rustle of dry leaves as he took in her sallow, jaundiced complexion. There was a hint of brandy on his breath.

'Is everything all right, Private Gallagher?' asked a slim young nurse, her officious English plumminess grating on Mary, despite the woman's obvious concern.

'Yes, it is. This here is my sister,' he replied. The nurse spared Mary a cursory look before rejoining her charges. Mickey sighed, unsure where to look; words somehow stuck in his throat.

'They said you were dead,' Mary said quietly as she touched his cheek. He shrank back.

'Look at me, I'm a monster. What good am I to my Janet now? She's better off without me,' he said, his voice hoarse.

'Holy Mary Mother of God, Michael Gerald Gallagher, you're a bloody great *eejit!*' He cocked his head, looking puzzled. 'Janet's lost without you!' A tear rolled down his cheek. 'We've got to tell her the army was wrong; tell her you're alive!'

'No!' he snapped, his eye wide in panic.

The nurse looked back. Heads turned.

'What about the wee ones, Davey and Lizzie and Daisy?' she asked, taking his gloved hand. It was stiff and immobile beneath the dark leather.

'Daisy?'

'Aye, Daisy. She's like a doll; all curls and big eyes. She's the spit of her ma,' she said, leading him gently by the hand to a nearby bench. They sat down. He was silent. 'They sent Janet her letters. They said they found them on your body. That's how they knew it was you. What happened?' she asked.

He looked at her. Where to begin? He took a deep breath and then spoke. 'It's a terrible thing is a battle, Mary, full of noise; full of screaming and dying and the guns...' His voice trailed away. It was all there, inside his head. Just saying it brought it back: the smells; the sounds. She squeezed his hand. He was shaking. 'We tried to stop them at Mons but there were too many of the buggers, wave after wave of them. Someone must have found my coat cos I lost half my kit when we pulled out. They dogged us all the way, day after day, never giving us time to rest. Then we got orders to stop, to turn and fight. Christ knows where we were. I was in a ditch, firing and firing and firing. It was slaughter. Then next thing I know I'm stark bollock naked in a ditch with some bastard trying to bury me! It was a miracle, they said, a bloody miracle, so they fixed me up as best they could. Couldn't save me leg; Fritz already got the other bits.' He held up his gloved hand, touching the eye patch. 'Good thing I've a spare, eh?' he joked weakly.

'So why didn't they say you were alive?' she asked.

'When I came to I had no idea who I was. It wasn't just me devilish good looks that the shell took. It took my memory too. No one knew who I was. I didn't know. I guess they must have found Janet's letters in some other fella's pockets, the one with my coat, and assumed it was me. By the time I knew differently, it was too late...'

'I don't understand. What do you mean too late? Too late for what?' she asked.

'It's better this way, Mary.' He looked up; the other soldiers were in the distance now. 'I best be getting back,' he said suddenly, levering himself awkwardly to his feet. 'Please, Mary, don't say anything to Janet. Promise me.' She opened her mouth to speak. 'Please.'

Reluctantly she nodded. 'I promise,' she said. Then she asked, 'Will I be seeing you again?'

He turned, round-shouldered, the weight of the world pressing on him. 'I've an early shift at the factory this week, so what if I meet you here the evening after next, about six, by this bench?' He nodded, then hobbled away. She watched until he vanished from sight, not knowing whether to laugh or cry. Everything had changed. Mickey was alive. It took her an hour to summon up the strength to leave, as if walking away would somehow put a lie to what had just happened. By the time she got home it was late.

'Did you do anything exciting?' asked Janet.

'Not really,' replied Mary, trying to avoid Janet's gaze.

'You were a long time doing nothing much, then,' added Janet, placing a cup of tea down on the table in front of her sister-in-law before sitting down opposite. 'You look exhausted.' Mary could feel Janet's eyes on her. She played with the tea, sipping occasionally in the somewhat awkward silence. 'I'm off to bed, then,' Janet finally pronounced. Mary remained silent. Janet rose and ambled to the door, pausing, her hand hovering over the brass knob. 'You're hiding something, aren't you?'

Mary looked up suddenly, eyes wide in alarm.

'W-what makes you think that?' she stammered, almost spilling her tea.

'You met someone today, didn't you?' Janet said, smiling sympathetically.

'How could you even think that, with my Kevin wounded and all?' Mary bridled.

'Come off it, Mary, what difference does that make? Good luck to you, I say; they work you too hard in that flaming factory as it is! You should jack it in while you can. Just look at you, worn thin. So why shouldn't you live a little? For all you know your fella's already dead,' Mary blanched, 'so for God's sake don't go ending up wasting your life like me, waiting, always waiting ... and for what?'

'You shouldn't go talking like that, Janet!' Mary snapped.

'Mary, just cos you want something don't mean it's gonna happen, does it?'

'You can't go giving up on Mickey like that. He'll come home; you'll see. I just know he will.'

Mary felt awful and over the next few weeks her behaviour did little to make Janet think she hadn't found another man – but she knew she couldn't tell her about Mickey. She'd promised. Then she had an idea.

'We used to come here. She was the most beautiful girl I'd ever seen. So slight and fragile and she thought me so handsome in my uniform,' he reminisced as they sat on the Chelsea Embankment watching the tugs and tenders wend their way up and down the busy Thames. Mickey seemed happier; easier with his words as he talked about Janet and how they met.

'Janet still needs you, and the wee ones,' she said.

Mickey sighed.

'They'll be discharging me soon, then what? Soldiering's all I've known and now ... and now, what good am I to anyone? Maybe if I sent money? I know a fella in the pay office who could make it look like she was getting a pension,' he offered. 'How could I expect her to spend the rest of her life looking after a cripple?'

'Because she loves you, you great *eejit!*' Mary averred. 'And you still love her. I'll tell you what, how about I fetch Janet and the weans over to the park next Sunday? We'll have a picnic. You could see them...' He looked scared, blinking back the threat of a tear. 'They'd never know you were there if you stayed by our bench, the one where we met in St James's. Then you could see they're all right.' His heart thumped against his ribs. 'She's a little darling, is wee Daisy.'

'All right then, but they mustn't know I'm here. Promise me, Mary, you'll not tell them,' he said, looking down at her with his clear blue eye.

'That's settled, then,' Mary said, smiling. 'You just make sure you're by our bench at one o'clock next Sunday, that's an order!'

'Aye, ma'am,' he replied, chopping off a mock salute. It was the first time she'd seen him smile.

'Now let's get you back to hospital before they set one of those wolfhounds of a posh English nurse on me,' she laughed, taking Mickey by the arm. She had a plan.

Janet wasn't keen when she suggested a picnic but the children loved the idea, squealing with excitement.

'It'll probably be heaving with rain, so why

136

go all the way to St James's Park?' Janet asked. 'Wouldn't it be easier just to go to the common? Besides, the tube ain't free. Lord, I've barely got the money for the rent.'

'Whist, woman, will you stop worrying yourself over trivia! It'll do the weans good to get some fresh air. I'll pay the tube fares,' Mary insisted. 'London's a grand city, the capital of the greatest empire the world has ever seen, Janet, and who knows, you may even have fun!'

Narrowing her eyes, Janet looked from Mary to the expectant faces of her children. 'Sod the flaming empire, it ain't done me no good,' she grumbled.

'Please, Mummy, please,' wheedled Lizzie, backed up by Davey whilst Daisy simply gazed at her mother with huge, saucer eyes, sucking her thumb.

'Oh, all right, then,' relented Janet. Resistance was futile. Mary smiled, tousling Lizzie's wayward auburn hair. 'I don't know what you're up to, Mary Gallagher, but Lord help us I know you're up to something.'

That night Mary didn't sleep, tossing and turning in her narrow bed, and by Sunday she was a bundle of nerves. It was threatening rain by the time they reached the park but by some miracle it held off. It would be Easter soon and the last thing they needed was yet another washout bank holiday weekend. There was a band adding cadence to the strollers' gait.

'That's what your daddy used to do,' Mary told Davey as they watched khaki-clad Life-guards ride down Horse Guards Road to change the guard outside Horse Guards Parade.

'Will you stop filling the boy's head with such nonsense? Mickey isn't a donkey walloper, he's Irish Guards, not the flaming Household Cavalry!' Janet corrected her.

'You said *is*, not *was*,' replied Mary, taking Janet by the hand. Together they crunched over the red gravel road to the fountain at the edge of the park. Davey hoofed his football over the grass, breaking free to chase after it. Janet spread out a musty old Stuart tartan travel rug that had seen better days, and started laying out their meagre feast. There were potted meat sandwiches and some plum jam ones too. Mary had acquired a pork pie from somewhere and there was a flask of strong sweet tea. It was all Mary could afford but if the look on little Lizzie's face was anything to go by it was good enough. She glanced at the bench. Mickey was meant to be sitting on it, but it was empty. There was no sign of him. The buzz of an aeroplane overhead distracted her, drawing her eyes upward. She had no idea what kind of aeroplane it was; Flynn would have known. She could see the pilot waving as he swooped over the park. Then Mary saw a figure in uniform, silhouetted by the sun; a shadow on the edge of the path. Watching; waiting. He leant heavily on a walking stick, watching Davey enthusiastically if somewhat inexpertly chase his football around the grass. Her stomach knotted. Without looking up, Janet dispatched Lizzie to fetch her brother to eat. Davey sent the ball wheeling awkwardly into the air. It bounced twice, landing awkwardly at the shadow's feet.

'There ye are, wee fella,' said the soldier, shoving the ball with his good foot. The boy picked it up, cradling it in his arms as he looked up at the man. Davey stepped closer. Mickey trembled, unable to contain the emotions welling up from within. There was a little girl with him now, a mass of wayward auburn hair and deep-brown eyes. 'And aren't you the spit of your ma?' he mumbled. The girl cocked her head. She reached out, touching his hand. A tear welled in his eye.

'Who's that with the kids?' Janet asked, getting to her feet, Daisy in her arms. Mary was up too, following her. 'I told you before not to go talking to strangers,' she called.

'It's all right, Mummy, it's not a stranger, it's Daddy,' Lizzie replied without taking her eyes off the soldier.

'I'm really sorry. Ever since their daddy went they keep calling every man in a uniform daddy,' apologized Janet, looking up at the soldier for the first time. There was something about him: the scars, the eye-patch, the clear blue eye. The eye. 'It's impossible,' she gasped.

'Hello, Janet, my darling,' said Mickey.

CHAPTER 12

Thursday 27 April 1916, British front line, Hulluch, north-west France

'Watch where you're going,' Fallon said, elbowing his way along the crowded communication trench. He was tired after a long night manning the front-line trench. The place stank like an overused public toilet on a hot bank holiday. He wasn't a happy man. It was barely 4.30 a.m. It had been a long night. At least he was heading in the right direction: away from the front line. Whoosh! A flare hissed, arcing overhead, bathing the line of soldiers snaking towards the front line in an eerie green glow. He could see Devlin leading his heavily laden platoon forward.

'Jerry's restless,' muttered Collins as he traipsed along behind Fallon.

'Look, it's that gobshite Gallagher and his la-di-da pal Flynn,' hissed Fallon, pulling the peak of his cap low over his eyes to shade his face as he strode through the chaos of humanity. He dropped his shoulder, catching Flynn in the chest and sending him flying.

'Hey, watch it!' Flynn snapped as the two ammunition boxes he was carrying clattered to the floor. Devlin cursed. Someone yanked him to his feet. Then his mystery assailant was gone, lost in the crowd and shadows. *'Bloody eejit,'* Flynn muttered before scurrying after the others.

'So what was that about?' asked Collins. Without breaking his step, Fallon held up something for Collins to see. It was a grey cloth PHG gas helmet. He had taken it from Flynn when he barged into him. It was a classic pickpocket's ruse. He crumpled the gas helmet into a ball and tossed it over the parapet. 'Let's see how yer man gets along without it.'

'Do you think they'll be gassed, then?' asked Collins.

'Let's hope so!' replied Fallon with a wink.

By 5.00 a.m. the entire Irish Division was in position and as the sun began to peep over the horizon it promised to be a clear day. A warm breeze played on Flynn's cheeks as he gazed across the flat, waterlogged wasteland that separated them from the Germans. Despite the chill morning air, he was sweating, a ball of excitement in his gut, and the scar tugging at the corner of his right eye itched. They were below the watertable so oily black water oozed into the trench, collapsing the

141

sides. They would be busy later. Lieutenant Colonel Thackeray was doing his rounds. He was their third commanding officer, drafted in from the Highland Light Infantry and a breath of fresh air. Captain Stirke and the adjutant, Captain Heffernan, were with him.

'Look,' said Flynn, pointing at the German line. 'What's that?'

'It looks like some sort of banner,' replied Cronin as he squinted through the telescopic sight mounted on his rifle. He passed the weapon to Flynn.

'It says: "Irishmen! Heavy uproar in Ireland! English guns are firing at your wives and children. Throw your arms away; we will give you a heart welcome!"' Flynn read.

'What's that about?' asked Gallagher. Flynn shrugged.

'Have you really not heard the news?' asked Doyle. 'There was an uprising in Dublin last Sunday. The Shinners seized the GPO. I heard that there's still fighting going on.'

'You're joking me?' scoffed Gallagher. 'Even the Shinners aren't that stupid, not with us fellas out here. They'll muck it up for everyone.'

'Look, I had it from old Hackett,' insisted Doyle.

'Then it must be true,' sneered Cronin to a chorus of laughter that was cut short by the rumble of guns on the horizon. The Germans were opening up. Flynn's gut tightened, his bowels loosening slightly, and as he pressed himself against the wet clay trench wall he realized there was nowhere to hide: the bunkers were flooded. He closed his eyes, impatiently awaiting his fate as the shells screamed over.

'Why aren't the bloody things exploding?' shouted Gallagher as shells plopped into the mud.

'Perhaps they're duds?' offered Docherty, looking pale, just as Captain Murphy staggered into view. He was coughing. Callear was with him, his eyes streaming.

'Are you all right, sir?' asked Devlin.

'B-blasted Boche is tear-gassing the support trenches,' coughed Murphy. The thunder of the guns was rolling across their front now like a drum roll. 'Best you get under cover, lads,' he added. 'I think we'll be getting a visit from Jerry any minute soon!' Then the high explosives began to fall, shaking the ground, jarring their insides. Hot metal hissed overhead, overwhelming Flynn's senses in an orgy of noise. He screamed. They all did. It helped ease the pressure throbbing through his skull. His nose began to bleed. Dirt showered down around them, fraying his nerves. He lost track of time. Someone screamed for a stretcher-bearer and as he pressed himself deeper into the wet mud he felt a pang of guilt that he was happy that someone else had been injured and not him. He noticed Cronin edging up to the parapet.

'What the hell do you think you're doing?' he shouted.

'There's a fecking great green cloud coming towards us,' said Cronin.

Devlin was up in a bound, by his side. 'Shit! GAS! GAS! GAS!' he screamed as the ominous green cloud billowed closer. The cry rippled down the line as Gallagher tore his gas hood free of its bag and pulled it over his head; others followed suit. It stank of chemicals and the mica eyepieces steamed up in an instant. Flynn was flapping around.

'I can't find my mask!' shrieked Flynn, teetering on the brink of panic as he scrabbled at his kit. All the while the silent green cloud ghosted nearer.

'What do you mean you can't find it?' barked Devlin. Trembling, Flynn pathetically held up the empty gas-hood bag. The sergeant muttered something but his words were muffled by his mask as he stomped off. Flynn could smell chlorine, nudging his panic closer to the precipice. He thought about running but before he could Devlin was back, stuffing a sodden lump into his hands. 'Strap it over your nose and mouth,' Flynn heard him say. He hesitated. It was a field dressing. Devlin shoved it onto his face. It smelt like an old toilet and his eyes smarted as the languid green cloud began to tumble into the trench. Gallagher tied it off then patted his friend on the shoulder. The gas swirled around them, plunging them into a green fug that crept into every nook and cranny, leaving shadows that flitted like wraiths through the gloom.

'Here they come!' shouted Murphy as loud as he could through his gas helmet. It looked like the cloud was being carried on hundreds of jackbooted legs. Men scrambled to the parapet as the Germans desperately raced across no-man's-land. Two men bundled a Vickers machine gun into place, then cocked it with a harsh, metallic click-clack. Flynn took up a firing position, slipping off the safety catch and taking aim. His eyes burned. He could hardly see. He felt the hard trigger on his finger and he took up the slack, the first pressure; he was halfway there. 'Fire!' shouted Murphy. He squeezed. It was like a storm breaking as every ounce of the Irishmen's pent-up fear, anger and frustration unleashed itself in a torrent of gunfire that tore across the front.

Palming the bolt, he fired, then fired again and again until the hollow metallic click told him it was empty, then snagged his fingers as he stuffed fresh rounds into the breech. The noise was deafening. Field-grey bodies hung in rags on the wire, staccato machine-gun bursts tearing chunks from writhing flesh. Cronin was back on the parapet carefully selecting targets. Devlin dashed to and fro replenishing ammunition. Someone wrestled with a misfire. He had no idea where Gallagher was, or anyone else for that matter; anonymous beneath the shapeless bags of their gas masks.

There was a flash. He staggered, ears ringing. His head hurt. He couldn't hear. He felt sick. Then, through the swirling mist he saw them: the Germans, their spiked helmets and respirators demonic in the gloom. Someone grabbed his shoulder. He turned, lashing out with his rifle. The butt thudded into a yielding skull. He heard it crack. Another shape loomed and he screamed, driving his bayonet into the shadow's core. He jabbed and jabbed again. Around him shapes swirled, grappling, living and dying. Devlin raged, flailing a gore-caked shovel like a two-handed axe: a throwback to some Irish legend of old. Then it stopped. They were gone, fleeing across the wasteland from whence they came. Cronin mounted the parapet once more, coolly picking out targets until the gas thinned, then he amused himself peppering the Germans' banner. Others joined in, reducing it to an indecipherable sieve. Slumping against the sandbags, Flynn couldn't be bothered; he was too knackered, emotionally and physically. Then he pulled the pad from his nose and mouth, sucking in lungfuls of foetid air.

'What was that?' asked Flynn.

'A Jerry attack,' replied Gallagher.

'Not that, this?' said Flynn, brandishing the sodden field dressing.

'Oh, that?' said Devlin. 'It's an improvized gas mask. Before the boffins came up with these things,' he held up his gas hood, 'some fella told me that if ye piss on a cloth and strap it over yer face it'll do the job.' Flynn dropped the pad.

'You pissed on a field dressing!' spluttered Flynn.

'Ach, don't be soft. I didn't have enough time so I dipped it in the piss bucket over there,' Devlin informed him, beaming, bloody shovel in hand as he pointed at an old tin bucket full of urine and fag ends. Flynn spat, wiping his mouth with his sleeve. Try as he might, the tang lingered. The others laughed, desperately seeking emotional relief; laughing too hard for the humour of the joke. 'Anyways, ye should be grateful ye didn't cop it. Now, maybe next time ye'll look after yer kit,' he chided before moving off to check on the others. The Duke dished out cigarettes from a battered tin; Carolan lit them.

'But I'm sure I had it,' Flynn grumbled. Docherty sat staring into space, trying to make sense of what had just happened. Fitzpatrick flopped down next to him. This was their first real taste of battle. Flynn tried to wipe the blood from his bayonet, trying to

147

ignore the hair-flecked smears on the butt of his rifle. There was a vile taste in his throat and he needed a piss. Someone groaned. A German writhed on the duckboards clutching his gut. Doyle jumped down, offering the man water. A medical officer appeared, working his way through the trench, assessing casualties. He gave the German a cursory once-over, shook his head and moved on, followed by weary stretcher-bearers; disentangling the living from the dead. A whistle shrilled and unthinking they scrambled back to their positions.

'Don't these fellas know when they're beat?' groaned Fitzpatrick wearily.

'Shut it and watch yer front,' snapped Devlin, who had reappeared minus his shovel.

'Come off it, Sarge, even Jerry isn't *eejit* enough to have another go today. They'll be as knackered as us,' observed Gallagher. The shelling was random now, the odd explosion rather than a rolling clap of thunder. Everyone's faces were pinched with strain. Flynn noticed Cronin was still on the parapet, straddling the sandbags, scanning no-man's-land for prey.

'Will you stop trying to win a VC and get your arse down here before you get a wooden cross,' said Flynn, but Cronin didn't seem to hear. He glanced, eyes shining exuberantly, flushed with victory. Despite his youth, Cronin was a master of his craft; an angel of death at home on the battlefield. Flynn was just thankful to be alive. 'You really enjoy this shit, don't you?' he'd once asked Cronin.

'What's not to like?' he'd replied with a shrug and a grin. 'It's fun.'

'Don't you worry about getting killed?' asked Flynn.

'Why? If you're alive there's nothing to worry about and if you're dead, well, you're dead.'

Flynn had to admit that there was an inescapable logic to what Cronin said, envying his stoicism.

'When in doubt, make tea!' Gallagher said, pulling a brew kit from his webbing and pottering over a petrol stove. Flynn took a drink from his water bottle. It tasted of chlorine. It reminded him of a swimming baths. He rinsed his mouth, spitting out the brackish water. It didn't make much difference, only making him thirstier.

'So, Joe, what's this about fighting in Dublin?' Flynn asked Doyle, keeping his eyes on the tattered German banner fluttering lamely in the slack air.

'Don't listen to him, he's talking shite as usual,' Carolan muttered.

'I'm afraid not, lads.' It was Lieutenant Callear. Murphy was behind him. Instinctively they braced but Callear gestured for them to relax. 'Sadly the papers are full of it. From what I hear the Fenians are holed up

149

in the city centre. The navy have shelled Sackville Street. It's madness, utter bloody madness.'

'We've enough to be getting on with here,' added Murphy, scowling at Callear. It was obvious that he didn't want his men dwelling on their home town's troubles at this precise moment. 'Now, Private Cronin, do as Corporal Flynn says and get down here before you get shot! We've lost enough good men today.'

'Very good, sir,' Cronin replied reluctantly. He looked disappointed as he turned to jump down, swinging his leg over the sandbags just as a shell erupted in front of their position, flinging the boy head first into the trench to land amid the filth and shattered duckboards. He lay still.

'C'mon, Pat, stop acting the goat and get up,' said Doyle, offering the boy a hand. He groaned. Doyle rolled him over. There was blood on his leg. 'You all right, Pat?' he asked. Flynn jumped down, running his hand over the boy's wounded leg. His trousers were rent. Cronin cried out. Someone shouted for a stretcher-bearer. Flynn's hands were slick with blood.

'It's all right, Pat, you've been hit. There's a bit of blood but...' Cronin struggled to sit, shoving Flynn's hands from his leg, but Doyle restrained him, pushing him back. Flynn tore open Cronin's trousers. His flesh was smooth and pale, milky from lack of sun. There was a ragged gash in the boy's thigh, coating everything in thick dark blood. It was deep but to Flynn's relief it wasn't an arterial bleed. Cronin twisted, thrashing his legs, desperately twisting away from Flynn's hands as he tore away the boy's underwear. There was a gasp of horror.

'Jaysus, Mary and Joseph, they've blown his fecking prick off!'

Cronin squirmed and so did several on-lookers. Flynn scowled, unable to fully grasp what he was seeing.

'Will you *eejits* get a grip?' snapped Devlin, elbowing Flynn aside and pressing a large field dressing to the boy's wound, blotting away the blood. Then he began to laugh.

'Don't you think you're being a bit heart-less, Sergeant?' asked Flynn, taken aback by Devlin's apparent callousness.

The Ulsterman shook his head. 'Suddenly it all makes sense,' Devlin muttered to him-self.

'What do you mean, Sergeant?' asked Murphy.

'Well, to be honest, sir, it's not like young Cronin here had a prick to lose, is it?' Mur-phy looked puzzled, then Devlin beckoned him over, pulling aside the gory pad. 'You see, sir, unless I'm much mistaken, young Cronin here's a girl!'

CHAPTER 13

Woolwich, London

Mary sipped her tea, staring at the glowing embers in the grate as they consumed the last of her old newspapers. The cold didn't bother her; besides, it would be payday soon. She could buy some more fuel then or work extra shifts and keep warm at the arsenal's expense. No, it was the loneliness that rankled. Ever since her brother had taken Janet and the children back to Ireland, she felt abandoned, isolated, alone. To make matters worse, Daiken had upped the rent. She'd been looking but lodgings were hard to come by. Events in Dublin hadn't helped, the Rising merely resurrecting anti-Irish prejudices that had only been partially buried by the war. Whenever she opened her mouth she attracted wary glances, despite the sacrifices of her family and thousands like it all across Ireland, as if she was the enemy within. Even the girls at work had become standoffish. Her father had written to say that everyone was fine and not to believe everything in the papers but the pictures said it all. British guns had laid waste to her home town.

Sighing, Mary put down her cup. The damp room smelt vaguely of old cabbage but thanks to the chemicals she handled every day at work she didn't really notice. They'd damaged her once frothy blonde hair as well as her sense of smell. Her hair was lank and brittle, her hands callused and worn. She felt old; old and tired. All she needed was a good night's sleep but sleep evaded her. Every time she closed her eyes her mind drifted back to her brother and Flynn, out there somewhere risking their lives for an ungrateful country. Flynn's letters were welcome relief but it had been a week since his last. It seemed like an age. She tried to tell herself that no news was good news but still she worried. A tap on the door disturbed her thoughts. It was quarter to nine, making her wonder who would call so late. It was Daiken.

'Good evening Miss Gallagher,' he said, fixing his watery eyes on Mary's chest. His tongue darted over his thin lips, reminding her of a reptile. Even her blunted sense of smell was overwhelmed by the stale odour that followed him in as he stepped, uninvited, into the room. 'I hope I'm not disturbing you.' His eyes remained on her chest, mentally peeling away her clothes as he stood with his hands thrust deep into his trouser pockets. 'It's about the rent,' he said. 'It's overdue.'

'It's payday soon,' answered Mary, forcing a smile. His tongue made another reptilian pass over his lips as he stepped closer.

'That may as well be but you're already late and there are plenty of people about who'd pay good money and on time for rooms like these,' he replied. He was closer still, wraithlike in the firelight, his cloying breath warm on her cheek. She stepped back, unhappy at his proximity, his violation of her space. 'You should count yourself lucky I've let you keep the roof over your head so far. After all, people like you aren't very popular these days,' he added, baring his crooked, stained teeth.

'What exactly do you mean, *people like me*, Mr Daiken?' snapped Mary, barely keeping her temper.

'Why, Irish, of course. Sadly, most people hereabouts think you are all just a bunch of troublesome Micks; drunken bog-trotters with your harsh accents and clacking worry beads,' he said, glancing at the crucifix on the wall by the window. 'They said I was asking for trouble, taking in Irish.'

'Asking for trouble? You were happy enough to take my money! I've a brother and an uncle in the army, you know!' she snapped indignantly.

'That may well be, Miss Gallagher, but you know how people are, especially with all the recent unpleasantness. Anyway, talking of money, what are we to do?' He made her uncomfortable and, worse still, he knew it. His tongue darted once more as his eyes drifted from her face. 'I think we could come to some sort of arrangement.' She looked at him, puzzled. He stepped closer, seizing her breasts with his thin, bony hands and squeezing them hard. She lashed out, her hand slashing his sallow cheek with a resounding thwack that brought a semblance of colour to his face. He grabbed her wrist, twisting her arm, deceptively strong for all his frail appearance.

'What sort of woman do you take me for?' she demanded. He laughed, pulling her closer so that his repugnant face hovered mere inches from hers. For an awful moment she thought he was going to try and kiss her.

'What sort of woman do I take you for? Why, the sort that is far from home; the sort that is short of money; the sort that is quite alone. *That*, Miss Gallagher, is the sort of woman I take you for and believe me I intend to take you! No one can help you, Miss Gallagher, no one but me. So what kind of woman do I take you for, Miss Gallagher? One who needs to think *long and hard*,' he emphasized the words lasciviously 'about my generous offer. The streets of London are dangerous, especially after dark. It would be a terrible shame for someone so young and pretty to end up on them. Wouldn't you agree, Miss Gallagher?' He patted her cheek and stepped back. She felt sick. He hovered by the door as if expecting some sort of reply, then realizing he'd get none stepped back onto the landing. 'You've got till Friday.'

Mary shut the door, leaving Daiken's words in the hallway. Then she cried. He was right. She was alone.

Even sleep abandoned her. It was raining when the sun came up, groping cautiously through the threadbare curtain. After she washed, she crept downstairs, eager to be away. There were letters by the front door in ramshackle piles on the sideboard. Then she recognized Flynn's unruly scrawl: a letter! It was battered, stained, its flap worried as if someone had tried to open it, but it lifted her spirits. She pocketed it quickly; she would read it later. She sensed Daiken's eyes on her but resisted the temptation to turn, denying him the satisfaction. 'Good morning, Miss Gallagher,' he said from the end of the hall.

She stepped outside, the morning air wet on her skin. They'd call it a soft day back home, the sort that got wetter as the day grew long. She paused at the corner where she and Flynn had joked about chips, sparing the house a quick glance. The curtain twitched. He was watching; waiting; biding his time like a spider in his web. Then she smiled.

'Bog trotter, am I, Mr Daiken? Just you try and lay a finger on me again and you'll see just what sort of woman I am,' she said to herself as the rain thickened, threatening to overwhelm her umbrella, and for a moment she wondered if it was raining in the trenches. She ran her fingers along the stiff length of Flynn's letter as she walked, anticipating the pleasures within. She knew it would be trivia – the censors saw to that – but it was Flynn's trivia and she kept it all in a box under the bed. Sometimes, when she read them she could almost hear his voice and that comforted her as she lay alone in her bed at night. At least he was alive. By the time she reached the sprawling Woolwich Arsenal, she was soaked through despite her umbrella and she spent the next twelve hours sniffling and coughing through her shift.

'What's that?' asked one of the girls who sat next to her during her tea break: a bird-like Londoner called Maureen, who was a nodding acquaintance.

'It's a letter from my fella at the front,' she announced proudly, emphasizing her Irish brogue, attracting the passing attention of one or two other girls.

'My old man's in the army too but he don't write much. He never was much good at school. Too busy getting into trouble,' replied Maureen, craning to see what was written on the rain-smudged page. 'What's your fella say?'

'Only that I shouldn't worry.'

'Easier said than done, dearie!' squawked Maureen.

'And that there's plenty of food,' Mary said. The censors made sure that there wasn't much else except a few lines about Gallagher being his usual cheery self. Gallagher was a bit like Maureen's husband; he didn't write much so she had to rely on Flynn to keep her informed. Satisfied, she put the letter back in her pocket. She would read it again later, when she was alone.

By the time her shift was over, the sun had long set. She was used to that as well as the gloomy, claustrophobic streets beneath the guttering streetlamps. She thought she could hear distant thunder; it could have been the echo of guns over in France. They said you could hear them sometimes. She took her time. She was in no hurry to get back to her lodgings. There was nothing there for her now except Daiken and she was certainly in no hurry to see him. The clatter of hoofs on the cobbles disturbed her thoughts as a cab trundled by. She liked the streets at night. She turned the corner at the end of her street and fumbled for her key. A shape loomed from the shadows, tall and dark.

'Bit late to be out on your own.' She stopped, startled. The shadow stepped closer. 'Who knows what could happen?' Fear raised the hairs on the back of her neck. She gripped the key in her fist so that it poked between her index and middle fingers, ready to gouge it into the man's face if necessary. He was wearing a uniform, the peak of his cap low over his eyes. He was smiling, his teeth glinting in the lamplight. 'Jaysus, Mary, do you not know me?' asked the shadow, and then it dawned on her that the man was Irish: a Dubliner like herself.

'Rory?' She stepped closer. 'Is that yourself?'

'So it is! Some fella in your house said you didn't live there any more but I could tell the oily little shite was lying so I thought I'd hang about and see for myself.'

She looked him up and down. It was Rory all right, she could see that now; a bit taller and filled out but her brother all the same. It was the uniform that puzzled her. 'That'll be my landlord. Anyway, I thought you were unfit for the army.'

Rory grinned. He reminded her of Gallagher; they had the same impish grin.

'Ah well, now that's a bit of a tale, so best we get inside and get the kettle on so I can tell you all about it!' he said, flinging his arm protectively round his sister's shoulder. 'I could murder a cup of tea!' The curtain twitched. Daiken was still up, she suspected awaiting her return. As usual the mildewed hallway was unlit, the stair carpet musty, but her rooms seemed less unwelcoming with her brother there. They drank the last of the tea. He told her how he'd gone to Cork and lied through his teeth to get into the Royal Army Medical Corps.

'At least Mammy's glad I'm not in the infantry like Terry,' he said and Mary agreed, relieved that at least Rory wouldn't be doing any fighting. 'So what's happening?' he asked, so she told him everything: about Daiken, about his proposition, everything, until the colour drained from his amiable face.

'Where are you going?' she asked as he sprung up.

'To have a word with your man downstairs,' he replied. 'Don't worry, I won't kill him if that's what you're afraid of.' She felt guilty.

Her attempt to stop him was a token effort and she couldn't help secretly looking forward to her brother giving the slimy old lech a good old-fashioned thrashing.

Rory hammered on Daiken's door.

'D-do you know what time it is?' stammered Daiken, opening the door a crack, his eyes darting from Rory to Mary over the chain. 'Clear off or I'll call the police,' he snapped, feeling braver behind his makeshift barricade.

'You'll be sorry for this!' Rory snarled, driving his hobnailed boot into the door, sending it crashing into Daiken's face, splitting his lip, before grabbing him by the throat and slamming him into the wall, sending his lank comb-over billowing.

'You're in serious trouble now, sonny,' squealed Daiken. 'That's assault and criminal damage–' Rory's knee in his groin cut him short, driving him up the wall and rolling his eyes into the back of his head. Then he went limp, like a rag doll in Rory's fist. Mary had never seen her brother like this before. Daiken moaned. Blood dribbled down his chin. Rory squeezed his cheeks, holding his face close to his own.

'You don't frighten me, you wee gobshite. Now you're going to listen and I'm going to speak. I'll do it slow so your little brain will cope. If you so much as look at me sister again, let alone try and lay one of your filthy little hands on her, I'm gonna tear your bollocks off and feed them to you. Nod if you understand,' he snarled. Daiken nodded, his eyes wide in terror as a dark stain spread across his crotch.

'And just in case you think you'll be safe when I'm gone there's a lot of us Irish in this shitty city – friends of mine and some of them really aren't as nice as I am.' He patted Daiken's cheek, letting him fall. He wiped his hands, as if he'd just handled something deeply unpleasant. 'There, I don't think you'll be getting any more trouble from him,' said Rory.

He didn't hear the Zeppelin, nor did Mary, as it ghosted over Woolwich high above the cloud. Nor did they hear the bomb as it crashed through the roof of the house, nor the blast as it tore through the ramshackle brick. All Mary saw was Rory's smile, then darkness.

CHAPTER 14

British rear area, Hulluch, north-west France

Gallagher poured him a glass of pale white wine. Most of them struggled calling it *'vin blanc'* so the locals had got used to hearing British soldiers ask for plonk to go with their egg and chips.

'Won't that put hairs on your chest?' declared Gallagher, pouring a second glass. They preferred it to the local pale gassy beer.

'Either that or take the enamel off your teeth,' spluttered Flynn, struggling to keep it down. Then he leant back to drink in the scene, making out familiar faces in the smoky haze. The estaminet was rough and cheap, like its wine, its food and especially its women but at least the food was hot and besides it was better than mooching around camp waiting to go back into the line. There would be trouble later, there always was when you mixed squaddies with drink, but Flynn didn't care. Doyle staggered away to the toilets to 'ease springs' just as a peroxide blonde wearing too few clothes and too much rouge plonked herself on his lap, wriggling and smiling as she waved to one of the waitresses for another bottle of wine. Although she may have been only twenty, her eyes were much older. Her English was as poor as Flynn's French but he got the gist of what she said and shook his head. She pouted, looking professionally disappointed before casting her eye around his companions.

Fitzpatrick had slumped across the table, snoring gently, after too much wine and too little sleep in the trenches. Gallagher winked, flashing her a cheery smile as he chased the debris of his meal around his plate with a chunk of bread, then he belched, flecking the back of Fitzpatrick's head with fragments of food. Devlin was with them too, ignoring her as he tapped his hand on the table in time to the tune kerplunking from a knackered old piano and drunken caterwauling. Docherty sat nursing a mug of gassy beer, already half cut, whilst Carolan avoided the girl's eye, acutely conscious that his wife, Elizabeth, wouldn't be impressed. Flynn didn't think Mary would approve either. Only the Duke didn't seem embarrassed by the girl's lack of subtlety. He didn't care. She took his hand and led him to the stairs in the corner, lasciviously swinging her hips as she went.

'Want not, waste not!' said Gallagher as he relieved the Duke's abandoned plate of its last chips. He farted loudly, chortling to himself as he declared, 'Better out than in.'

'Christ, you need pulling through,' spluttered Devlin, unimpressed. Gallagher beamed, revelling in his schoolboy delight in flatulence. Flynn poured another glass of wine. It was something to do and better than being back in the trenches. Maybe it would help him sleep.

'Fecking Yank never could take his drink,' said Gallagher, helping himself to Fitzpatrick's glass as the American unconsciously snuffled the table. Doyle sat back down, picking up the nearest glass and draining it. There was a raucous cheer from one of the tables as two drunken soldiers lurched up onto it, wobbling precariously as they attempted to perform 'the dance of the flaming arseholes'. Flynn knew it wouldn't be long before fists began to fly as alcohol-sodden tempers frayed. He noticed Fallon a few tables away deep in conversation with his cronies – discussing the fate of Ireland, no doubt – and resisted the urge to walk over and punch him. He didn't like Fallon. He knew the feeling was mutual. He was pretty sure that it was Fallon who'd tried to push him under a train back in London. It wouldn't surprise him if he'd had something to do with his missing gas mask too but without evidence there was nothing he could do. He noticed Fallon was watching him, not too obviously, but every time he looked up he just saw the weaselly little man's rat-like eyes flick away.

'Is there any news of Cronin?' Flynn finally asked Devlin. It was the elephant in the room, the subject they had all avoided ever since they'd discovered that he was really a she. He still found it hard to think of Cronin as a woman, making him realize that even after a year and a half he knew nothing about her. To be honest he knew very little about the others either; only what they let slip. He knew Devlin was married but knew nothing of his family, nor Mahon's. Even Carolan said little of his domestic life except he missed what little of it he'd had.

'He ... er ... I mean, she, is in a field hospital down the road, last I heard,' replied Devlin without looking at Flynn. 'The captain says she'll be fine, just a blighty, that's all. It's not right a girl being as good with a rifle as she was,' he added, before upending the last of his drink down his throat.

'Doesn't it make sense though,' slurred Fallon, suddenly leering drunkenly over them with Collins, 'that the best soldier in your platoon was a fecking girl!' Without so much as a backwards glance, Gallagher drove his elbow hard into Fallon's groin,

165

poleaxing him face first into the table, sending glasses and plates flying. Fitzpatrick woke with a start. Someone caught Collins with an almighty haymaker. Then the dam burst. Fists began to fly, fighting flaring across the bar like wildfire. There would be black eyes and sore heads in the morning.

'Let's get out of here,' suggested Gallagher, sloughing away Fallon's groaning form. The military police had arrived, in red caps with shrieking whistles, flailing truncheons.

None of them needed convincing and together they ploughed through the fray, heading for the back exit. The Duke would have to fend for himself. Their way was barred by a snarling highlander with a face like a bad day in the Gorbals but Gallagher dropped him with a well-aimed headbutt to his broken nose. Flynn ducked a wine bottle. It smashed into the back of some unknown squaddie's head and then they were out, safe in the garbage-strewn alleyway behind the estaminet. 'Quick, before the monkeys get here,' said Gallagher, relieved that the MPs had forgotten to seal off their escape. Then they ran.

News of the fight in town had reached the camp before them – rumours were funny like that – and as they staggered through the gate the orderly sergeant, Mahon, turned a blind eye. By the time they found their tents they were sober and grinning like fools. Spud did his best to ignore them, curled down on Carolan's bunk, whilst Gallagher retold dropping Fallon for the umpteenth time until the epic tale had become embellished like a legend of old. On the other hand, Fallon wasn't quite so lucky and spent the night under arrest, confined to an old barn with a dozen or so other unfortunates picked up by the MPs.

The next morning Sergeant Major Clee came looking for Devlin and the others.

'Corporal Gallagher, Captain Murphy wants to see you,' snapped Clee, throwing back the tent flap, letting the morning sunlight flood in. Gallagher squinted up from his bunk, unsure what was happening. 'Now!' barked Clee. He was up in an instant and doubling smartly towards company HQ. Devlin thought it best to go with him especially as Murphy didn't look pleased to see him when Clee marched him in.

'Lance Corporal Gallagher,' said Murphy from his makeshift biscuit-box desk. 'Private Fallon has made a serious allegation. He says that you assaulted him and started a riot. Striking a subordinate is a very serious offence, Corporal, so what do you have to say?'

'The thing is sir ... the thing is...' Gallagher began to say, squirming uncomfortably, guilt plastered across his guileless features.

'The thing is, sir, Private Fallon is lying, sir,' interrupted Devlin, his face deadpan. Clee scowled. Murphy raised a sceptical

167

eyebrow but the Ulsterman was adroit at making sure officers only knew what they needed to know.

'Is that so, Sar'nt? You know Fallon says that he's a witness, a Private ... er...' He shuffled through the papers on his desk. '...Collins. He says you struck him in the groin in an utterly unprovoked attack.' Gallagher couldn't help grinning, the memory too sweet. Clee glowered, moustache twitching, and Devlin jabbed him sharply in the back of the ankle with his boot, wiping the grin from his face.

'Collins is lying too, sir,' Devlin added as he stared blankly into the middle distance, properly at attention like Gallagher.

'Is that so, Sar'nt? And you are willing to give me your word that there is nothing in Private Fallon's allegations?' asked Murphy, fumbling with his pipe.

'Aye, sir, I am,' declared Devlin, snapping to attention himself. Murphy sighed, leaning back and letting out a long stream of blue-grey smoke. 'We were nowhere near the estaminet last night, sir. Just ask Sergeant Mahon, sir. He was orderly sergeant last night. He saw us in camp when the fight started, sir,' said Devlin. Clee narrowed his eyes. He knew that Devlin was covering for Gallagher and he knew that Devlin knew that he knew but as long as the sergeant was willing to defend his corporal then Fallon's word was meaningless, even if Collins backed him up. After all, the word of a sergeant and a lance jack trumped two privates every time. That's how the army worked. That's how discipline survived.

'Very well, Sergeant Devlin, Corporal Gallagher, I hope that I will hear no more of this nonsense. Sar'nt Major, find Private Fallon for me and in the meantime, Corporal Gallagher, try and keep out of trouble.' They were dismissed. Outside, Flynn and the others were waiting.

'And?' asked Flynn.

'And what?' replied Gallagher.

'And now we make ourselves scarce,' said Devlin, watching Mahon trotting red-faced towards them. 'Why don't we visit Cronin in hospital? It's not far.'

'Oi, Sar'nt Devlin!' shouted Mahon. 'I've been looking for you. Mr Callear has a little job for you.' Devlin rolled his eyes – life had taught him to be wary of officers who had *'little jobs'* – but Callear wasn't bad as officers went. 'By the way, thanks for dropping me in it with the captain, saying I knew where you lot o' drunken *eejits* were when half the battalion was rioting down town. Don't worry, I covered for you, so you owe me,' he added, shoving his cap to the back of his head and mopping his sweaty brow with a crisp white handkerchief. He didn't look too upset.

'Good man!' said Devlin, slapping the

ageing Guardsman on the shoulder, winking conspiratorially. Mahon rubbed his arm and was about to reply when they heard the abrasive tones of the provost sergeant, a beast of a man from Dublin's north side, bellowing abuse that would make even the most jaded whore from Dublin's notorious Monto red-light district blush. He was haranguing a squad of men under full pack, rifles held high above their heads as they stumbled towards the battalion's makeshift parade ground. Provost corporals snapped at their heels like a pack of feral dogs. Fallon was there with Collins, sweating away their hangovers. 'Kevin, do me a favour. Keep Terry here out of trouble and take him with you. Give my regards to Cronin. The rest of you come with me,' said Devlin before striding away smartly with Mahon at his side.

The walk cleared Flynn's head, exorcising the last of his hangover. It took hours to find the hospital: a collection of tents and huts in the grounds of a small chateau that could deal with around a thousand casualties at a time. A convenient railway siding made casualty evacuation easier and a cemetery provided for those unfortunates beyond help. Flynn asked a worn-out-looking Medical Corps sergeant where reception was. He looked at them with the eyes of a man one step ahead of his past and pointed at a large, off-white tent sporting a huge red cross on its roof.

'We've come to see Private Patrick Cronin, 9th Battalion, Royal Dublin Fusiliers,' Flynn told the corporal at the reception desk, a scrubbed, folding wooden table strewn with files. The corporal flicked through a list, then sat back looking at Flynn and Gallagher. Flynn was conscious of how clean the corporal was and how shabby they were, especially as Gallagher was sporting his tatty 'Gor Blimey' hat and vacant grin.

'Sorry, mate, there ain't no Private Cronin on the list,' he replied.

'Are you sure? She was brought in a couple of days ago,' said Flynn. It felt funny saying she. The corporal watched Flynn, expectantly fiddling with a lighter. Reluctantly, Gallagher tossed a battered packet of Woodbines onto the table.

'She, did you say, mate?' he answered, deftly palming the cigarettes into his tunic pocket. 'Well, there is a female patient over in the big house. Talk of the town, it is; we don't have many of them here, mate.' His tone irritated Flynn. 'Now let me see, I think she's called Louise Dempsey. If she's your girl then you've got no hope of seeing her. Rumour has it she's a brigadier general's daughter,' he added, rather too smugly.

'Good job there's a hospital nearby, *mate*,' growled Gallagher, stepping forward, but Flynn blocked his way with his arm. The corporal paled, the smug look sliding from his face as he leapt to his feet, knocking over the chair.

'Look, it ain't up to me, mate. You need to find a fanny–' Gallagher balled his fists, assuming he was making some obscene comment about Cronin. 'Er ... you know, someone from the First Aid Nursing Yeomanry. They're the girls looking after her,' he gabbled, pointing in the direction of the chateau. They were beginning to attract unwanted attention. A white-coated medical officer with a neatly clipped moustache and slicked-down hair began walking over, accompanied by two burly orderlies.

'Quick, let's get out of here,' said Flynn. They ducked behind a wooden hut, some kind of store, then Flynn noticed a slim young woman in some kind of khaki uniform standing by one of the chateau's side doors finishing her cigarette. She looked like an officer, her raven hair pulled back in a bun beneath a shapeless khaki cap. She was watching them. 'Maybe she knows where Cron ... er ... I mean Dempsey is.' The name felt strange, unfamiliar.

Nursing Sister Jane Carmichael wrinkled her nose, downwind of the two approaching scruffy soldiers. The smell shouldn't have bothered her – she'd been in France long enough – but it did. She couldn't abide filth, which was probably why she made such a good sister, but they looked friendly enough: a tall, dark-haired corporal and a stocky lance corporal about her height wearing a tatty old cap, who reminded her of a half-witted dustman. 'Can I help you, gentlemen?' she asked in an aristocratic drawl. Gallagher grinned, looking straight into her hazel eyes, obviously liking what he saw and heard. She noticed the tall corporal's sad, intelligent grey eyes. A scar ran from the tip of his right ear to the corner of his right eye, giving him a rakish look, like some sort of swashbuckler. They saluted and, whilst she wasn't really an officer, Jane saluted back.

'We're looking for a friend of ours, ma'am.' Jane looked sceptical. 'He, I mean she, copped a blighty a few days ago and we were told she was here. The fella at reception said Miss Dempsey was over here.'

'I'm not sure that would be at all possible,' she replied, biting her lower lip. She seemed a little unsure of herself. The tall one looked disappointed but there was something strangely compelling about the short one with his cheeky wry grin and chocolate-button eyes. He seemed friendly enough despite his shabby uniform and somehow endearing as he screwed his cap in his hands, setting his bizarre glib flapping in the breeze. There was a vulnerability to him utterly missing in his melancholy friend. Then Gallagher said please. She relented. 'All right then, but only one of you can see her, understand?'

'I think I'm in love,' Gallagher whispered to Flynn, imbibing her musk of starch and soap as they followed her up some narrow stairs. Flynn rolled his eyes. The stairs smelt of bleach. It felt strange to be around someone so clean.

'You'll have to wait here with me,' Jane told Gallagher when they reached the door to Louise Dempsey's room. Gallagher couldn't help grinning. She smiled. 'You've got five minutes and then you'll have to go,' she insisted. Flynn tapped on the door and disappeared inside, leaving Gallagher with Jane outside. It was an airy room, well lit and clean. A gentle breeze wafted in through the open window. Louise Dempsey lay propped up on pillows on a large, ornate brass bed clad in a flannel nightdress whilst a cage kept the weight of the blankets from her damaged leg. She looked small, pale and vulnerable, her haircut the last vestige of who she used to be. She looked up.

'Kevin! How on earth did you get here?' she gasped. Even her voice had changed, Cronin's rough Dublin brogue erased by an upper-middle-class Anglo-Irish one that some would sneeringly call West Brit. He felt strangely awkward, unsure for the first time why exactly he was there despite all they'd been through together. He didn't know what to say. 'Look, I've still got my leg!' she

174

offered, throwing back the blankets, making him blush and look away. It was foolish really; he'd seen her legs before but things were different now. 'I'm sorry I lied to you chaps but I had no choice.'

'Who are you?' he finally blurted, the words sounding brutally blunt. 'And is it true your old man's a brigadier? And more importantly, who the hell is Pat Cronin?' he asked. She pulled the blanket back over the cage, flopping wearily against the pillows and gazing into his eyes.

'If you must know...' The look in Flynn's eye said he must. 'I'm from Newcastle West over in Limerick. My old man isn't a brigadier, he's a major general. Major General the Viscount Dempsey to be precise and I'm the Honourable Louise Victoria Dempsey, though I have to admit it was more fun being plain old Pat Cronin of the Royal Dublin Fusiliers.' It didn't make sense. She patted the bed, inviting Flynn to sit down. He sat. 'My brother Charles was killed right at the start of this business. He was cavalry, like Papa; shameful use of good horseflesh if you ask me. Anyway, I wanted to make the Boche pay but the blessed army doesn't let girls join up, do they, so I had to cheat a bit. Poor Pat Cronin thought he was on to a sure thing, cheeky beggar! He was off to join the Munsters; met him at the railway station. He had a letter from his parish priest and

175

everything, so I led him on a little, plied him with drink, and then when he passed out I took the lot, got a haircut and hopped it to Dublin. After all, I couldn't join my local mob, could I? Someone might have recognized me and, besides, that's where the real Pat Cronin was headed, so I joined the Lambs.' Flynn was speechless. 'Now Papa knows I'm here so they're evacuating me in the morning.' She smiled, touching Flynn's hand. It felt strange. Wrong somehow. 'I'm glad you came.' So was he.

'Look, I've got to go,' he stammered, getting up suddenly and backing to the door. She smiled, her face softening as she held his gaze. 'I'll write,' he added, opening the door. There was a commotion outside as Jane and Gallagher hurriedly disengaged, untangling what Flynn recognized as a passionate embrace. He didn't know how Gallagher did it but the girls seemed to like him despite his dishevelled appearance. 'When you've quite finished,' he stammered, flustered, trying not to watch Jane blush as she straightened her uniform, fiddling with her tunic buttons. 'We've got to get back and it's a long walk to camp.'

'I'll catch you up,' replied Gallagher as he held on tightly to Jane's hand, a beaming grin plastered across his face. He winked. Jane was smiling too. Suddenly, he felt very alone; missing Mary terribly.

CHAPTER 15

Woolwich, London

It was a miracle that Rory was alive; at least, he thought he was. It was hard to tell buried in claustrophobic darkness. He could see nothing, his eyes clogged with grit, his nose and mouth clogged with fine brick dust that he couldn't wipe away. His arms were pinioned. He couldn't move his legs either. Something sharp dug into his back; he had no idea what. There was a draught near his left foot. Managing to expel some of the dust in his mouth, he chewed his tongue, then dribbled; it trickled down his cheek. He was upside down. Then there were voices. He tried to shout but something pressed down on his chest. Rubble groaned, beginning to move. He fought to stay calm. Something seized his leg and for a moment he thought he was going to be crushed, then he was out, gasping for air as he was dragged free. Someone draped a blanket over his shoulders as he gasped for breath. His face hurt. Someone handed him some water. He sluiced his mouth before spitting it out. The sunlight stung his gritty eyes.

The air stank of burnt wood and brick dust. There was ash everywhere, coating the rubble-strewn street. Soot-stained firemen were clearing up whilst others picked over the rubble of Daiken's house. The houses on either side were in ruins too and the street's windows were out. Rory couldn't remember what had happened. He wasn't sure why he was there. There were policemen holding back a small crowd and for a moment he thought he was in Dublin until a woman emerged with a tray of tea from one of the standing houses and offered him one in a broad London accent. He took it.

'You're lucky to be alive, sonny,' said a weary-looking St John Ambulance Brigade sergeant wearing an old Victorian campaign medal on a filthy, rumpled uniform. The tea was laced with rum. 'Bloody Zeppelins!' he cursed.

'Over here!' someone shouted and Rory looked to see firemen tearing away at the rubble. Others joined him whilst the silent crowd looked on, swaying like wheat in the wind. Then Rory remembered Mary. This was Mary's street. It was coming back to him now. He had been with Mary. He'd been looking at her. The firemen were bundling something onto a stretcher; keeping it out of sight as they covered it with a thick red blanket that did nothing to hide the mis-shapen lumps beneath. He felt sick.

'Friend of yours?' asked a policeman as Rory watched the stretcher pass. A charred arm flopped out, hanging limply in a greasy old cardigan. He thought he could smell boiled cabbage but it must have been his mind playing tricks. The sleeve looked familiar. Then he remembered; he remembered all of it.

'I think that's some fella called Daiken,' he said. The policeman scribbled a note. He took Rory's details too – name, rank and number as well as his unit. 'Have you found anyone else? My sister was with me.' The policeman gave the St John ambulanceman a quizzical look that was far from reassuring.

'We've pulled out five – no, six – including the last fellow and you're the only one we've found alive so far,' said the ambulanceman, avoiding his gaze. There was a row of bodies draped with red blankets, feet protruding from the ends. Some of the lumps were tiny, childlike even, and then he saw a woman's foot. He felt sick, struggling to his feet. The shoe was charred black. There was another shout, then the firemen lifted something else. It was floppy. He couldn't see as they manhandled it onto a stretcher beneath another red blanket.

'Stay here!' ordered the policeman as he and the ambulanceman scrambled up the rubble just as an ambulance clattered around the corner, bell ringing, horses hoofs clattering on the cobbles. Rory ignored it, intent on the firemen. 'She's alive!' shouted the copper and Rory felt a rush of relief. It had to be Mary. They had her by the ambulance. He staggered over. The policeman was smiling, talking softly to whoever lay on the stretcher. They were sliding the stretcher into the ambulance. Then he saw her face, all ash and bloodstains, but it was her.

'Thank God you're alive!' he gasped, squeezing her hand. She managed a strained smile.

'At least I've still got my teeth, I think,' she said after testing her mouth and fat lip with her tongue. Rory couldn't help laughing. She tried to laugh too but it hurt too much. Her left arm was numb like her face. She tried to be brave as Rory ran his hand down her arm, his training kicking in. It was broken. The ambulanceman agreed and began to splint it. 'Where's Daiken?' Rory shook his head. She tried to look upset but it wasn't working.

'You'll have a proper shiner,' he commented, changing the subject. 'Now let's get you to hospital and get you sorted,' he said, climbing into the ambulance beside her.

'What happened?' she asked.

'A couple of bloody Zeppelins must have sneaked over,' said one of the ambulance crew. 'They normally have a pop at the docks but I reckon they were after the arsenal last night. Jesus, but it would've lit the place up like a flipping Christmas tree if they'd hit it. Your street took the brunt. It's a bloody miracle you survived, if you ask me. Flipping shabby way to wage war, dropping bombs on women and kids in their beds like that. I heard we got one of the little bleeders; came down in the Channel on its way home. I hope the bastards burned all the way down!' he added.

'Shame they didn't get it before it got here,' moaned Rory.

'They're quiet little blighters are your Zeppelins. Unless someone gets lucky and sees them coming over, the first thing you know is wallop! They're dropping all sorts on you.'

'You'd've thought it'd be easy to shoot down a great bag of gas,' said Rory.

'You're joking, right? Our aeroplanes can't get high enough and there aren't enough anti-aircraft guns. It's pathetic. You'd have thought someone in the bloody government'd get a bloody grip, but who am I, eh? What would I know?' grumbled the ambulanceman as they jolted towards the hospital, doing their best to keep Mary comfortable. There wasn't much they could do so Rory gazed out the window watching the streets go by. Then they were there.

'I think it best that you wait here,' ordered a formidable-looking nursing sister in a heavily starched uniform as they took Mary inside. Rory couldn't help thinking she looked like she'd swallowed a bees' nest. She didn't look like contradicting her was an option so he didn't bother. Instead, he slumped against the wall, lighting a cigarette. He would wait. Someone brought him a mug of tea. People always seemed to bring him tea. Not that he was complaining; it helped pass the time as he watched people come and go. Some spared him a curious glance in his dirty, dust-stained uniform while others didn't look past the red crosses on his sleeves. He noticed his toecaps were scraped pale grey, devoid of the gleaming shine he'd lovingly built up with spit and polish.

'Can I tempt you?' said an awfully well-spoken young redhead in a Volunteer Aid Detachment uniform, smiling at him and proffering a plate of sandwiches. She looked clean, making Rory realize how dirty he was in his grimy uniform and unwashed hands. He wiped them on his thighs. It was a token gesture; they were still filthy. He laughed, sidestepping the obvious innuendo, and took one. She appreciated his gallantry.

'You've lovely eyes,' he blurted, making her blush.

'I saw you out here and thought you may be hungry. You look like you've been through the mill.' She was right. He was famished. It had been ages since he'd eaten. The corned beef tasted good as he tore into the sandwich. She held up a cup of tea.

'You're an angel,' he said with a wry grin. She looked away, fiddling with her hair.

'Was that your girl you came in with?' she asked.

'My sister,' he replied and he couldn't help seeing a brief sparkle in her eye. He was about to ask her if she could find out what was happening when the formidable nursing sister thrust her head out of the door; scanning the area. She looked stern as ever, scowling at the young nurse. She beckoned her over.

'When you've quite finished, Miss Chapman!' she barked in a voice like nails down a blackboard. Miss Chapman treated Rory to an apologetic smile. She had good teeth. Then, as she scurried back towards the hospital, he couldn't help watching her backside, hoping he would see Miss Chapman again, but it was not to be. Instead, he was left to his own devices until the streetlights flared into life. A chill wind scudded in off the Thames and he flipped up his collar, gleaning scant warmth from yet another cigarette. The clock over the main entrance struck nine. If he didn't go soon they'd think he'd deserted. At least he had a note from one of the policemen explaining his predicament, so hopefully he'd get past the guard with little difficulty, despite his dishevelled appearance.

'Still here?' asked Mary, as she stepped into the street, her arm in a sling. 'I've a bit of a broken arm and save for a few cuts and bruises the doctor says I'll be fine.' She was pale and drawn and looked like a vagrant in her dirty, torn clothes. 'Will you look at me and I've nothing but the rags I'm wearing,' she complained.

Rory gave her a hug, doing his best not to crush her plastered arm. 'Will you stop your moaning? You're alive, aren't you? Now let's find somewhere for you to stay,' he said, leading her by her good arm. Everywhere seemed to be shut or had signs saying 'No dogs, no blacks, no Irish' stuck in the window, and it was gone ten by the time they finally found somewhere to stay. It was shabby, tucked in a back street, and Rory thought it looked like the sort of place that rented rooms by the hour. Mary didn't bother to ask him how he knew what that sort of hotel looked like. The man behind the counter didn't ask questions; he just grunted that it would cost two shillings for the night. 'That's outrageous!' gasped Rory.

'Take it or leave it,' replied the man indifferently. 'Bedding is thruppence extra. Do you want the bedding?' he asked with a crooked, insincere smile, exposing blackened, broken teeth. Reluctantly Rory slapped two shillings and thruppence down on the desk top. They vanished into the man's pocket, then he handed Rory a big brass key followed by a bundle of greying sheets.

'Jaysus knows what you'll be sharing a bed with, sis,' he said, sniffing the sheets. They smelt of stale sweat with a hint of other things he couldn't quite identify. Deep down he couldn't help thinking he was better off not knowing. The landing reminded him of a urinal. The door to the room was stiff. He forced it open. It was damp and draughty and there were stains on the bare floorboards. The rickety bed groaned under his weight. At least the door had a bolt so Mary would be safe as she slept. 'So what now, sis?' he finally asked, handing her a ten-bob note. 'You'll need this. After all, you can't stay here again, it's a fleapit!'

'Whisht, it's not so bad,' she said, glancing out of the window to the street below, but she could tell Rory wasn't convinced. The problem was she wasn't either. He was right, it was a fleapit! 'All it needs is a wee bit of a clean and it'll be grand.' Then she sighed and flopped down onto the bed next to her brother. The bed creaked ominously; not long for this world. Then she relented, laughing. 'You're right, it's a dump all right, but I'm thinking the fleas would be extra like the sheets!' Rory couldn't help laughing. 'I guess I don't really have much choice but to go back to Ireland,' she finally said. 'I've nothing left here now.'

'Well, you've cleaned me out, sis, and ten bob isn't going to get you very far,' he said.

'Tell you what, I know of some fellas over in Kilburn who'll help.'

'What fellas?' Mary asked.

'Just some fellas I met in the pub. They said they looked out for us Irish in this old town. They're always sniffing around Aldershot looking out for Irish soldiers, keeping us informed about what's what back home. You know the ones.'

'You mean Fenians, don't you? Oh Rory, you're not mixed up with Fenians, are you, not after last Easter?'

'Of course not, but if they can get you back over the water then I couldn't care what their politics are! Now, you get your head down. I'll bivvy here and I'll take you to them in the morning.'

'Won't you be in trouble with the army?' she asked.

'What, because of the Fenians?'

She rolled her eyes, hitting him with a limp pillow. 'For being late, of course, you *eejit!*'

'Technically I'm already absent without leave as it is. My pass expired yesterday so another day won't make much difference. Besides, one of the peelers gave me a chit,' he said, brandishing a crumpled piece of paper. 'Worst comes to the worst I'll get jankers and a wee fine. It doesn't matter.'

'Jankers?' she asked. It was as if soldiers spoke a foreign language.

'You know, jankers: punishment. I'll be given a bit of extra work and some running around. I'll be fine,' he explained as he settled onto a wobbly old chair, folding his arms and closing his eyes. Mary slipped out of her dress and curled up under the covers and was soon asleep, snoring gently. Rory didn't sleep; he couldn't. The chair was too uncomfortable and he was afraid it would collapse from under him, so eventually he lay down next to his sister and slept. The next morning he was up early; it was a habit he'd got into. Without a razor, shaving was out of the question and smartening up was pointless. He looked like he'd slept in his clothes, which of course he had, and his cap was gone. Mary looked just as bad; except she didn't have stubble!

They left before sunrise and Rory decided it best to remove his tunic and puttees, hoping that in the half-light he'd be mistaken for a labourer. There were military policemen at the tube stations so they had to walk, keeping to the back streets and alleyways to try and avoid undue attention as they crossed the city. It took hours to reach Kilburn. Rain battered down on them, making their trek more miserable. The Golden Harp was tucked down an alleyway, taking Rory another twenty minutes to find it. He'd never been there before. He hammered on the back door. It opened a crack, secured by a heavy chain.

'What do you want?' asked a hard-faced man with a thick Cavan accent.

'I was told to come here and ask for Mick if I needed help,' replied Rory.

'Mick's not here, but you best come in,' said the man, opening the door.

None of them noticed the man in the shadows further down the street watching them. In fact, Detective Constable Rawlins of Special Branch almost missed them too. He was bored, poring over *The Times* crossword, when he'd noticed a man in what looked like the remnants of a uniform – a deserter, no doubt – and a scruffy blonde slip down the side street trying not to be seen; being cautious but not cautious enough. It was the first suspicious thing Rawlins had seen since he'd been assigned the Golden Harp. Everyone knew the place was crawling with Fenians but no one took them seriously until that business in Dublin. He tucked his paper under his arm and settled back to watch and wait. Half an hour later the deserter emerged from the back door clutching a brown paper package under his arm. He was wearing an old overcoat and a battered fedora hat pulled low, shading his features. The girl was no-where to be seen. The deserter took a quick, furtive look up and down the street then set off in the direction of the High Street. Raw-lins turned up his coat collar – it was raining heavily now – curious to know what was in the package, so he decided to follow.

Rory wasn't happy leaving Mary in the pub but he didn't have much choice. He needed to get back to camp whilst the people in the pub would sort her out some fresh clothes and a ticket home. It was a no-brainer and besides, if he didn't get back soon he'd be in serious trouble. A few days confined to barracks wouldn't hurt but going to chokey was another matter. He was just about to enter the tube station when something made him look around; he didn't know why but he thought he saw a smartly dressed man duck into a doorway. Maybe it was the Fenians keeping an eye on him. He shrugged, joining the queue to buy a ticket. Then he noticed the man in the doorway was speaking to one of the policemen by the entrance. They were looking at him. He resisted the irrational urge to run. After all, he'd done nothing wrong. The man walked over, accompanied by the policeman. There was something unnerving about him, like a man who knew exactly what he was capable of.

'Excuse me, sir, but I think you better come with me,' said Rawlins, holding up his warrant card.

CHAPTER 16

13 May 1916, British front line near Hulluch, north-west France

It was a moonless night. It was his first trench raid.

'It's time to go,' Devlin whispered to Flynn, who took one last drag on his cigarette before flicking it away. Around him others were doing the same all along the trench, needles of light piercing the darkness. A flare soared skyward bathing them all in eerie green light. It was almost midnight.

'Do you suppose they know we're coming?' asked Gallagher as he watched the flare drift lazily back to earth. 'Because if they do, I can think of better things to be doing of a night,' he added with a grin.

'I bet you can and I can imagine who with,' replied Flynn.

Gallagher had spent much of his off-duty time with the nurse they'd met when they visited the hospital.

'You know, I don't know what she sees in me,' said Gallagher.

'Well, you're not alone there,' answered Flynn, earning a reproachful scowl and an elbow in the ribs from his friend. Somewhere in the darkness, a machine gun spluttered into life. 'Sounds like one of ours,' Flynn added, sounding like a veteran. He fumbled in his pocket for a fresh cigarette.

'They'll be the death of you,' Gallagher joked, heaving his Lewis gun onto his broad shoulder. He was the obvious choice to hump the twenty-eight-pound machine gun and despite huffing and puffing like a steam train, he easily managed the weight.

'When you ladies have quite finished,' grumbled Devlin testily. He was on edge and who could blame him? After all, he was about to lead a trench raid. Flynn stopped rummaging and shuffled after Devlin along the greasy duckboards. They were travelling light. Raiders always did.

'Join up, they said. See the world, they said. Good food, they said,' grumbled Gallagher as he followed them. 'You know I should be catching up on me beauty sleep.' He wasn't looking forward to lying out in no-man's-land half the night waiting to give the withdrawing raiders covering fire.

'For the love of God, will ye stop yer fecking bitching, Corporal Gallagher? Ye're more of an optimist than I took ye for if ye think sleep'll help looks like yours!' rebuked Devlin. 'Now shut up or I'll have that stripe off ye!' Gallagher flashed him an oafish grin, making Devlin roll his eyes in despair.

191

'What's his problem?' Gallagher whispered to Flynn, who gave him a long-suffering look that rivalled Devlin's. A wet canvas-ripping crescendo reverberated off the trench's walls, filling the air with the sulphurous stench of rotten cabbage and a ripple of nervous laughter. 'What?' Gallagher protested.

'Do you do that sort of thing in front of Jane?' spluttered Flynn, wrinkling his nose in eye-watering disgust. Gallagher jiggled his leg as if checking he'd only farted.

'Devil's a bit windy,' said Gallagher.

'You're not trying to blame him for your rotten guts, are you?' asked Flynn

'No, I mean your man seems a bit windy about all this,' replied Gallagher.

'Can you blame him?' said Flynn, who was glad that he wasn't responsible for leading the raid. Devlin looked round, scowling furiously enough to devastate a small bunker. He gestured them forward. Viscous slime oozed over the tops of Flynn's boots and it took several tugs from Gallagher and Devlin to work him loose from its cloying grip. The sentry on the fire step spared them a cursory glance before resuming his vigil. Flynn thought the sentry looked like Fallon but in the gloom he couldn't be sure. His hand drifted to his gas mask bag, checking it was there. It was.

'Wait here,' ordered Devlin. They were outside a dugout. Flynn already felt tired. It was always the way before the cocktail of adrenalin, caffeine and nicotine kicked in. It was quiet. He wallowed in the silence, languishing in it like someone luxuriating in a hot bath. In a perverse way it was beautiful. Devlin flipped back the gas cape that served as the dugout's door, splashing them all with amber light, unmasking the foetid trench in all its squalid glory before darting inside. Another flare burst into life overhead, sending shadows scuttling for cover as the aroma of frying bacon and tobacco wafted up from below. Flynn's stomach grumbled loudly. He hadn't eaten in ages, not properly anyway, and was pretty sure that a hard-tack biscuit smeared in Marmite didn't count.

'I suppose this must be C Company's command post,' observed Gallagher quite unnecessarily, as there was a large sign declaring as much by their heads.

'You don't say?' replied Flynn, keeping deadpan. He was hungry and he let his mind wander to what he would eat when they got back: if they got back. Moments later, a fresh-faced subaltern sporting a baggy cricket sweater emerged unleashing another surge of smells. Flynn didn't recognize him. The machine gun ripped into life once more as if fanfaring the officer's appearance. Flynn thought the officer painfully young, which was ironic considering they were all quite young compared to their regular army counterparts. Distant guns joined in the machine gun's concerto, rumbling like a summer storm. Someone else wouldn't get much sleep, he mused.

'It's a piece of cake really,' Flynn heard the officer saying to Devlin in a middle-class Irish accent that contrasted starkly with the sergeant's harsh Derry brogue. 'Just pop over to Jerry's place and crash his party; find out what you can and bag a prisoner or two. Make sure you get you and your lads back before sunrise. There'll be hot scran and a tot of rum waiting.'

'Very good, *sir*,' replied Devlin, placing the sort of emphasis on the word 'sir' that only a senior NCO could – utterly devoid of deference. The sergeant touched the peak of his cap in a lacklustre semblance of a salute. The officer responded in kind, but then officers weren't meant to salute properly: it was bad form, part of that studied amateurism most officers cultivated.

'Who's the Rupert?' asked Gallagher after the officer had ducked back inside.

'Buggered if I know,' said Flynn, shrugging.

'You'd make a passable Rupert, you know,' observed Gallagher. 'After all, you're work-shy and talk all posh. You'd fit in grand!'

'Will you two *eejits* stop yer blathering!' hissed Devlin. 'If you hadn't noticed, we're about to pay the Hun yonder a wee visit; so Corporal Flynn, get along the line and

194

check that no one's kit rattles. I don't want us crossing no-man's-land sounding like a bag of spanners!' He scowled, jumping up and down to test his own kit. 'Well, jildy, quick smart! Oh, and try and make it look like you know what you are doing.'

'Oh well, people to see, places to go. You know how it is?' chirped Gallagher, but Flynn ignored him. Instead he focused on the task in hand, diverting his mind from what was to come. He pulled off his woolly cap comforter, raking his fingers through his greasy hair before checking the line. Most of them wore woolly cap comforters although some wore balaclavas and one for some reason wore a bobble hat, a present from his mum. All of them had gas masks, just in case, but not their webbing. Instead their pockets were crammed with everything they needed, or thought they would need. None had rifles – they weren't looking to get bogged down in a fire fight – just a vicious array of clubs, knives and shillelaghs, like throwbacks to an earlier age. Carolan had a pickaxe handle swathed in razor wire, Fitz-patrick a cosh and Doyle a machete. Flynn had a shovel, honed to a razor edge, and a service revolver just in case. Gallagher had his Lewis and the Duke a sawn-off shotgun to cover their withdrawal. Devlin had a shovel and pistol like Flynn.

'Right then, follow me,' whispered Devlin

once he was satisfied they were ready. Flynn felt light-headed as fear began to build in his gut. He tried hard not to show it, unable to tell if the others felt the same. Soldiering was like that; you learnt to hide your feelings. His boots skidded on the wet clay as they scrambled up the sally port into no-man's-land. The smell of chlorine lingered on the yellowed grass as the raiders crept forwards, ethereal in the darkness as they passed through the wire.

'I've an idea,' said Fallon as he watched them fade into shadow. 'Keep your eyes peeled,' he added, looking up and down the deserted trench.

'Where are you going?' asked Collins. 'They'll shoot you if you run.'

'I'm not running, I'll be back in a sec,' he replied, skipping down from the fire step. Collins watched him flip open a box of trench stores and rummage inside. Then he jumped back up, holding something bulky in the crook of his arm.

'What's that?' asked Collins, doing his best to keep his voice down.

'You'll see,' replied Fallon before slipping into the darkness after the raiding party. Collins was confused, unable to work out what his friend was up to. Fallon kept low, crawling along the same narrow path the raiders had used to get through the British wire. When he reached the other side he stopped, drinking in the scene, straining to hear. It was unnaturally quiet. He felt unnaturally alone. He decided not to dwell on it. Instead he put his weight behind pushing a wooden stake into the thick clay soil before fitting a flare to its top. He carefully stretched a tripwire from the flare to a picket post, closing off the gap in the wire. He smiled, satisfied with his handiwork, then slithered back to his post. It had taken ten minutes at most. For Collins it seemed like an age. 'Now, with a bit of luck all we have to do is sit back and wait,' Fallon told Collins when he got back. Collins still didn't understand. 'Let's just say that Devlin and his band of merry men will regret getting me in the shit with Captain Murphy.' Then Collins noticed Fallon had begun humming softly to himself as he gazed off into the darkness waiting for the show to begin: 'A Nation Once Again'.

Out in the quiet, ever-shifting shadows of no-man's-land, Flynn's nerves were being steadily frayed. At least the Germans were on the ridge above them, masking their move-ments in darkness. They'd frozen a couple of times as green flares fizzled overhead but other than that their crossing had been uneventful. Devlin stopped them short of the enemy wire with a curt hand gesture which Flynn assumed meant 'keep an eye out'. He wasn't as good as he should be at 'monkey talk' – the hand signals they were supposed to use in the field. The sweat cooled on his back as he lay watching shadows morph into imaginary Germanic hordes, gripping the haft of his spade. His cap comforter was sodden too but at least it stopped the sweat stinging his eyes. Whoosh! He fought the urge to run. To move meant death; it was a lethal game of statues, nothing more, nothing less. He kept one eye closed in an attempt to preserve his night vision. A salvo of shells ploughed into the German line a mile or so away and more flares arced skyward. The diversion had begun. The light fizzled into darkness.

'Move!' snapped Devlin. The ground began to rise and Flynn suddenly realized that he needed to pee. He could hear Clee's sage advice rattling around his mind – never go into battle with a full bladder or an empty stomach. It would have to wait and if he wet himself, so what. He was past caring. Gallagher slipped to one side with the Duke, setting up the Lewis on the lip of a small crater.

'Flynn, take Fitzpatrick and clear a path through the wire. Once ye get into Jerry's trench, hoot like an owl and then we'll get after ye,' said Devlin without looking at him. It was a battlefield habit, not looking at who you were talking to. It didn't make much difference in the dark but in daylight doing so could inadvertently show an enemy sniper who was in charge. Snipers liked shooting people who were in charge.

198

'Hoot like an owl? You are taking the piss, right?' replied Flynn. Crestfallen, Devlin shot him a quick, narrow-eyed glance.

'All right, wave then,' Devlin muttered. 'I assume ye can do that?'

Flynn nodded, quick and curt. This was it. His stomach convulsed as if wrestling with an indigestible meal. Blood pounded in his ears as he crawled slowly towards the German wire through the whispering grass. His chest constricted as if some invisible tourniquet was slowly tightening. Christ knows how Devlin stayed so calm. He nestled beneath a strand of wire, fumbling for the wire cutters. The ground was wet. Something kippery nearby stung his nostrils.

Fitzpatrick grasped a razor wire strand, pulling it taut. Flynn snipped. For a moment it resisted, then parted, making a noise that seemed like thunder but in reality was barely audible to anything without the hearing of a bat. Fitzpatrick eased the severed strands back, tucking them out of the way before he shuffled forward with Flynn to deal with the next strand of wire.

They had no idea how long it took to clear a man-sized gap but it seemed like ages until they finally lay close to the lip of the German trench. There was a whiff of coffee in the air: real coffee, not the vile chicory slime they mixed with water to pretend was coffee. Someone was laughing, deep in the muffled depths of a bunker. There was something else: that wet-dog smell that the Germans' furry backpacks gave off when exposed to the elements. Steeling himself, Flynn shifted his grip on his shovel, slipping silently over the precipice until his boots crunched softly on the enemy fire step. A gramophone crackled into life just as Fitzpatrick slipped silently next to him. The traverse was empty.

'What now?' the American whispered, bright-eyed with fear and excitement. Flynn put his finger to his lips; a childlike gesture for silence, as if they were playing some kind of game, which indeed they were. He turned and waved. Something rose, a mass of darkness against the night sky, and moved towards him. It was Devlin. He thudded gently onto the step beside Flynn, his teeth white against the shadow of his face. Then one by one the others joined them until they were squatting nervously in a line. Flynn couldn't help noticing how well made the trench was as he moved towards the edge of the traverse, spade held ready. They really knew how to dig trenches. In fact, he was so distracted he almost walked straight into the shape that stepped into his path.

'*Was zur Hölle ... Scheisse!*' spluttered a startled German. Flynn felt painfully conspicuous, foolish even, like a naughty schoolboy caught scrumping apples, staring at the unfortunate German. They stood like gunslingers waiting for the other to draw. It seemed like ages; it must have been a matter of seconds. Then the German moved, fumbling with his rifle strap, but Flynn was quicker, swinging the razor-edged shovel like a two-handed axe and driving the blade shoulder-jarringly deep into the man's face. He fell like a rag doll, dragging Flynn's spade with him, and he had to push down hard with his foot to wrench the bloody blade free. Something warm flooded Flynn's trousers. He'd wet himself. No one noticed. Devlin prodded the body with his toe. The German was dead.

'That was close. Now give us a hand to get him out of the way,' muttered Devlin as he rummaged through the dead German's pockets, liberating his pay book and wallet. He left the dog tag in place so the body could be identified and recorded properly before it was buried. 'Now let's see if we can get ourselves a prisoner.' It was obvious from the tone of his voice that he was enjoying himself. They lugged the body onto the fire step. Devlin draped a gas cape over it, making it look as if the unfortunate man was asleep rather than dead. 'There, that'll have to do,' he said, surveying his handiwork. Flynn's hands were shaking, overdosing on adrenalin. It was a rush. Suddenly, light flooded the trench as a gas cape screen was thrown back and a scruffy-looking German in a crumpled

Feldmütze stepped out, stretching his arms, looking around, not quite able to take in the scene unfolding before his eyes. He froze. Everyone froze.

'*Alarm! Engländer!*' he screamed, going for the pistol that hung from his belt. There was an almighty bang and a stabbing flash that stripped Flynn of his vision, lancing his brain with needles of light. The German tumbled backwards, clutching his face. There were more cries. A whistle blew. Another flare shot skywards. A machine gun burst into life. The line was waking.

'Shit, that's torn it!' cursed Devlin, smoking pistol in hand. He pulled a Mills bomb from his pocket and, tugging the pin loose, lobbed it into the bunker. There was a dull crump; cries of pain. 'The bastards will be all over us in a minute!' He looked worried. 'Well, don't just stand there catching flies, follow me!' Then he ducked into the bunker's entrance. Fitzpatrick dithered in the doorway until Flynn shoved him hard and together they skidded down the steps. The heavy gas cape fell back into place behind them just as the trench above began to fill with the sound of heavy boots and startled cries.

'Jesus,' Flynn cursed, skidding on something slimy coating the ramshackle stairs that led down into the bunker. It was long, the bunker deep; much deeper than the ones in their own trenches. It was crowded. In the lume of Devlin's torch he saw that the room at the bottom was smoky and cramped; low-ceilinged and stinking of sweat, tobacco and garlic sausage, mixed with the sulphurous, rotten-egg stench of cordite. There were bunks against the wall and a couple of bodies sprawled across the floor. He tried to avoid looking down but he couldn't help himself. 'What now?' Flynn asked, trying hard to avoid the blank, fish-eyed stare of the mangled corpse at his feet.

'Christ knows,' replied Devlin quietly.

'It's a dead end,' said Flynn.

Devlin sighed heavily. 'Thanks for that,' he growled irritably. Darting into the bunker had seemed like a good idea at the time but now it looked like they'd only delayed the inevitable.

'Fitzpatrick, collect what you can,' ordered Devlin, determined not to give up hope. The American did as he was told, rummaging through the dead Germans' pockets collecting pay books and wallets.

'Bavarians,' said Fitzpatrick, as he tore off a blue-piped epaulette.

'Jaysus, we're trapped in this fecking place!' wailed Doyle despondently. He slumped against the wall, letting his machete hang limply at his side. He was close to breaking. Devlin knew he had to do something or they'd all go the same way soon. Panic and despair was like that. Flynn looked at the

Ulsterman, whose face had become hard, devoid of emotion. Pistol in hand, Flynn crept up the stairs, stopping at the bend halfway up. There were voices and for the first time in his life he regretted not paying attention in German lessons in school. Someone shouted and he knew a grenade would follow. If it did they were finished.

'Hang on, what's this?' asked Carolan as he pulled back a tattered canvas sheet that was strung across the wall. It was a tunnel.

'Keep an eye on the stairs,' Devlin told Flynn before elbowing his way to join Carolan. The Germans had dug deep, lacing their front line with subterranean walkways and chambers that kept their soldiers safe and sound. A pale amber light flickered in the distance. 'Do ye reckon it leads anywhere?'

Carolan shrugged. 'It looks pretty narrow but it's better than staying here,' he said. Devlin agreed.

'Joachim, Pieter, sind sie noch abgestiegen?' shouted the voice from above. It was nearer, louder, closer.

'I think they're coming down,' whispered Flynn, cocking his revolver. *'Wir sind ... wir sind ... shit!'* He couldn't remember what to say.

'Quick, follow me!' barked Devlin, leading the way, pistol held high. Carolan followed. The bunker trembled and dust fell as shells began to pound the ground above them.

Flynn couldn't help thinking about Gallagher and the Duke out in no-man's-land. He hoped they were all right. Fitzpatrick had darted into the tunnel, leaving Flynn with Docherty and Doyle. There were footfalls on the stairs. A grey shape loomed around the bend. Flynn raised his pistol and fired, filling the confined space with a deafening roar and blinding light. He fired again. The shape tumbled, landing at his feet. He fired once more, barely able to control his panic. Doyle was rooted to the spot, staring at the dead German. Docherty dithered by the tunnel entrance.

'What the hell ye waiting for, an embossed invitation?' snapped Devlin, poking his head back into the room. It was enough to break the spell, galvanizing Flynn into action. He shoved Docherty towards the sergeant and, grabbing Doyle's sleeve, he dragged him behind him into the tunnel. They'd got thirty yards when there was an almighty blast, searing Flynn's ears like a hammer blow. Doyle sagged and he lifted him up, virtually dragging him. Thankfully the canvas curtain had taken much of the blast. Someone shouted. He cursed, blundering into a low beam as a bullet gouged at the wood near his head. He fired blindly behind, emptying his pistol in three rapid bangs until it clicked forlornly.

CHAPTER 17

14 May 1916, German front line near Loos, north-west France

As Flynn fumbled to reload his revolver, an image of his mother popped into his head. He didn't know why. It wasn't as if they'd been close although he had no doubt that his parents loved him in their restrained, Catholic middle-class way. He kept thinking of the dead German and wondered how his mother and father would take the news of his death. With all the infuriatingly fatalistic, middle-class Catholic calm they could muster, no doubt. His mother would light a candle and clack her rosary beads. He could almost hear her voice muttering, 'I told you so'. He wondered whether the German's mother would miss him too but he didn't get to wonder long. Devlin grabbed his sleeve.

'C'mon! I think I've found a way out!'

Flynn followed him around a corner, following a cluster of dark telephone lines fixed to the damp planked wall. Devlin paused, taking the edge of his shovel to the wires, parting them easily. 'There, that should confuse the bastards!' Then he expertly flicked open his revolver, checking his ammunition. 'Are ye loaded?' he asked. Flynn nodded. He had six shots and then he'd be out. They hadn't come prepared for a fight. 'Here, take this and see if ye can keep them back a while,' Devlin added, handing him his own revolver and Doyle's machete. Great, thought Flynn, just great.

As he watched the others vanish up the tunnel, he thought he could hear something: muffled footfalls from whence they had come. Crouching low, he peered around the corner. The Germans were coming. He fired two rapid shots, thundering in the shadowy confines of the passageway, stinging his ears. He ducked back, expecting a salvo in return. Instead there was nothing, not even a muffled cry. Then the tunnel plunged into darkness. Steadying his nerves, he lay down, easing his head back around the corner. He could see a thin halo of light squeezing itself around the edges of the tattered gas curtain, and he thought he could make out shadows flitting behind. At least they couldn't see him. Maybe they'd think twice before they resumed their pursuit. He hoped so.

A stream of bullets shredded the canvas, tearing up the corridor to flay the planks on either side. Flynn pressed himself into the floor, pulling his head back out of the way. The Germans had a machine gun. He fired blindly around the corner, his shots a pathetic response to the fusillade being unleashed in his direction. Someone squealed. It was a fluke but he didn't care. The machine-gun fire slackened.

'Sod this,' he muttered, belting off into the darkness after Devlin. Cursing as he smacked into the walls more times than was dignified, he finally blundered his way into a long stretch of tunnel. There was a red glow ahead. He slowed, holding his revolver ready just in case as he eased his way towards the light. It flickered. There were shadowy figures. The hammer clicked noisily as he thumbed it back. The shadows froze.

'Who's there?' challenged Devlin.

'It's me,' replied Flynn, easing the hammer forward, making the revolver safe.

'Where's Jerry?' asked Devlin, shining the light in Flynn's eyes.

'Back up the tunnel. I think I got one of them but I don't think they'll hang back for long. The bastards have got a machine gun,' he explained.

'Grand!' wailed Doyle but it was Fitzpatrick not Devlin who told him to get a grip. They were obviously all getting sick of his whining. Then Flynn noticed Carolan and Docherty loitering cautiously at the foot of a staircase. He asked where it led. They shrugged.

'You stay here,' Devlin told Doyle. 'We'll be back for ye in a minute. The rest of you come with me.'

'Do you think it's a good idea leaving Doyle on guard?' Flynn asked Devlin quietly as they climbed the first couple of steps.

'Look, no one knows what's at the top of these stairs so if yer man Doyle's going to funk it it's better he does it down there out of the way than up here with us.' Flynn had to agree there was a ruthless logic to it and in the end Devlin was in charge; it was his call. 'Now give me my Webley back,' he instructed, taking the revolver from Flynn. He cocked it, steeling himself to move onwards and upwards, the treads groaning ominously beneath his feet as he climbed. After ten feet, the passage canted to the right.

'What is it?' asked Flynn.

'How the hell should I know? My mind-reading powers are a bit weak right now!' snapped Devlin, rubbing his temples and throwing Flynn an irritated stare. Then the sergeant looked around the corner before stepping gingerly onto the next stair. Flynn followed, head pounding as more adrenalin flooded his system. There was a glimpse of starlight. They eased into the fresh air, keeping low. A green flare hissed high into the sky. Shells fell randomly all around, the aftershocks of battle. Between explosions Flynn thought he could make out snippets of German gusting on the breeze.

'Do you know where we are?' asked Flynn.

'Jaysus, but ye ask a load of questions,' snapped Devlin, close to the edge of his patience. There was an empty machine-gun mounting at one end of the pit, nestling between two neat piles of sandbags. Naturally, the machine gun was elsewhere, safe underground, and would only be brought to the surface to repel an attack. Fitzpatrick squatted down beside them followed by Carolan. Flynn looked up at the stars. He liked the stars.

'We must be somewhere near Jerry's support line,' whispered Flynn quietly, doing his best to ignore Devlin's testiness, thankful he wasn't in charge. Devlin nodded, his face strained. 'I think our lines must be that way.'

'So, what now, Sarge?' asked Fitzpatrick. Devlin sniffed, scratching his chin, deep in thought as his brain whirred into gear, working out a plan. Docherty had joined them now.

'First, someone needs to go fetch Doyle,' said Devlin, giving Flynn one of those 'you go do it' looks that senior NCOs were so good at.

Reluctantly, Flynn slithered back towards the stairs, his boots skidding on the muddy steps as he picked his way down in the darkness. He regretted not bringing Devlin's torch. The hairs prickled on the back of his neck. Something was wrong. It was like entering a tomb. 'Doyle, where are you?' There was no reply so he worked his way along the tunnel, feeling his way with his fingers. The silence was deafening. 'Stop pissing about and get over here.' He waited a few more minutes, then went back. There was no point hanging around. Doyle was gone.

'What the feck do ye mean, he's not there?' grumbled Devlin, his voice brittle with frustration and fatigue. 'Jerry must have him.'

'Do we go get him?' asked Fitzpatrick.

'What with? We've less firepower than a bunch of boy scouts,' replied Devlin. 'Doyle's going to have to look after himself; we've got more pressing problems. We were sent to get information and now we've got it we need to get back.' No one disagreed with him. 'Besides, for all we know our boys are still lying out there somewhere in no-man's-land waiting for us to get back.' Another flare zipped skywards and Flynn glanced at his pocket watch. It was ridiculous; the sun would be up soon. He didn't know where the night had gone. If they didn't get back soon, whilst it was still dark, then surrender would be the only realistic option left. Maybe Doyle had grasped the nettle, letting himself get caught. At least he'd be safe if he did. Maybe they should do the same. For a moment it was tempting but he shook off the idea, deciding he didn't really fancy spending the rest of the war in a POW cage even if his parents would probably be happier if he did.

They could hear movement, something in the dark. Another incandescent streak of green shrieked into the night sky, bathing everything in jittery light. Angular shadows lunged at the fear lurking in the back of Flynn's mind. He was cold, foetid water seeping through his clothes as they cowered in the sodden machine-gun nest. The Germans would start stirring soon. They had to move. Devlin slunk over the sandbags, keeping low. Fitzpatrick slipped after him. Flynn froze as the word *'Schweinhunde'* was caught on the breeze and hurled towards them. He didn't speak German but someone had told him it meant 'pig-dog'. It was a strange sort of curse. Nothing happened. Carolan and Docherty were next, followed by Flynn. It was an agonizing crawl, inch by inch, pressed flat against the earth until they reached the parados of the German front line. Devlin peered into the trench. It was deserted.

'Quick, down ye get,' Devlin whispered to Flynn as he crawled up beside him. There was no point in arguing. He slid over the edge, easing his way down the reverting into its depths. His boots thudded softly on the damp wood as he landed, squatting down, shovel in hand. A match flared. His heart skipped a beat as he saw a sentry huddled nearby beneath a *Zeltbahn*, lighting a furtive cigarette, seemingly oblivious of Flynn or the others. Devlin dropped down beside him, a knife glinting in his hand. He moved like a phantom, gliding towards the crouching figure. The blade flashed in the starlight as Devlin grappled the unfortunate gently to the ground. 'I could murder a drink,' he grumbled, wiping the wet blade on his cuff as if cutting throats was a mundane chore. The stink of blood hung in the air as the others climbed down to join them.

'Just in case,' said Fitzpatrick, picking up the dead German's rifle.

'Good man,' replied Devlin as he watched the American fiddle with the weapon's un-familiar mechanism. Carolan squinted into no-man's-land, desperately seeking a gap in the wire: their only hope of escape. Then when he saw one he pulled himself up onto the parapet, keeping flat. Devlin scrambled up with him. Flynn couldn't help staring at the dead man's glasses, askew across his sur-prised face. He tried not to look but some-thing drew him inexorably back as he helped Docherty climb up over the top. Click! Clack! Clack! Click! The metallic noise of a cocking rifle echoed down the trench.

'Will you stop playing with that thing!' Flynn snapped at Fitzpatrick.

'*Halt, oder ich schiesse!*'

There were Germans in the trench, bayonets flickering menacingly in the eerie glow. Fitzpatrick stood, unsure what to do, the sentry's rifle slack in his hands.

'Go!' hissed Flynn, hoping Devlin had heard him. The Bavarians eased forward, cautious, poised, ready, their spike helmets menacing in the flickering shadows. One of them broke ranks, his luxuriant walrus moustache making him seem more bestial. Flynn noticed the medal ribbon looped through his tunic buttonhole and the NCO lace on his collar and shoulder straps.

'I would put up my hands if I were you, Tommy. I would hate to have to shoot you,' he said, pointing his Mauser pistol almost casually at Fitzgerald. His English was excellent with the merest hint of a Germanic accent. The Bavarian was calm, collected and firmly in control, betraying not the slightest suspicion that he would be disobeyed. The rifle slipped from Fitzpatrick's hands, thudding to the floor. The Bavarian smiled, nodding approvingly. One of the Bavarians stepped forward, picking it up.

'Believe me, I should hate you to have to shoot me too!' said Flynn as he dropped his shovel, and he sensed the Bavarian relax slightly.

'You British and your ironical understatements, how I miss them,' the Bavarian answered rather light-heartedly. 'I worked in Bristol before the war ... ah, happy days, happy days.' The man's eyes were hard despite his comradely smile, whilst his pistol never wavered. One of his men was staring at the dead sentry, muttering something aggressively guttural before lunging at Flynn. A bayonet flashed past his face as he swerved to avoid his assailant, twisting and lashing out with an iron-shod boot. The soldier grunted, unable to riposte as the NCO wrenched him angrily aside in a tirade of abuse. Seizing him by the collar, he backhanded him savagely with his pistol, sending him reeling.

'I must as you say apologize for my man,' said the NCO, ignoring the beaten soldier. 'Now you must come with me. I believe one of your friends is waiting to see you again,' he added, and Flynn assumed he meant Doyle. The NCO cocked his head in a faux-deferent bow, gesturing the way. By the time they reached their destination, the sun was up, the Bavarians were stood to and Flynn's boots were sodden and his feet blistered and torn, making each torturous step agony.

The Bavarian headquarters wasn't what Flynn was expecting. He could see through the swirling tobacco smoke filling the air that the walls were papered, making it look like a cheap bar rather than something hacked from the wet clay. Doyle was in the corner, crestfallen beneath the gaze of a sallow-faced guard sporting one of those oversized moustaches the Germans seemed to love, who leant on his rifle like a crutch. The guard's washed-out pale eyes followed Flynn and

Fitzpatrick across the room to a desk where a round-faced officer sat puffing on a glowing cigar. The NCO coughed politely. The officer looked up, distracted from his pile of papers. The NCO said something: a situation report, Flynn assumed, as he chopped off a crisp, professional salute. The officer glanced at the Irishmen with red-rimmed eyes, irritated that the *Englanders'* unholy fixation with trench-raiding had cost him yet another night's sleep. He couldn't help thinking war would be a much more orderly affair if everyone stopped trying so damned hard to kill each other!

'So, tell me, Corporal, what is your name and unit? What are your orders?' he asked in passable albeit heavily accented English.

Flynn stamped loudly to attention.

'Kevin Michael Flynn, Corporal, number 4982,' he reported, staring woodenly into the middle distance. The officer sighed, turning to Fitzpatrick, who predictably recited his name, rank and number like they'd been told to do if captured.

The officer smiled. *'Sehr gut,* Corporal Flynn, Private Fitzpatrick. I am much impressed. At your ease, *bitte.* You are playing your part well, yes, but I am afraid that your friend here is not so ... er ... as you say, diligent. No?' He gestured towards Doyle with a casual flick of his hand. It was only when Doyle gave an apologetic shrug that

Flynn noticed his black eye and he did his best to reserve judgement. Then the officer said something to the NCO, who clicked his heels, chopping off yet another immaculate salute before rounding on Flynn, his dark eyes softer than before.

'You are to be taken to the rear, my friends, for … er … questioning, then you will be sent to a prisoner of war camp.' Flynn didn't like the way the NCO had paused before saying 'questioning' but then maybe he was just being paranoid. 'Please, *Herr* Flynn, do not look so alarmed,' said the NCO, noticing Flynn's expression. 'We Bavarians are not barbarians, whatever your government may have you believe. Nothing will happen to you. Look on the bright side, my friend, you get to sit out the war in a prison camp. For you the war is as good as over; you get to survive, after all. Surely that has to be a good thing? Now, I have instructed this *Gefreiter* here to take care of you.'

'*Ja wohl, Herr Unteroffizier,*' barked Doyle's guard, suddenly conscious that his superior was watching him. Then he hauled Doyle to his feet.

'What did you tell them?' asked Flynn but before Doyle could answer, the *Gefreiter* shouted at him, spraying spittle as he shoved the prisoners towards the door. Then a thought crossed his mind. He would make the three Irishmen pay for ruining his plans for a quiet morning, snug in the command bunker. Now he faced the prospect of a long walk to regimental headquarters followed by a very long walk back after next to no sleep. The *Gefreiter's* face split into a broad, disquieting grin that set Flynn's teeth on edge.

CHAPTER 18

14 May 1916, German trenches near Loos, north-west France

Flynn wandered along beside Fitzpatrick with his hands thrust deep into his pockets. He didn't like the way the *Gefreiter* kept glancing furtively in his direction and whispering to the other guard. Doyle kicked along like a petulant teenager, which is really what he was, ignoring the others.

'Well...' started Flynn but the *Gefreiter* cut him short with a sharp blow with his rifle butt and if it hadn't been for Fitzpatrick catching his arm he would have fallen.

'No talking, *Engländer!*' he barked in heavily accented English.

'Hey, we ain't English, bud,' replied Fitzpatrick testily, attracting a glower and a threatening bayonet beneath his nose. 'Just saying,' he added with a disarming shrug.

Flynn glanced back at Doyle. He looked drawn and pale in the morning sunlight. 'You can't blame the young fella, Kev. He's just scared,' whispered Fitzpatrick from the side of his mouth.

'Aren't we all scared?' replied Flynn unsympathetically.

'Silence!' squealed the *Gefreiter*, glowering imperiously, irritated that they were defying his authority. 'No talking or I shoot!' he snapped, jabbing his rifle at the two men, who lapsed begrudgingly into silence. The shock of capture was wearing off and as his despondency receded, giving way to anger and frustration, Flynn thought of Mary and decided he would try and escape. It was obvious the *Gefreiter* was a pompous little buffoon and as he glanced around he began to try and work out how they could use the man's idiocy to their advantage.

'What you thinking, Kev?' asked Fitzpatrick quietly, his face serious.

'That we get out of here.'

'What's the point? If we go into the cages then we'll survive this crappy war, won't we?' said the American.

'I thought you were here fighting for the old country?' replied Flynn, looking surprised.

'Yeah, right! Like that's such a great idea. If it hadn't been for this war we'd be beating the hell out of the English and the Prods over Home Rule. As it is they've turned

Dublin into a pile of rubble that wouldn't look out of place over here.'

'Well, the blasted Fenians shouldn't have started their bloody stupid uprising,' replied Flynn.

'I don't mean the Fenians, I mean the English! They shelled the city centre and then shot the ringleaders like they were common criminals!'

'Look, the Fenians knew the risks when they rebelled and if they didn't then they're *bloody eejits,* all of them!' replied Flynn, irritated by the way so many of his comrades seemed to condemn the Easter rebels on one hand and then vilify the army – the same army they belonged to – for putting the rebellion down the only way they knew how. He'd even read that the bulk of the soldiers who'd been involved were Irishmen anyway – something the more nationalistically minded of his comrades were rapidly forgetting.

'I'm just saying *they* shouldn't have shot the ringleaders, that's all,' grumbled Fitzpatrick.

'We don't know for sure they shot them,' replied Flynn.

'Old Hackett in stores said.'

'Why didn't you say so? It must be bloody true, then!'

'Look, those guys were in the Volunteers, like most of us. It's different for you, Kev, you weren't in the organization. I probably know some of the fellas who took part. Doyle's cousin was there. I heard him say so. You know he ain't been right since we heard about it.' Flynn resisted pointing out he had a cousin in the Volunteers; he didn't see the point of being drawn into an argument with his friend. Besides, he had no idea whether his cousin had been involved in the Rising or not. To be honest he didn't care. He'd never subscribed to some of his countrymen's romanticized obsession with a rebellion in every generation; unsure what real difference being governed from Dublin rather than Whitehall would actually make to his life, or anyone else's for that matter. Politicians were all a clique of middle-class frock coats as far as he was concerned.

'Séamus is right. We're just a load of thick-Mick cannon fodder,' snapped Doyle. 'When the war's over the lying English bastards won't give us our country back, you'll see!'

'No talking!' barked the *Gefreiter*, cocking his rifle with a fluid flick of the wrist.

'I'm just saying we can't just leave the lads to it. They need us,' whispered Flynn. Fitz-patrick nodded, mouthing OK.

'Shut up!' shrieked the *Gefreiter*, raising his rifle so that it pointed straight at Flynn's head. His comrade was aiming at Fitzpatrick, flicking the muzzle occasionally towards Doyle to hold them at bay. They walked on in sullen silence and as they finally left the maze of communication trenches, Flynn surreptitiously lengthened his stride to annoy his guards. The guns were a distant rumble now, barely audible over the twitter of the birds, as they moved along a cratered gravel road through a decimated wood. Behind them the German trenches burrowed into a low ridge that both shielded their rear area and exposed that of the British to their scrutiny. Slag heaps dotted the countryside, betraying its mining heritage. Supply wagons hauled stores towards the front line and with every step in the other direction he felt himself getting more and more tired and hungry. Something buzzed overhead, making weary pioneers in black-piped *Feldmützen* squint anxiously into the sky. The sun was brighter now and Flynn felt its warmth playing on his skin. It was almost pleasant, stirring distant childhood memories of family outings visiting relatives in the Wicklow Mountains, and for a moment he drifted away to fantasies of strolling along leafy Irish lanes hand in hand with Mary. Then he thought of Gallagher and Devlin, wondering if they'd made it. He hoped they had.

'Hey, Fritz, is it much further?' asked Flynn. The *Gefreiter* scowled, brandishing his rifle with an expression that made him look like a man who had bitten a dog turd, before scuttling over to his companion. He whispered something; Flynn couldn't hear what. Even if he had it wouldn't have made any difference: he didn't speak German. Flynn didn't like the way the other guard nodded, keeping his eyes on the prisoners.

'*Hände hoch*, Tommy. *Hier*, stop now, Tommy! We rest, yes?' barked the *Gefreiter* after they'd walked on for a few more minutes. He gestured towards a sparse, flayed copse by the roadside whilst his companion fumbled with his own rifle.

'I got a bad feeling about this,' said Flynn. For some strange reason their expressions reminded Flynn of sheepdogs herding sheep. Doyle and Fitzpatrick were already in what had once been a small clearing about thirty feet from the road. He hesitated.

'*Raus! Raus!*' growled the *Gefreiter*, shoving him after them, making him stumble. His ankle snagged on a tuffet, twisting his foot and sending jarring pain shooting up his leg. The buzzing was louder. The *Gefreiter* was aiming at him, a cruel sneer on his lips, his pale, lupine eyes demonically ablaze. '*Wiedersehen*, Tommy!' Flynn tensed, closing his eyes. So this is it, this is how it ends, he thought as despair washed over him and he felt his lips begin to move.

'Hail Mary, full of grace...' There was a flash, an almighty bang and then Flynn was flying through the air before landing heavily on his shoulders, driving the air from his lungs. Groaning and gasping for breath, he opened his eyes, prising himself awkwardly into a sitting position. The *Gefreiter* was face down, moaning. German soldiers were dashing for cover. It was chaos. There was a gory, greasy streak across the charred grass and Flynn could feel blood pouring from his nose.

'Son of a bitch, what the hell was that?' spluttered Fitzpatrick, his face blackened like an escapee from a minstrel show. Bloody lumps of tattered flesh hung from them both. The *Gefreiter* was levering himself from the ground.

'Where's Doyle?' asked Flynn, looking around.

Overhead three spindly, two-seater pusher biplanes with their engines behind the pilot's cockpit streaked overhead, the British roundels clearly visible on their wings as they strafed the road. They flared upwards, engines straining as they turned for another pass. As they passed by, their gunners sprayed the road but the element of surprise was gone and here and there Germans were firing back.

'Doyle's bought it,' said Fitzpatrick, pointing to where Doyle's shattered corpse lay; killed by a British bomb, the victim of war's cruel irony. The *Gefreiter* was on his knees now, blinking and shaking his head to clear his vision. Then he looked up. His rifle was just beyond reach. He stretched out his hand just as Flynn skipped forward, driving his size nine boot into the side of the German's head like a full-back trying to convert a try.

'Way to go! Come on, the Dubs!' cried Fitzpatrick as the *Gefreiter* flew sideways, grunting as he landed and lay still. 'Is the son of a bitch dead?' he asked, but Flynn wasn't listening, already trying to see if there was a way out.

'Let's go. I don't know about you but I don't fancy hanging around here waiting to get shot. If we're quick we might just make it,' said Flynn before he broke into a trot through the copse and away from the road. They paused at the treeline, catching their breath as they scanned the rolling meadow beyond for signs of the enemy. There was a waterlogged nullah about a football pitch's length away, edged with tufting long grass. 'There!' They kept low, moving as fast as they could, half-expecting gunshots to snap at their heels. Flynn's side began to hurt as a stitch set in and as he skidded down the side of the slimy ditch he promised God that he'd give up smoking.

'So, what now, buddy?' gasped Fitzpatrick, making Flynn feel secretly satisfied that his friend was as unfit as he was.

'Look, over there,' wheezed Flynn, pointing at a dense patch of woodland a few hundred yards away. 'Maybe we can hide out there?'

'Then what?' asked Fitzpatrick.

'Christ knows but it's better than hanging around here,' replied Flynn, glancing back at the road with its burning supply wagons and panicking horses. He felt sorry for the horses. It was still chaos but they both knew it wouldn't last much longer. After a few gulped breaths, they got up and ran and by the time they reached the wood the British aircraft had gone. Fitzpatrick vomited, sucking down air whilst Flynn rolled onto his back, panting. He could see dots high above; presumably the aeroplanes making their escape. Several more dots swarmed towards them and they began tumbling and weaving across the sky. One of them billowed smoke, spiralling downwards, growing bigger and bigger until it swooped low overhead, its engine spluttering as the pilot wrestled with the controls. It was British and from where they lay they saw the gunner slumped in the front cockpit. They watched horrified as the stricken aircraft yawed sideways, bucking violently before skimming the sparse canopy above them and bouncing heavily through the long grass beyond, where it slewed to a halt, its engine stuttering to silence.

The pilot jumped clear, hurling his flying helmet to the ground, looking to Flynn as if he was cursing his machine. There were field-grey figures emerging from a wood on the other side of the meadow, waving and shouting. Something flashed and Flynn winced as the familiar crack-thump of gunfire sent rounds zipping harmlessly overhead. It wouldn't be long before they started trying to hit. A dark shadow passed overhead, their senses overwhelmed by an almighty roar as a gaudily painted German fighter plane screamed low overhead like some kind of bird of prey, waggling its wings before tearing up into the blue.

'Well, it sure looks like we ain't the only ones up shit creek!' observed Fitzpatrick. Flynn was up, intent on the drama unfolding before them. 'Hey, what's up?'

'I was just thinking–'

'Always worrying,' interjected Fitzpatrick.

'Like I was saying, if–'

'Dangerous word *if*,' opined the American.

'Like I was saying, if we could get to your man there and help him get that thing working again, then maybe we'll be able to get a lift out of here?' said Flynn.

'You know, I had a feeling you were going to say something dumb-ass like that.'

'Well? What do you think?' asked Flynn.

'I don't think you'll like what I think,' answered Fitzpatrick.

'So you're up for it, then?' replied Flynn, grinning wryly when Fitzpatrick rolled his eyes.

'You know in football they'd call this a *Hail Mary* play,' said Fitzpatrick.

'C'mon then,' said Flynn, crossing himself

before he moved. He didn't really know why. Unlike his parents, he wasn't much of a Catholic and, much to his mother's chagrin, he'd studiously avoided going to church whenever possible since his chrismation. Then they ran, hell for leather towards the downed aircraft. The pilot didn't notice them, absorbed as he was with his frantic attempts to restart the engine. Stray bullets plucked at the machine's tattered canvas and as they neared Flynn couldn't help wondering how the hell the thing got off the ground in the first place. A bloody body sprawled half out of the cockpit.

'Do you think you can get it started?' asked Flynn, sucking wind. The pilot swung round, obviously startled as his hand snatched at the revolver slung from his hip like some sort of Old West gunfighter. 'Hey, whoa there, we're on your side,' gabbled Flynn, holding his hands up high. 'Look, Jerry will be here in a minute, so do you think you can get this bloody thing started or are we gonna be feasting on sauerkraut tonight?' The pilot's eyes narrowed, his pinched young face pale and drawn, his leather trench-coat and face stained with oil. He hesitated, unsure what to make of the two filthy soldiers who seemed to have come from nowhere. The pistol slipped back into its holster. 'Will it take the three of us?' asked Flynn. The pilot was looking over Flynn's shoulder at something in the distance. They looked. It was the *Gefreiter* staggering down the field, rifle at the trail. On the other side of the field the Germans were closer. It was a toss-up who would kill them first.

'Well ... er ... the FE2 is a temperamental old kite,' he said in a mild Kentish accent that made him sound more NCO than officer. 'I may just be able to get it started. Now, help me get the blasted crate into wind.'

The Germans were closer.

'C'mon, Séamus,' called Flynn. 'Jump to it!'

'They're almost on top of us!' shrieked Fitzpatrick, pointing wide-eyed at the approaching Germans. Then Flynn noticed the Lewis gun hanging from its pintle mount at the front of the aircraft's nacelle.

'Séamus, get your arse up there and keep the bastards' heads down,' he ordered. 'We'll crack on down here.' Almost reluctantly, the American tore his eyes from the field-grey figures looming closer and scrambled up the side of the aircraft. He eased past the limp gunner, squeezing into the cockpit and cocking the machine gun. Unleashing a ragged burst, he scattered the Germans as they dove for cover. The noise thundered through Flynn's skull, making his ears ring. Fitzpatrick swung around, aiming at the *Gefreiter*, and fired again, a short staccato spray of bullets that sent him scurrying for cover too.

Over the noise Flynn heard the crack of passing rounds as the Germans began to fire back, making his head swim in a cocktail of fear and excitement. It would all be over soon.

'Look,' shouted the pilot over the din, 'I'm going to get back in and when I do this,' he held up his fist, thumbs up, 'I want you to heave the bloody prop as hard as you can, understand? If the bloody thing starts then get back round here and get in PDQ. I don't think we're going to get a second shot at this. The old girl wasn't designed to take four so we're going to have to ditch everything to get off the ground.' More bullets zipped by, closer still. Flynn could feel them plucking at his clothes as they passed. The pilot gave the signal. Flynn heaved on the propeller, using every ounce of heart, soul and muscle he could muster. It turned. Acrid smoke belched in his face as the engine coughed, then spluttered, then banged, then whined, then died. The enemy were less than a hundred yards off.

'Shit!' cursed the pilot. Fitzpatrick let off a long, rattling burst that tore up flailing clods of earth. 'Do it again!' he shouted. 'Do it again NOW!' Flynn tried again, flinching as a bullet tore a jagged splinter from the propeller blade that barely missed tearing his cheek. The engine backfired, belched out more acrid smoke, then erupted into deafening life. He ducked out of the way, weaving around the machine just as it lurched forward, and for one heart-stopping moment he thought he would be left behind. More bullets zipped by. He grabbed a strut, hauling himself off the ground.

'Ditch the bloody gun!' he shouted at Fitzpatrick as he hooked his elbows over the edge of the front cockpit, one foot in the metal stirrup below. It would be a tight squeeze.

'Tell me you're kidding,' snapped Fitzpatrick as the aircraft lurched across the rutted field.

'Do I look like I'm bloody kidding?' replied Flynn angrily, clinging desperately to the side of the plane. The noise was deafening, coursing through Flynn's body. Fitzpatrick let off one last long burst, then unhitched the Lewis, reluctantly tossing it over the side, then he ditched the magazines. Flynn's foot slipped as the plane bounced before thudding back to earth and for a fraction of a second he could see himself being thrown through the churning airscrew to be shredded and scattered like so much bloody chaff. His fingers ached, losing purchase. He could feel panic taking grip. Then he felt Fitzpatrick's hands on him, reeling him in until he squirmed awkwardly, head first, into the cockpit. It was only when he'd managed to wriggle past the inert observer that he realized they were airborne – just. Below, Germans were sprinting forward, muzzle flashes silently twinkling beneath the roar of the engines, then he noticed a filth-coated figure on the edge of a ditch brandishing his fist like a pantomime villain. It was the *Gefreiter*.

The engine flared, changing pitch as the FE2 lurched upward, its engine belching more dark smoke and flame. Flynn tried his best to ignore the fist-sized holes appearing in the wing as they skimmed the treetops. He'd never flown before and as the plane groped skywards he was overwhelmed by the living diorama unfolding beneath him. He'd never felt so alive. Then the observer groaned. He was alive. They were all alive and as the spluttering flying machine struggled across no-man's-land, Flynn began to let himself believe that they would make it.

CHAPTER 19

Dublin Bay, Ireland

Mary leant against the ferry's guard rail, the wind ruffling her hair as she watched the screeching gulls circle above the foam-capped expanse of Dublin Bay. It was choppy and the swell of the deck beneath her feet felt almost reassuring as the land of her birth drew nearer. She could see fishing boats and pleasure boats tugging listlessly at their moorings as if eager to be at sea. She could see Dublin, a dark, smoky smear in the distance as the ferry eased its way into Kingstown harbour. Excitement balled in the pit of her stomach as she began to make out buildings and people. She felt like a thoroughbred champing at the bit at the Fairyhouse races, eager to be ashore, eager to be home. There was a saying: may you die in Ireland. She'd always thought it a stupid thing to say until now; after eighteen months in London she was determined never to leave her homeland again.

The briny air was making her hungry. Her stomach grumbled but eating would have to wait. She had things to do.

'It's time,' said a Scouse accent behind her. She turned around. He was stocky, his face lived-in and weather-beaten; one of those faces that told of a lifetime of privation and travel. She had never met him before. They had never spoken but she knew he would come. They'd told her he would. They said to keep an eye out for a man with a blurred harp tattoo on his arm. He would make contact before they landed. She guessed he was one of the crew. She'd seen him on deck but had paid him no mind during the crossing. The smell of cheap tobacco and cooking oil hung around him like bad aftershave.

'Just do what the fella tells you and you'll do fine,' the Golden Harp's barman, Charlie O'Connell, had told her back in London. To be honest, the first time she'd met Charlie, when Rory had left her at the pub, she'd been terrified of the hulking Irishman but he was a gentle giant, a pussy cat really, and she had no reason to doubt him. After all, he'd taken her in in her hour of need; letting her stay in his family's tiny, red-brick terrace just around the corner from the pub.

'Well, we've got to look after our own, don't we?' said Charlie's wife, Maude, making Mary welcome. She sounded English to Mary but she was Irish enough to her own satisfaction: the great-granddaughter of a Wexford man. She had a temper too, especially after a gin or two, that kept Charlie on his guard – but they loved each other. That much was obvious. That they were both dedicated revolutionaries was less so.

She didn't bother going back to the arsenal. What was the point? The way Maude told it, it didn't seem right making shells for the British, especially as some of those shells had been fired on Dublin back at Easter. At least she was getting her colour back now that she wasn't handling dangerous chemicals all the time. She began helping out, making tea and the like for the men who met in the Golden

Harp's back room, shrouded in smoke and hushed talk of next time. She guessed they were Fenians and if her mother wouldn't have approved she didn't care. All the war had done for her family was cripple her older brother and send two others off to God knows what. The sooner it was over the better. Then at least they would come home.

'Then we'll make the English listen and be a nation once again,' said Maude at the end of one of her many impromptu lectures about Irish freedom. Charlie had just gone to work and she was fussing about her kitchen when she added, 'There are some people I'd like you to meet.' She handed Mary her coat and led her to a crumbling old Catholic church a few streets away. There was moss on the stained, cobwebbed windows. They crunched down the gravel path past an imposing granite angel staring sternly down on them as they made their way to the parochial house next door.

Maude knocked a staccato tattoo, and the door opened a crack. They were ushered in by a grey-haired priest whose voice sounded fresh off the boat from Belfast despite years in London. He led them to a back room. The curtains were closed, blotting out the sunlight, and through the gloom Mary could make out the shape of a woman sipping tea in the shadows. Mary sensed the woman's eyes on her.

'Is this her?' asked the woman, her voice soft and very Irish. Maude nodded. 'Mrs O'Connell says that you would be a valuable recruit.'

'They don't take women in the army,' said Mary, looking puzzled.

'Ah, now that would depend on whose army, now,' replied the woman.

'She means a recruit for the organization, for *Cumann na mBan*,' interrupted Maude.

'Cooman nah what?' asked Mary, guessing the words were Irish. She didn't speak Irish; hardly anyone did any more except to prove a point.

'*Cumann na mBan*,' repeated the woman. 'It means the Irish Woman's Council. We do our bit to help our boys in the Volunteers. Mrs O'Connell here says you're just the sort of girl we're looking for. You've not been in trouble with the peelers, have you, Miss ... er ... Gallagher?' asked the woman. Shaking her head, Mary wasn't sure where this was going but she could see the woman smile, her teeth a splash of white in the darkness. 'Well, that's just grand! What we need now is people the peelers don't know, especially after last Easter. Most of the boys are banged up or on the run so it's vital we tread carefully, make sure that next time we're ready. We could do with some fresh blood.' Mary was uneasy with the phrase 'fresh blood' but she didn't comment.

'And what is it you want me to do?' Mary asked cautiously.

'Oh, this and that,' replied the woman rather evasively and that was how she found herself on the Liverpool–Kingstown ferry doing *this and that* for the cause.

'Well, are you coming?' asked the Scouser, indicating that she should follow him below deck. He led her down a white-painted passageway to a store. It smelt of food and stale sweat. 'Stay here,' he ordered before disappearing inside, leaving her loitering conspicuously outside. A few moments later he emerged clutching a package in his hands. He handed it to her. It was heavy. She'd been told not to ask questions. 'Hide it in your suitcase. The bizzies don't stop women,' he added confidently. She wasn't so sure. 'Take this,' he produced an envelope, 'and stuff it in your knickers. They really won't search there.' Her cheeks coloured. 'Now clear off and don't draw attention to yourself. Understand?' Then he was gone.

She stowed the package in the bottom of her bag and went back on deck. Kingstown, or Dunleary, as Maude and Charlie insisted on calling it, was much closer now. They would be ashore soon. She could see people on the quayside; eagerly awaiting loved ones, no doubt. Her parents wouldn't be there. They didn't know she was coming. Maude had told her it was better no one knew. Even the ticket had been bought at the last minute. She hadn't heard from Flynn either. He hadn't answered her last letter. As she stepped ashore she didn't know whether it was the crossing or her nerves that made her legs wobbly. There were men in the crowd in smart suits, hats pulled low as they watched the throng. She'd been warned that there'd be G-Men waiting, looking for *'players'* – known Republicans – but Maude had assured her she was a *'cleanskin'* – an unknown. No one would stop her. She hoped they were right. A man stepped into her path. Her heart skipped a beat. Maude had been wrong!

'Do you have it?' he asked, sparing a quick glance round. She stared at him blankly, knees weakening. He was tall, dark-haired, about thirty, handsome after a fashion and way too scruffily dressed to be a plain-clothes man. 'Don't just stand there gawping. Do you have it?' he repeated just as a scuffle broke out on the ferry's deck. It was the Scouser. He was fighting with one of the suits. Whistles shrilled and she could see blue uniformed constables barging their way through the crowd to help the detective. She nodded. 'That's grand! Now, come with me,' he added, throwing his arms around her in a warm embrace. His face was close, hovering inches from hers, and for a moment she half-expected him to kiss her. Then, as he relieved her of her suitcase, she realized that she

238

wouldn't have minded if he had. 'Subtle, aren't they?' he said, nodding his head in the direction of a man in chalk-stripe and a bowler who was all too obviously pretending to read his newspaper. Outside the terminal, the street was teeming. Cabbies and porters vied for trade whilst here and there soldiers stood guard, bayonets gleaming wickedly in the sun. It felt strange to think that two of her brothers were wearing exactly the same uniform: the uniform of the enemy.

'Where are we going?' she asked but the man ignored her, leading her calmly by the hand across the street, using the distraction of the Scouser being dragged into a waiting Black Maria to cover their retreat. She felt like running but he simply strolled along as if he hadn't a care in the world: just a man meeting his sweetheart off the boat. She squeezed his hand; it felt warm and safe. Without looking, he squeezed back. She didn't even know his name. That wasn't unusual: since doing *this and that* she'd met plenty who'd not given their names. Maude said it was safer that way; for her and them.

'Will you be quiet, woman,' he rebuked, smiling roguishly and winking. She couldn't help noticing his eyes. They were clear and blue like water on a bright day. She liked his eyes. 'They call me Sweeney, Gerard Sweeney,' he eventually said when they were several streets clear of the terminal.

'Do they now?' she replied, unsure who *they* were or whether he was lying. Not that she cared. She liked him; she had no idea why. He seemed so different from Flynn, who was all books and awkward charm. This one was different. He made her feel safe. 'Well, they call me Mary Gallagher,' she told him.

'I know,' he replied as they entered an uninviting, garbage-strewn alleyway. Plump rats foraged amongst the filth, sparing the couple only the most cursory of glances as they waddled about their business. 'Don't you go worrying about the smell,' said Sweeney as he stopped outside a shabby door set in a large, windowless wall. 'It keeps the peelers away.' He rapped on the flaking woodwork. There was silence. He knocked again, making what almost sounded like a little tune. The door peeped open. There was an unshaven face. Sweeney shoved the door, throwing it open.

'Does she have them?' asked the unshaven man. Sweeney held up the suitcase and the man took it, testing its weight. He seemed satisfied.

'I've my things in there,' said Mary, suddenly afraid that the unshaven man would disappear with her suitcase. The man rolled his eyes, plonking the suitcase on the floor before squatting down and flipping it open. She didn't like the way he rummaged through her things but there was nothing she could do as he retrieved the package. It vanished into unseen hands.

'And the rest?' the man asked. Mary blushed; she'd done as the Scouser had said.

'It's in my underwear, like the man on the boat said,' she replied. She didn't like the way the unshaven man suddenly perked up, leering at her with a lascivious glint in his eye. He held out his hand. 'What? Here?' she asked but the man didn't say anything, he just grinned.

'Feck off, you pervert!' snapped Sweeney, elbowing the man aside. The hallway smelt suspiciously of damp plaster and urine. 'Now if you don't mind you can turn around and give the lady some privacy!' She liked the way Sweeney called her 'the lady'. Reluctantly the man turned around. Sweeney did likewise and just as Mary began to hike up the front of her dress they heard snickers from up the stairs. Without looking Sweeney snapped, 'And you little feckers can look away too!' There was a groan of disappointment from the shadows and the sound of a door slamming. Mary resumed rummaging. 'Are you done yet?' asked Sweeney after a few moments

'Er, yes, sorry,' replied Mary and the men turned around. There was a disappointed look on the man's face as he snatched the envelope from Mary's hand but then he wafted it beneath his nose, breathing deeply. She shuddered.

'Don't mind him, he's an *eejit*. A useful *eejit* but an *eejit* all the same,' apologized Sweeny, leading Mary by the hand back into the alleyway. 'Now then, Miss Gallagher, let's get you home, shall we?' he said. She smiled. She liked the way he called her Miss Gallagher. 'But first I think you could do with some breakfast, on me,' he added with a smile. 'I know a place.' She was ravenous. They headed towards the seafront and ate in a café where Sweeney seemed well known. An anonymous collecting tin sat on the counter and she watched him drop a few coins in it as he ordered their food: bacon, eggs, soda farls, potato bread and mugs of thick brown tea. The food was filling and she couldn't help noticing how attentively he listened as she talked, cocking his head to one side and nodding appreciatively. When they'd finished she fiddled with her hair, conscious that his eyes were still on her. She realized she hadn't mentioned her brothers or Flynn, especially Flynn, all the time they'd been chatting. Somehow, it didn't matter. All that mattered was the here and now. All that mattered was being with this man.

They took a tram back into Dublin. He carried her case, walking her to the corner of her street. They were arm in arm. She couldn't help thinking how ordinary it looked, how unchanged, yet deep down she knew that everything had changed. Nothing would be the same again.

'I best be off,' said Sweeney. He could see that she was disappointed, which pleased him. He'd enjoyed their afternoon together.

'Will I see you again?' she asked, gazing into his eyes.

He gazed back; so unlike Flynn. He smiled. 'Oh, I expect so, Miss Gallagher,' he replied nonchalantly. Then they both laughed for no other reason than they could. It was good to laugh. 'I'll tell you what, Miss Gallagher–'

'Please call me Mary,' she interrupted.

'Mary, then. Why don't I meet you here at three o'clock tomorrow?' She liked the idea and leant forward to kiss him. She aimed for his cheek but somehow their lips met and he kissed her back, passionately, before pulling away. 'Three o'clock it is, then!' He beamed. For a fleeting moment she thought of Flynn and felt a twinge of guilt but sloughed it off. Flynn was in France. Besides, Sweeney was here and now. For all she knew Flynn was probably already dead and if the war had taught her anything it was that life was for living.

She looked around but Sweeney was gone and to her embarrassment she couldn't help feeling that she was missing him already. The feeling soon evaporated as she pushed open the door, remembering all those long-forgotten smells of childhood as she entered the house. She could hear voices in the kitchen so she followed them. Her mother looked old, washed out like clothes put too many times through the mangle. She was holding a letter in her hands.

'Oh, it's you,' she said, looking up.

CHAPTER 20

May 1916, near Hulluch, north-west France

The FE2's engine spluttered, banging violently as the aeroplane dropped suddenly before swooping back up. For a moment Flynn thought the pilot was showing off but the look on his grimy face showed he was fighting with the miscreant machine, locked in a life-or-death struggle over the wasteland below. It was a long drop and even the thought of it was at once exhilarating and terrifying. The plane lurched, flicking the gunner's lolling head back in a jarring head-butt that sent white daggers lancing through Flynn's brain. He could taste blood. There was a flat metallic bang, ominously louder than the last, followed by the oily reek of hot metal. The ground was closer, faster. Fitzpatrick had wedged himself down, squeezing his eyes shut as if not being able to see danger would make it go away. He was praying and Flynn felt an overwhelming urge to join him.

Then Flynn noticed something dark, like an angry swarm of bees, tumbling through the trail of smoke that traced their swirling trail across the leaden skies. The swarm grew bigger so he waved at the pilot, jabbing an open palm in its direction. Then he jerked his thumb downwards, hoping that the young pilot would recognize the infantryman's hand signal for 'enemy'. For the briefest of moments the pilot looked confused, then he nodded, trawling up distant memories from his time in the Engineers before craning over his shoulder into the lume of the sun: fighters. His heart sank. Flynn wasn't much of a lip-reader but even he was good enough to decode the pilot's expletives. The plane lurched sideways, slipping downwards. Flynn felt like his stomach was being forced into his throat and as the machine swerved he caught a glimpse of bodies and a burnt-out aircraft smeared across the blackened ground below. He tried not to dwell on them.

Mesmerized, Flynn watched one of the swarm break away, careering closer: death on the wing. He tried to look away – to close his eyes like Fitzpatrick – but he couldn't and as the blob slowly took shape before his eyes he felt his guts turn to water. It had wings and wheels and he could even make out the bulge of the pilot's head. Silent flashes winked from its nose, stitching jagged holes along the FE2's wing, chipping wood and cracking struts. They lurched again as wires parted. Another swarm cascaded downwards, jumbling with the first. They were feet from the ground now. The swarms were swirling, reeling through the air, locked in combat. Another strut parted. They were at rooftop level now, the muddy ground streaking by. Flynn wondered what it would be like to die, to feel the ground crashing into him as the plane shattered across the ground. More importantly, he wondered if it would hurt.

For an awful moment he thought he'd wet himself, his trousers suddenly drenched, then it dawned on him: he was soaked in petrol, its overpowering reek flooding his senses, making him light-headed as if drunk. A stray bullet had fractured the fuel tank, marinating them with petrol. Tracer rounds sped silently by. One spark and it would be over. Then they lurched lower still, below the level of the broken trees. He could see pale faces staring up from the trenches as they sped over them, the aeroplane's wheels mere inches from the ground. There were more holes in the wings as bullets stitched through the canvas, then their pursuer broke off, chased by a smaller version of their own plane: a British DH2 fighter. Shells began to fall, splaying gouts of flame and smoke, buffeting their plane. The engine stopped. The rush of the wind filled Flynn's ears. Fitzpatrick was still praying, eyes screwed shut, knuckles white. Flynn joined him. He felt helpless, awash on the fickle sea of fate. He could hear horses; he could hear shouting; he could hear wood splintering as the ground rose up to crumple the undercarriage. They were down, skidding wildly along, sending searing pain jolting up Flynn's spine. Then they stopped.

'Quick! Run!' screamed the pilot as he jumped from the cockpit and sprinted away as fast as he could. Flynn tumbled to the ground, banging his head on something hard. He didn't care. Fitzpatrick was spluttering, struggling to his feet. Then Flynn remembered the observer.

'Séamus, give us a hand! Quick, before the whole bastard thing goes up!' he shouted, grabbing the observer's shoulders and heaving him clear, his fingers slipping on the man's petrol-soused leather coat. The plane began to burn. They staggered clear, suddenly tired and aching now the adrenalin surge was ebbing. They lowered the unconscious observer to the ground. Flynn's back hurt but he'd rather be in pain than on fire.

Fitzpatrick slumped to his knees, vomiting noisily before sheepishly wiping his mouth on his sleeve and muttering 'Sweet frickin Jeezus' again and again. Flynn flopped down beside him, grinning inanely like a schoolboy who'd just done something inordinately stupid and got away with it. He felt like puking too but didn't. Then they noticed Fitzpatrick's puttees were engulfed in flickering blue flame like a Christmas pudding. He screamed.

'Calm down!' Flynn cried, wearily shoving his friend down into the steaming pool of vomit and rolling him on the grass, beating at the flames, momentarily oblivious that he too was soaked in petrol. Then the flames were out.

The aircraft was a raging inferno, its heat tight on their skin. Flynn edged away, unwilling to take chances. Spooked horses careered here and there being chased by angry skinners across the fields beside a ruined village: a scarred pile of tortured brick. He had no idea where they were but at least from the khaki uniforms they were safely on the British side of the line. One of the ramshackle buildings had a large Red Cross banner stretched taut across its shale roof. There were men coming towards them, wearing Red Cross armbands. Two carried a stretcher and after a cursory examination by one that appeared to be a doctor, the observer was bundled onto it and spirited away. One of them hung back, a round-shouldered officer wearing a dog collar and half-moon reading glasses. He was probably about thirty but looked much older.

'Son of a bitch, it just ain't goddamn right,' cussed Fitzpatrick, smelling of burnt vomit.

'It's all right, they'll look after him,' replied Flynn.

'Not them! That!' he said, pointing at the blazing aeroplane. 'It just ain't frickin' right, flying like that! It just ain't natural. If God had wanted us to fly he'd've given us frickin' wings, for Chrissake! I'm telling you if I ever come across those frickin' Wright brothers I'm gonna give them what the hell for!'

'Would you rather we'd left you behind?' Flynn spluttered, laughing as tears rolled down his sooty cheeks whilst the American floundered, fumbling for a throwaway line. He couldn't. He was overwhelmed, flopping down in befuddled silence. 'Thought not,' said Flynn, watching the pilot approach.

'James McCudden, 20 Squadron, Royal Flying Corps,' he said, thrusting out his ungloved hand, grinning cheerfully. He'd shed his coat, exposing his sergeant's stripes, and despite him being the pilot it was the observer who'd been in charge of the aircraft. McCudden was merely the wounded officer's chauffeur. After all, officers didn't drive. That wasn't the army's way. Flynn took his hand, shaking it firmly.

'Kevin Flynn, 9th Battalion, Royal Dublin Fusiliers.' He didn't bother with ranks. 'This is Sean Fitzpatrick, one of our colonial cousins.' Fitzpatrick prised himself up and, wiping his filthy hands on his thighs, shook McCudden's hand.

'Well, seeing as that was definitely not one of my better landings, I'm grateful for the luck of the Irish, if you don't mind me saying. It's good to see that you are both in one piece,' said McCudden.

'McCudden's a good Irish name. I'm sure you've enough luck of your own without us. How about the other fella?' Flynn asked.

'Christ knows, he's shot up pretty bad and the landing must have shaken him about a bit. This was only the second time we've flown together. Anyway, let's hope he's all right, eh?' McCudden replied. There was a faraway look in the pilot's eyes as if he were struggling to recall something he'd forgotten. Then he relaxed, his mind drifting as he scanned the roaring pyre of his machine. 'Shame, she was a good kite.'

'Well, what now, Sergeant?' Flynn asked.

'Mac. Please call me Mac,' McCudden corrected gently with a smile. 'I guess we need to let someone know we're here.'

'I don't know but I think they might already know we're here!' chipped in Fitzpatrick.

'Not this lot, you *eejit*, the battalion,' Flynn added wearily.

'I may be able to help you lads there,' said the padre. His uniform was grubby, his dog collar rimed with sweat, but compared to Flynn and the others he was spotless. Dull bronze lieutenant's pips decorated his shoulder straps in Foot Guards fashion and Flynn noticed the Military Cross ribbon over the man's tunic pocket. 'You chaps must be exhausted after all this excitement,' he added with a warm smile and welcoming, outstretched arms. 'Let's see if I can rustle up some scoff and a hot brew, eh?' He produced some cigarettes but then, noticing the stink of petrol, smiled apologetically. 'Maybe later, eh chaps?' he added.

'That'd be great, sir,' replied McCudden. 'I missed breakfast this morning.' Flynn could not help thinking how cool and collected the aviator seemed as they strolled towards the field hospital, considering all they'd just been through. The padre led them to a single-storey outbuilding butted onto the end of the one sporting the Red Cross flag. Flynn could see telephone lines snaking down the wall and across the yard to a nearby wood. His stomach grumbled. The last thing he'd eaten was a dog biscuit smeared in Marmite but that was hours ago. Maybe McCudden was right. He needed to eat. Fitzpatrick looked hungry too, his eyes hollow with fatigue.

The room smelt of disinfectant and cheap tobacco laced with tea but none of them seemed to care. It had chairs, the sort you hired by the hour at the seaside, and a black, pot-bellied stove cracking out heat. Fitz-patrick flopped into a deckchair, luxuriating in the stove's glow with feline pleasure. Flynn and McCudden sat at a scarred and scrubbed table, the heat making them drowsy. The padre disappeared and moments later, or at least it seemed like moments to Flynn in his soporific state, a clean-looking soldier wearing Army Service Corps flashes appeared carrying a tray of steaming tea in chipped enamel mugs and a pile of thick bully-beef sandwiches that made their stomachs growl more fiercely.

'There's plenty more,' said the soldier as he set down his burden on the table.

'That'll do nicely,' said Flynn, helping himself to a mug. The tea was sweet, heavily laced with condensed milk as well as rum, and its warmth flowed easily into his fingers and toes. Fitzpatrick burrowed into a sandwich whilst McCudden took his time, savouring his tea as he cradled the mug in his cupped hands. Flynn could feel the hot liquid through the thin sides of his mug but didn't mind, despite the growing discomfort. It was almost as if he took some perverse pleasure from the pain. Weakness leaving the body: God's way of letting you know you were still alive. That was how their physical training instructor, a bull of a sergeant called O'Connor, had described it during one of his many beastings during training back in

Ireland. He drained the mug, scalding his mouth. He didn't care. The padre re-appeared, nursing a brown china teapot, and topped up their mugs before setting it down and pulling out a battered notebook.

'We'd better get a message to your units that you are all right. They must be worried sick about you chaps,' he said, pulling out the stub of a pencil. Somehow, Flynn didn't think they would be worried sick. This was the Western Front: people went missing every day, thousands of them. After scribbling a few details, he disappeared once more.

'So, Mac,' said Fitzpatrick between mouth-fuls of food. 'What the heck makes you want to go up in one of those goddamn flying machines, then?'

'Flying's the future,' replied McCudden, pushing a mop of brown hair from his eyes.

'Well, it ain't my future. Nothing's gonna get me back in one of those frickin' death traps,' spluttered the American before clearing his throat with a slug of rum-laced tea.

'Look, I admit your introduction to the noble art of aviation wasn't all it could have been but just think about it, chaps: where would you be now if it wasn't for my poor old kite, eh?' asked McCudden with a wry smile. He was right. Without McCudden and his aeroplane they would still be prisoners of war or worse. 'Me? I love it. Always have, ever since my brother took me for a flight over

Salisbury Plain before the war. Look, why don't you chaps pop round to my squadron? It's just north of here, I think, and I'll take you up for a spin.' Fitzpatrick's eyes widened. 'Do a few circuits and bumps and then see how you like it without Jerry trying to knock seven bells out of you, eh?'

'Hey, I think I've had enough circuits and bumps, as you put it, to last a lifetime,' said Fitzpatrick as he scooped up the last sandwich. 'Anyhow, I heard most of you guys don't last a week. I can see why now!'

'Maybe, but I've been in this game for two years now. I was a sapper before the war, digging latrines and playing with explosives mostly, until I transferred to the RFC. Now, I get to sleep in a bed most nights – a bed with clean sheets and blankets – and three hot meals a day. There's even hot water to wash and shave. Believe me, it beats dog biscuits, bully beef and the smell of your own armpits!'

Flynn scratched his stubbly chin, ruminating. It was hard to disagree. Despite the queasy, gut-wrenching terror of their flight, he had to admit that it had been exhilarating; in hindsight, fun even. 'It all seems a bit bloody dangerous, Mac,' he finally replied.

'And the trenches aren't?' He had a point. 'When was the last time you had a night out to a café? I tell you, the *mademoiselles* love a flyer.' He was grinning now, warming to his theme. 'Look, none of us know when we're going to cop it in this war so if I'm going to cop it I want to do it after a good night's sleep in clean clothes and with a full belly. Any old fool can be hungry and uncomfortable.' In the warped logic of the war, Flynn knew he made sense.

'Do you think there'll be more?' asked Fitzpatrick.

'What? Aeroplanes?' answered Flynn, looking puzzled.

'No, sandwiches,' said the American as he rubbed his greasy hands down the front of his filthy tunic, eyeing the empty plate. There was a whizz-bang as shells began to fall outside in a nearby field. They could see them through the window. Horses neighed, shying and bolting as their drivers darted for cover.

'Somehow your offer suddenly seems tempting,' said Flynn.

'What? Of more sandwiches?' said Fitzpatrick but both sergeants ignored him, shaking their heads as dust cascaded from the ceiling like a biblical plague of dandruff.

'You'll be pleased to know that I've managed to make contact with your units,' announced the padre, re-entering the room. 'Your squadron's sending a car, Sergeant McCudden. It should be here within the hour.' Then he shrugged apologetically. 'I'm afraid it's not such good news for you chaps, though. I managed to get through to your battalion and the gentleman I spoke to said you'd have to walk.'

'Poor bloody infantry,' muttered Mc-Cudden, loud enough for them to hear.

'They're expecting you back by morning,' added the padre, adopting his best, professionally comforting smile, the one he'd obviously been taught at seminary school. Then he beamed unaffectedly. 'Time for more tea and sandwiches.' A salvo of shells came down nearer, scabbing plaster from the cracked walls, making the padre wince.

'It's only harassing fire, Father. Try and ignore it or you'll go stark raving mad. It's the sons of bitches you can't hear that'll do for you, not these ones,' said Fitzpatrick, doling out advice like a grizzled veteran, seemingly oblivious of the man's medal ribbon. The irony wasn't lost on the padre, who resumed his professionally concerned smile before disappearing once more. 'Seems a decent enough sort for a Prod.'

'How do you know he's a Protestant?' asked Flynn.

'Gotta be, ain't he? He's English. Aren't all English God-botherers Prods?'

'Tell you what, chaps. Why don't I give you a lift back to your unit? Then at least you'll be able to get some decent kip rather than spend all night wandering about,' said McCudden.

'It's a plan,' agreed Flynn just as the shelling eased off and the soldier returned with some blankets and pillows. McCudden built a nest in one of the deckchairs and began to drift off, as did Fitzpatrick, leaving Flynn alone with his thoughts and cooling tea. He wondered where Mary was. He missed her. She'd written but he hadn't read her letter. Foolishly he'd put it in his pocket to read after the raid. They weren't supposed to carry personal items in case the Germans learnt something important from them. He didn't think Mary knew much that would shake the empire to its foundations but he'd never know now. The Germans had taken it when he'd been captured. One of them would be reading it now. His cheeks flushed. He hoped there was nothing embarrassing in it, which was foolish really as the chances of him ever meeting the German who'd read it were slim to non-existent. Fitzpatrick was snoring and Flynn felt his head nod as he finally crumpled across the table in a deep, dreamless sleep.

'It's here,' said McCudden, shaking him awake. It seemed like moments. The driver, a very clean RFC corporal, disdainfully watched the two filthy infantrymen climb into his immaculate Model T Ford, followed by McCudden.

'It's almost like the fair's come to town,' announced Flynn as he stretched out in the back.

'What fair?' asked Fitzpatrick, banging his chest with his fist. He regretted wolfing down quite so many sandwiches. He was looking around. 'My pa told me to be careful with carney folks.'

'There isn't a fair, you *eejit*,' said Flynn, playing up his Irish accent.

'Then why'd you say there was one?' he asked petulantly.

'I just mean that I've flown in an aeroplane for the first time ever and now I get to go in a car. It's like a bank holiday. All I need is a ride in a train and a trip to the seaside and I'll be made up!' quipped Flynn, then he noticed the fields and trees, almost for the first time. 'You know, it looks so different from back here, the countryside. Whenever we're on a march I just stare at the fella in front's back and switch off. I don't suppose sappers do much marching? Me and the fellas back in the battalion, we must have marched the length and breadth of this bloody country and, you know, this is the first time I've ever seen it!'

'That's what I love about flying,' Mc-Cudden chipped in from the front passenger seat. 'When I'm up there,' he pointed at the sky, 'it's like you're free and, let me tell you, at eleven thousand feet the view is, well, out of this world.' There was a faraway look on the pilot's face as if transported to a happier place. Fitzpatrick began to sing, belting out a chorus of 'The Ragtime Infantry'. The driver didn't look amused. Flynn and McGudden joined in. *We cannot march, we cannot shoot; what bloody use are we...*'

They had lapsed into silence by the time the car jerked to a halt outside yet another anonymous brick farmhouse, attracting the attention of curious onlookers. There was a sign. It read 'HQ, 9th Royal Dublin Fusiliers'. They were home.

'Out you hop, then,' said the driver, ignoring Flynn's rank as he skipped out and opened the door. He was keen to be rid of the ill-smelling fusiliers who'd made such a mess of the back of his car.

'I meant what I said – look me up if you're ever in the area,' called McCudden, waving cheerilyas the car sped away.

'And where the bloody hell do you think you've been?' bellowed Clee belligerently. Instinctively, they braced, spinning around to confront Clee in all his neat, compact and immaculate splendour. His boots were unnaturally clean; his moustache bristled; his stick quivered beneath his arm as his all-seeing eyes seemed to scour their souls. 'I should have you two shot for bloody desertion!' he growled, making Flynn begin to regret escaping captivity. Then Clee's hard eyes softened, ever so slightly, and he stepped forward. The mask slipped, revealing the genuine concern beneath. 'Where's young Doyle?'

'Copped it, sir,' said Flynn. 'We got caught. Doyle copped it when we made a break for it. Didn't he, Séamus?' He didn't see any point in elaborating, in telling Clee that it had been a British bomb that had killed him. What would be the point? Doyle was gone. The truth wouldn't bring him back and he seriously doubted that it would make his parents feel any better about their loss. He could tell from the look on the American's face that he agreed. Clee nodded, guessing that there was much left unsaid. Then the mask was back.

'You'd better report to Sergeant Devlin so he can finish his report.' Flynn felt a surge of relief that Devlin had made it. 'Then, I've no doubt Captain Murphy will want to speak to you.' They dithered, unsure what to do, where to go. 'Well?' sniffed Clee. 'What you waiting for? Get away!'

They found Devlin outside an old barn, a Woodbine hanging limply from his lips as he dawdled with his hands thrust deep into his pockets. He looked pale and drawn, distinctly out of sorts. His sunken eyes were fixed on the ground at his feet like a man awaiting his own hanging. Crushing the cigarette beneath his boot, he turned to enter the building when he noticed Flynn and Fitzpatrick approaching.

'Thank Christ ye made it!' he gasped, genuinely pleased to see them. 'Let's get ye inside and get yous sorted.' He ushered them inside. The room stank of kerosene and sweat.

'Doesn't the army love paperwork?' muttered Mahon, newly elevated to the heady heights of Company Quartermaster Sergeant, from behind a makeshift desk piled with forms. An old copy of the *Irish Times* lay tea-stained beside them, announcing the executions of the Easter rebels' leaders. Captain Murphy was nowhere to be seen.

'So where's Terry?' asked Flynn, half-expecting to find his friend hanging around in the makeshift company office. Mahon became unnaturally engrossed in his forms, as if trying to avoid eye contact. Even Devlin seemed strange as the atmosphere in the room thickened, like lead on Flynn's shoulders. 'Where's Terry?'

'He's gone,' said Devlin quietly.

'Gone? What do you mean gone? Terry wouldn't do a runner. He must be with that Carmichael woman,' replied Flynn.

'No, Kevin, he's gone. Him and the Duke...' Devlin was staring listlessly into the middle distance as if trying to work through a problem in his head. 'Damnedest thing. They must have got lost getting back, set off a flare coming through our wire. Jerry machine gun got them. They're dead, Kevin, both of them.'

CHAPTER 21

British rear area, Hulluch, north-west France

Flynn woke with a start, his ears still ringing with the sound of phantom guns. His mouth felt like sandpaper and tasted like something had died in it. He was drenched in sweat; stale whiskey sweat. It had been Devlin's idea to christen his stripes. He had no idea why on earth Captain Murphy had made him a sergeant. Some people would have loved the power and he could picture Fallon strutting like a cockerel if anyone had been stupid enough to make him up. Instead, Flynn just saw responsibility and he'd already had enough of that. Every time he closed his eyes he saw Doyle's bloody carcass smeared across the grass or Gallagher and the Duke floundering on the wire. Whiskey helped, blotting out his dreams, but the mornings always hurt: a dull ache inside his head. At least he didn't have to do fatigues any more, only supervise them, and he saw another side to Devlin and Mahon; a side he'd never seen when he was in the ranks and now he understood why Mahon sometimes buried himself in his paperwork. It was somewhere to hide.

The latrines were somewhere to hide too when he was on a work evasion scheme. He'd washed and shaved, cutting his chin in several places before relaxing on one of the rudimentary thunderboxes, doing his best to keep his boots clear of the thick brown porridge seeping around his feet. A work party marched by, picks and shovels shouldered. This was their rest period. Flynn didn't see why because they seemed to spend most of it back in the line repairing wire or raiding the enemy. He looked at his wristwatch – spoils of yet another raid – before turning his face to the warm June sun. Work could wait.

'If ye've not got a sense of humour, ye shouldn't have joined,' he remembered Devlin saying when they were recruits, and he made a mental note to look up 'sense of humour' in the dictionary when he got a chance, just to check whether they were both working off the same definition. Then he picked up a piece of old newspaper and skimmed it over, not understanding a word. It was in French: blurred words in cheap ink on cheap paper but it would do for what he had in mind. Surely *The Wipers Times* would have been a more appropriate publication for the task.

Then he took out Mary's letter, the words leaping from the page as he read. She was sorry but she couldn't walk out with a

British soldier, not after what British soldiers had done in Dublin. For a moment he toyed with the idea of using it instead of the newspaper but the proper place for 'Dear Johns' was the company noticeboard. It wasn't as if her letter would be alone: there were literally dozens of them as long-cherished sweethearts dumped their boyfriends, sick of waiting. Succumbing to tradition, he opted for the newspaper, as oblivious of the passers-by as they were of him. He'd learnt a long time ago that privacy was rare in the army and to be honest he was amazed that Cronin, or should he say Dempsey, had managed to get away with her deception for so long. He'd just finished when he noticed Fitzpatrick sauntering over, carrying two steaming mugs of tea. He was wearing corporal stripes, incongruously new and clean on his shabby old tunic.

'Here you go, Sarge,' said Fitzpatrick. 'Get this down you,' he added, seemingly sickeningly fresh despite consuming copious quantities of whiskey with Flynn and Devlin the night before.

'Can't a man take a crap in peace?' grumbled Flynn, taking one of the mugs. Fitzpatrick was right; it made him feel better although he couldn't resist commenting that it tasted like shit.

'Hey, that was crafted by my own fair hand,' protested the American.

'Not literally, I hope?' replied Flynn with a face that could curdle milk.

'Hey, don't take the piss out of my special Irish breakfast tea,' he said.

'Why's that, Séamus, because there'd be no flavour left if you did?'

'So what do you think of the big push, Sarge?' asked Fitzpatrick, changing the subject.

'Well, army biscuits do have a habit of blocking you up, but this tea of yours should certainly help.'

'Not your frickin' bowels! I mean *the big push* – you know, the knockout blow we've all been waiting for, the thing everyone's talking about, the thing that will end this darned war. You know, *that* frickin' big push!' said Fitzpatrick.

'Séamus, my boy, people have been going on about a big flaming push ever since we got here! Jesus, do you remember when we joined up? They said it'd all be over by Christmas!' said Flynn between sips of tea.

'Sure they did, but no one said which year, did they?' answered Fitzpatrick. It was an old joke, guaranteed to raise a laugh from the most jaded of squaddies. 'OK, very funny, but seriously, though, this is different. The Frogs have been taking a pasting down in Verdun since February. The place sounds like a meat grinder; those guys have lost thousands. Old Hackett says they can't last much longer unless we do something ... and soon!' He was referring to the massive battle that was bleeding the French army white and although they didn't know it, it was bleeding the Germans white too.

'And?' asked Flynn.

'And that is precisely why we need to give old Kaiser Bill a smack on the nose,' enthused Fitzpatrick. 'Just think. If Jerry's burnt himself out against the Frogs then it'll be a walkover!'

'Don't you think that if everyone is talking about this big push that Fritz will know all about it too, eh?'

Fitzpatrick's smile wavered slightly. 'OK, so we won't have the element of surprise. Maybe Division's been pulling all these stunts recently,' he meant raids, 'to draw Jerry in, get him to reinforce here and overstretch at Verdun. After all, have you heard how much stuff the gun bunnies have brought up around Albert, wherever that is? There ain't no way anyone's gonna survive the bombardment those guys are going to throw at Jerry, poor buggers.'

Maybe they were right. For several weeks the Brass had been throwing at least a battalion a night at the Germans in their sector. They said it was good for morale, kept Jerry on his toes, but it was a dripping tap. So far they hadn't fought a proper battle and yet over twenty men were dead and dozens more had been wounded. He thought of Gallagher. Devlin had said Gallagher's death hadn't made sense. That night was the elephant in the room. The thing they were all aware of but none of them could talk about. It didn't do to dwell on the dead. That was the theory anyway; shame it didn't quite work in practice. Maybe that was why he'd started to drink too much.

'I don't know what you're getting so excited about anyway,' said Flynn. 'If, and I mean if, old Hackett's right and this big push comes off, it won't happen here. Most of the army's up at Wipers,' he meant Ypres, 'so it stands to reason that's where it'll be.'

'Hell, no, Wipers is too goddamn obvious. That's what Fritz will be expecting. No, I think Haig will pull something out of the bag – after all, that guy knows what he's doing. Stands to reason; he wouldn't be in charge otherwise. No, old Hackett says it'll be on the Somme. It's in all the papers. They say it's a bit like Salisbury Plain, all rolling chalk downs. It's where our line ends and the Frogs' begins: stands to reason really. Perfect attack country and once we've got Fritz on the run, well, we'll be able to chase him all the way back to Berlin, you see.'

'And old Hackett told you all this?' Fitzpatrick nodded. 'Don't you think that if old Hackett's worked out that the big push will be at this Somme place then it's reasonable to assume that Messrs Hohenzollern and Falkenhayn,' he meant the German kaiser and his chief of the general staff, 'may have worked all this out too?' Fitzpatrick narrowed his eyes, mulling Flynn's words over in his head. Flynn glanced at his watch before handing back the empty mug.

'So, my special breakfast tea wasn't so bad after all,' said the American, upending the empty mug and peering inside.

'Well?' asked Flynn.

'Well what?' replied Fitzpatrick.

'Are you going to stand there all day?' asked Flynn, conscious that he was still sitting on the toilet. The American braced, knocking out a mock salute before turning and swaggering away smartly towards their tents. A small shape charged from the nearest tent, yapping excitedly. It was Spud, their unofficial mascot. He noticed the word 'Verdun' in blotchy print. When he'd finished, he pulled up his trousers.

'Cleanliness is next to godliness,' he mumbled to himself as he scrubbed his hands as best he could in the scummy-soaped water in a galvanized trough nearby. Bugs travelled fast in the close confines of the camp and even the slightest relaxation of strict hygiene discipline would lay half of them low with what the army referred to rather innocuously as 'D and V' diarrhoea and vomiting.

He'd found it amusing during training that they'd taught them how to wipe their own backsides, even brush their teeth, until it dawned on him that some of the recruits knew how to do neither. Out of the trenches life was one long, endless cycle of work and sleep punctuated by bodily functions in or out and Flynn couldn't help thinking the rudimentary toilets that played such a part in their world were a metaphor for army life.

June had been wet, reducing their trenches to glorified sewers that could put even the most ardent roast dinner eater off gravy for life. Trench foot cases were up as men's feet rotted in their sodden boots. That was why he checked his boys' feet every morning and night; by torchlight if needs be. An infantry-man with rotten feet was no good to anyone. At least he didn't have to check Gallagher's feet any more, he thought. It never ceased to amaze him how long Gallagher had seemed to be able to eke out a pair of socks.

'If they stick to the wall, it's time to change them,' Gallagher used to say and for a second he half-expected to see his friend's oafish grin waiting to greet him. Instead there was Spud, sprawled on the grass making the most of newly arrived sun. Gallagher was gone, along with the Duke and a lad called Mahoney, who Flynn didn't know. They were buried together – at least that was something – in the corner of the makeshift cemetery a few miles

269

up the road. Jane hadn't taken it well. There was no reason why he should but he'd felt he had to tell her. It hadn't been easy watching the aristocratic nurse crumple before his eyes and he'd been unsure what to do. He could hardly take her out and get her drunk. That's what squaddies did to dull the pain. Instead he'd mumbled a few awkward words and left, feeling a coward and a failure, routed by her sobs. He'd written to Gallagher's parents too, choosing his words carefully. Captain Murphy had also written, using the usual platitudes: brave soldier, well-liked NCO. They were just words, and for the first time in his bookish life he'd realized that words just weren't enough. Spud didn't need words, sprawled in the sunlight watching the world go by with expressive brown eyes, not a care in the world. In a way, Flynn envied the scruffy little Yorkie. He was fed, people fussed him and he didn't have to go into the line. What more could anyone want?

'There's plenty more fish in the sea,' said Fitzpatrick as he eased the letter, *that* letter, from his hand. He hadn't realized he was still holding it. He watched his friend walk over to the company notice-board and pin it up with all the others. It was like it was official: the decree absolute dissolving their relationship. It didn't make it any easier. 'Don't beat yourself up about it. If the dame won't wait for you then she isn't worth worrying about,' declared Fitzpatrick, with all the certainty of a man who'd never had a girlfriend.

'It wasn't the waiting,' replied Flynn. 'It was the fact that I'm out here in the British Army, propping up the *English* Empire, she said.' It was a sentiment they'd all heard before, which was ironic considering almost everyone in the battalion, even the division, was some sort of Irish nationalist. 'She says we're all traitors.'

'Sounds like she's been knocking about with Shinners,' said Fitzpatrick, referring to the Irish Republican *Sinn Féin* party, who were agitating for a complete break from Britain and the empire. So much so that the government were convinced, wrongly as it happened, that *Sinn Féin* had been behind the ill-fated Easter Rising.

'Knocked up by a fecking Shinner more like,' snapped Carolan, who was worried what effect all the adverse comments back home about soldiers was having on his wife. He hated being away from her. Flynn chose to ignore him although deep down he had an awful feeling he was right. Mary had never mentioned politics before the war, not even in London, and it was obvious to anyone with eyes to see that someone else had filled her head with all the rebel claptrap she'd spouted in her last letter. To be honest, he was amazed that the censors hadn't black-inked most of it.

271

'Yer man's right,' said Devlin. 'There are plenty of braw colleens out there and if this one won't wait then find another. Ye've got to bury yer dead and move on,' he added, churning out yet another martial cliché. They talked a lot in clichés; it made life easier, numbed the pain. They exemplified that all-important principle of war – economy of effort. You bought the farm; caught a blighty; went west; neutralized the enemy; targets fell when hit. No one actually said what they were doing: killing and dying, maiming or being maimed.

Flynn liked economy of effort: as a principle it was a soldier's friend and they all tried to live by it. It was a way of staying sane and as he sat listening to Devlin and the others he realized why NCOs and officers seemed to play a part, keeping everyone at arm's length. Everyone he'd let close – well, almost everyone – was gone: Gallagher, the Duke, Doyle, even Cronin and Mary. What guarantee was there that Devlin and Fitzpatrick wouldn't follow them down the long, long trail? Then he noticed Devlin was watching him, his dark eyes burrowing into him as if the Ulsterman knew that he was experiencing some sort of epiphany.

'Sergeant Flynn?' It was a young corporal. Flynn thought his name was Dooner. He wasn't sure. 'The CO wants to see you.'

Flynn felt his heart sink. 'Did the colonel

say what he wanted?' he said rather too testily. It had been a long day already and being summoned to the CO's office was rarely good news. That said, it could have been worse. The RSM could have been looking for him.

'Don't know, Sarge.' Dooner shrugged. 'They just told me to fetch you.' Flynn stood up, letting out a deep sigh as he buttoned up his tunic and rubbed the toecaps of his boots on the backs of his puttees. It didn't really make much difference but it was the thought that counted. Battalion HQ was busy, a beehive of activity, and he couldn't help noticing some red-tabbed staff officers chatting away with Major Stirke and the adjutant. Thankfully, the RSM was nowhere to be seen.

'The colonel wants to see me,' he told one of the HQ clerks, who led him down a narrow corridor to a door that said 'Commanding Officer' on it. The clerk knocked. The RSM opened the door and gave Flynn a withering once-over that made him think he really was in the shit.

'Uniform,' was all he said. It was enough.

'Sergeant Flynn to see the colonel, sir,' said the clerk. Flynn marched in, stamping loudly to a halt in the middle of the colonel's spartan office. He chopped off his finest, elbow-wrenching salute before staring woodenly into the middle distance.

'Please, stand at ease, Sergeant,' said

Colonel Thackeray. 'I'm so glad you were able to join us,' he added, as if Flynn had actually had any say in the matter. 'The general here would like to speak with you.'

The general! It was worse than Flynn thought. He had no idea why a general would want to speak with him. He allowed his eyes to drift. There was an immaculate figure by the window sporting major general's rank tabs and glittering spurs. He was exquisitely tailored and although Flynn couldn't put his finger on it, there was something vaguely familiar about the man. He assumed he'd seen him during one of their parades; after all, they were often paraded in front of visiting senior officers. The man was playing with his clipped moustache, watching Flynn like a hawk. Flynn avoided his gaze, which seemed to amuse the general. He was a man used to power.

'Thank you, Colonel, that will be all,' said the general, dismissing the CO and RSM without so much as a glance. They closed the door. The general strolled around the room with a bandy horseman's gait. Flynn resisted the urge to turn. He knew better, standing properly at ease, staring at some imaginary point in the distance. 'So, you're Flynn,' said the general, finally coming to rest on the edge of Thackeray's desk. He was pure Anglo-Irish ascendancy. 'You know the colonel speaks very highly of you.' He couldn't think why.

'Anyway, enough chit-chat, eh? I suppose you're wondering why you're here, eh, Sergeant?' Flynn didn't answer. 'My daughter speaks very highly of you too,' he added. Flynn wasn't sure what he meant. Then he almost laughed as he realized who was talking to him. The general snorted, braying like a stallion; obviously enjoying himself. 'You've probably guessed that I'm Major General Viscount Dempsey.'

'How is ... er ... your daughter, sir?' Flynn asked, at a loss what to call Louise Dempsey.

'Please stand easy, Sergeant, relax,' he added, but Flynn didn't really feel like relaxing. 'Unfortunate business, what, eh? Lady Dempsey and I were worried sick about Miss Dempsey after she disappeared. My daughter said that you took good care of her. Actually, she said that you took good care of all your chaps. Anyway, I've something to ask of you, Sergeant,' he put emphasis on the word 'sergeant', 'something rather delicate.'

'I had no idea that Private Cronin was a woman, sir, until she was wounded!' blurted Flynn, suddenly afraid that the general was about to accuse him of doing something improper with his daughter. 'None of us did!'

'I don't doubt it,' replied the general. 'If I thought you had...' He left the sentence hanging. 'Anyway, as I was saying, I'd rather people didn't know that my daughter has spent the last year and a half playing at soldiers.' Flynn couldn't actually remember Cronin *playing* at soldiers. 'We told everyone she'd gone to visit relatives in Canada. Now, seeing as my daughter speaks so highly of you, I'm willing to recommend you for a commission, so long as you keep her little jaunt to yourself.'

Dempsey's offer seemed to Flynn to smack of shutting the stable door after the horse had bolted but he kept his opinion to himself. Officers rarely actually wanted a soldier's opinion, even when they asked, unless of course it reinforced their own.

'Well, man? What do you say?' asked the general, slapping Flynn hard on the arm in what he assumed the general meant to be a comradely gesture. Flynn thought there was something unsettlingly vulpine about the man.

'But I don't want to be an officer, sir,' replied Flynn. He didn't want the responsibility, the expense of a new uniform, the mess fees – but more importantly he didn't want the short life expectancy that junior officers had in the trenches. It was the general's turn to look confused. He was a professional officer. It was beyond his ken that anyone would turn down the chance of the King's Commission and all the social kudos that came with it. More importantly, he wasn't used to people contradicting him.

'What do you want then, Sergeant?' the

general asked, suddenly suspicious of the tall NCO standing before him. Everyone wanted something, he thought, as he looked Flynn up and down. It had to be money. His sort always wanted money.

'Nothing, sir,' Flynn replied after a slight pause. The general sniffed, looking more than a little puzzled, unsure that he had heard correctly. 'I don't want anything. You don't have to worry, sir: no one talks about your daughter. Not any more.' Which was true; they rarely spoke about those who had gone. 'And if you say she was in Canada, sir, then I'm sure she was in Canada.'

The general looked satisfied as he picked up his expensive gold-braided cap, fiddling with it momentarily before looking back at Flynn. There was something of Cronin around the general's eyes.

'Excellent! Well, Sergeant, off you go! I doubt we shall meet again.' Flynn hesitated. 'Yes, Sergeant?' The general couldn't help thinking the sergeant was going to ask for something after all. They always did.

'Please give my regards to Miss Dempsey, sir,' Flynn said.

'I don't think that will be necessary,' replied the general and without the need of another word Flynn knew he'd been dismissed. He saluted, about-turned and marched smartly from the office, pausing briefly to open the door.

The RSM was in the corridor, scowling fiercely. 'And what did the general want with you, Sergeant Flynn?' he asked after the colonel had gone back into his office. The RSM didn't like his NCOs talking to officers, especially senior officers, without him, just in case they aired a little too much of the battalion's dirty laundry in public.

'Nothing, sir,' replied Flynn, emphasizing the word 'sir' in a way that few soldiers ever did for mere officers. The RSM leant in closer, his brows furrowing more deeply, his eyes blazing more savagely. Flynn could smell his breath: tea, tobacco and a hint of rum. He looked unconvinced and as Flynn marched away he decided it would be best to avoid him for the next couple of weeks.

CHAPTER 22

1 July 1916, Thiepval, the Somme

Everything was noise, like ripping canvas punctuated by savage, ear-rending bangs.

'What now?' shouted Rory Gallagher. Screwing his eyes shut, he forced his face deeper into the chalky soil as a fusillade of machine-gun rounds zipped overhead. Private Andy McNee stared blankly, doing a passable impression of a pancake. It had been a busy day for the stretcher-bearers. The Ulster Division had made good progress, overrunning its objectives, but now they had stalled, fired on from three sides. They would have to pull back soon or risk being cut off and at this precise moment Rory was beginning to regret Special Branch not arresting him. At least a prison cell would have been infinitely safer than the shallow depression that he and McNee were hiding in.

He had no idea why they'd sent him to the 36th Ulster Division. He'd asked for a posting to one of the Irish divisions, one of the proper Irish divisions, not one full of Ulster Prods who wouldn't have been seen dead in the company of a Catholic Jackeen like him back home – which was ironic, really, when he thought about it, as there were plenty of dead Prods around him right now. All he could think was that the postings clerk had been English; it was the only explanation.

'What's so funny, *ye taig eejit?*' growled Mc-Nee, a dour Ulster Protestant from Ahoghill in County Antrim. Rory had grown used to being called a *taig,* even a croppie, by those who preferred their sectarianism more traditional. The division had been built around the loyalist Ulster Volunteer Force and whilst he certainly wasn't the only Catholic in the division, there was no doubt that it was overwhelmingly Protestant, overwhelmingly

Presbyterian and definitely much too Orange for Rory's tastes. Usually they rubbed along, shoulder to shoulder, giving as good as they got, but when they were away from the front line, alcohol usually resulted in violence between the two Irish tribes.

The ground shook as a flurry of shells sent shards of hot steel zinging by, joined by renewed bursts of machine-gun fire. An almighty clang set Rory's ears ringing as his head was snatched backwards, the chinstrap of his ill-fitting helmet biting into his throat. His hands were already raw and shoulders stiff from heaving stretchers but that was nothing compared to the searing pain that shot down his neck into the base of his spine, sending his vision into a kaleidoscope of black and white stars.

'They got me!' he shrieked, his head flopping forward. He lay still. McNee slithered closer.

'*Eejit!*' snapped McNee. 'They've dented your tin hat, that's all.' Rory reached up, cautiously running his hand over the battered steel. The dent felt huge but was probably no bigger than his thumb. The helmets, like oversized soup bowls, were a new idea. They all wore them now. If he hadn't, he'd be wearing his brains down the back of his tunic. He couldn't help grinning. It was stupid, really, but it was the only thing he could think of to disguise the queasiness churning his gut.

'We can't stay here,' he said.

'Really?' replied McNee, who was huffing like an old shunting engine. Foolishly, Rory raised his head, attracting a fresh salvo of gunfire that kicked up dirt around them. He shuffled sideways, away from where he'd last been seen, and poked his head up once more. There were bodies everywhere and through the swaying grass he thought he could make out what he assumed was the German position: a fortified redoubt on a piece of rising ground some 300 yards off. He could be wrong – after all, he was a Medical Corps private, and no one told him anything. Shells were still falling, almost randomly it seemed, and he couldn't tell whose they were. Not that it mattered. Dead was dead no matter where the shells had been made. He could see men moving in a depression about a hundred yards away. They looked wounded, cowering from the machine gun behind a berm of flayed chalk. The machine gun shifted its fire to probe the edge of a shattered wood, seeking out Ulstermen hiding behind splintered trunks.

'Do you have any water?' asked Rory. He was parched, his lips dry, feeling as if every drop of moisture had been sucked from his body.

'The water's for the wounded,' said Mc-Nee.

'So it is,' said Rory. 'Now give me what

you've got.' Reluctantly, McNee handed over the three water bottles he was carrying. They were full; heavy. Rory slung them around his neck, then crawled over to another stretcher-bearer who sprawled dead nearby and relieved him of his canteens. McNee didn't really approve of his partner genuflecting but in the circumstances he let it pass as Rory heaved himself onto his knees.

'Cover me!' barked Rory as he leapt to his feet and sprinted towards the berm, no longer feeling guilty about visiting that brothel back in Albert. He'd never have dared back home, his mother would have killed him if she'd found out, but here was different. At least he wouldn't die a virgin, which was something!

'What with, a bloody stretcher?' shouted McNee in confusion but Rory had already gone. Except for their gas masks, haversacks full of bandages and spare water, they were completely unarmed.

'Hail Mary, full of grace...' Rory murmured. He kept low, as low as his tumbling gait would allow without overbalancing, side-stepping randomly. He expected to die; after all, movement attracted attention. That's what people saw from the corner of their eyes and right now he was about as conspicuous as a turd in the middle of a dining-room table. Bullets tore at the ground at his feet. 'Pray for me now and at the hour of my death...' he said as shell-bursts showered him in dirt. It was a miracle they missed. As he reached the berm, something thudded into his back. He fell. Rolling over, he half expected to see his own ribcage protruding from his chest but instead it was McNee.

'Well, I couldn't let an *eejit taig* take all the glory, now could I?' said McNee as he started rummaging through his medical bag. Nearby lay an officer with a severe head wound. Next to him were two ashen-faced privates who stared expectantly at the new arrivals. One clasped his wrist, slick with blood as he held up his shattered hand, staring at it as if he couldn't quite work out how he'd lost so many fingers. The other lay on his side, his left arm hanging limply at his side.

'We need to get this one to a doctor,' said Rory, examining the arm. It was a clean wound. He would live; if they got out, that is. Then he cursed. 'We'll have to carry him!' The man's legs were riddled with shrapnel. Another salvo of machine-gun fire streaked overhead, making him duck.

'What now, big fella?' McNee asked, liberally scattering iodine powder over the officer's head and bandaging it.

'I'm not sure,' Rory replied. He hadn't really thought that far ahead when he'd made his dash. He gazed back at the stretch of exposed ground they'd just crossed and realized he was more than a little annoyed that McNee had followed him. There was no need for the two of them to die. 'We carry them back, I guess,' he finally said. McNee nodded. Crack! Crack! Crack! Another burst flew overhead. 'Mind you, if we want to get back there, we really shouldn't be starting from here,' he added with a juvenile grin. McNee frowned, the sort of frown he reserved for people who talked in chapel, wondering what he'd done to be stuck in the middle of no-man's-land with a Jackeen *eejit* for company. There was movement on the edge of the wood and for a moment he thought the Germans had flanked them but the soup-plate helmets told him they were friendlies. The machine gunner saw them too, shifting his aim. Rory heaved the officer over his shoulders in a fireman's lift. 'I might just be able to make it to that shell hole,' he said, indicating a crater about thirty yards away. 'Stay here. Keep an eye on these fellas. I'll be back.'

The men in the wood were firing. Rory could see their muzzle flashes. He staggered forward, eyes firmly on the shell hole as he blotted everything else out. The officer groaned, writhing awkwardly as Rory staggered under his weight. He was a heavy bugger but the adrenalin had kicked in, speeding his steps. Then they were there; in the crater; alive. Oily slime lapped at his knees as he arranged the unconscious officer beneath its lip. His lungs were on fire as he gasped for breath and his helmet, pressing down on his skull, was giving him a head-ache. The machine gun was still preoccupied so he took his chance. Seizing the officer by the lapels, he dragged him back into the open and down into a second crater twenty feet further on. Then he took a look. Shells were still falling. He ducked down, at a loss what to do.

'Hey, over here!' shouted someone in pure East Belfast. Screwing up his courage, Rory poked his head up once more, looking for the voice. He saw soup-plate helmets less than twenty yards off. They had a Vickers machine gun. 'We'll cover ye!' shouted the voice again. He saw a thin face, ludicrous beneath an oversized helmet, sporting a droopy walrus moustache. He was waving, beckoning Rory over. 'Just give us a sec to get this thing set up!' he shouted. Rory nodded, then watched the men fumble with the machine gun until the man stuck a thumb up. 'Right-o, sonny, after three! One! Two! Three!' The Vickers spewed into life, sending tracer rounds arcing in the direction of the German machine-gun nest. The men in the wood joined in and the Germans' fire slackened. Grabbing the officer, Rory was up, staggering to safety. By the time he reached the Vickers he was drenched in sweat, muscles quaking. He felt sick. Then he vomited, thanking God he hadn't wet himself instead. He was in an old communication trench. There were others there, bayonets wavering like barley in the wind. The Vickers let off another long burst that set his ears ringing. He noticed the gunner's tongue poking out the corner of his mouth in childlike concentration.

'Well, now, that'll turn their bloody gas down!' crowed the man with the huge moustache. He was a sergeant, obviously the gun commander. Several men cheered then, anxious-eyed, scrambled over the top, vanishing into the howling maw of battle. 'Ye done good, sonny,' added the sergeant, slapping Rory on the shoulder. 'Now let's get yer man here to the doctor, shall we?' He tasked off two riflemen to take the officer to the rear before handing Rory a water bottle. He took a long swig, regretting it instantly as fiery liquid seared his throat. It tasted like paint stripper; or what he assumed paint stripper tasted like.

'Jaysus, Mary and Joseph, what the feck was that?' spluttered Rory, handing back the canteen to the sergeant, who seemed momentarily taken aback by both his Dublin accent and distinctly Catholic outburst.

'Sure now, ye're jammy wee *taig*,' he said. 'I thought ye'd cop it.'

'You and me both, then,' replied Rory with a weary smile, choosing to ignore the sergeant's sectarian jibe. After all, the man probably hadn't even given it a thought. It was a reflex action, like swearing was to most of them. 'My mucker's still out there,' he added. Whatever the sergeant had given him had revived his spirits slightly but he still felt very, very tired as he leant against the trench's side. 'Can you give me covering fire whilst I go get him? He's some wounded fellas with him.'

The sergeant nodded and as the Vickers laid down a blanket of fire, he hauled himself out of the trench once more, feeling awfully exposed. Then he ran, noise thundering through his skull, overwhelming his senses, as he kept low, zigzagging back the way he came. Something snatched at his sleeve, sending him tumbling. He patted his arm, searching for the tell-tale slickness of a wound, but there was nothing save a jagged tear in the cloth. Then he was up again, running, careering headlong into McNee's position. He'd made it.

'You didn't think I'd leave you, did you?' gasped Rory, panting for breath. He could see McNee was afraid, close to breaking, looking like a sheep in the abattoir yard. Taking a deep breath he said, 'I don't know about you, big fella, but I think it'd be a good idea if we got out of here.' Unsurprisingly, McNee and the others didn't look keen to abandon the relative safety of the berm. 'Sure, it sounds worse than it is. It's not so bad once you're out there,' he lied, amazed at how easily the words had come. It was obvious that it was what McNee and the others wanted to hear. Rory grinned. They were buying it: another little miracle. 'Now, give us a hand,' he said, checking over one of the casualties' bandages. Then the Vickers opened up again just as the four of them made their dash. 'There now, that wasn't so bad!' panted Rory when they reached the first crater. McNee didn't look convinced. Neither did the man with the shattered forearm, whilst the one who had lost his fingers just rocked back and forth, keening gently as he stared into space, eyes shining brightly against his milk-white face. 'Not much further.'

They were all running on empty. He knew he had to keep them moving. He seized the fingerless man's webbing and ran, pulling him behind him. He didn't look back, praying that McNee had followed. Then they were down in another shell hole, panting for breath. More shells fell, masking them from German fire. Seeing his chance Rory was up again and running, dragging the wounded man behind him. One went down, wrenching Rory's arm. He cursed. More bullets zipped by. A surge of relief washed over him as he realized the man had only stumbled.

'Let's go!' he shouted, seeing McNee hard on his heels with his own man. The Vickers was covering them as stray rounds groped at their feet, making the wounded man do a panic-stricken jig. Then they ran. It was the longest thirty yards of Rory's life and his feet felt like they were made of lead, too large and cumbersome for his legs.

'Ye really are a Jammy wee *taig*,' said the sergeant, who seemed genuinely pleased to see that Rory had made it back.

'Aye, Gallagher here's a good man, Sarge,' replied McNee, unsure whether he liked anyone but him calling Rory a *taig*. Unfazed, the sergeant handed Rory his water bottle. Rory gratefully took a long pull on the fiery liquid before passing it to McNee. He sniffed it suspiciously, declining to drink. McNee wasn't much of a drinker – not exactly tee-total but he declined his rum ration on the rare occasions they were given one. He'd seen too many good men ruined by drink. The two casualties were less circumspect, gulping down the spirits, much to the sergeant's chagrin.

'There's an aid post about a hundred yards down that way,' said the sergeant to the two walking wounded, prising loose his precious canteen from one of their hands. They stumbled away, looking more than a little relieved to be out of the fight. Then the sergeant turned to Rory. 'Well, sonny, I reckon you deserve a flaming medal for all that,' he said, extracting a notebook from his tunic pocket along with a stubby pencil. He licked the end, preparing to write.

There was an almighty flash.

When Rory opened his eyes, he was on his back. His ears were ringing, the noise flooding his senses. He was soaked. He sat up. The sergeant was gone. So was the Vickers team. He looked round. All that remained was a steaming hole where they once had been, littered with twisted metal and sodden lumps. He stood up, his legs wobbly. Someone groaned. It was McNee, sitting nearby, cradling his head in his hands, his face masked by his helmet brim. He went over to him.

'Let's get out of here!' shouted Rory.

'There's no need to shout, ye *eejit!*' McNee shouted back, obviously temporarily deafened as well. His hands were red. Rory knelt down beside his friend. McNee's face, or what was left of his face, was soaked in blood, a tattered mass of flesh exposing bone. His eyes and nose were gone and Rory felt a bitter taste rise in his mouth as he bit back the urge to puke. He struggled to stay calm, to sound calm.

'Ach, it's not so bad,' he lied as he wrapped a field dressing around McNee's face, then he took his blinded friend gently by the hand, helping him to his feet. 'C'mon, Andy, let's get you home.'

CHAPTER 23

Wicklow Mountains, Ireland

Mary couldn't quite put her finger on it but Dublin had changed somehow since she'd left. It wasn't the damage to Sackville Street, although that was bad enough; it was subtler than that. It just felt different: sadder somehow.

She knew Sweeney had been involved in the Rising – he didn't really say how but whenever they strolled past Dublin's Liberty Hall he seemed to look at it like an old friend. In fact, he was a bit of an enigma; cagey about his past. She rarely saw him excited, except when he started talking about someone called Marx – she'd never heard of him – but she happily sat and listened to him going on about a time when everyone would be equal, when war would be abolished. That sounded good to her.

'It's his sort that keeps the Magdalene Laundries and the gallows in business,' her father had said after meeting him, which she thought a little unfair. It was obvious they preferred Flynn but she didn't care. Flynn was the past; men like Sweeney were the future and the war had taught her that that's all that mattered. She didn't tell them about *Cumann Na mBan:* she knew they wouldn't approve. They'd only blame Sweeney for leading her astray. Anyway, she liked Sweeney leading her astray. She knew her parents really wouldn't have approved of *that!* She knew he would ask her to marry him; he just hadn't got round to it yet.

'Will you come away from the window,' she said from the comfort of the bed. 'People might talk!'

'Isn't that the curse of Ireland?' he replied somewhat bitterly. 'That people talk.' He was naked, sipping tea as he leant from the croft's window, gazing at the lush green hills peeping over the surrounding treetops, oblivious of his nakedness. She'd never known anyone quite like him; someone devoid of all that Catholic guilt and angst, someone so at ease with himself. 'Will you stop your fretting,' he said, turning and smiling. 'We're in the middle of nowhere.' Of course he was right: there was no one for miles. He seemed to like it that way.

Mary smiled back, still half-asleep, snuggled beneath the blankets. The remnants of a turf fire smouldered in the grate, filling the croft with a homely, earthy smell. It was Sweeney's home, or at least he said it was, tucked away in the Wicklow Mountains; where they had come when they left

Dublin, when she had left home, sick of the frosty atmosphere and endless fights. It was spartan, its uneven walls daubed with whitewash, accentuating the dusty shafts of sunlight thrusting across its one room. She'd baked some bread; it lay hacked and discarded next to some empty stout bottles and a jar of blackberry jam. A Webley revolver lay nearby along with a box of cartridges. Sweeney never left home without it. Sometimes she went with him. He said they were less likely to be stopped that way. There was a car in the yard, a black two-seater Riley 10. She didn't know where Sweeney had got it from; she didn't ask nor did she care because it had brought them to this island of calm after the hubbub of Dublin and that's all that mattered.

'Isn't it too early to be up and about?' she said, patting the bed. 'Come back to bed, you'll catch your death like that.' She stretched languidly, letting the blankets fall away to expose her naked breasts.

'You're shameless, utterly shameless,' he said, shaking his head in mock disapproval as he crossed the room. His bright blue eyes twinkled mischievously as he ran them over Mary's exposed contours. She looked healthier than when they'd met, no doubt because she didn't play with explosives any more. 'What would people think if they could see you now?'

She blushed slightly, making him grin all the more. She liked his grin; she'd liked it ever since they'd met that day at Kingstown. She didn't know why; she just did. 'Well, from the look of you it's easy to tell what's on your mind! Is it all you think of?' she replied, unable to take her eyes off his groin.

'I've not heard you complaining,' he quipped.

'My parents said you were trouble. Called you a Fenian corner boy.'

'I'm shocked,' he quipped mockingly. 'I've never been a Fenian though I've been called worse!' She didn't doubt it as he pulled back the blankets, fully exposing her nakedness to the light of day. She stretched, accentuating her curves.

'Your parents aren't fans?' She didn't contradict him. 'So whatever we do won't change their opinion of me.' He was right. 'Anyway, it's not what *they* think of me that counts,' he added, leaning over her. Her skin tingled with excitement. He was exciting. He was a good listener too. She liked that. He asked her what she thought. She liked that too. Her parents never asked her what she thought; it was as if London had never happened, as if she wasn't supposed to have an opinion. Even when the news had arrived saying Terry was dead. For all she knew, Rory was dead too. The papers were full of the names of poor Irish lads duped into dying for the English crown when they should have been at home, dying for Ireland if there was any dying to be done.

She didn't regret sleeping with Sweeney. How could she? He was kind and gentle and in his arms she felt safe. In his arms the nightmares had gone, the spectre of falling rubble and children's screams that had stalked her dreams since that awful night when Daiken's house had been bombed. He'd insisted on using a condom. He always did. When he'd first suggested it she said that the Church wouldn't approve but she dropped the matter when he pointed out that condom or no, the Church definitely wouldn't approve of what they were doing. She didn't care. He'd given her life meaning and now she had no regrets, none, about giving herself to him. Life was for living.

'What's it like out?' she asked, gazing up at him.

'Can't you see for yourself?' he answered, beaming cheekily.

'Not *that!* The weather, you cheeky *eejit!*' she replied.

'Ah now, you know what Oscar Wilde said about people who talk about the weather,' he said.

'Oscar who? Is he one of them fellas at HQ?' she asked, looking puzzled. Sweeney was always meeting people from the local Volunteer HQ. He rarely mentioned names.

He said it was better that way; safer.

'You're kidding me, right? Are you seriously telling me you don't know who Oscar Wilde is?' he asked in astonishment. 'Oscar Wilde: the great Irish writer.' Flynn would have known. He always had his nose buried in a book of some sort.

'Ah well, you read too much. I was never one for books,' she replied.

'You know they say that a man who reads books lives a thousand lives, whilst a man who doesn't only lives one,' said Sweeney. Their faces were close now. He liked her face; it was her mind that wasn't up to much but he didn't mind. It wasn't really her intellect he liked.

'Well, I'll settle for one life. Now, will you shut the window. It's letting in the cold,' she said, twisting to one side and swinging a pillow at his head. She was quick, but he was quicker, rolling to one side and rolling her on top of him as they entwined in a raucous tangle of laughter. 'So what did this Wilde fella have to say, then?' she asked. It was his turn to look puzzled. 'You know, about people who talk about the weather.'

'He said they had no imagination!'

Mary frowned, pouting childishly.

'I'll show you who's got no imagination, Gerard Sweeney!' she squealed, planting a passionate kiss on his lips. Sweeney grinned, pinning Mary to the bed. Later she lay with her head on his chest, listening to the gentle beating of his heart. Then Sweeney glanced at the clock on the mantelpiece.

'We're late,' he suddenly announced, their recent frolic seemingly forgotten.

'Late for what?' she asked

'You'll see,' was all he said in reply. It was what he always said whenever they went out, especially if they were off on an operation. At first he'd been reluctant to get her too involved but she'd persuaded him that the police were less likely to stop a courting couple out for a drive than a man or men in a car on their own. He knew she was right, especially after Easter, and so far the police always waved them on with a smile and a polite 'good day'. He sometimes wondered how on earth the British had managed to build an empire in the first place with such naïve servants to police it.

They dressed quickly and in silence. He slipped the revolver into his pocket.

'Just in case.'

He was wearing the same worn tweed suit he'd been wearing when they first met. She'd asked for a gun too but he'd drawn the line at that. He didn't approve of women and guns, not after watching Countess Constance Markievicz waving one around like a toy during the Rising. He'd later heard that she'd begged for her life during her trial, wailing from the dock that 'you cannot shoot a woman'. He had no idea if it was true, but it fitted with his low opinion of an aristocrat playing at revolutionary. Besides, if the peelers lifted them it would go better for Mary if she was unarmed. She watched him take a map from an old biscuit box and stuff it in his other pocket before slipping into a voluminous beige gabardine riding coat. A flat cap finished the ensemble, shading his eyes, obscuring the details of his face. She took longer to dress but he didn't complain, merely thumbing through a hefty-looking book with the curious title 'Capital' emblazoned on its spine. She assumed it was about Dublin.

Thankfully, the car started easily, despite the damp.

'Where are we going?' she asked as Sweeney crunched the Riley into gear.

'To meet a man in Aghavannagh,' he replied as the car lurched into life, fighting for traction on the muddy yard before bouncing up a narrow track between the trees that led to the main road.

'Now doesn't that sound like a song if ever there was,' Mary quipped light-heartedly, but Sweeney ignored her. He seemed preoccupied. 'So what man will we be meeting?' she asked more seriously, hoping he would open up. He didn't; not even when they finally swung out onto the county's old military road. Sweeney clunked the car into third gear, putting his foot down, and Mary couldn't help but enjoy the sensation of cool mountain air ruffling her hair. There were sheep on the hills and hazy rain in the distance. It'd be a soft day, after all; typically Irish, neither wet nor dry despite the early promise of sunshine.

She caught her breath as they rounded a wooded bend, squeezing Sweeney's thigh involuntarily. There were policemen by the side of the road. Three of them with bicycles and stubby carbines, their rifle-green uniforms almost black in the shade of the trees. They looked unconcerned, probably taking a breather mid-patrol. Sweeney seemed unperturbed. Cool and collected as usual. He honked the horn, waving cheerily. They looked up, waving back.

'Bunch of bloody traitors,' he muttered through his forced grin as they passed them. She relaxed her grip, releasing his thigh but leaving her hand lingering on his leg. Sweeney spared her a sidelong glance but made no effort to remove it.

'You're a cool one,' she said.

'Now, a wise fella once told me that if you act suspicious people will get suspicious, so I don't see any point in upsetting the peelers for no reason by creeping about,' he said by way of explanation. She laughed. He didn't and after a few moments they lapsed once more into awkward silence. He seemed on edge.

'What's the matter?' she asked, afraid that she'd done something wrong.

'Mary, darling, everything's just grand,' he replied without conviction. Something was obviously on his mind. Ever since the Rising, Sweeney had been running around trying to keep the revolution going, keeping men together, resurrecting the cause from the ashes of failure. It was a heavy burden and she wanted to share it but he wasn't much for sharing. She squeezed his thigh once more, less urgently this time, and laid her head on his shoulder.

'Are we there yet?' she asked almost dreamily as they passed beneath the shadow of Lugnaquilla, the largest mountain in eastern Ireland. She could see crofts, like Sweeney's, littering the glens.

'Aye, this'll be Aghavannagh,' replied Sweeney.

'What's the big house?' asked Mary, pointing at a large, imposing granite building that squatted ominously on the edge of the hamlet.

'That'll be the barracks,' he replied almost casually and he couldn't help but laugh when he saw the colour wash from Mary's face.

'Will there be soldiers there?' she asked.

'They say there were fifty peelers living there when old Charlie Parnell owned the place.' Mary frowned. 'Your man Redmond bought it back in '91 when Parnell snuffed it.'

'So this place is crawling with peelers, then?' she said before adding, 'How come a politician owns a barracks?'

'Because Redmond owns the land round here, but you don't need to worry, the peelers are long gone. It's just a house now, though it's a terrible waste leaving it empty most of the time. They say your man Redmond uses it at the weekends to go blasting the bejaysus out of the local wildlife.'

It was Mary's turn to relax.

Then the house was gone, lost behind a thick screen of trees and hedges as they swung around an open bend past a small country school. Beyond it stood a man in a shabby dark-brown suit, grey collarless shirt and cap. He was reading a newspaper, or at least pretending to. The headline was about the Somme. The headlines were always about the Somme, Mary thought. The man looked up, deftly folded the paper and tucked it under his arm before grinding out the cigarette he was smoking beneath his foot.

'Yer feckin' late,' the man snapped irritably, casting a disapproving glance at Mary. 'What'd you bring her for?' She thought he had a look about him of a man who wanted people to think he was more than he was and she quickly decided she didn't like him. She had no doubt that the feeling was mutual.

'Will you stop your whining, Danny,' replied Sweeney tersely. 'Mary's sound and I'm here now so can we get on with it?' The man Sweeney had called Danny scowled, his lupine eyes reminding Mary of a wolf she'd once seen in Dublin zoo. He climbed onto the running board. 'So?' It was Sweeney's turn to sound angry. 'I assume you've dragged me all the way out here for a purpose?' Danny squeezed into the car next to Mary. He stank of tea, tobacco and sweat. She shuffled closer to Sweeney, trying to avoid Danny's touch, which was difficult: it was a tight fit. Sweeney clunked the car into gear and they were off.

'Take a left at the next junction,' said Danny, waving vaguely off into the middle distance. 'It's up there,' he added as they approached a break in the hedges lining the old military road. Sweeney swung left and the car bounced awkwardly into a waterlogged pothole, hurling up a sheet of filth as they climbed a gently sloping track towards a scattering of low grey buildings in the lee of an overgrown rath. It was a farm; or used to be. Beyond it, yellow gorse speckled the rolling peat bog.

The track was hard going, making the car's suspension groan as it lurched from pothole to pothole. Mary used the jolting as an excuse to snuggle closer to Sweeney; Danny used it as an excuse to frot himself against her thigh. The man kept looking over his shoulder, like he was expecting to be followed; Sweeney kept glancing at Danny like he'd found a dog turd on his car seat. As the car jolted, Danny's jacket fell open revealing the grip of a pistol thrust in his inside pocket. Both men were armed. She wasn't sure why it was a surprise, but it was.

The air was heavy now with the stink of something faecal and as the car slewed to a halt she felt a wave of relief as the last few hundred yards had felt as if some invisible giant had given her a shaking. Danny leapt out, his boots slurping in the viscous dark goo around them. Sweeney looked less keen to get his feet dirty. He always cleaned his shoes. There were pens at the far side of the yard: pigsties, she guessed.

'You stay here,' Danny ordered Mary. She looked up. It was cloudy and a scree of rain was idling its way steadily down the hillside towards them. Sweeney tossed Danny an angry glance that could have felled an ox. Danny made a brief bid to meet Sweeney's gaze but baulked, staring awkwardly at his feet.

'Tell you what, Mary darling, why don't you get inside and make me and the fellas some tea?' Sweeney said. He said fellas. There were more, thought Mary. He flashed her an indulgent smile although his eyes were hard, far from happy. Something was

303

worrying him. She toyed with asking him outright but thought better of it. He held out his hand, ever the gentleman, and led her through the filth to the farmhouse. There was a low iron bracket, weathered brown by rust and rain, by the door. He scraped the filth from his shoes on it, adding to its distemper. Ducking her head, Mary went inside. A turf fire blazed in the fireplace but the air was damp, betraying the fact that the building was rarely used.

'This way,' Danny said, flicking his head towards a door in the back wall that Mary assumed led to the back of the building. There was a dark wooden crucifix nailed to the wall above it. Sweeney nodded. He paused at the door, almost as an afterthought.

'Best you stay here, Mary darling,' he said, his voice unnaturally flat. She started fussing by the stove, filling the brass kettle, overwatched by a gaudy picture of the Virgin Mary.

Danny led Sweeney through a labyrinth of passages and across another muddy yard to a lone, thick-stonewalled outbuilding some distance from the main farmhouse. Sweeney noticed another grey man in a nondescript suit standing slightly in the shadows, cradling an old-fashioned muzzle-loading shotgun in the crook of his arm. It had been sawn off short, like a bank robber's. They exchanged nods before trooping inside where the air was cool and it took a few seconds for Sweeney's eyes to adjust to the gloom. A shape sat in the middle of the dirt-floored byre; a man tied to a chair. He was hooded with an old potato sack; rocking slightly and keening pathetically. Sweeney walked closer. He was shabbily dressed and stank of urine. It was obvious he'd soiled himself.

'Jaysus, the bastard's shat himself,' jibed Danny with a stupid grin. The man with the shotgun was grinning too, following Danny's lead. Sweeney ignored them, circling the tethered man. He understood ruthlessness, that was inevitable in revolution, but he'd never understood cruelty; wallowing in other men's suffering. All he wanted was for the suffering to end – one day. 'The shite says his name is Michael Grogan though the little fecker's probably lying. Says he's a tinker and aren't all tinkers liars?' Sweeney couldn't follow Danny's logic, selectively sifting truth from lies to slake his own bigotry. 'He showed up a few days ago but there's no one around here can vouch for him. One of the boys saw him having a wee chat with the peelers up on the main road.' Sweeney was in front of him now. 'Then we found him poking around up here, out in the barn.' The hooded man grunted. 'The bastard wouldn't stop squealing so we gagged him,' explained Danny.

Sweeney yanked off the hood, exposing

Grogan's face. He'd been beaten, badly beaten, his lived-in face swollen and bloody beyond recognition. He couldn't tell his age. It didn't matter; he wasn't going to get much older anyway. He'd been scoured by wind and rain and too many nights beneath the stars. There was something pathetic about the way his watery eyes watched Sweeney with desperate hope. Sweeney pulled the gag free from Grogan's swollen mouth. He whimpered.

'Are you Michael Grogan?' Sweeney asked gently.

'In the name of God, sir, I swear I was only looking for a place to sleep,' gabbled Grogan in a brogue that was neither here nor there and hard to place. Sweeney calmly repeated the question. Grogan nodded.

'You know, Michael, spying for the enemy is a serious crime,' said Sweeney.

'I was only looking for a place to sleep, sir!' protested Grogan but Sweeney merely held up his hand to silence him.

'Michael, I just want to help you out of a tricky situation. Now, you look like a decent enough fella but you were seen talking to the peeler and now you turn up here. Look, if you tell me everything then I can help you. Just tell me what they said to you,' Sweeney asked calmly.

'They were moving me on, sir! I swear it!' There was panic in Grogan's voice.

'He's lying,' growled Danny. The man with the shotgun agreed. They looked agitated, overexcited by the man's suffering. Sweeney made a note to deal with the pair later. He didn't like working with fools, especially sadistic fools – they were a liability. Grogan was weeping, blubbering like a child as fat tears rolled down his unshaven cheeks.

'For God's sake, can you not at least act like a man?' complained the man with the shotgun, brandishing it at Grogan's head. 'Can't we just shoot the shite now and be done?' he added, cocking his gun. Sweeney threw him an angry glance that made him step back.

'Look, Michael, if you cooperate, then you've nothing to be afraid of,' said Sweeney softly as he squatted down in front of Grogan, doing his best to ignore the smell. 'Your only hope is to tell me what you told the peelers. What did they want to know? Did they ask you to keep an eye out for anything strange, anything unusual?'

Grogan nodded, hanging his head.

'They said I was to tell them if I saw anything but I swear to God I was just looking for somewhere to get me head down! I'd never go grassing anyone up to the peelers, sir,' he gabbled. Sweeney nodded and stood up, pulling the sack back loosely over Grogan's head. 'W-what's happening?' spluttered Grogan, twisting his head from left to right.

'Don't you go worrying yourself, Michael, we'll be done soon,' said Sweeney as he walked behind the chair, pulling his pistol from his jacket pocket. He pointed it at the back of Grogan's head, steadying the weapon as he took aim. The noise was deafening, ricocheting off the thick byre walls. Danny flinched, crossing himself as Grogan's body was thrown forward, a jagged hole torn in the back of the hood. He stepped forward, placing the muzzle against Grogan's head, and fired again; the *coup de grace*.

'I thought you boys might–' gasped Mary from the doorway, dropping the tray of tea she was carrying. She screamed. The man with the shotgun jumped, spinning around and snatching the trigger in fright, refilling the small room with flame and noise. Sweeney felt the shot fly past his face, some of it peppering Grogan's head whilst the rest tore a bloody hole in Mary's chest, sending her flying back from whence she came. Then came silence; a terrible, echoing, sulphurous silence that hung like a shroud over them, filling everything.

'What the feck have you done, you fecking *eejit?*' shouted Sweeney, running over to Mary, pale with shock. Reaching down he touched her face – it was still warm. He wanted to hold her but somehow resisted the urge because of the blood. It was everywhere. He could see her ribs poking through the tattered remnant of her breast like some grotesque toast rack. 'What have they done to you, Mary darling?' he whispered, gently brushing lank strands of blonde hair from her wide blue eyes, disturbing her look of surprise at death's swiftness.

'It just went off,' the man with the shotgun whimpered pathetically, as if the weapon had a life of its own. 'Jaysus, I'm sorry.' Sweeney hated working with amateurs; half-trained idiots who seemed to think revolution was some kind of a game. 'I ... I ... it just ... it just went off,' he repeated. Sweeney stood up, feeling his shock turn to rage. He had liked Mary a lot, maybe even loved her; he would never know now. He turned, his face like a demon from the depths of hell, and stepped towards the shooter, who let the weapon slip from his fingers. Danny stepped in the way.

'What are you going to do now?' asked Danny, looking very afraid.

'You're going to fetch a shovel and bury them,' he said, his voice dangerously calm and quiet. 'And then I will decide what to do with you two culchie *eejits*.' He would deal with them later. No one would ask any questions. People disappeared all the time.

CHAPTER 24

28 August 1916, Chocques, Hulluch Sector

The shunting yard was in chaos.

'Bloody rain,' cursed Fallon from beneath the meagre shelter of his tin hat, greatcoat and gas cape. 'I could have stayed at home for a soaking like this!'

Nearby, his friend Collins sat with the rest of the company looking equally forlorn. It was cold, it was wet and they were all tired and hungry. Everything was *on the bus* then *off the bus* and always *rush, ready, wait*, typically army. No one had a clue what was going on but far too many people were willing to shout about it. He could never work out why the army insisted on doing things in the middle of the night, as if the War Office was run by insomniacs; but it did. He couldn't remember when he'd last slept in a bed. It would be hours before they ate, he just knew it, and he regretted not snatching a bite when he'd had the chance – but the letter from his wife had thrown him. Well, technically she was his wife, although he'd not seen her in years, not since he went to India and she stayed in Kildare. Now she was demanding money: a cut from his pay. She even threatened to write to the CO about it. He'd deal with it later. Right now he had more pressing matters on his mind.

'Old Hackett says we're off to the Somme,' said Collins authoritatively. Old Hackett was uncannily well informed for a store man. 'No good will come of it,' he added, trying to light a soggy Woodbine.

Fallon could see that Collins wasn't happy.

'I reckon you're right,' he agreed wistfully. 'I hear tell the Brass have made a right balls-up down that way. Worst cock-up since ... since ... ah, well, just pick one, there's been so many. Anyway, they wouldn't be sending us if they weren't going to attack again. By Christ, why couldn't they have sent me back to one of the mobs they sent out east?' His eyes lit up as he remembered the first time he'd passed through Suez. 'I could be living it up in the sunshine with some sloe-eyed bint and a couple of sherbets.' He was watching Mahon approaching, ramrod straight, holding a clipboard that he'd inverted in a desperate attempt to keep his precious paperwork dry.

'Sloe-eyed bints and sherbets, my arse, you'd've shat yourself to death at Gallipoli if you'd gone out east,' replied Collins.

Mahon was looming over them.

'All right, then! You lot follow me,' he growled, then he led them over the tracks to a string of cattle wagons on the far side of the goods yard. 'In you hop,' he said, chalking a series of numbers and letters on the wagon's side. Fallon unslung his rifle and scrambled inside. The wagon smelt of wet straw and flatulence but at least it was shelter from the slashing rain. He hunkered down in a corner, greatcoat steaming, as the wagon began to fill with men bringing the musk of wet serge with them.

'How come the officers get decent carriages whilst we get packed into this shite like animals off to the knacker's yard?' grumbled Collins.

'It was ever thus,' Fallon replied rather stoically.

'Well, it fecking well shouldn't be!' snapped Collins, attracting more than a few curious glances.

'Will you keep your voice down?' hissed Fallon. 'If old Hackett's right and it's the Somme we're after then you'd best get some sleep, cos God knows there'll be little enough to be had when we get there!' He closed his eyes, nestling back with his hands thrust deep in his pockets.

'Do you think old Hackett's right, then? Do you think it'll be the Somme?' asked Collins. Fallon opened his eyes. It had to be; why move them otherwise? 'The army does as the army does, Aiden, me old mucker, and we'll go where they send us, that's for sure. So I wouldn't go worrying your wee head about it if I was you. Now get some sleep.'

Collins didn't feel like sleeping. To be honest, he couldn't understand how easily Fallon fell asleep, almost at will. It was an old soldier's trick. There was a rumble in the distance. He didn't know whether it was thunder or guns and as he listened to the metallic rattling of the train, he lost track of time. Eventually he nodded off, lurching awake as the train squealed to a halt, the steam engine sighing like a runner coming to rest. His backside was numb, cold against the hard wood floor, and he was hungry. He could hear boots on gravel, then an avalanche of light flooded his brain as the doors flew open. It was Mahon.

'Out!' he snapped, waving his omnipresent clipboard. At least it wasn't raining. Fallon eased up the brim of his helmet, taking a look around. There were muffled crumps in the distance and he began to feel his age as he jumped down onto the railway embankment. All around NCOs bellowed, hapless squaddies doubled, forming the semblance of platoons and companies. It was the usual chaos. Devlin and Flynn were there too, pointing and shouting. His feral eyes lingered on the pair for a moment too long, savouring the thought of the reckoning to come.

He saw the RSM on the other side of the tracks talking to Clee, the man an island of

313

calm amid the cacophony. The CO was near-by along with Stirke and the other officers, buzzing around the colonel like flies round a cowpat. He had no idea who the subalterns were. There was no reason why he should. They came and went, usually wrapped in a groundsheet after having some pointless brain-fart about 'sticking it to the Hun'. Collins elbowed him in the ribs.

'Ain't that fella Tom Kettle?' Collins asked, pointing out one of the new officers.

'Tom who?' he replied.

'You know, *Tom Kettle!*' said Collins. 'He was a Member of Parliament; big man in the Volunteers before the war. He's the one who said we weren't fighting for England but for small nations like Belgium and Ireland. You know, *that* Tom Kettle!'

'Oh, *that* Tom Kettle. Why didn't you say? Never heard of the man,' he sniffed dismissively.

'And who's the fella with him, then?' asked Collins, ignoring Fallon's studied indifference. Kettle was deep in conversation with a slightly built young lieutenant sporting a neatly clipped blond moustache. Fallon made a theatrical show of looking around, bemused.

'I'm sorry, Aiden, but for a moment there I thought you were talking to someone else, because you really have mistaken me for someone who gives a shit!' growled Fallon.

314

He was bored with Collins's meaningless prattle, too preoccupied with the sounds of battle wafting over the horizon.

'That young gentleman, Private Collins, is Mr Dalton.' It was Mahon. It was uncanny how he managed to sneak up on people. It was a gift. 'He's been assigned to C Company so he'll be nothing to do with you, now, will he? So when you two *gentlemen* have finished your little *tête-a-tête*, would you be so kind as to fall in with the rest of B Company.' There was a slight pause. 'Now, bloody jildy!' he barked, his booming parade-ground voice chasing after them like a wolfhound as they sprinted away.

'What now?' asked Collins when they found B Company stretched out along a chalky track that was rapidly turning to grey mush beneath the combined assault of boots and rain. It looked like they were going nowhere and so the two of them flopped down, trying to ease the weight of their kit on their shoulders.

'How should I know?' replied Fallon. 'Hurry up and wait, I guess.' Collins lapsed into silence, smoking quietly. Flicking away his dog-end, Fallon was about to speak when a young sergeant – too young, in Fallon's eyes, to merit his stripes – came storming along the track, hurling out a tirade of expletives, imperatives and spleen, rousing them to their feet. Resigning himself to a long walk, Fallon was pleasantly surprised that they only trudged along for ten minutes at most before wheeling past a sign that read 'Sandpit Camp'. Rain lashed horizontally across the camp, stinging his face.

'Great, no bloody bunks,' grumbled Fallon when he was finally allocated a tent. At least he was sharing with Collins and a dozen other sodden wretches. He threw his kit down, tugging out his gas cape. The others did likewise. Within minutes water was trickling over the edge, soaking his backside. It would be a long hard winter. He lit up, shoving a young fusilier aside so that he had a clear view of Devlin and Flynn getting their own platoons under cover, making a mental note of where they were camped. It might prove useful later.

The rest of Fallon's day passed miserably despite fleecing his tent-mates of their meagre pay with a marked deck of porno-graphic playing cards, the pictures suffi-ciently explicit to distract his hapless victims. Night-time was no better and for once sleep didn't come beneath a sodden greatcoat. He felt the damp cold seep into his bones as he lay listening to the ever-present rumble of the guns. Reveille was almost a relief so he rose and shaved before scavenging for breakfast – thick, sweet tea and a slice of bread and margarine. It wasn't much but it was better than nothing. Then they formed up in full fighting order, swaying like cornstalks before hurriedly running through company and battalion battle drills.

'Keep up! Hug the barrage. Stay as close as you can – that way Jerry will still have his head down when we get in amongst them!' shouted Captain Murphy with a flourish of his blackthorn cane. They'd done it all before, back in Ireland, trudging along behind men waving flags, pretending to be a creeping barrage.

'I don't like the look of this,' complained Collins when they broke for lunch. Fallon didn't feel hungry. Everything was far too serious, not like the stupid game they played back in County Cork and Aldershot. No, this time everything was real, even more real than at Hulluch. This time the battalion was going to war. This time they were going to attack. It was the first time for all of them and Fallon knew full well that for many – God knows how many – it would be the last. 'Will you look at the grinning *eejits*,' added Collins, shoving the last of the stew around his mess tin. 'You'd've thought Hulluch was bad enough. We'll be in the thick of it soon.'

'So what do you suggest? We can't run. They'd shoot us for sure,' Fallon said between forced mouthfuls. He didn't find the prospect of being shredded by German shot and shell terribly appealing either. He'd just finished his tea when he noticed Kettle strolling amongst the men, chatting. He didn't look well. There were rumours that he was too fond of the drink; to be honest, who wasn't? thought Fallon. Only an *eejit* would want to stay sober amongst all the insanity. They spent the rest of the day practising more attacks, trudging back to camp only after the sun had fled into the western skies. At least it had stopped raining.

'Well, I'll sleep tonight,' grumbled Collins between mouthfuls of tea. Somehow Fallon just knew his friend had spoken too soon and as they marched through the darkness he could feel the rumble of the guns rising up through the ground. Here and there shells exploded, showering them with light as they stumbled to a halt at a place someone called Billion Farm. Sandpit Camp seemed lovely by comparison. Everything was relative. Then it started to rain again and someone started to sing, *'We're here because we're here because we're here because we're here...'* and soon everyone was belting it out including the CO and RSM. Then they lapsed into silence.

'All right, chaps, gather around,' called out Colonel Thackeray. There was a buzz, an air of excitement as the battalion formed a loose horseshoe around an old GS wagon he was using as a podium. It was times like this that Fallon regretted losing his stripes; after all, NCOs usually knew what was going on, not just what the officers told them. They were the battalion's backbone, the glue that held the battalion together, and that brought power and privilege. He liked those; what he didn't like was responsibility or the fact that most of the NCOs seemed barely old enough to shave, not like in a proper regular army battalion. Then he saw Flynn looking up at the CO, thinking it a travesty that they'd made him a sergeant. War was ruining the army.

Looking down from the wagon, Temporary Lieutenant Colonel Frank Thackeray felt tired but strangely content with his lot. Never in his wildest dreams, not even as a cocky, overconfident gentleman cadet at Sandhurst, had he ever imagined he would command a battalion in his twenties. It was unheard of in the old, peacetime regulars and yet here he was, a substantive captain from the Highland Light Infantry, the 9th Battalion's third CO in two years. He knew he wasn't alone. There were hundreds of junior officers holding temporary field rank. Some even commanded brigades. Maybe he would one day. It would look good on his record. Operational commands always did. War was a hard school.

The battalion wasn't what he'd expected. In fact, he hadn't really known what to expect, but it hadn't taken long for his Regular Army prejudices to slip away as he got to know his officers and men. They were a garrulous bunch and even the ordinary soldiers seemed to have an opinion about something, especially Ireland; but so far they had fought like devils and he liked that. In a way, they reminded him of his Jocks – hard fighting, hard drinking rogues. He missed his Jocks but these were his rogues now and that's what counted.

'I just thought I'd let you chaps know what's going on,' he began without a scrap of Scots in his voice. He was from Monmouthshire, but that wasn't obvious either from his crisp, Regular Army diction. Shells screamed overhead, heading for the German lines, cutting him short. He waited, then resumed. 'You'll be pleased to know that as we speak our chaps are sticking it to the Boche at Guillemont.' It was obvious that the name meant nothing to most of the battalion.

'Didn't they try and take that place back in July?' whispered Collins out of the side of his mouth. Clee shot him a hostile look. He shut up. The CO continued.

'Now, the general,' he meant Major General William Hickie, the tough, chain-smoking Irish Catholic who commanded the 16th Irish Division, 'has decided that the English lads need some help, so he's sent a brigade to help out.' There was a cheer. 'Sadly it's not us, chaps, but rest assured we'll get our chance soon enough.' More cheers. 'So in the meantime, make the most of it and get some rest!' He climbed down from the wagon, turning to Major Stirke, who was still the second in command. 'Henry, there will be work parties for sure and I want everyone bombed up by four pip-emma.' He meant 4 p.m. There would be little rest.

'Best to keep the lads busy, sir. Stops them thinking too much, even if they grumble about it,' replied Stirke, who didn't seem to resent calling a man half his age 'sir'; after all, he was only a lieutenant himself, winkled from retirement despite his white hair and the major's crowns on his cuffs.

'We both know Thomas Atkins Esquire loves to grumble, Henry. It's when he stops moaning we're in real trouble, eh?' replied the colonel, raising a laugh from the gathered officers.

'Look at the la-di-da bastards,' muttered Fallon, wondering what the officers were finding so funny. 'Bloody Ruperts are probably laughing at us.' Clee was staring at him, moustache bristling. He decided to shut up, knowing it was best not to give the sergeant major any rope to hang him.

Then the RSM cracked out a bone-jarring salute which the CO returned with a vague wave somewhere in the vicinity of his helmet brim. It was what the men expected. Officers weren't meant to be terribly soldierly. That didn't mean they didn't expect him to know what he was doing – after all, their lives were literally in his hands – but most soldiers liked their officers to be more than a little idiosyncratic. Thackeray's first platoon sergeant had taught him that, so he gave them what they wanted. So did the RSM when he unleashed the full fury of his lungs. It was as if the army was one great big lethal pantomime, each with his part to play.

'I don't know what bloody dictionary the army used to look up the word "rest",' complained Collins as he and Fallon collected heavy wooden boxes of Mills bombs. Around them NCOs were organizing fatigue parties.

'Same one they used to look up "sense of fecking humour",' replied Fallon. 'So I'd take my time if I were you, lugging this lot, cos if we finish too soon they'll just give us another shitty little job to do.' He was right, of course, it was the army's way; and no sooner had they finished than they were put to work doing something else, then something else again, until evening stole unnoticed out of the east. Then it was time to move.

'I'm too old for this shite,' grumbled Fallon as they stumbled towards the fiery horizon through the ankle-twisting debris of Trones Wood. Splintered tree trunks jabbed accusingly at the sky, broken and blasted by weeks of battle. The air was so thick with the stench of battle – spent ammunition and spent lives – that even the torrential downpour couldn't dilute it. Fallon wasn't sure he'd ever be able to face kippers again. He'd seen action out in India; not much but nothing like this. This was beyond his wildest nightmares, beyond all their nightmares, making his mind ache. His joints ached too and he'd already 'lost' some of the trench stores they'd piled on him when they'd set out for the front.

'Shut up and keep moving,' Devlin hissed, using his duties to divert his thoughts from the freezing rain and shells coming down around them. Fallon scowled from the shadows of his helmet. He disliked Devlin almost as much as Flynn, with his harsh northern accent, but he didn't dwell on it. There were other things playing on his mind as they crossed the moonscape of flares and fire into the trenches on the other side of the wood. He'd overheard Kettle call it Sherwood Trench. The rest of the battalion was nearby in Fagan and Dummy Trench. The British liked naming their trenches; it brought a sort of suburban banality to the madness. The British seemed to like suburban banality.

'So, Martin, where's this blessed village we're meant to take?' asked Collins. He was scratching his head, peering over the parapet towards the German lines. Fallon scrambled up beside him, curious to see what was there. It was morbid curiosity, nothing more, nothing less, that made him squint into the blood-red dawn. Smoke and flashes swirled ominously in the distance, masking the ruins of Guillemont and Ginchy beyond as the air above laboured and parted beneath the weight of shells like tearing canvas. Fallon could feel the heat on his face, like looking into an oven when it's on full heat. Tracer arced overhead, adding to the carnage; overwhelming his senses; overpowering his ears. Something balled in his stomach, something hard and small, but he felt it grow, like a cancer, until it threatened to consume him. His mouth was dry, suddenly desiccated, then he started to laugh; a short, dry cackle subsumed by the guns. He felt like crying.

'What's so fecking funny?' asked Collins.

'What's so fecking funny? Holy Mary mother of God, I'll tell you what's so fecking funny! This is, that's what. Cos I'm telling you, Aiden, my old mucker, if the Brass wants us to go there,' he jabbed a bony, nicotine-stained finger in the direction of the two shattered villages, 'we really shouldn't be starting from here!'

CHAPTER 25

Saturday 9 September 1916, Ginchy, the Somme

Guillemont was a shambles in every sense of the word. The place was full of enemy dead. The Germans had not let go easily; instead they'd been prised from the ruins one bloody finger at a time. It had been a winnowing, leaving over thirty-nine fusiliers dead and as many wounded, despite the fact that it was the 6th Connaught Rangers, not the 9th Dublin Fusiliers, who'd borne the brunt of the fighting. Instead the Dubliners had occupied a wood in support of the Rangers before pulling back once more to the relative safety of Fagan and Sherwood Trenches.

Their company commander, Captain Callear, was down, hit by a shell, leaving Kettle in charge. Flynn didn't envy him. It was a lot of responsibility and so far nothing had made him regret turning down General Dempsey's offer of a commission. It was bad enough being a sergeant. To make matters worse, the colonel was down too, caught in a sunken lane near Trones Wood. He'd been giving his orders. Stirke, the adjutant and

Captain Good, along with a slack handful of other officers, had been hit too. It was a mess. Captain Murphy was in charge now and as he sat in the dugout listening to the captain issue his final instructions for the attack, Flynn did his best to blot out the banshee cries of shells outside.

He'd been shelled before, they all had, but not like this. Nothing could have prepared him for the anguished keening steel rending the air as if all the tormented souls in the underworld had been unleashed from the homicidal abyss opening its maw outside. Spud whimpered, cowering beneath a flea-bitten old bunk in the corner of the foetid, muggy dugout, unable to make sense of it. All around him scruffy, careworn NCOs slumped together behind a nicotine smoke-screen, listening just a little too intently to Murphy's warbling.

'Bloody long-range snipers are dropping short again,' muttered Devlin as the dugout trembled beneath an ill-aimed British shell. Several men coughed, clearing their lungs of the dust cascading from the rafters like dandruff. Flynn shrugged, filling his lungs with Woodbine smoke. Popular wisdom had it that chain-smoking neutralized the effects of gas, so ever since Hulluch Flynn smoked far too much. Ever since Gallagher's death he drank too much. He wasn't alone. There was a nip of rum in the air over the fug of tobacco. He fiddled with the hessian-covered tin hat he'd been issued. None of them wore them, not in the dugout. There was no point: if the roof came in a steel helmet wouldn't help. The ground shuddered again, the shock wave rumbling up through the soles of his hobnail boots.

It wasn't that Flynn wasn't scared; only a fool or a lunatic didn't feel fear. It was just he couldn't be bothered, it was too much effort, and wasting effort was pointless. Everything he valued was gone. It was as if he had nothing left to lose and if Gallagher's death had set him on the path to that realization, Mary's letter had been the epiphany. It had sealed the deal. It made no difference whether you were good or bad, cruel or kind. Death didn't care and if it sought you out there was nothing you could do about it, absolutely nothing. The sad truth was that shit happened; that was that. Nothing more, nothing less, and the sooner you accepted it the better.

He sat back, staring down at his helmet, feeling detached, lightheaded even, as the rumble of the guns reduced Murphy's voice to an annoying buzz in the background. It all felt like it was happening to someone else, as if he was some sort of voyeur vicariously eavesdropping on someone else's nightmare. Unthinking, his hand delved into his pocket, grazing the edge of the envelope. It had been an unexpected letter and his skin tingled as his finger probed inside. It was from Louise Dempsey, crafted in neat copperplate that made Mary's looping scrawl look childishly illiterate. He still found it hard to think of her as Dempsey, his mind defaulting to Cronin. But Cronin was gone, like Doyle, like the Duke, like Gallagher, consigned to oblivion. Instead there was Louise Dempsey, the general's daughter, and despite the shared intimacy of military life, the shared intimacy of war, she was a stranger to him. She'd written to apologize for her father's boorish behaviour. She said she missed the battalion but Flynn wasn't sure she'd recognize it any more – so many had died. She said she was a nurse now, volunteering as soon as her leg had healed, and was back in France. She didn't say where – the censor's pencil would have put a stop to that anyway – but Flynn couldn't help thinking she would be some-where near the Irish Division. He didn't know why but he kept the letter, neatly folded and stowed in his pocket. He'd ditch it later.

'The attack will commence at four-forty-five pip-emma.' Murphy's words flèched through Flynn's thoughts, making him sit up. 'Mr Kettle will continue the briefing.' He saluted. The RSM shouted, 'Sit up!' and then the temporary CO departed. Flynn wasn't sure about Kettle. He was an unknown quan-tity, a Johnny-come-lately, whereas Callear had been with them from the start. He liked Callear, he was a good boss. Old Hackett said Kettle drank too much. He certainly didn't look well but Flynn refrained from judging. They all drank too much, alcohol's amnesia sheltering them from the storm.

'Bugger, we've got flaming ages yet,' Flynn muttered, glancing inconspicuously at his watch. It was a good watch with luminous hands, made in Switzerland. Closing his eyes, he could still feel the adrenalin buzz through his system at the memory of taking it, making him feel for a fleeting moment so alive, when most of the time he just felt empty; like a car running on fumes. He felt no remorse about killing its previous owner. Why should he? Besides, if he hadn't cut the watch's previous owner's life then right now some German somewhere would have been playing with some trinket stolen from Flynn's blood-soaked corpse.

'I do hope that I'm not boring you, Sergeant ... er ... Flynn?' asked Kettle.

Flynn opened his eyes, his face flushing pink, exaggerating the paleness of the scar tugging at the corner of his eye, feeling suddenly conscious that all eyes were on him as nervous chuckles ricocheted around the dugout. They meant no harm, his discomfort merely a momentary reprieve from the shadow of the gallows hanging ominously over them all. He shifted awkwardly, then someone farted, raising a ragged cheer, more laughter and a feeble chorus of 'Gas! Gas! Gas!' as well as ribald comments about needing to be 'pulled through', before Clee's disapproving gaze reduced them to reverent silence. 'Er ... hem ... as I was saying,' Kettle persisted. 'We've had a hard few days, I'm sure you'll agree, but we've got Jerry on the back foot at last–'

'Excuse me, sir,' interrupted a young soldier who stamped rigidly to attention in the doorway. It was Kettle's servant, Private Rob Bingham, whose relatively clean uniform and Belfast accent marked him out as an outsider. He looked terrified. He held a note. Devlin reached over, relieving him of it before handing it to Kettle.

'Thank you, Bingham,' said Kettle. The boy saluted again, then darted away, leaving Kettle to skim the note, frowning intently as he read.

'Is something the matter, sir?' asked Clee.

'I'm afraid it's bad news. Captain Good is dead,' replied Kettle, his voice almost a whisper. Flynn couldn't hear Clee's reply; it was drowned by the thunder of shells. He was glad he was underground, safe from the bombardment. He remembered when they passed through Guillemont he'd come across a group of Guardsmen, tall and smart, sitting with their heads lolling as if asleep where they sat in a neat little row. But they were dead, torn from life by the blast of a shell without a scratch. He would never get used to the shells. Then he had a premonition, that Kettle wouldn't make it through the day, but he sloughed it off. It didn't do to dwell on such things.

'The RSM says the CO will be back with us soon, sir,' Clee informed them, puffing casually on his pipe, staying calm for appearances' sake. Sergeant majors were supposed to be calm. Kettle nodded, understanding the game.

'The RSM is absolutely right, Mr Clee. With luck the CO should be back with us in a few days so until then Captain Murphy has the ship, as they say in the navy,' Flynn had no idea why he'd brought the navy into it; the sea was miles away, 'and I'm sure you will be pleased to hear that Captain Callear is recovering nicely. They're sending him back to Blighty so you are going have to put up with me as your OC for the foreseeable future.' There was a ripple of gentle laughter, which Kettle indulged, awaiting its subsidence before pressing on. 'Major Stirke and Lieutenants Purden, Kirk and Lee are also being sent home to recover from their injuries.'

'Jammy beggars,' came a voice from the fug, whipping up a second volley of laughs. Clee looked up from his notepad, clenching his pipe-stem in a thin-lipped frown as he cast his eye over the gathering in an overly theatrical show of disapproval. They expected nothing less.

Let them laugh, Kettle thought. He felt like a charlatan, an outsider. His men had already been through so much together, so much without him. People called the Royal Dublin Fusiliers 'the Old Toughs', but he preferred their other nickname, 'the Lambs'. It summed up their gentle stoicism, that soldierly fatalism glinting in their hollow, prematurely aged eyes. Something squirmed inside and he struggled to stay calm, terrified that he was out of his depth, leading his lambs to the slaughter. It was a shadow clouding his mind. Only last night he'd written a poem for his young daughter; it felt like a goodbye. The army had offered him a way out: a staff job or even sick leave. He was too well known to be left to die in the trenches – it would look bad in the papers – but he'd refused. Such an expedient would have only made him feel even more of a fraud, even more undeserving of the lieutenant's pips sewn to his cuffs.

'We shall be supporting 7th Royal Irish Rifles on the left flank of the attack,' he continued, slapping a map on the dugout wall with his blackthorn cane. 'Once they have secured Ginchy it will be our job to pass through their positions and take the ground on the far side. Jerry has dug in deep but Intelligence thinks we may not have to face too stiff resistance.' There was a ripple of forced laughter as men tried just a bit too hard to grasp at something funny. 'A Company will naturally be on the right flank. We'll be on their left with C Company on our left. We go in on a platoon frontage.' NCOs scribbled copious notes. They were being given much more information than was usual but then they were painfully short of officers. 'With luck the Gun Bunnies will keep Fritz's head down until we are right on top of them,' more laughter; they were infantrymen sharing an infantryman's lack of regard for the artillery, 'securing our objectives, here, here and here, by five-twenty-five pip-emma.'

'Wouldn't it have been better to hop the bags earlier this morning, sir?' asked Devlin, using the soldier's expression for going over the top. Kettle smiled. It was one of those professionally reassuring smiles of a barrister turned politician. Devlin didn't like it. He wasn't a subtle man.

'That is exactly what Jerry would have been expecting. If we'd gone over at dawn we'd have had the sun in our eyes, and besides, the lads would've been tired and hungry after spending all night getting ready. This way we're fresh and,' a salvo of shells screamed low overhead, 'it's Jerry who's been up half the night in a funk over what the hell's going on.' Devlin nodded, satisfied with the answer. 'Now, I'm not going to

333

patronize you chaps. Brigade seems to think we are up against Bavarians in Ginchy.'

'Aren't they the bastards who did for yer man Doyle?' Devlin asked Flynn quietly. Flynn nodded, keeping his eyes on Kettle, who was still speaking.

'They seem to think that they won't put up too much of a fight, not like the Hun over in Guillemont ... Prussians, I think. But you know as well as I do how much the enemy likes to counter-attack, so keep your wits about you. Now, I've no doubt you chaps will give the Boche a bloody nose and once we're all snug for the night the CQMS will bring up some hot scoff.'

Mahon made a scribbled note. It would be a bugger of a job getting enough Dixies of stew across no-man's-land in the dark but he'd make it happen somehow. They all knew he would.

'Oh, and make sure that the lads get a tot of rum before kick-off,' added Kettle, prompting a flurry of crooked grins and muffled cheers. Flynn licked his lips, anticipating the fiery communion of army rum. 'Of course, I will go over with the lead platoon,' added Kettle, feeling a little vainglorious as he surreptitiously ran his hand over the contours of the flask full of Jameson's in his tunic pocket.

'Which platoon will go first?' asked Clee.

'I want Sergeant Devlin's platoon to open the ball,' replied Kettle.

'Aye, sir,' answered Devlin emotionlessly as he ruffled Spud's greasy, black and tan fur.

'Sergeant Flynn. I want your platoon to go next. Keep forty yards back.' Flynn nodded. There was nothing else to say or do. What would be the point anyway?

'Where do you want me, sir?' asked Clee.

'The CO needs a safe pair of hands in the forward trench so I want you there to feed in reinforcements and take care of casualties,' answered Kettle, thrusting his hands deep into his tunic pockets, massaging the hip flask like some sort of sacred talisman. Clee harrumphed quietly, obviously unimpressed with his assignment. 'Well, gentlemen, I think that that is about it, so I would like to wish you all good luck and God bless. This is it, what we've all been waiting for. Today we shall write yet another glorious chapter in our country's history. Remember, today we fight for neither king nor empire but for Ireland and our regiment's motto – *Spectemur agendo* – let us be judged by our actions! All Ireland's eyes are on us as we speak; Ireland's and England's too! Believe me, chaps, after today no one will be able to doubt the justice of our cause or deny us Home Rule! After today we *will* be a nation once again!'

'No pressure, then,' Flynn whispered, loud enough for those around him to hear, raising a muffled chorus of sniggers. Kettle paused, glancing up momentarily before dismissing them.

The cold light stung Flynn's eyes as he blinked his way from the dugout into the relatively fresh air of the stinking, over-crowded trench. Pendulously swollen rain-drops lashed down around them, a brief distraction from the chuntering shells.

'*Lacrimae mundi*,' muttered Flynn, turning up his collar.

'I didn't know you could speak Irish,' said Devlin, giving his friend a curious look.

'I don't,' replied Flynn.

'It's Latin,' said a disembodied voice. It was Father Doyle, the kindly, middle-aged Jesuit attached to their battalion. 'It means "the tears of the world". I didn't know you were a classical scholar, Sergeant ... er ... Flynn?' It was uncanny how he knew their names.

'Shouldn't ye be back at Brigade? It's far too dangerous for ye here, Father,' said Devlin, ignoring the priest's attempt at conversation.

The Jesuit spared them a warm, mildly reproving smile.

'And where else should I be at a time like this than with my flock? he asked quietly. Devlin nodded, feeling suddenly guilty for questioning the priest's presence. It wasn't as if Father Doyle was a stranger to the trenches. Unlike the Anglican padres, who'd been ordered to stay away from the front line by the chaplain-general, Father Doyle made

336

it his business to share his parishioners' ordeals. That's why the boys liked him. Even the divisional commander, General Hickie, had a soft spot for the man. 'Would either of you like me to hear your confession?' he asked. It was Flynn's turn to look uncomfortable, deliberately avoiding the Jesuit's gaze. He wasn't much of a Catholic.

'Maybe later, Father. Me and Sergeant Flynn here, we've work to do,' said Devlin, coming to the rescue. The priest made the sign of the cross, muttering a blessing. Instinctively Devlin genuflected. Flynn didn't, but only just.

'Yes, maybe later,' replied the priest before sloshing away.

'Yer man there's gonna get himself killed one day,' observed Devlin with what sounded like genuine concern. He had a soft spot for the padre which Flynn put down to the taciturn Ulsterman's northern roots; as if he was somehow compensating for growing up in Ireland's Protestant heartland.

'I didn't know you were religious,' said Flynn.

'I'm not, but where's the harm in covering your arse, eh? Ye don't find many atheists in the trenches unless ye count them Prods, of course!' Devlin replied with a wink and a lopsided grin. Then the mask dropped, the smile gone. He looked old. He held out his hand. 'Good luck, Kevin. See you on the other side.'

Flynn took his friend's hand, gripping it firmly in a wordless embrace, and as their eyes met he thought he could see the fear flicking in their depths. They knew they were gazing into the abyss. There was nothing to say; nothing.

'Hey, fellas, what's happening?' asked Fitzpatrick, breaking the spell.

'Haven't ye got anything to be getting along with instead of standing there prattling, Corporal?' rasped Devlin, snapping the mask back into place. 'Now, will you leave Sergeant Flynn here in peace to do his job? There's a lot to do.'

Devlin was right: thankfully there was much to do, which made sure that Flynn, that all of them, had no time to dwell on what was to come; to divert their attention from the deafening drumfire mauling the German lines. Men cleaned weapons; some slept. Most just stared blankly into space, chain-smoking away the time. Here and there someone scribbled a last, brief note. Flynn had no one to write to; not now. He thought about writing to Dempsey but to write what? *'Dear Louise, Just a short note to say we're about to pop over to the German lines. Wish you were here. Regards, Kevin.'* He thought better of it. Maybe later. He tried reading but the words became meaningless squiggles on the page. He gave up. Nearby,

Carolan sat petting Spud, feeding him fragments of hard-tack biscuit smeared in Marmite. He offered Flynn a piece. He took it, chewing methodically as he smoked.

'Them things'll kill you, Sarge,' joked Carolan, puffing on his own 'coffin nail'. Flynn ignored him, his mind churning around other things. Making it to old age was the least of his worries.

'Hey, Private Keegan, can you spare a grenade?' he asked as a teenage bomber carrying two sandbags of grenades tried to squeeze past. The lad stopped, then rummaged through one of the sacks like a child rifling his stocking on Christmas morning, before plucking out one of his precious bombs.

'There you are, Sarge.' Keegan's voice betrayed his humble, north-side origins as he handed Flynn a grenade. 'You be careful now, Sarge, them's tricky little bastards if you don't know what you're about.' Flynn carefully placed the bomb in his tunic pocket. It might come in handy.

Around three o'clock Mahon arrived to dish out tablespoons of rum from brown stone jars marked SRD. Someone once told him it stood for 'Special Reserve Depot' but given the jar's contents most believed it meant 'Seldom Reaches Destination'. He liked army rum. To be honest, right now he'd've liked anything with a kick to it and he savoured the thick, cheek-tingling distillation as he sluiced it around his mouth. Then he noticed a group of stretcher-bearers fussing over their equipment. They would follow the attack; clear up the mess. One of them, a corporal with the ribbon of the Distinguished Conduct Medal on his tunic, looked vaguely familiar.

'Good God, is that you, Rory?' asked Flynn.

'Holy Mary mother of God, if it's not Kevin Flynn!' Rory beamed, looking up from the haversack he was rummaging through.

'What are you doing here?' said Flynn.

'And there was me thinking it pretty obvious,' quipped Rory. 'It's a long story but the short of it is the medics took me. I was with the Orangies up at Thiepval until I managed to persuade them to send me to a proper Irish division,' he replied with a cheeky grin.

'Have you heard from Mary?' asked Flynn. He didn't know why, it just came out.

'Not since she took up with that fella in Dublin. If it's any consolation, my parents weren't happy when she ditched you. In fact, they chucked her out, said she was a disgrace. They'll come around, I'm sure, as soon as they find out where she's run off to. I'm not sure where she is now but the folks are worried sick about her. Things haven't been good at home since Terry and all...' His voice faded. Flynn placed his hand on Rory's arm.

'How's your brother Mickey?' Flynn asked, changing the subject.

'Strangest thing – some woman called Dempsey got him a job in Limerick so he took the family with him. They're doing fine. Ma wasn't impressed with him traipsing off to the other side of the country but beggars can't be choosers, eh? After all, there's not a lot of call for cripples back home.'

'There'll be plenty of them when this is over,' observed Flynn wearily.

'Over? It'll not end here. That business last Easter was just the beginning. Ireland's changed since you left. Christ, Kevin, it's a right mess back home–'

'Hey, looks like something's happening,' interrupted Carolan, just as Kettle emerged from his dugout fiddling with the holstered pistol on his hip. Flynn glanced at his watch. Four forty-three. It was almost time. Then there were whistles and cheers. Machine guns cackled. Stray rounds zipped menacingly overhead. Flynn shoved Carolan back to the fire step and as the shelling intensified they could hear bagpipes skirling, taking the Irish to war.

'That'll be the first wave,' observed Flynn beneath the weight of his helmet pressing down on his head, making it ache. He noticed Devlin further down the trench; smiling, reassuring his boys. Docherty was with him, dishing out ammunition and advice. Spud was flat on the fire step; ears back, eyes wide. Carolan gave him a biscuit. Kettle was talking to Clee, a study in nonchalance. Then the sergeant major swept his bayonet into the air. There was a pause; a terrible, intoxicatingly electric pause in the buzz of excitement.

'Com-PANY will fix BAY-o-nets!' Clee's words echoed along the trench. Flynn felt his flesh tingle. 'FIX BAYONETS!' The command echoed down the line. There was the merest hint of a pause, then a sea of blades flashed, rippling and waning in the sunlight like a silver wheatfield. Spent metal zipped harmlessly overhead. Heads buzzing with adrenalin turned to Kettle, eyes shining, drunk on fear and excitement. Flynn's mouth was dry, the memory of rum's sacrament gone. Carolan's hands were shaking, his bayonet wobbling erratically as he struggled to slide it home.

'There you go,' said Flynn as he clicked Carolan's bayonet into place.

'Christ, I don't know if I can do this,' Carolan quailed, red-eyed and pale.

'Sure you can, Joe. It won't be so bad once we're started,' Flynn lied.

'I should never have let Terry talk me into this shite,' muttered Carolan.

'You and me both,' replied Flynn, trying to make light of it all.

'No, I mean it, Kev. Lizzie said there'd be

hell to pay,' he grumbled. 'You know, I'd be coming back from work about now. She'd be in the kitchen sorting my tea. Maybe we'd have wee ones of our own by now if I wasn't here. Christ, Kev, she's too young to be a widow!' He looked like he was about to cry.

'There'll be plenty of time for that when we're done here,' replied Flynn.

'Who are you trying to kid, Kev? Our fellas have been trying to turf Jerry out of this place since July so what makes today so different, eh? Face it, Kev, we're not soldiers, not really. We're just a bunch of *eejits* who thought this ward be a *craic!*' Flynn shifted awkwardly, unsure what to say. 'If I don't make it–'

'Of course you'll make it,' interrupted Flynn.

'What? Like Terry or Mickey or the Duke? Like all the others, eh? Stop shitting me, this isn't some fecking game! Look, if I don't make it tell Lizzie that I loved her ... love her. Tell her I want her to get on with her life. She's too young to waste it moping over me. You'll tell her that for me, won't you, Kev?' pleaded Carolan.

'You can tell her yourself, Joe,' said Flynn but Carolan didn't look convinced as an awkward silence fell like a veil between the two men. Flynn looked away, wondering briefly who would miss him if he fell. It was a very short list. Carolan was right: most of

343

their friends were already dead. More would be dead before the day was out.

He noticed a piper squeezing himself through the cluttered trench, his bagpipes incongruously anachronistic amid the modern technology of war; a throwback to an earlier, maybe more heroic, age. Then the piper scrambled up onto the parapet, standing upright, ignoring the blast furnace as he filled the tortured air with strains of 'Let Erin Remember'.

A shiver passed down Flynn's spine, the hairs prickling on the back of his neck as the primordial intoxication of the Irishman's war-pipes swept like a flame along the ramshackle trench. Then Kettle mounted the parapet next to the piper and looked at his watch, pistol in hand, his blackthorn cane clamped under his arm. His whistle hovered near his lips like a referee waiting to call full-time.

'Hail Mary, full of grace...' muttered the young bomber, Paddy Keegan, as he fumbled through the stations of a worn old rosary, a parting gift from his mother. Carolan crossed himself, eyes blurred with tears, and for a brief moment Flynn felt like praying too, the words rising subconsciously in his throat. Devlin was right: there were no atheists in the trenches. '... be with me now and at the hour of our death, Amen.'

'This is it,' muttered Flynn.

All around him men strained like rabid dogs on a short leash. Nearby he could see Devlin reassuring his men; calm before the storm. Fitzpatrick looked miles away, staring blankly into the distance, then he saw Fallon's pinched features poking through the crowd. He needed a leak. Men were peeing against the back of the trench. Flynn joined them, quickly emptying his bladder.

'Do you have to?' someone asked.

'It's not like we'll be coming back,' quipped someone else just as Spud began yapping around Carolan's ankles, sensing his master's distress. Flynn got back to the parapet. Kettle's whistle blew – a shrill knell rolling along the line. Then there was a pause – a fraction of a second at most – before the dam burst, sending cheering Dubliners swarming over the top.

'Come on, the Dubs!' bellowed Kettle, brandishing his revolver. Devlin was with him, pale as death, keen bayonet flashing.

Flynn scrambled up for a better view, hot air washing over him from the German lines. Somehow Spud had managed to get up next to him. His guts churned as he watched Devlin's platoon vanish, engulfed in a shroud of smoke and flame, lost in the chaos. He gripped his rifle, white-knuckle tight to control the trembling that fear and adrenalin had unleashed. Someone vomited.

'All right, it's time to go, fellas,' he called

calmly. 'Just stick with me and watch your spacings!'

'Jaysus, Kev, I can't do it!' cried Carolan, burying his head in the parapet.

'They'll shoot you if you don't,' replied Flynn, holding out his hand. Carolan looked up, crying.

'I'm scared,' he replied. Sergeant Major Clee placed his hand on Carolan's shoulder.

'We're all scared, Joe. Now, up you get,' he said quietly, helping Flynn pull Carolan up over the parapet. Then the sergeant major scrambled up to join them.

'I thought Mr Kettle wanted you to stay here?' said Flynn.

'Like that was ever going to happen, Sergeant Flynn,' replied Clee with a wry grin.

CHAPTER 26

Saturday 9 September 1916, Ginchy, the Somme

The attack had been a nightmare, a bloody shambles as they pushed on to the outskirts of Ginchy. Tortured by shellfire and fought over since July, the town was little more than a name on a map: a shattered pile of bricks easily missed. Disorientated, Flynn staggered along, rapidly losing any sense of time or direction. He had no idea where Clee was: last seen leading a party of men, hunched as they pushed into the teeth of the storm. He had no idea what had happened to Fitzpatrick but he remembered seeing Carolan go down, wounded by a shell fragment as they reached the edge of the village. He could still hear him crying 'Don't leave me!' but he'd had to. Orders were orders and, besides, Carolan's wound didn't look too bad. A blighty, that's all. He left him for the stretcher-bearers. At least Spud had stayed with him, nuzzling his wounds so he wasn't alone. Anyway, Flynn had enough worries of his own.

By the time he'd found shelter in a large, flooded shell hole, he was sure he had pissed himself. It was hard to tell. Not that he cared; not that anyone huddled in the crater cared. They were all more concerned by the fragments of steel scything through the air above them. For some reason the words of the 'Hail Mary' barged themselves to the front of Flynn's mind and out of his mouth as if he no longer controlled it. Several others joined in, looking to him like frightened children for some sort of lead. He was sweating and despite the proximity of so much water his mouth was bitter and dry, accentuating his raging thirst.

The ground trembled, deafening blasts

drowning their prayers and curses. Someone was sobbing, dark blood oozing through
grimy fingers clutched at a shattered face.
Bullets crackled overhead, spitefully hurled
from a German machine gun that had them
well and truly trapped. He was shaking as
fear and adrenalin pulsed through him, the
world speeding up and in slow motion at the
same time. Keegan was there, looking painfully young.

'What now, Sarge?' he asked Flynn, eyes
pleading, making him suddenly feel old,
bone-weary old, as he sat forcing down gulps
of rancid air, desperate to steady his nerves.
They were looking to him to take charge.
That's what sergeants did. He wished that
Devlin was there instead of him. Devlin
would have known what to do. Then he got a
grip.

'Right, lads!' shouted Flynn. 'If we stay
here, we are as good as dead. When I say, we
move – clear?' He sloshed across the viscous
pool and slithered up the side of the crater.
He peeked over. 'Shit!' Hot air kissed his
cheek as a bullet brushed past and he
tumbled back, all arms and legs, noisily, into
the filth. Slumping against the crater's side,
he fought to stop his hands shaking, gripping
his rifle until his knuckles bulged white.

'You all right, Sarge?' asked Keegan.
Flynn looked up, grinning sheepishly at the
lad, who looked scared, and at that moment

Flynn cursed the stripes that squatted mockingly on his sleeves, building up everyone's expectations except his own. They were all teetering on the precipice of fear; nerves brittle, stretched taut. He knew they would panic soon and strangely the thought calmed him, giving him purpose. They wanted – no, needed – him to tell them what to do. It was down to him.

'Right, lads, listen in,' he said, affecting his best sergeant's voice, clear, calm, in control – play-acting. 'Fritz's got a machine gun about a hundred yards up on the left. If we move right, it looks like there is a trench about thirty to forty feet away. If we can get into it then we're home and dry. You, Corporal,' he pointed at a burly lance corporal opposite him, 'I want you to give covering fire. Then, when I shout; you follow. Clear?' The lance corporal nodded, sloshing thigh-deep across through the slime into a fire position.

'So, fellas, when I say move you lot go like hell and don't stop until you reach the trench and if you find any Jerries in it when we get there then give 'em what for, clear?' barked Flynn. 'Just remember your drills and you'll be all right.' He couldn't believe he was spouting the same old claptrap he'd heard back in training; unsure who he was trying to reassure, them or him. He tried ignoring the frightened eyes boring into him but couldn't. 'PRE-pare to move!' The lance corporal opened fire. 'MOVE!'

Flynn lunged forward, adrenalin tunnelling his vision as he dashed for the ruined parapet. There were bodies everywhere, tattered shreds of khaki. Thankfully he didn't have time to register faces, all too conscious of the lack of cover as he ran. Then he was down, cowering as best he could behind a thicket of rusting barbed-wire pickets, blazing away at the machine-gun nest, palming his rifle's bolt – sensing rather than seeing the others belt pell-mell past into the sanctuary of the trench. For a moment his eyes were drawn to the eviscerated remnants of a German nearby, his youthful face strangely calm in death.

'Move!' Flynn bellowed over his shoulder, seeing the man rise and sprint forward as he covered him. He let him pass, snapped off a few more shots before charging after him to plunge feet-first into the trench. Landing heavily, his boot skidded, sending him crashing onto his backside. He looked down. There was something pale and rubbery clinging to the sole of his muddy boot, something strangely familiar, and for a moment it didn't quite register what it was. Then he grimaced, shaking the tattered shreds of someone's face from his foot. He took a deep breath. The air stank, a sickly cocktail of cordite and God knows what. Keegan vomited, smiling sheepishly as he wiped his mouth on his sleeve. Flynn was glad he'd made it; so had the big lance corporal and three others. The rest were gone. 'Right, follow me!' said Flynn as he stood up. There was no point hanging about. They needed to find the others and he needed to find someone else to take charge; someone to take away the responsibility.

They passed a dead German, his face sallow and grey, eyes staring, vaguely surprised. A briar pipe smouldered in one hand and a mug of coffee steamed in the other, tugging at Flynn's taste buds. The top of the man's head swarmed with flies where something had sheared away the top of his skull, his leaking brains reminding Flynn unnervingly of an underdone boiled egg. Keegan posted a grenade into a nearby bunker doorway, the dull crumps urging them to move on. Heavy footfalls taunted them from around the next bend, and the next; always just out of sight. 'To thee do we send up our sights, mourning and weeping in the valley of tears,' muttered Flynn, recalling yet another long-forgotten prayer from his Catholic childhood. It amazed him how much he remembered.

Then he skidded to a halt, convinced he heard voices just around the next corner. Keegan thudded into his back. He grunted. The voices stopped. Keegan handed him a grenade; his last. He could hear people whispering, moving cautiously. They were looking to him, his pathetically small band – for all he knew, the last of the 9th Battalion, the last of the brigade; or even the division, for that matter. They expected him to go first. He loosened the pin, gripping the spoon tight. The last thing he wanted was to kill himself fumbling the grenade. He slipped forward, the bomb heavy in his fist. Sweat trickled into his eyes, stinging them as the sound of his heartbeat blotted out everything as he willed himself forward. Pressing the bomb to his chest, he crouched, taking a quick peek. BANG! A bullet gouged into the woodwork near his head. He ducked back, unsure whether he was alive or dead as he yanked the pin half-free.

'Jesus Christ! We're British!' he shrieked loudly, carefully pushing the pin back into the grenade.

'Come out slowly if you don't want to get shot,' someone snapped, tersely.

'We're coming out. There are six of us. 9th Dubs! Don't shoot!' shouted Flynn as he approached the corner, forcing himself to at least look relaxed, raising his hands as he stepped into the open. A saucer-eyed youth squatted on the duckboards, holding a smoking rifle. The muzzle lowered, fear easing its grip on the boy's mind. Flynn could see others huddled behind him, making the most of what cover there was. A surge of relief washed over him. One of them was an officer, a very young officer but an officer none the less, and as he lowered his hands he could feel the weight of responsibility slip from his shoulders like a discarded pack.

'It's good to see you, Sar'nt. Whoever you are,' said the officer calmly, in an accent that sounded very similar to Flynn's: middle-class Dublin. 'We could use your help.' The officer paused, awaiting a response, but Flynn's attention was fixed on the corpse at the officer's feet. 'Do you know him, Sar'nt?'

'Knew him, sir,' Flynn corrected, instantly regretting his brusque tone. 'It's Mr Kettle, sir. My company commander, or at least he was. B Company.'

'I know,' sighed the officer, dropping his guard momentarily, raking his fingers through his grubby blond hair before plonking his helmet back on his head. 'He was a friend of my father.' Then the officer held out his hand. 'Lieutenant Dalton. Acting OC, C Company. I guess I'm OC B as well now,' he added as they grasped hands. Then a shell burst uncomfortably close by, sending them both sprawling in the muck beneath a hail of chalky debris. Flynn cursed. Dalton grinned boyishly. Then the shooting started. 'You lot, hold your position here! We'll be back in a minute!' screamed Dalton over the din. 'Sar'nt. You come with me!'

Then he was off, dashing down an old communication trench which emerged in the middle of what had once been one of Ginchy's streets. Flynn followed him and together they took cover behind a low, broken wall whilst Dalton did his best to locate the enemy. 'That way!' he said as they leapt up and ran through a deluge of bullets that crackled by from all directions. Then they were down once more, sprawled behind another shattered wall. Flynn was about to speak but Dalton hushed him, looking bizarrely childlike in the circumstances with his finger to his lips. Then the officer pointed, open-palmed. Flynn slithered forward. He could see Germans mere yards ahead, a nervous undulation of coal-scuttle helmets cresting a nearby shell hole. Flynn could see what looked like an officer barking commands.

'On my word, we attack,' whispered Dalton, pulling out a grenade. He was grinning. It was madness, sheer bloody madness, but Flynn couldn't help grinning too. Then Dalton threw the grenade and they attacked, screaming like madmen. Stunned, the Germans' resolve crumbled, leaving Flynn, ears ringing, at the crater's edge, threatening the huddled mass with bloody bayonet and loaded rifle as they pleaded wretchedly for their lives. Dalton pointed his pistol at the officer, who meekly unbuckled his gun belt, letting it drop at Flynn's feet. Blood poured from a face wound but he ignored it, raising his hands. Flynn squatted down, picking up the belt without taking eye or aim off the officer, and tossed it over to Dalton. 'A keep-sake for my little brother,' said Dalton, slipping the German's Luger automatic pistol into his pocket.

'Best be getting them back, sir. Before they work out there's just the two of us,' prompted Flynn. Dalton nodded. 'C'mon, Jerry, let's go,' Flynn said to the German officer, gesturing with his bayonet just to make sure he understood.

'Soldaten, hande hoch! Raus! Raus! Schnell! Mitt me kommen! Raus!' Dalton ordered in poor, schoolboy German. For a moment they hesitated, then, much to Flynn's relief, they obeyed, allowing themselves to be herded like sheep back towards the British lines. He couldn't help noticing that most of them looked happy to be prisoners, relieved to be out of the fight, and for the first time it dawned on him that the last few months must have been as much of a nightmare for the Germans as it was for them. Soon they could see familiar soup-plate helmets poking over the tops of the trenches. Someone fired. 'Cease firing, you bloody idiots!' shouted Dalton, waving his arms. Thankfully, the shooting stopped even if the shelling didn't.

'We bagged twenty-one of the little buggers by my reckoning, sir,' Flynn informed Dalton when they'd finished handing the prisoners over to the lance corporal, who seemed quite

355

happy to escort them to the rear. He was conscious that his hands were shaking so he balled his fists, hoping that no one would notice. Then he saw that Dalton was shaking too, making a mess of feeding fresh rounds into his revolver. Their eyes met, both grinning like mischievous schoolboys who'd just got away with doing something unfeasibly stupid, and they started to laugh. Dalton grimaced, clutching his side. He was bleeding. 'Stretcher-bearers! Mr Dalton's been hit! Stretcher-bearers!' shouted Flynn, feeling suddenly very old and tired again.

'Don't worry, it's nothing,' insisted Dalton, putting on a brave front as he fended off a medic who was trying to manhandle him onto a stretcher. 'What's your name, Sergeant?' he asked.

'Sergeant Flynn, sir. Kevin Flynn.'

'Well, Sergeant Flynn, it looks like you're in charge now,' he said before letting the medics carry him away, leaving Flynn to slump on the fire step under the dead weight of renewed responsibility. He lit a cheap, ration-pack gasper, wondering for a moment what had become of Devlin; better still Clee. 'Bugger!' he spat, hoofing an old tin can across the trench. 'Why can't you find a bloody sergeant major when you need one?' A shadow passed over him, disturbing his thoughts.

'What now, Sarge?' asked Keegan. Flynn flicked away the half-smoked dog-end and picked up his rifle, looking around.

'What do you think? We press on, of course. The rest of the battalion have got to be somewhere around here, so let's go find them.' Then he walked off, praying the others would follow. He didn't look back but somehow he knew they would.

CHAPTER 27

Saturday 9 September 1916, Ginchy, the Somme

'Sarge! Sarge! Are you all right?' shouted Keegan, his voice distant and dreamlike somewhere in the back of Flynn's mind, dragging him back from the abyss. The sound of machine-gun fire wrenched him back to consciousness. He couldn't really remember what had happened but Ginchy was behind them. His neck was sore, his nose and mouth full of blood. He was sure one of his teeth was loose. He opened his eyes. There were bodies everywhere. Then it came back. He'd found the company. They'd been advancing, renewing the attack. Then all hell had broken loose. Something moved, catching his attention. It was Keegan waving from a shell hole nearby. He looked terrified.

Who could blame him? A stream of fluorescent green tracer buzzed overhead, cleaving the thinning daylight. It would be dark soon.

'For Christ's sake, will you shut up? Do you want to get me shot?' snapped Flynn as more tracer zipped overhead. He pushed his face into the wet, chalky soil, eking out every scrap of cover from the shredded, limbless torso that lay in front of him. 'On the count of three give me some covering fire,' ordered Flynn. 'One! Two! Thr–'

'Sarge, I'm out of fecking ammo!' Keegan called out apologetically as another burst of tracer ambled lazily by.

Flynn froze in disbelief.

'Is there anyone else in there with you?' he asked, feeling rather awkward trying to sustain a conversation in the circumstances. Keegan nodded. 'Well?' The boy looked puzzled. 'Do they have any bloody ammo?' Flynn snapped angrily. Keegan's head disappeared as if dodging Flynn's words just as several more rounds churned up the ground, groping to find him, then he reappeared.

'Quick, Sarge, move!' Keegan shouted, waving his arms just as someone started firing, keeping the Germans' heads down.

Flynn didn't need asking twice. He leapt to his feet, keeping low as possible as he belted for cover. Bullets tore up the ground around his feet, urging him on until he finally tumbled headlong into a thigh-deep pool of effluent next to Keegan, disturbing a headless corpse that bobbed languidly on its surface. The icy liquid seeped through his trousers as he lay panting for breath. Nearby, a lanky corporal lay face down in the mud, a filthy Red Cross haversack and a number of water bottles hanging from his slack, blood-soaked shoulders. 'He's copped it,' Keegan told him just as a fresh salvo of tracer clawed at the crater's rim.

'Blast! I've lost my bundook!' cursed Flynn, realizing that he'd left his rifle out in no-man's-land. He felt strangely naked without it; as vulnerable as Keegan looked. Then he noticed the rifleman who'd covered his escape slide down the side of the deep crater and slosh over to join them. It was Fallon.

'So, what are *you* going to do now?' Fallon sneered, making no attempt to hide the malice in his voice. 'I could have been a sergeant by now if it wasn't for you and your friends. Instead, I'm stuck here,' he added. There was a look in his eye, the same look Flynn had seen in it on the tube station all those months ago. Flynn chose to ignore him.

'Are they full?' asked Flynn, looking at the water bottles around the medic's neck. He was thirsty and his face hurt. Freeing one of the canteens, he lobbed it over to Keegan, who fielded it expertly. The boy drained it with one noisy gulp.

'Greedy little bastard!' snapped Fallon.

'Leave him alone. There's plenty more,' Flynn snapped, throwing a second canteen at Fallon, who caught it awkwardly, letting his rifle squelch into the muck. Without so much as a thank-you, he pulled the cork with his nicotine-stained teeth, keeping his cold, serpentine eyes on Flynn. He took a drink, gulping noisily before theatrically smacking his lips.

'Thirsty work, killing,' he finally announced but Flynn carried on ignoring him, reaching instead for a third water bottle. The medic stirred, groaning. Flynn rolled him over. It was Rory. One of his eyes was bruised, blackened and closed, his bloody cheek ripped open, exposing the chipped bone beneath. He'd been shot through the thighs too but the dark blood oozed: it wasn't an arterial bleed. Rory opened his eyes, forcing a weak smile.

'It's all right, Rory, we'll get you out of here,' said Flynn. 'Here, give us a hand,' he said as he rummaged through the haversack for some bandages.

'Why bother? He's finished anyway,' replied Fallon coldly as he started to reload his filthy rifle, pushing the bullets slowly, deliberately into the breech, keeping his eyes on Flynn.

'We're going to have to take out that machine gun if we're going to get him to a dressing station,' said Flynn, folding back the ragged flap of skin over Rory's broken cheek and dressing his wounds. By the time he'd finished, Rory's head reminded Flynn of a picture of an Egyptian mummy in one of his old history books.

'You're fecking joking, right? Take out the machine gun? Is that the best you can come up with?' Fallon barked incredulously as he snapped the bolt of his .303 closed. Keegan looked worried. He'd never heard anyone speak to a senior NCO like this before.

'Will you wind your bloody neck in, Fallon?' snapped Flynn before turning his back on him and crawling up the side of the crater to try and locate the machine-gun nest. Keegan joined him but Fallon stayed where he was, cradling his rifle. 'So, what have you got?' asked Flynn.

'This,' replied Keegan, lifting the bayoneted end of his rifle up to show Flynn.

'That's more than me. Hang on a minute,' said Flynn, remembering the grenade in his tunic pocket, the one Keegan had given him earlier. He pulled it out, holding it beneath his chest as he searched for the machine gun. Fallon couldn't hear what they were saying. He didn't care. They were barking mad if they thought he was going to get himself killed attacking a machine gun. 'Fallon, get your arse up here,' said Flynn, looking back at Fallon. He froze. 'What the hell do you think you are doing?' Fallon was aiming at them. Keegan turned his head. Fallon shot him, the bullet taking him between the shoulder blades, throwing him flat. Fallon fired again, the second round shattering Keegan's skull. 'What the fu–'

'And there I was, thinking this was going to be a shite day; but here we are, alone at last,' Fallon sneered as he re-cocked his weapon. 'Not so clever now, are you, Sergeant la-di-da fecking Flynn, without all your little mates around you, eh? I'm going to enjoy killing you. Now turn round and show me your hands. I want to see the light go out in your eyes when I shoot you.' Flynn rolled over, yanking the pin from the grenade.

'Shoot me and you're dead too.' He held up the grenade. Fallon hesitated, unsure what to do.

'Stay where you are,' he snapped as Flynn stepped closer, ignoring him.

'Not such the big man now, eh? Go on, shoot me!' demanded Flynn, past caring whether he lived or died.

'I said stay where you are!' replied Fallon. 'If you let that thing off you'll kill all of us all right, even this fella,' he added, flicking his head in Rory's direction. Flynn hesitated. Fallon smiled. 'Throw the grenade away.'

'You'll leave him to die anyway. At least this way it'll be quick,' Flynn replied calmly, stepping forward once more. He could see fear in Fallon's eyes.

Fallon took a step backwards, then another and another, hoping that if he could just put some distance between him and the bomb he might survive the blast. It was a long shot. He raised his rifle, aiming at Flynn's face, and flicked off the safety. The German machine gunner couldn't believe his luck. There was a shape, a head poking up from where the Tommies had fired at him. A squirt of lurid green tracer flayed the gloom, plunging onto the lip of the shell hole, mangling Fallon's flesh and bone – tearing the life from him as he tumbled back down.

Flynn threw himself flat, then lay staring, not quite able to grasp what had happened. He felt the grenade slip in his hand, greasy with filth. He threw it away to detonate harmlessly outside the crater, then he waded over to where Fallon lay and poked him with his boot, making sure he was dead. Then he picked up his rifle. It would come in useful. He took Keegan's pay book and one of his identity disks; he didn't bother with Fallon. There was no point searching the headless corpse.

'Stick with me, kid, and you'll be fine,' he told Rory as he cradled him gently in his arms like a baby. He would wait until dark before trying to get back; it would be safer that way.

Shells continued to fall all night and by the time Flynn had managed to carry Rory back to Ginchy, what was left of the battalion had gone, relieved in place by the Welsh Guards.

CHAPTER 28

Tuesday 12 September 1916, Corbie, the Somme

It was a subdued gathering beneath a sombre sky; the entire battalion, or at least what was left of it, waiting patiently for Father Doyle to begin the drumhead service, his vestments contrasting starkly with the gathered khaki. They'd piled the drums to make an altar and whilst it wasn't Sunday that didn't matter. They'd been in the line on Sunday and a week was too long to wait for what needed to be said. Even those Protestants amongst them were there, showing solidarity with their Catholic kin. It was the first church service that Flynn had attended through choice in years. It seemed right, somehow.

'*Dulce et decorum est,*' said the priest, his gentle voice frail from behind the drums. He looked worn down, a husk of the man he'd been, reliving his Calvary. They all were, a sea of pale faces trying to make sense of the last few days. Even the RSM seemed lost for words as the battalion came to terms – indeed if it ever would come to terms – with the carnage of the last few days. '"It is a sweet and fitting thing to die for your country," said the Roman poet Horace, but I feel his words do little justice to our recent loss of so many friends,' continued the priest. He had known them all, made it his business to know them, and whilst he knew all men were born to die, such loss still grieved him. How could it not? 'Ireland has paid a heavy price. We have all paid a heavy price...'

Murmurs of agreement rippled through the hollow-eyed ranks of the congregation and Flynn felt his clasped hands begin to tremble '...*there are few die well that die in battle...*' as memories of the butcher's bill flooded back. Devlin was missing – so was Spud, for that matter – but at least Docherty and Fitzpatrick had made it. He felt bad about Spud. Roll call had been a sorry affair of awkward silences, uneasy shuffling amongst thinned ranks, and even the double rum ration supplied by Mahon did little to numb the pain or deaden the shock. It had helped Flynn sleep though. Rum always helped him sleep.

'...but it is up to us to make sure that theirs was no mean and wasted sacrifice. It is up to us ... it is up to us...' The priest's voice faltered, then he seemed to regain himself. 'It is up to us to make sure that the people back home remember those who gave their lives

365

for Ireland's future...' Flynn began to sweat, his back clammy beneath his shirt. 'I'm minded of what St John said, that greater love hath no man that lays down his life for his friends...' They said the attack was a victory. It didn't feel like it to Flynn. Then, as the Jesuit began naming the dead, it started to rain.

'Captain William Murphy...' He'd liked the captain; they all had. '...Lieutenant Thomas Kettle...' Little more than a name. '...Second Lieutenants William Boyd, Ernest O'Kearney-White and Thomas Tyner...' It was a litany of sorrow; he'd never seen the RSM so shaken. '...CSM William Clee...' He could picture him still, spur jangling in City Hall, an Englishman amongst the Irish. '...Sergeants Patrick Elmur, Charles Mills, Edward Wall and Jack Wilson...' He'd drunk with them all in the sergeants' mess. '...Corporals Thomas Connell, Stephen Dooner, Joseph Fitzpatrick, John Maloney, Patrick Murphy, John Neary, Michael O'Driscoll, Ralf Read...'

Flynn's mind drifted and for some reason the words of the poem 'The Charge Of The Light Brigade' came to mind, making him smile. *Was there a man dismayed?'* He'd been scared witless. *'Not tho' the soldiers knew someone had blundered...'* He still felt guilty about Carolan; he shouldn't have left him. *'Theirs not to reason why, theirs but to do and die ... cannon to the right of them ... cannon to the left of them ... cannon in front of them ... volleyed and thundered...*' Too right, they had. '*Back from the mouth of Hell ... left of six hundred...*' It seemed appropriate somehow.

'What?' Fitzpatrick asked. Flynn hadn't realized he was speaking out loud.

'...Lance Corporals James Byrne, Joseph Corrigan, Michael Donnelly and James O'Neill; Privates James Boylan, Edward Brown, James Burke, Michael Byrne...' He'd heard Carolan was in hospital, that was something. '...Joseph Carter, John Connell, Dennis Curran, Michael Curran, John Delaney, Patrick Dempsey...' Any relation? he wondered. '...John Devlin...' He'd not bothered reporting Fallon's death. '...Christopher Fanning, Myles Flood, James Forristal, Michael Gallagher, Henry Garland, Albert Goude, Alexander Gribben, Frederick Hegarty, Patrick Higgins, Thomas Jordan, Peter Kane, Patrick Keegan, Peter Keegan...'

'*When can their glory fade?*' Flynn mouthed bitterly but it was already fading as he struggled to put faces to the names.

'...James Kelly, Gregory Kinahan, Peter Lawless, Charles Linton, Thomas Morgan, Joseph Murphy, Thomas McCormick, Richard McDermott, Hugh McPhail, James Nulty, Martin O'Brien, Patrick Parr, Patrick Quigley, Edward Quinn, James Quinn, Michael Rafferty, James Rathband, John

Rawson, Patrick Redmond, John Shannon and Peter Tully...' Then it was finished, the battalion's litany of woe. Flynn didn't really remember the rest of the service, just a string of genuflection and trawled-up Latin scraps from his childhood until the RSM dismissed them.

'We are Fred Karno's army; we're the ragtime infantry...' someone started to sing as they began to disperse. One by one other voices joined in. 'We cannot fight, we cannot shoot, what bloody use are we?' They were all singing now. 'And when we get to Berlin we'll hear the Kaiser say, *Hoch, hoch! Mein Gott,* what a bloody rotten lot are the ragtime infantry!' Then they cheered, and cheered and cheered. It was better than crying.

'Old Hackett says you're up for a medal,' said Fitzpatrick as they ambled back to the tents. Flynn grunted. He wasn't listening, his mind elsewhere. 'Tell you what, why don't we nip over to the hospital and see what Joe is up to?' he added before steering Flynn towards the camp gate. It wasn't far and no one spared them a second glance as they strolled down the sunken lane that led to the casualty clearing station. No one cared who they were, no one cared what they were doing, and as long as they were back before lights out no one would ask any questions. Anyway, Mahon would cover for them. After a while they knew they were close, the overflowing cemetery a sure-fire sign that the hospital was nearby.

'Private Joseph Carolan?' asked the nurse as she flicked through a stack of paperwork. She looked old before her time, her blonde hair lank for need of a wash. 'No, we don't have a Private Carolan I'm afraid.' She seemed more interested in the arriving ambulances than speaking to Flynn.

'But he's got to be. He would have been brought in a couple of days ago. Big fella; red hair. My sergeant major said he was here,' replied Flynn, looking worried. They could hear guns in the distance, ominous evidence that the battle went on. There were more ambulances. She seemed eager to go. Then she placed her hand on Flynn's, the first time a woman had touched him in ages. She met his eyes and held them, pale-grey wells of sorrow.

'It's all right, Sarah. I'll take care of these gentlemen,' said a slightly built nurse with short dark hair who had walked over to join them.

'If you don't mind me saying, you look kinda familiar, ma'am,' said Fitzpatrick, trying desperately to place the face behind the crisp, Anglo-Irish accent.

'I should fecking well think so, Séamus Fitzpatrick! Did we not go through training together?' she replied, affecting the thickest of Dublin accents. Fitzpatrick furrowed his brow, scrutinizing the nurse's face. Then the penny dropped along with his jaw. It was Louise Dempsey. She touched Flynn's hand. 'I'm glad you made it, Kevin. There's so many didn't. It looks like the division's lost over two thousand–'

'And for what?' he interrupted.

'To win the darned war, that's what for,' said Fitzpatrick, making Flynn smile at the American's boundless optimism. He wished he shared it. He did once. Dempsey took some papers from Sarah and flicked through them, chewing the inside of her cheek. Flynn found it diverting.

'Now, let's go and see if we can find Joe, shall we?' she said. Flynn noticed her limp, legacy of her wound, as she led them over to the main administration building, an old chateau. 'Wait here,' she instructed before stepping inside. She was gone for ten minutes, maybe more; it was hard to tell.

'I shouldn't have left him,' said Flynn. 'He begged me not to leave him.'

'Hey, don't say that,' replied Fitzpatrick. 'You had a job to do. Anyway, he's here now. Surely that's what matters.'

'I guess you're right,' he said just as Dempsey stepped back out.

'The chaps on reception say he should be over in B Ward so come on, keep up! Jildy!' she said, leading them off towards a line of marquees in the chateau's grounds. Someone was walking towards them and for a moment Flynn thought it was Carolan. The top of his head was swathed in a lumpy mass of crisp white bandages, exposing one eye, reminding Flynn of some mummy in a museum.

'What are you doing here?' It was Rory.

'We're trying to find one of our fellas called Joe Carolan. I don't suppose you know him?'

Rory shrugged.

'Look, I'm glad I caught you, Kevin,' he said. 'This thing's a proper blighty; they're sending me home later today. I just wanted to say… I just wanted to say, do you mind me tagging along whilst you look for your mate?' he asked, lapsing into awkward silence. For an awful moment Flynn had thought he was going to thank him for saving his life. He wasn't sure how he'd cope if he did. He'd have done the same for any of them. He wished he'd been able to do so for Gallagher but it was no good wishing.

'And who is this chap?' asked Dempsey.

'This is Terry's brother Rory,' said Fitz-patrick.

'I knew your brother. He was a fine fellow,' she replied, shaking Rory's hand.

'Who's she?' asked Rory as Dempsey skipped off purposefully towards the tents.

'It's a long story,' said Flynn, watching her go, seeing her for the first time for what she was: a woman; an attractive woman, not the sliver of a rifleman he'd known in training.

Ignoring the others, he ran after her, catching up and taking her hand. She squeezed it, sparing him a sidelong glance and the hint of a smile, then let his hand go for the sake of appearances. Carolan wasn't in Ward B. In fact, no one had heard of him except a harassed-looking doctor who said if they wanted to find him they'd better go over the road. It didn't make sense. There was nothing over the road, nothing that is except a cemetery – a field of churned earth and wooden crosses, row after row of them.

'But he can't be dead!' spluttered Flynn. 'They said he was here ... you said he was here...' His voice faded as something caught in his throat, stifling his words. She took his hand, regardless of appearances. 'He's not here, is he?' he asked, looking at a long row of bootless bodies laid out under old blankets awaiting burial. 'It's my fault. I shouldn't have left him,' he muttered. 'I shouldn't have left him.'

'Don't talk rot,' snapped Dempsey, her voice a slap in the face.

He pulled himself together.

'What's that?' asked Fitzpatrick, pointing at something beyond a group of tired-looking pioneers digging fresh graves. It was small, a scruffy bundle of black and tan, curled up atop a newly piled mound of earth. They walked towards it. The bundle moved, watching their approach with large, sad brown eyes. Flynn's feet felt like lead. It was Spud. Dempsey took his hand, its comforting warmth giving him the strength to move on. He had found Joe Carolan's grave.

By the time they got back to camp, Devlin had shown up.

EPILOGUE

Dublin, April 1919

Flynn knocked back the glass, pouring the last tint of whiskey down his throat. As breakfasts went it wasn't the best but it would help take the edge off the day, maybe even keep the memories at bay. Some hope; they waited in ambush on every street corner, ghosts of happier times. Every time he wandered past City Hall their faces flooded back. He couldn't even go near St Stephen's Green without remembering the day the battalion had formed. He still felt guilty about Carolan, even after all this time. He felt guilty about the others too; the men he'd been in charge of, the men he'd been responsible for. He could just about cope with that, thanks to Messrs Jameson and Bushmills, but no matter how hard he tried he still missed Gallagher, with his stupid grin and schoolboy antics. But Gallagher was gone now, never coming back, like so many others who were never coming back. It wasn't supposed to be this way.

'It's a real shame about young Gallagher, he was a good lad,' Mr Byrne had said when Flynn had called around to see if he could get his old job back. After all, he needed a job. Everything looked the same, it just felt different. Gallagher's chair was empty. What did he expect? Byrne had seemed surprised to see him, awkward even, as he puffed nervously on his pipe.

'You said you'd hold our jobs for us,' said Flynn.

'Look, you're a good fella, Kevin, but things have changed since you left and I'm afraid there isn't a position for you here any more,' he added with a weary, almost apologetic sigh.

'So what am I supposed to do now?' he snapped, face darkening as his fists balled. Byrne stepped back, afraid Flynn would lash out, almost dropping his pipe. Flynn didn't move, just stood there scowling. Byrne started fussing over some papers, hoping that his ex-employee would get the message and go away. 'Well, thanks for nothing, then,' Flynn finally snarled before storming out, slamming the door. He didn't understand. Byrne may have been a bit of an old woman but he thought they'd got on well enough.

Obviously he was wrong.

'What about you, Mr Flynn? Back from the war, is it?'

'I am that,' said Flynn, looking round at the man who had spoken, narrowing his eyes in thought. 'Good God, John Riley, but haven't you grown!' he declared, recognizing the man. 'Did you join up in the end?' he asked.

Riley raised an eyebrow, as if it were a stupid question.

'Nah, by the time I was old enough the war was as good as over,' he replied, shaking his head. 'Besides, I'm a junior clerk now,' he said proudly.

'It's all right for some, John, but that old bugger Byrne won't give me my job back!'

'Have you not heard?' said Riley, smiling sympathetically. 'It's the Shinners. Ever since they set up shop in the Mansion House last January they've been throwing their weight around like they run the place. Don't you know that the old fella would have you back for sure if it was up to him but it ain't?'

'What's that?' asked Flynn.

'It's them Shinners. They told him, they did, told everyone hereabouts.'

'Told him what?'

'That those who went to fight for the English are traitors to Ireland and that anyone who gives them a job is a traitor too. Some fellas came by and told Mr Byrne so.

They were Rah, I tell you, I'd put a tanner on it...' He meant IRA, the organization that had risen like a phoenix from the ashes of the Irish Volunteers. 'I hear them talking and this one fella tells Byrne that anyone who betrays Ireland best look out. The Shinners don't like being disobeyed. They shot some peelers down in Tipperary last January and another in Limerick last week so a fat old knacker like Mr Byrne isn't going to bother them.' Things started to make sense. 'Well, I best be going,' said Riley, shaking Flynn's hand. 'I'm sorry there's not more Mr Byrne could have done,' he added before going inside.

Poor old bugger, thought Flynn as he strolled away from the office along Eden Quay, feeling guilty for thinking bad of Byrne. It wasn't his fault. Instead he felt anger at men who hid behind patriotism to intimidate an old man. He thrust his hands deep into his pockets. He could feel the hardness of the medal case against his hand; the Military Medal he'd won at Ginchy. He didn't know why he'd brought it with him; he just had. It was like a talisman. There was graffiti on the wall: *'English go home'* and *'Up the Republic'*. 'Yeah, right, up the bloody Republic,' he muttered, louder than intended, drawing reproving stares from a bunch of young men hanging around on the waterfront. 'And what the hell do you think you're looking at?' he snapped angrily, taking a step towards them. Experience had taught him attack was the best form of defence, sheer aggression counting for much in a fight. The men shuffled anxiously. 'I fought for my bloody country and I'm as Irish as any Fenian,' he snapped. They looked away, anxious to avoid his gaze.

By the time he'd reached the O'Connell Bridge he'd calmed down. Sackville Street was a mess, the GPO a burnt-out shell even though wreckage of the Rising had been swept away years ago. Nothing had been done to make good the damage, almost a metaphor for the state of the country. At least the river still stank. That much hadn't changed, thought Flynn, as he crossed, heading for Grafton Street, watched by a constable who loitered at the southern edge of the bridge. His partner was peeling an army recruiting poster from the wall and Flynn stopped to watch. He'd seen the poster before. It was one of those ones with a couple of smiling squaddies drawn on it, having fun. *'Join the Army and see the world,'* it announced. This one had been defaced by some Republican wag who'd written beneath: *'Join the RIC and see the next one.'*

'Nothing to see here, son,' said the policeman.

'I was in the army,' said Flynn. He didn't really know why, it just seemed like something to say.

'I'd be keeping that to myself these days,' said the policeman. 'This isn't a good time for ex-soldiers.' Not a good time for peelers either, thought Flynn, but he kept his thoughts to himself. The policeman gave him a quick once-over, then added, 'Maybe you should think about re-enlisting.'

'No, thanks,' was all he could think of saying. He'd had enough of soldiering. Devlin had signed back on. You'd be mad not to, he'd said. Peacetime soldiering was a doddle compared to what they'd just been through. Maybe Flynn was mad. Last he'd heard, Devlin was somewhere in the Middle East with the Dubs 2nd Battalion. He wasn't sure about the others. Someone had said that Docherty was back working as a chippy somewhere round Parnell Square. They'd never been close but maybe he'd look him up sometime. He'd left Fitzpatrick in a pub down by Liverpool docks looking for a ship to take him back to the States. For some reason he'd swung by Royal Barracks a couple of times just to take a look. Once he almost walked through the gates but he'd never quite made it. Instead he usually ended up in a pub nearby, killing time with the rest of the demobbed outcasts that the city pretended didn't exist.

'Can I fetch you another?' asked a warm, comradely voice at the bar next to him, gesturing for more drinks without waiting for Flynn's response. He didn't recognize the man but assumed he was an old soldier, like almost everyone else in the smoky bar. 'Would you be the Kevin Flynn who won a medal at Ginchy?'

'What's it to you?' Flynn asked the stranger, his alcohol-clouded mind suddenly on guard. The stranger handed him a frothy pint of stout. He sipped it, eyeing the man cautiously.

'The army could do with men like you, Mr Flynn,' said the man. He didn't look much like a recruiting sergeant to Flynn but then these were worrying times; it paid to be cautious. Then he laughed, shaking his head.

'And which army would that be? Haven't you noticed the fecking war is over?' He was slurring slightly, barely bothering to hide his contempt for the IRA man.

'Oh no, the war has only just begun to get the bastard English out of our country, out of Ireland for good.' The man's eyes were shining with fanatical zeal as he warmed to his theme. 'Our army needs experienced soldiers like you, Sergeant Flynn.'

'Do I know you? I don't remember you at Ginchy, or anywhere else for that matter.' He looked around the smoky bar as the murmur of conversation dropped away amongst the gathered ex-soldiers. 'You're not one of us, that's for sure,' he said, sweeping his arm around the room. 'What do you and your so-called army know about war? What you're doing isn't a war, just *eejits* waving guns, playing at soldiers. War is squalid and dirty and if you had a fecking clue what war was like you wouldn't be so keen to fill the streets of your own country, my country, with blood! Where were you when I needed a job, eh? I was a bloody traitor, we all were,' he was angry now, feeling the killing rage welling up inside him, 'but now I'm good enough for your bloody army. That's a joke. You think I'd fight for you when all filth like you have done since I got home is treat me – us – like something you've trodden in! Now do yourself a favour and piss off before I kick the shit out of you, you pathetic shite!'

'Leave it, Kev,' said an ex-fusilier called McCurtain who'd been in Flynn's platoon at Messines Ridge. 'Let the bugger go,' he added, before turning to the IRA man and saying, 'Get away whilst you can. Can't you see you're not wanted here?'

It was dark by the time he left the pub and his pockets were empty. It would be a long walk home. He didn't hear the footsteps closing in from the shadows, nor did he get a chance to fight back as they put him on the ground, raining kicks on his head and back. He curled up into a ball, the alcohol thankfully killing the pain. Then as he lay battered and bleeding, a familiar voice hissed in his ear. 'Kick the shite out of me, will you, soldier boy?' Then there was white light followed by darkness.

'Well, well, well.' The voice was kindly, with a familiar, washed-out tint of Mayo. Flynn blinked and opened his eyes. He was still in the gutter. He'd been there all night, left for drunk or worse. There was something about the face hovering over him, then he worked out what it was – or who it was, to be precise. It was Mahon. 'It's heart-warming to see you've readjusted so well to civvy street, eh?' he joked. Flynn struggled to sit. 'I think we need to get a brew and a piece down you,' added the ex-CQMS, reverting to type.

They found a café. Flynn ate; Mahon paid.

'So what are you up to these days?' asked Flynn. He hadn't seen Mahon for over a year; not since the 9th Battalion had been merged with the 8th back in October 1917.

'I work up in Phoenix Park,' he replied after taking a quick look around.

'Doing what?' asked Flynn, none the wiser. 'Have you got a job tending the grounds, then?'

'For a clever fella, you're a wee bit dim sometimes, Sergeant Flynn,' he replied with a deep sigh. 'I work at the depot.' Flynn frowned, still not getting it. 'I'm a peeler.'

'But I thought you were Irish Guards,' said Flynn.

'Aye, I was, for twelve years, then RIC.'

'You never said you were a peeler.'

'You never asked,' he replied jovially. 'Anyway, when the war came I was asked if I'd help out when they formed the battalion. You know the rest. When I demobbed the constabulary took me back and even promoted me. I'm a sergeant now, which is more than I was when I left. The money's good and there's a pension too.'

'Aye, if you live to draw it,' quipped Flynn.

'And by the look of you, Kevin, you'll not be much longer for this world yourself.' Flynn shifted uncomfortably. Mahon was right. His liver wouldn't take much more. 'Tell you what. Seeing as you seem to be at such a loose end, why don't you get yourself cleaned up and meet me at the depot at three this afternoon?'

'Why?' asked Flynn.

'Because I think the police would do you good. It's a bit like the army but without the shite bits. They're a fine bunch of lads, the best in the business, and the way things are going we're going to need all the decent blokes we can get.'

'Why not?' replied Flynn. 'What's the worst that could happen?'

The publishers hope that this book has given you enjoyable reading. Large Print Books are especially designed to be as easy to see and hold as possible. If you wish a complete list of our books please ask at your local library or write directly to:

Magna Large Print Books
Magna House, Long Preston,
Skipton, North Yorkshire.
BD23 4ND

This Large Print Book, for people
who cannot read normal print,
is published under the auspices of

THE ULVERSCROFT FOUNDATION

... we hope you have enjoyed this book.
Please think for a moment about those
who have worse eyesight than you ...
and are unable to even read or enjoy
Large Print without great difficulty.

You can help them by sending a
donation, large or small, to:

**The Ulverscroft Foundation,
1, The Green, Bradgate Road,
Anstey, Leicestershire, LE7 7FU,
England.**
or request a copy of our brochure for
more details.

The Foundation will use all donations
to assist those people who are visually
impaired and need special attention
with medical research, diagnosis
and treatment.

Thank you very much for your help.